Kiss Me Deadly

13 TALES OF PARANORMAL LOVE

Edited by Trisha Telep

RP|TEENS
PHILADELPHIA • LONDON

Library of Congress Control Number: 2010926067
ISBN 978-0-7624-3949-2

Cover photo: Clayton Bastiani / Trevillion Images
Cover and interior design by Whitney Manger
Edited by Trisha Telep
Typography: Beyond Wonderland, Caslame, and Caslon

Published by Running Press Teens
an imprint of Running Press Book Publishers
2300 Chestnut Street
Philadelphia, PA 19103-4371

Visit us on the web!
www.runningpress.com

Y

Table of Contents

Introduction

Love in the Time of . . . Zombies?

Somehow that just doesn't have the classic ring of Nobel Prize–winning author Gabriel Garcia Márquez's famous novel, *Love in the Time of Cholera* (read it if you haven't!), but my bet, after titles like *Sense and Sensibility and Sea Monsters* and *Queen Victoria: Demon Hunter*, is that this is likely in some publisher's pipeline somewhere, probably slated for publication next year, or the year after that.

Welcome to the *other* side of love. If love has a dark side (and, thank the sweet heavens, it does), then this is it. We're through the looking-glass here, people. This is where Alice got into all that trouble. And who can blame her? The other side of everything is always the best, and conventional love will only get you so far. (And don't let the "deadly" fool you. It's not all *that* bad. It's more like "bad" in that good Michael Jackson–type way. But then sometimes it is . . . bad—really, really, truly bad, in the horrifyingly not-so-good, totally unfun way.)

Deadly kisses are light and bright, and full of magic—light enough to dispel all the evil in the world, light enough to make you invincible and be your lifeline in a world of chaos and uncertainty. Deadly kisses are also pitch black, full of desire, deadly desire—dark as midnight, as dangerous as deception, as deadly as uncontrollable, heart-stopping, desperate addiction (that stealing-car-stereos-and-rifling-through-your-Grandma's-pocketbook-for-spare-change kind of addiction). These are kisses given and taken in the shadows, anonymous and unsaid, locked away from prying eyes. All secrets. And you know what they say about secrets . . .

Better to just steal a kiss and head back to the light, to the land of the living. Best not to stay too long in your paranormal lover's arms when the lights go out or you'll never find your way home in the dark. This is the *other* love, the flip side of love, love with a capital "*L*": Love. Who told you that it was all going to be so *nice*? Didn't you realize that love is a trap, a lie, an evil deed, a spell woven by magical creatures for nefarious purposes to soften you up for the death blow?

Choose to dabble in a little paranormal activity and your home life will become intolerable. Your parents will probably frown on double dates with demons ("*Shouldn't you be doing your algebra homework rather than learning to communicate with the dead, young lady?*"). Everyone knows that pretty boys with glowing eyes only whisper words of love so you'll taste better when they finally gobble you whole. Surely you've read enough fairy tales to know this by now? (Oh, but it's not *all* bad. Remember Michael Jackson . . . see above.)

After death, mortal love lives on in the lover's memory, a sweet, gentle reminder of the life-affirming splendor of everlasting devotion (aw . . .). But, is that it? Is that really love? A love that can . . . die? What kind of cruddy love is that?

Choose paranormal love and make your relationship last forever! I mean, shouldn't all true loves be able to survive a reanimation . . . or two?

—TRISHA TELEP

The Assassin's Apprentice
BY MICHELLE ZINK

I made my way through the crowd, trying not to be jostled by the men around me. It was always difficult to get my thick, blond hair under a hat, and I was never quite certain it would stay there. If it came loose, I would be a beacon not only for the rough men in the room, but for the demon lurking among them.

And be revealed as both a female and a Descendant, either of which could get me killed—or worse—in company such as this.

The men were filthy, wound tight with an energy that rippled through the crowd. I could feel their agitation. Their rising excitement. Their despair. They would work their whole lives through and find little more than a meager wage, an occasional night at the street fights, and an early death. I felt a moment's pity for them as I made my way along the outskirts of the crowd, but my sympathy quickly dissipated.

Perhaps these people would never rise above their station. Perhaps they would die young from breathing coal dust or in an accident at one of the factories in our New York town.

But they would never see their families executed by a demon like Bael.

And that, in my opinion, made them far better off than I.

The closer I came to the front of the crowd, the more the men pushed and shoved. Their shirts hung limply against their skin, sticking to their sweaty bodies as they angled for a better look at the makeshift ring in the middle of the derelict building. The first two contestants had not yet entered the patch of ground reserved for the fighters, making this the best chance I would have of spotting Bael. Once the fight began, the men would surge forward and pack even more tightly together.

I made my way to the front, looking for a place to hide and finding it in the shadows that lurked near the wall. It was too far back to see the fight properly, but perfect for surveying the room in its entirety. Stepping into the darkness, I leaned back against the crumbling wall.

I scanned the crowd, my eyes skipping over the bearded, dirty men until I spotted Bael, standing against the wall opposite mine. He stood in the shadows, much as I did, his face only half-visible through the broad shoulders and bearded faces of the mortal men. Even so, it was easy to be certain of his identity, for his skin was as smooth as a child's, his clothes crisp and unsoiled.

I knew it for the lie it was. There was no doubt in my mind that the demon who had murdered my family lay under the guise of the handsome blond gentleman leaning against the wall. Fury rose in me like a tide, beginning at my feet and continuing until my face was hot with it.

The time for waiting was passed. Now it was time to be done with it. With him.

Now it was time for him to pay.

My fingers found the hilt of my Blade without looking, and I had a flash of Father, standing near me as I assumed the ready position. I could still feel his hand on my shoulder, steadying my arm as I focused on the targets across the field in the distance.

Hit your mark, Rose. Hit your mark.

I stepped forward, itching to drive the Blade through Bael's black, black heart.

"I wouldn't do that if I were you." It was not the murmured voice in my ear that gave me pause, but the hand, tightly clenched around my upper arm, that made me stop in my tracks.

I knew better than to expose my back to Bael. Instead, I tipped my head so that my body was still facing forward, glaring from under the brim of my hat at the young man who had spoken.

"And *I* wouldn't do *that*." I let my eyes skip to his hand, still encircling my arm. "If I were you, I mean."

In the noise and activity of the room, the young man's face was a series of quick impressions. Angular cheekbones, dark hair curling at his ears, deep blue eyes flashing even in the dim light of the room.

"I understand," he said, loosening his grip on my arm. "But he'll kill you, too, if he sees you."

For a moment, everything seemed to still, and all I heard were his words.

He'll kill you, too, if he sees you.

As if he knew about the murder of my family.

I removed my hand from the hilt of the Blade, looking at him in surprise. "First of all, you don't understand. Couldn't possibly understand. And second of all," I pulled my arm violently from his grasp, "who are you?"

• • •

"Let's go." The young man still had a hold of my arm, despite my best efforts at freeing myself.

I should have been frightened, for even now we were making our way to the entrance of the building. But he was moving me away from Bael, and this made me believe that we were somehow on the same side.

The crowd seemed to part as we moved through it, the young man commanding a strange, unspoken respect as everyone stepped aside.

"I can walk on my own, you know." I tried one last time to wrench free of his grasp, but his fingers were like a vice on my arm.

"I have no doubt," he said. "But I think you should stay close. It seems we may have company."

It took me a minute to understand what he meant, but as we reached the door, I looked back to where Bael had been standing.

Then I understood.

He was no longer there.

I felt a rush of utter fear followed quickly by shame. Fear could not co-exist with vengeance.

"Can you at least tell me your name?" I asked as the young man pulled me out the door and into the cold night.

He sighed, and I marveled that he could sound so bored when it seemed we were both on the run. "It's Asher. Now will you be quiet until I think of a way to get us out of Bael's sight?"

His words silenced me as nothing else could. They were confirmation that he did, indeed, know Bael by name. I had never heard the demon's name spoken aloud except by my Mother and Father.

That meant the young man holding my arm could only be one thing.

I knew there were other Descendants, though they were scattered far and wide. Underground for their own protection against filth like Bael. And though we knew the Assassins were among us, attempting to quell the execution of the Descendants, we did not speak of them. They moved silently among the shadows of our world, doing their duty without worldly aplomb or association.

I was pulled from my thoughts when the young man named Asher hurried me down the crumbling stone steps and onto the darkened streets, smoke rising from the streetlamps that flickered every few feet. He looked back only once, cursing softly under his breath.

"We have to hurry. I think he might have spotted you. We have to find a place to take cover until we lose him."

I stopped suddenly, forcing Asher to a stop as well. "I don't want to lose him. I want to kill him." I silently cursed the quaver in my voice.

"Yes, well, I'd say he'd probably like to kill you too." He leaned in, his face mere inches from mine. I felt a blush heat my face, though I could not have said why. "And he'll get the chance if you do not come with me right now." He pulled me forward, grumbling. "We can debate your chances of killing him before he kills you once we've found a safe place to hide."

His unwavering determination gave me pause. I wasn't used to being strong-armed. Mother had once told Father that he was the only one who held sway over me, and I had been forced to admit on more than one occasion, if only in the privacy of my own thoughts, that I was not always agreeable.

But Asher did not seem intimidated by my stubbornness. His arm was strong on mine, and I had the sense that I could not escape him if I tried. It might have been frightening if not for the fact that he was so clearly trying to save my life.

Now, the knowledge of his strength held a secret thrill.

We passed two drunkards, singing loudly and off-key, and Asher pulled me into a dark alley, glancing around until his eyes settled on a pallet stacked high with wooden crates. As we made our way to it, I contemplated pointing out the obviousness of such a hiding place, but as soon as we stepped around it to the back, I knew why he'd chosen it.

"Here. It is far from perfect, but it will have to do." His voice was quiet as he stepped into a deep door frame behind the pallet, tugging me back into the shadows, pulling my body to his.

I did not have time to protest. I could feel Bael's presence in the alley beyond our hiding place. It was almost as distracting as the press of Asher's body against mine, the faint smell of woodsmoke and spring rain clinging to his shirt. My hands came up against his chest, and in the quiet of the night, I felt the steady thrum of his heart.

It came as a surprise. I did not realize Assassins had beating hearts while in the mortal world.

He tipped his head, bringing his mouth to my ear. The kiss of his breath was soft against my skin as he whispered. "Don't move a muscle."

And then Bael was there, moving around the pallet, the sickly sweet stench of him seeping into our hiding place, making me want to gag. I fought the urge, burying my face in Asher's shirt and calling myself a coward.

Take him now! You wanted him. There he is, I thought.

But I could not. It was all I could do to stand, immobile and full of fear, while Bael scoped the small space behind the pallet outside the doorway where we hid. His boot steps fell, heavy and purposeful, stopping only feet away. I was shocked when, a moment later, he spoke.

"I can smell her, Apprentice." The last word was spat with venom, his voice low and guttural. "I could take her now, but I must admit, I'm enjoying the game. It's always entertaining to toy with someone who thinks they stand a chance of winning. Besides, you can't be with her every minute."

The blood pumped through my body with extraordinary speed, and I looked up at Asher, wondering what he would do.

The answer was nothing. He only gave a small shake of his head as if to say no.

Bael remained a moment longer as if reveling in our predicament. Then his boots fell on the hard ground once again, growing farther and farther away until there was only my breath mingled with the muffled beat of Asher's heart.

● ● ●

"I want to go home." I willed my voice steady, aiming the words at Asher's back.

"It would be foolish to do so now." He prodded the logs with an iron poker, his voice partially lost in the quickening flame of the fire.

After making our way carefully out of town, Asher had brought me to a cottage at the edge of an empty field. It had seemed desolate at first glance. Abandoned. But once inside, it was surprisingly comfortable, though very small. The rugs blanketing the floors were similar to the ones in my own fire-damaged home, the ancient furniture covered with worn blankets and tapestries.

Asher stood, rising to his full height, and I realized that he was quite tall. His shoulders strained at the fabric of his shirt, and I had a moment's memory of my face pressed against his muscled chest, the scent of him nearly as distracting as Bael's footsteps in the alley. A ripple of excitement passed through me.

"I have been sleeping at home since the fire." I said, lifting my chin with conviction.

"Perhaps." Asher grabbed a rag from the mantle, wiping his hands on it as he spoke. "But that does not mean it wasn't foolish. You have only lived this long because Bael thought you had died in the fire. Now that he knows you're alive, he will come for you. Even more so now that he knows you are under my protection."

I crossed my arms over my chest, looking away as the truth of his words rang through my mind. It had been an unnecessary risk to remain in my home, despite my precautions to go unseen. But it was all I had left. My parents were gone, the servants released the day after the fire. My home, crumbling and sooty though it may be, was the only thing that remained of my other life. A life I knew I would never lead again.

Still, I recognized the facts. It would be impossible to destroy Bael if he killed me first.

"Fine." I turned back to Asher, meeting his eyes. "I'll go back one last time to pack my things before taking a room in town."

Asher sighed, setting the rag back on the mantle before turning to look at me. "You cannot go back now, in the dark, and none of the lower-profile inns and boarding houses are fit for an unescorted young woman."

"That is all well and good," I snapped. "But I need to gather my things, and I've nowhere else to go."

My voice cracked at the end, and tears stung my eyes. I forced myself to blink them away, hoping Asher had not seen them.

He crossed the room, stopping in front of me. "If I promise to go with you tomorrow to gather your things, will you agree to stay here until my business is done?"

"Here? In your home?" It seemed scandalous even in light of the situation.

"It is not my home, exactly. I'm only renting it until I am finished here." He nodded slowly. "But yes. Here. In this house. I realize it is not proper by your standards, but who is to see?" He looked around the room, glancing back at me with a shrug. "There is no one here but you and me, and I don't plan to tell anyone."

I looked around the room. "But . . . where will I sleep?"

"Under the circumstances, I think it best that we stick together in case Bael reconsiders and comes after you tonight." He gestures to the sofa in front of the fire. "You sleep here. I'll take the floor."

It did not take long to consider the offer. The room was very warm, and it would be a lie to deny that Asher's presence was reassuring.

"All right," I said.

His nod was almost imperceptible, but he moved to a trunk against the wall, removing a stack of blankets from its interior to create a makeshift bed on the sofa. A few minutes later, I lay atop it with my head on a musty-smelling pillow, while Asher settled onto the floor next to me.

I told myself he was only protecting me, as was the task of any Assassin.

And besides, I thought, he's right. It would be foolish to risk my safety in the dark of night when a more practical option is available. I'll simply take advantage of his protection right now, and then I'll go after Bael myself, just as I planned.

I made argument after argument in the hallows of my mind. It all made perfect sense. But with Asher's steady breath so near and my own heart beating like a drum, I knew it for the lie it was.

We approached the house cautiously, doubling back several times to ensure that we were not being followed. I heeded Asher's every instruction, allowing him to take the lead as we made our way to the only home I had ever known.

The home that would no longer be mine.

It was not as I remembered it. After the fire, I avoided it until nightfall when I was forced to find a place to sleep. Shrouded in darkness with a small fire crackling in the grate of the parlor, it had seemed only slightly shabby. I had slept amid layers of blankets piled before the firebox and had forced from mind the soot staining the walls. The smell of smoke that hung in the rooms like a ghost.

But now, in the harsh light of day and with Asher by my side, I was forced to confront the full measure of the destruction wrought by Bael. As we climbed the steps to the front door, I avoided looking into the yawning emptiness of the windows above. I did not wish to remember the things that had happened in the rooms beyond.

I pushed open the massive front door, and we stepped across the threshold into the entry. I did not linger. The terror and loss of the great house seemed to reach out to me from the soot-blackened walls, and I suddenly wanted nothing more than to leave as quickly as possible.

Asher followed me into the parlor, stepping carefully, as if aware that every floorboard, every piece of carpet, held precious memories.

"I'll just be a minute." I headed for the valise on the floor, knowing that everything I could salvage would be there where I left it. I had always been prepared for a quick getaway.

"Take your time." I did not turn to look at him when he said it, but I was surprised by the gentleness in his voice.

It took only a moment to pack my meager belongings. The shawl Father brought back from India for Mother. The ivory comb he'd given me. The brush and mirror set that had been my grandmother's, and the few items of clothing I had pulled from the wardrobe in my chamber when preparing for the flight I always knew would be necessary.

I closed the valise, marveling that everything I owned could be contained in the small click of its latch. Straightening with the bag in hand, I took a last look around the room.

"Tell me." Asher's voice was soft, and when I looked up, I saw that he was leaning against the wall on the far side of the room, his eyes dark and unreadable.

"Tell you what?"

He tipped his head into the room. "Tell me what you see."

I swallowed with difficulty, shaking my head.

"It will help you remember."

Licking my lips, I looked around the room, taking it all in for the last time. "I see the piano in the corner where Mother played when I would sing. I was never in key, but she never seemed to mind."

"Go on," he said.

I pointed to a chair near the fire. "That was where Father would sit, smoking his pipe while Mother attended to her needlework. She didn't like the smell, but it gave him so much pleasure that she rarely complained."

"And what about you?"

I looked away from the chair, meeting Asher's penetrating gaze. "What about me?"

"What would you be doing? When your father was smoking and your mother sewing?"

I looked back to the chairs, seeing my parents as clearly as if they were really in front of us. Seeing myself, too. "I would be reading. Something from the library."

He tilted his head, narrowing his eyes as if he could see it all in the moment before he looked back at me. "What else? What else do you see, Rose?"

I was surprised to hear him speak my given name. It was a caress on his lips.

"I see Father and me playing chess. I see him teaching me."

The silence lengthened between us, and he pushed off from the wall, crossing the room toward me. "Teaching you what?"

I watched the ghost Rose with her father. Saw him point out the obvious moves. And the not so obvious ones.

"Teaching me about chess. About strategy. About life." My words became softer as I said it. As I began to understand.

Asher nodded, taking a finger and tipping my face up so that he could look into my eyes. "That's right. And because of that, he is with you. Will always be with you. As will your mother. You'll carry them with you, Rose. You'll see."

For a moment, I was lost in his eyes. In the feel of his fingertips on my skin. The nearness of his body to mine.

Then I got my bearings, nodding and stepping away. "Thank you." I did not look back as I headed for the door. "Now let's leave, please."

•••

Asher threw another log on the fire as I tucked my clothes into the valise, trying not to feel self-conscious. My hair, loose and curling at my shoulders, was no longer bound by my hat. But that was not the worst of it.

The worst of it was that the men's clothes I wore to track Bael were dirty. The only other outfit I'd managed to salvage from the fire was a gown—hardly proper, or comfortable, sleeping attire. My lack of choices had forced me to don the white cotton nightdress hand-sewn for me by Mother's seamstress. As unseemly as it was, I was grateful I'd thought to pack it. Otherwise, I might very well be sleeping in nothing but a chemise, with mere feet between Asher and me.

It was odd being in the company of a young man, and with so few clothes, but these were, if nothing else, odd circumstances.

There was nothing to be done about it. I tried to banish thoughts of Asher's nearness and my own bare skin beneath the nightdress by focusing on the task ahead.

"Tomorrow, I must seek Bael and finish what he started." I rose from my valise.

Asher stood, turning to me. His voice was full of tenderness. "Why don't you let me handle Bael? It is what I was sent to do, and it is your right as a Descendant to have my protection."

"Thank you, Asher. I . . . Well, I am grateful for your offer. But this is something I must do. Vengeance for the death of my parents is a matter of honor. Surely, you understand that."

He favored me with a hesitant nod. "But it is no vengeance if their only child is killed in the process. And make no mistake about it, Rose; you almost certainly will be killed. Bael is the worst of the remaining demons. You have seen that which he is capable."

"Perhaps. But next time I will be ready for him. And I will not allow you to stop me." Even to myself I sounded like a defiant child, determined but ultimately delusional.

To my surprise, Asher did not name my foolishness. He simply asked the only question that really mattered. "I assume you have a Blade?"

My hand dropped automatically to the sheath at my waist. I nodded.

He held out a hand. "May I?"

It was a bold request. Each family of Descendants was given only one Avenging Blade. My father had entrusted ours to me just before Bael's entry into our home, and I was loathe to let it leave my hands.

Asher's expression softened. "It's all right. I have one of my own. See?" He reached for a belt around his waist, pulling something from its scabbard.

I knew what it was even from across the room. It did not shine in the minimal light of the fire, but I felt its power, a companion to the weapon still around my waist. I moved toward him without thinking, my eyes on the Blade in his hands.

"Do they give you one when you become an Apprentice?" I asked.

Asher nodded, holding the Blade in the flat of his palm.

I could not deny my curiosity. I knew Apprentices had to prove themselves before being elevated to full-fledged Assassins, but Father had never explained exactly how they went about it. I had never expected to meet one face-to-face, and though we trained and prepared for the possibility that the remaining demons would find us, deep down Father always believed the Assassins would eliminate the danger before we were forced to defend ourselves.

I continued to cross the room, coming to a stop in front of him. I looked down at the indecipherable symbols and words etched into the solid silver hilt and blade, surprised to see that they were slightly different from those on my family Blade.

"It's beautiful." The words came out in a breathy whisper. Without thinking, I reached out, running a finger along the engravings crisscrossing the weapon, feeling the dips and whorls of the ancient script.

Before I knew what had happened, my hand was encased in the iron grip of his fingers, the Blade back in its sheath. "You don't touch an Assassin's weapon without permission. Even you must know this."

His face was mere inches from mine, the strange electric current pulsing between us as it had in the alley.

I straightened my back. "You are not an Assassin. Not yet."

I saw a flash of fury in his eyes in the moment before he spoke. "Perhaps not. But I am closer than you. Killing Bael is not a task for a pampered Descendant, however much you might think you have prepared."

It took effort to pull my arm from his grip. He seemed surprised by my strength.

I glared up at him. "We will see about that."

"What is that supposed to mean?"

"It means," I said, "that this is all talk until one of us kills Bael."

He shook his head. "You are being utterly foolish, Rose. You'll be killed."

His lack of confidence in my ability and my need to avenge the death of my family only increased my determination. "Perhaps. Perhaps not. But either way, you cannot stop me."

I spun around, stalking away from him. I didn't know where I was going. The truth is, I had no place to go. I only knew that I needed to escape him. To escape his words and his gaze and the truth I did not want to hear.

But I did not get far.

A moment later, he was spinning me to face him. I expected him to shout. To tell me again all the reasons why I could not kill Bael.

Instead, his mouth was on mine before I could register what was happening.

I did not even consider resisting. His mouth, soft and firm, moved against mine, and then I was falling into light—spinning faster and faster toward the heat of a sun I could only feel, blazing at the center of my body. His hands found their way to the back of my neck, sliding into the hair cascading down my back. My mouth opened under his without a thought, a rosebud tightly bound and waiting only for this particular ray of light.

●●●

"Why weren't you killed?"

Asher's voice was so soft, I could hardly hear it over the faint crackling of the fire. We were lying amid an assortment of cushions and blankets that Asher had found. I felt returned to myself, brought back from the dead by Asher's tender but passionate kisses, his hands learning the curve of my neck, my jaw, my shoulders.

Now, with my head against his chest, I contemplated his question, thinking back to the night of my family's death. The screams tearing through the night. The moment's hesitation before I fulfilled my promise, climbing out of the window and making my way along the roofline until I could drop to the dewy grass and run.

Run without looking back, as Father had instructed should such a thing come to pass.

"Bael came for my parents first." I was glad he could not see my face, though I refused the tears that fought their way to my eyes. "I heard them screaming."

"How did you know to run?" His voice was sincere and filled with a sadness that took me by surprise.

"I've always known what I was. What we were. My parents didn't keep it a secret." I hesitated, wondering if my parents had disobeyed an unknown code of the Descendants. "Does that shock you?"

"Well, it is not forbidden to illuminate the next generation of Descendants . . . " His voice trailed off, and I knew he had left something unsaid.

"But?" I asked.

"But," he continued, his chest rising under my ear. "It is difficult to predict how the mortals would behave if they knew the offspring of angels walked among them. Most of the Descendants wait until their children are of age to tell them. You cannot be more than—"

I lifted myself up on my arms, looking into his eyes. "I am eighteen, thank you very much! Besides, you are hardly 'seasoned.' How old are you?"

His eyes shone with something like amusement. "My age is not measured in mortal years."

"Well, then," I tipped my head, not even trying to hide the sarcasm in my voice. "Why don't you tell me how old you would be if it were."

"Nearly twenty."

"Twenty?" I laughed aloud. "Well, I suppose I should feel safe in the hands of one so experienced!"

He sighed. "Yes, well, I'm in the final phase of my Apprenticeship. Bael is my last individual kill. I need only destroy him, and I'll be a full-fledged Assassin. The Council would not have sent me if they didn't have faith in my abilities. It is an important task."

"Yes, it is. One that is rightfully mine." I heard the steel in my voice and felt the warmth of the past hours slipping away.

"If you wanted to destroy him so badly, why have you been following him for nearly a week without moving in to kill him? You have had more than one opportunity." The earlier affection in his voice was replaced with frustration.

I tried to hide my surprise. Obviously, Asher had been observing me longer than simply one night. And there was something else. Something I was afraid to voice, though I knew I must if I was to honor whatever strange and beautiful thing had happened between us.

I nodded, looking into Asher's eyes. "I have had chances to take Bael."

Asher shrugged. "What stopped you then? Fear?"

His question did not surprise me. I had wondered on more than one occasion if it was fear that held me in check. Fear that, despite all the training my parents had bestowed upon me before their death, I would be no match for Bael.

But in the end I had been forced to admit that fear wasn't the problem.

I shook my head. "No. Not fear, though I know it would be justified when faced with a demon like Bael."

"Then what?" Asher's voice was soft but firm. I knew he would not let it go until he had an answer.

I tried to think of a way to tell him that my reason for hesitating was far darker than fear and infinitely more dangerous. I waited because I relished my hatred for Bael. It was the only thing that made me feel alive, and I held it close like a freezing man clinging to the dying flicker of a fire.

I sat up, hugging my knees to my chest and looking away from Asher's eyes. They already saw too much of me.

"Once Bael is dead, what will be left of me?" I asked the darkened room. "What reason will I have to wake up each morning? To put one foot in front of the other? To go on while every single person that I cherished is cold and dead in the ground?"

It took him a moment to speak.

"Hate will be a cold consolation for the losses you have endured," he said softly.

I looked into the fire. "Perhaps. But I have nothing else."

He sighed. "Rose." When I turned toward him, he was looking at me with such tenderness that it caused my breath to catch in my throat. No young man had ever looked at me in such a way. "If I agree to aid you in destroying Bael, will you promise to wait until tomorrow when we are both rested and I can fight by your side?"

It took me a moment to speak, so speechless was I by his offer. "You would . . . You would do that?"

"It is our task to protect the Descendants. Allowing you to go after Bael on your own would increase your odds of being killed and Bael's chances of escape, thereby rendering my own mission unsuccessful."

I tried to mask my hurt. "So that is the only reason you would agree to help me? To ensure that your mission is successful and to see me out of the way so that you might earn your place as an Assassin?"

He reached up to stroke my cheek, his eyes clouded with something I already knew was desire. "You want me to give voice to what has happened between us. To explain it." He took a deep breath, shaking his head. "I cannot. I have traveled the world over. I have slain frightful demons and been faced with questions that have no answer. Yet none of those questions come close to the one I have found in you."

I lay my head back on his chest, embarrassed at the intensity of his gaze. "After we destroy Bael, you will have to leave, won't you? You will be an Assassin in your own right and must continue the Council's quest to rid the Earth of the remaining demons."

"Yes," he said softly. My heart warmed to him further for his honesty. "We should sleep. Tomorrow will be a challenging day for us both."

I nodded, trying to memorize the feel of his arms around me, the rise and fall of his muscled chest as he breathed. And then, just as I fell into the mystery of sleep, I was flooded with complete and total peace.

...

His absence was not the first thing I noticed upon waking. It was the weak slant of light spilling from a crack in the parlor's curtains, casting everything in the unfamiliar room a soupy gray. It took me a moment to remember; Bael at the street fight, Asher's hand on my arm, our hiding place in the alley, my last visit to the house.

And then, Asher's hands in my hair. His mouth on mine. The chiseled plane of his chest under my hands.

I sat up, the blankets falling away as I looked around the parlor. The embers were still hot in the fireplace, but there was no one else in the room.

Asher was gone, as I should have known he would be.

...

The streets were nearly empty as I made my way through town. It was too early for civilized people to be about, though I came across a few laborers and a drunkard passed out cold on the side of the road.

I was no longer nervous in the more questionable neighborhoods Bael preferred. In the past week, I had followed him to brothels, fights, seedy drinking establishments, and of course, the boarding house in which he rented a room. I saw it now, rising before me in crumbling brick, and thought back to all the times I stood in the shadows, cursing myself for allowing him to live another day.

But now I understood. Now I knew.

Those moments all led to this one. This was the moment when Bael would finally fall. And if I had anything to say about it, he would not do so at the end of the Apprentice's Blade, but at the end of mine.

I made my way up the steps, eyeing the dark places along the buildings on either side. Bael was a creature of habit and would likely still be asleep in his bed, but it would not do to be careless now. Not after all I had been through to reach this moment.

The front door was unlocked, as it always was, and I made my way inside, closing the door softly behind me. I started up the L-shaped staircase to the right of the entry, stepping over the second squeaky riser. I was grateful my initial fury at Asher had passed. I could not afford to have anything cloud my judgment. Besides, I should be angry at myself for trusting him.

Even still, we were on the same side. We both wanted the demon dead, and I was happy to allow Asher the glory. I wanted only the knowledge of my vengeance.

The thought caused me to move faster. It was quiet in the boarding house, and I began to worry that I was too late. That Asher had already dispensed with Bael. But a moment later, a loud *crash* beyond the top of the staircase told me I had arrived just in time.

I raced up the last few stairs, stopping at the top of the landing, trying to follow the sound. There was a muffled grunting and cursing, punctuated by a slamming that seemed to shake the very house. I turned my head to the right, following a terrific *bang* that brought to mind an overturned wardrobe or chest of drawers. It was a testament to the nature of the boarding house that no one opened a door to ask about the noise or demand quiet. Fights were not uncommon in this part of town. It was dangerous to involve oneself with quarrels that were not one's own.

Passing by the first door on the left, I continued down the hall to the second as the crashing grew louder. I stopped in front of the second door, gathering my wits and trying to calm the slamming of my heart against my chest. Then, all at once, it grew quiet, the noise from within the room stilling as quickly as it had started.

There was suddenly no time to wait.

I flung open the door, quietly but swiftly, not wanting to give Bael an advantage. It took only seconds to assess the scene before me. I calculated my options at lightning speed the way Father had taught me.

The disheveled room. Broken glass on the floor. An over-turned writing desk two feet in front of me. And fifteen feet away, Bael and Asher, their bodies frighteningly still and close, against the wall across the room.

Then, the most important thing of all; Bael, one arm shoved up against Asher's neck, choking him as he held a glistening Blade against the throbbing pulse at Asher's throat. My fingers caressed the handle of my dagger, raising it as I felt Father's hand on my arm, heard his voice in the recesses of my mind.

Hit your mark, Rose.

Instinct took over, and the knife left my hand before I could contemplate my chances. It sailed through the air, the ancient words inscribed on its hilt writhing and swirling as the weapon cartwheeled toward its target.

Everything slowed down, and Asher's eyes grew wide, meeting mine over Bael's shoulder. I did not see the fear I expected. Nor was there anger that I had come despite his obvious desire that I remain at the cottage.

No. There was only relief and gratitude and something deeper and too complex to name.

It all happened in the instant before the knife hit Bael between the shoulder blades, a sickening *thud* sounding at the moment of impact. For a moment, the demon did not move. Asher still struggled against his grip, and I wondered if it was all a dream. If I had not, in fact, just hit Bael with the only weapon that could kill him—an angel's Avenging Blade.

But then a crimson blanket began to spread outward from the knife protruding from his back. Bael's arm loosened and then dropped from Asher's throat as he staggered backward, falling to the floor, his eyes roaming the room desperately for a glimpse of his killer.

When he saw me, still standing in the doorway, his eyes flashed.

"You." It was not an accusation but a declaration.

A second later, flames erupted at the center of his body, a flash of purple fire rising from them in the moment before the flames disappeared in a muffled whoosh, leaving nothing in its place save the faint smell of burning mortal flesh.

Asher slid down the wall, his breath coming in ragged gasps, a fine line of blood trickling from a small cut in his neck. I knelt beside him, waiting for his breath to steady and wondering if he would be angry after all. Finally, he opened his mouth to speak, and I braced myself for his wrath, my arguments at the ready.

"You have good aim," he croaked.

I nodded, my shoulders sagging in relief. "Thank you."

I do not know how long we sat in the now-quiet room. Time had warped and slowed in the aftermath of Bael's destruction. Finally, I could not wait any longer.

"I suppose you'll be going now? Moving on to the next demon? Attempting to protect another family of Descendants?"

He nodded, pushing himself to his feet with effort and making his way to the door. Turning back, he managed a pained smile. "You coming?"

My heart lifted. I was at his side in seconds. He took my

hand, leading me out the door and down the stairs. Opening the front door to the boarding house, the morning light was a flash of brilliance. And then, we were out of the darkness at last.

Errant

BY DIANA PETERFREUND

The unicorn hunter brought her own unicorn, which was good as none had been seen in the countryside for years. Everyone in the château paused in their duties as she entered the courtyard; they stared in open fascination at her dusty traveling cloak and the equally dusty unicorn at her side.

If they'd been expecting the lithe, elegant monster they'd seen in tapestries and paintings, they were destined for disappointment. The unicorn was a rickety, goat-like creature with a bedraggled tail and tangled, mud-caked mats in her shaggy silver coat. She was missing a few teeth, and one of her eyes had already begun to cloud over with age. But her horn was as long and proud as ever, thrusting upward from her brow in a tight spiral half as long as a man's arm.

The hunter led the unicorn to the empty hitching post, and tied a length of chain first about the unicorn's neck, and then around the post. "*Bleib*," she told the beast, and the unicorn hung its head, its pink tongue lolling slightly from heat and thirst. The workers in the courtyard scattered. Chains and fatigue might slow the animal down, but they'd heard the stories. They knew the danger.

The unicorn hunter was shown into the parlor with little delay. Gathered there were four people: two strangers, plus the man with whom the unicorn hunter had business, and a petite girl a few years younger than the hunter, with skin the color of white roses and hair that curled softly about her face like a golden halo. She was dressed in a fine blue gown that would likely tear like tissue if she bent the wrong way, and she stared at the hunter with a mixture of fascination and revulsion.

"Sister Maria Brigitta of the Order of the Lioness," said the unicorn hunter, giving a curt nod to the man she'd come to see. "I am here about the hunt."

"Indeed." His eyes widening slightly at her accent. "I didn't realize you were German."

"Bavarian by birth," Gitta replied. "But I lived in Rome with the Order since my fifth year." And she'd wager her French was better than his German.

The man's name was Adolphe Dufosset, but as far as Gitta could tell, he was not the lord of this house. Neither was the tall, dark man in the corner, who, Gitta learned, was the Vicomte de Veyrac, the father of the young man who turned out to be the girl's betrothed.

No one bothered to introduce the girl.

Gitta wasted no more time and laid out the terms of her services. "For two ounces of gold, I will provide a unicorn and protection from the unicorn for the duration of your ritual. That includes teaching the maiden her duties. The price increases to two and a half should the maiden not pass the test." The Vicomte stiffened at these words, but Gitta felt no need to clarify. After all, he was not the one to pay her fee. "And the price quadruples should you wish to actually kill the unicorn."

"A mark of gold!" the Vicomte spat. "Absolutely not."

"Of course we must kill the unicorn," said Dufosset. "That is the purpose of the hunt!"

"Not at that price," said the Vicomte. "It's outrageous."

Gitta remained impassive. "And yet it is the price. Unicorns are scarce, in France and elsewhere, and this one has been with the Order for quite some time. She's very well-trained. I assure you, she can feign an excellent death, should you desire."

"I desire—" said Dufosset, "to see the creature's head on a pike."

"That will cost you eight ounces of gold," Gitta replied, keeping her voice even. Outside at the hitching post, Enyo felt her distress, and Gitta sent soothing thoughts in the unicorn's direction. She had been through these negotiations before. Officially, the price for a dead unicorn was only four ounces of gold, but these French squires did not know that, and Rome was very far away.

The Vicomte turned to the girl. "My dear, I shall not have this interloper wasting your father's money on some trifle."

"And I shall not allow our family tradition to be reduced to some cheap bit of playacting," said Dufosset. "If we are to have a unicorn hunt, then by God we shall kill a unicorn."

No, *Gitta* would kill Enyo, if they paid her price. Adolphe Dufosset could give her one mark of gold or twenty, but he would never deliver the death blow himself.

The girl looked at Gitta. "Perhaps," said she, her voice trembling, "the hunter has a suggestion for pursuing this alternative. I do not relish the thought of anyone butchering an animal in my lap."

Ah, so she was fastidious as well as soft. The perfect combination for disaster. The girl would be lucky if Enyo didn't run her through at their first meeting. "Most families are satisfied with a symbolic slaying," is what Gitta said aloud.

The girl gave her a look of annoyance, which Gitta ignored. Far too good to sully her silk gowns with unicorn blood, but still concerned with family pride? Ridiculous. Had the girl any real family pride she would have learned to be a hunter. But it was unlikely she had the ability to do so—so few maidens did anymore, despite what their family crests might say. And then there were those like Gitta: no surname of distinction, but still worth ten of these silk-encased porcelain dolls.

"Shall we carry symbolic spears and knives, then?" said Dufosset. "Perhaps wooden swords. Or toothpicks? Is this whole thing to be nothing more than a pageant?"

"Ideally," grumbled the Vicomte. "Right now it is nothing more than a delay tactic."

"I am trying to honor our family heritage, my lord. Traditionally, a de Commarque wedding is marked with a unicorn hunt. Surely you cannot begrudge my cousin and me of that, given our recent tragedy."

The Vicomte snorted and turned away.

Adolphe smiled at Gitta in triumph. "We will pay the mark. Make what preparations you must."

Gitta kept her face impassive. "Yes, sir. I will need a few days to prepare—the maiden." She gestured awkwardly at the girl.

"My name," said the girl, "is Elise de Commarque."

Gitta merely bowed her head.

• • •

Elise de Commarque, the daughter of the former Le Seigneur de Commarque, stood before her wardrobe and frowned. The unicorn hunter had summoned her down to the courtyard to test her against the unicorn, whatever that meant. She'd told Elise to wear something she didn't mind getting dirty.

As if Elise owned the type of rags that this Sister Maria Brigitta traveled the countryside wearing: that worn brown bed-skirt and scarf, and that horror of a torn gray petticoat. This was absurd. Elise had half a mind to call down to the servants' wing and ask them to send up a smock.

Eventually she compromised on her oldest gown and a torn apron she'd been meaning to deliver to the rag basket. As her maid helped her dress, her pug dog, Bisou, wove in and out between her feet and tugged on the bottoms of her skirts. She scooped him up in her arms and buried her face in his soft fur. Bernard had already informed her that his father the Vicomte did not allow dogs in his house. She would have to leave Bisou behind. And who knew if she and Bernard would ever return here? Perhaps, once they had children . . .

With Bisou safely stashed in the crook of her arm, Elise went down to the courtyard to meet this hunter and her animal. The servants were still nowhere to be seen. The woman stood holding the unicorn on a chain, and as Elise entered, it looked up and began to growl.

"I knew it," the older girl grumbled, then stopped. "Wait. Is that a *dog* in your arms?"

"Of course." Elise patted Bisou on the head. The poor thing was trembling and clawing at his mistress's sleeve.

"Take it away!" the hunter exclaimed. "You are destroying the test. You might as well have brought Enyo a bloody ham."

The unicorn snapped its jaws and lunged. Bisou squealed. Elise grasped him and fled, racing through the house and back up the stairs to her room. Bisou leaped from her arms and darted beneath the bed. Elise gasped, yanking at her stays until she could breathe again. The hunter had *set* the monster on her.

Eventually, she squared her shoulders and marched back downstairs. Sister Maria Brigitta of the Order of the Lioness could have as much contempt as she wished for her French hosts. But she could not mistreat her in her own house. Elise's father never would have stood for it, so neither would Elise de Commarque.

Back in the courtyard, she found a scene of carnage. The unicorn had caught one of the lawn peacocks and was engaged in tearing it to shreds. The hunter stood apart from the spatters of blood and calmly sharpened her knives.

Elise screamed, covering her hands with her mouth. The unicorn paused, its snout a mess of gore and green feathers, dropped the carcass of the bird, and began to approach her. The hunter glanced over. Spikes of greasy black hair had escaped her scarf and hung in her amber-colored eyes.

"Sister!" hissed Elise, freezing where she stood. "Your . . . animal."

"Sorry," said the hunter. "Enyo was hungry, and after the dog . . . well . . ." She shrugged. "Was the peacock worth so very much?"

But Elise had forgotten about the peacock entirely. She backed up a step, whimpering as the beast drew near. If she reached out, she could almost touch its long, sharp horn. But then the unicorn stopped, lowered its head, and knelt. Elise was so surprised, she almost curtsied in return.

Across the courtyard, the unicorn hunter stood, her knife gripped firmly in her rough, weathered fist. "Touch her," she commanded.

Elise obeyed, not for the sake of the hunter, but for that of the unicorn. There was something in its eyes. Something she'd seen before in Bisou, or in her father's horse Templar, or in Noir, the cat who lived in the kitchen. She leaned and slid her fingers along the unicorn's brow. Its hair was softer than she'd thought it would be. Tangled and filthy, to be sure, but silky and fine. The unicorn, still bowing before her, bleated.

"I don't believe it," said the hunter. "You are a daughter of the blood." Her tone was one of awe, but her expression remained locked in a scowl.

Elise withdrew her hand and somehow resisted wiping it off on her apron. "Of course. We traditionally hunted unicorns. That is why you are here."

The hunter laughed. "My lady, do you know how many great houses I visit where they claim their girls are daughters of the blood?"

Elise chose not to respond. The de Commarque claim was true. What did she care about some other house? "Does this make your task easier? To—train me for this, I mean."

"Yes," replied the hunter stiffly. "It shall be easier if you hold Enyo still while I kill her."

"Enyo," said Elise. "That is the animal's name?"

The hunter looked away. "Yes."

"Enyo," repeated Elise. The unicorn looked up at her, its eyes watery with age. "I have never heard that name. Is it German?"

"Greek." The unicorn hunter made a small sound in her throat, and the animal snapped to her side, a move so quick Elise was surprised she could follow it. "It is the name of one of Ares's companions."

Elise smiled as the hunter crouched low over her unicorn, pressing her scarved head against the animal's neck. "That is nice. I am not familiar with this Ares. My doggie's name is Bisou. You know—"

"I know what it means," the older girl hissed, straightening. "And Ares, you illiterate prig, is a god of war."

Elise blinked in shock. No one had ever been allowed to speak to her in such a manner. And now, this—this *nun*, with her dirty clothes and rusty-handled knives and filthy animal with its strange, foreign name—

"Forgive me, my lady," said the hunter, her rage vanishing as quickly as it had flared up. She bowed her head. "I should not have said that. It was uncharitable."

And untrue. Elise had read—well, a large part of the Bible. And a whole book on herbs. In Latin, no less! Plus her elementary readers, and a history of France. Lots of books. "You forget yourself, Sister," she said, her tone haughty.

The hunter nodded, eyes still cast downward. "I beg your pardon, my lady. I am used to a degree of camaraderie among my fellow hunters. Your power took me by—" she trailed off. "You're right. I'm very sorry. I am tired, from my travels. And . . . hungry."

Elise sighed. "Go around to the kitchen. They'll see to your food and find you a place to sleep. It's two days yet until the wedding and the hunt. I assume you will be able to teach me better starting tomorrow?"

The hunter stared at the ground.

Elise snapped her fingers and the older girl looked up. "I trained for ten years to become a unicorn hunter," Gitta said. "But if we only have a day, we will have to settle for teaching you how to stay alive."

The cook gave Gitta a pallet in a room with two scullery maids—
an offer Gitta might have accepted if she didn't have Enyo to
think about. Her living arrangements in the Cloisters hadn't been
better, but there, at least, she and the other hunters kept their pet
zhi by their sides at night. If left unchecked, Enyo would eat the
scullery maids, and Gitta might even let her. After all, the poor
thing deserved a good last meal, and from the look of the scullery
maids, they wouldn't mind shrugging off their miserable mortal
coils.

Enyo remained hungry. That peacock had been nothing
more than a scrawny snack. Perhaps she should have let the *zhi*
eat that stupid dog as well. With any luck, Elise de Commarque
would have had Gitta and Enyo driven from the house, and then
no one could blame Gitta for her failure to complete her mission.
They could take off again—go somewhere new. Somewhere wild.

Instead of the pallet, Gitta took Enyo out into the forest
beyond the fields and gardens surrounding the château, and slept
with her there, her arm curled tightly around the animal's throat.
She'd only had the unicorn for a year, but Enyo had lived with
hunters for all her life. She'd been given to Gitta by Sister Maria
Artemisia when she'd left the order to care for her widowed niece.
Gitta had recently lost her third *zhi*, Brunhild, to a village festival
near Seville. The villagers had attempted to eat the meat of the
corpse. Gitta had refrained from warning them against it, for
which her superiors in the Order had reprimanded her harshly,
though the villagers' illness had only lasted a few weeks.
Artemisia took pity on her, though. The old nun was pushing
fifty, and knew what it was like to outlive one's unicorns. Enyo,
Artemisia had explained when she passed the animal over, was
old and wouldn't mind dying so much. Gitta soon learned differently. Enyo might be old and frail and nearly blind, but she was
every bit as fierce as her namesake. Together, they'd survived
three of these so-called hunts thus far.

How sad, then, that Enyo would be sacrificed for some petty ceremony that no one in this de Commarque house seemed to actually want.

This wasn't what a hunter was, Gitta reflected as she lay in the dim forest and let the scent of the earth wrap around her. Not what it used to be, anyway. Once upon a time, her sisters had *protected* estates like this one. They'd come when the residents were threatened by wild unicorns. When a hunt was necessary. Now there was nothing but playacting. It was a disgrace, not only to the Order of the Lioness, but also to the families, whether truly of the blood or otherwise.

The unicorn moaned softly and kicked its hooves in its sleep. Its belly rumbled. It would need to eat something soon. Gitta hoped there were deer in these woods.

She curled her body around the beast's for warmth. Gitta could speak seven languages and had traveled all over the continent. Why then, here in this little French woods, did she suddenly feel so small?

...

As he did every evening at sunset, Bernard de Veyrac appeared beneath Elise's bedroom window with a flower twined round a little scrap of paper. And every day, Elise lowered a little basket for him to put the flower in, pulled it back up to the window, and read the poem he'd inscribed on the paper. Today's was very good, comparing Elise's breath to violets and her complexion to a lily's. It was almost as good as the one that said she was more fair and lovely than a summer's day. It would have been better, perhaps, had he thought to use a violet or a lily as the flower, but instead, he'd tied the note to a morning glory. Odd. Though Bernard seemed to have a way with poetry, her betrothed was sorely lacking when it came to that sort of planning. Foolish trifles of a boy in love, her father had said, but Elise knew better. She'd heard the way the servants talked about Bernard. She'd heard the stories about the peasant girls. Still, the poems were an unnecessary token, given their parents' wishes. That he took the trouble gave her comfort. Theirs would be a pleasant marriage.

She blew a kiss to Bernard from her window, and he pretended to catch it and press it to his heart. "Six days, my fair Elise!" he cried from the garden, his eyes shining in his handsome face. "Six days until you're mine!" And then he turned and left, and Elise smiled at him until she noticed he was trampling all the seedlings in her garden with his big brown boots.

"Bernard!" she shouted. "My tarragon!"

He leaped off the plants as if burned and landed squarely in the lavender.

Elise sighed and shook her head as she returned to her supper.

There was a knock at her door and a moment later, Adolphe appeared, powdered and wigged to within an inch of his life. Elise sat calmly by the window as he approached and stooped to kiss her hand. He towered over her, but it was an illusion. The heels of his coral satin shoes had to be at least six inches.

"My dear cousin," he said. "How are your spirits this evening?"

"Well enough," she replied. They would have been better had she not heard that five more of Adolphe's men had arrived at the estate this evening. She hadn't bothered writing to the Vicomte, though. He no doubt knew already, in that way he had of knowing everything that happened here. Her wedding couldn't come quickly enough.

She tossed a piece of chicken to Bisou, who was still hiding beneath her sofa. Perhaps the treat would draw him out.

"I worry for you, my dear," said Adolphe. "Left all alone, in this cruel world—"

"Not for long." She toyed with the flower in her lap. "Bernard and I shall soon be wed and then—"

"Such a pity your poor father did not live to see that day." Adolphe's voice betrayed not the slightest hint of human pity, though he'd shown up quickly enough the day after they'd placed Le Seigneur in the ground. "Do you not think it wise to delay this marriage? We have hardly had the chance to set his affairs in order."

"My marriage contract is in order," Elise said, allowing her tone to betray no hint of her annoyance. "My father signed it the day before his accident."

"Your father no doubt expected to live to see you bear him a grandson." Adolphe cast his eyes about the room. Elise wondered if he was sizing up her belongings, setting a price on every vase and handkerchief. "But now . . ."

"Nothing has changed." Elise's voice wavered slightly. How she wished he would not address her without the Vicomte or her other friends present! The Vicomte had been most specific about what she was and was not allowed to say to Adolphe Dufosset. "And when I am married, the contract will be executed as my father intended. Will that not be nice?" she asked hopefully. "To see his last wishes carried out?"

Adolphe did not respond and as the silence stretched, Elise began to grow uneasy. Bisou darted out from underneath the upholstery and pounced on the scrap of meat. Adolphe looked at the pup with disdain, and Elise frowned.

"I believe I am a bit tired, sir. Perhaps I should rest."

"Indeed." But he did not move to stand. "So much weight on your shoulders, my dear cousin."

Elise swallowed.

"It's a wonder you have not been overwhelmed by it all. Indeed, it seems you hardly know which way to turn, now that your father is gone."

Elise kept her eyes on her lap. "I trust in the opinion of the Vicomte. He was my father's dearest friend, and he will be my father, too, once I am married."

"The Vicomte would add you to his collection, and include our family lands if he can. Elise, do you not see this? It's impossible that you are so stupid that you cannot."

The stem of the flower crushed beneath Elise's fingers. "I want only to fulfill my father's wishes," she said, though it felt as if her own throat was equally mangled.

Adolphe's shadow fell across the silk of her dress. "We shall see, my dear cousin. We shall see if you marry this boy of the Vicomte's, and we shall see, if you do, whether you take with you this estate."

Elise raised her head. "Monsieur Dufosset, you would do well to remember that you are here on my invitation."

"I am at that," he replied evenly. "How curious that you fashion yourself the mistress of this house."

She caught her breath at the rage burning behind Adolphe's placid expression. Her father had refused to see the man during his lifetime. Elise didn't know the exact nature of their quarrel, but at the very least she understood from the Vicomte that Adolphe's claim to their estate was not as valid as Adolphe would have her believe.

"It's . . . best that you leave now," was all she managed to say.

"You think this is your home, that you can tell me where I may or may not go?" he asked, his tone turning dangerous. "That this is your room? Your china? Your dinner?" He shoved at her tray, and the glasses clinked. He was practically shouting now, and Elise shrank back against the cushions of her chair. "Do you think this is your *dog*?"

And with that, he snatched up Bisou and threw him against the wall.

Elise shrieked as the dog bounced off the plaster and landed on the carpet. "Bisou!" She threw herself from the chair to the floor. The dog tried to raise itself and fell, whimpering. "*Mon petit chien*! Bisou!"

The door to her room opened and in rushed her maid, along with one of her father's old valets. "My lady, is everything well?"

Bisou crawled toward her, crying pitifully. He dragged his back leg. Elise scooped the animal up in her arms. "My poor sweet thing . . ." she bawled. "My angel."

Adolphe let out a little snort. "Pathetic."

"Leave me," she whispered.

"Sir," said the valet. "You shall depart my mistress's chambers at once."

The maid crouched near Elise. "My lady, let me see to it for you."

Elise tightened her grip. "No. Bring me bandages. Bring me . . . something." A splint? Could a dog's leg be healed once broken? Above her, the valet was attempting to force Adolphe from the room.

"Remove your hands from me, filth," said Adolphe as he was shoved into the hall. "Or you shall know my wrath once I am master of this house."

The valet slammed the door and threw the bolt. Then he joined them near the floor. "My lady, I shall send for the Vicomte's men at once. We will install a guard at your door. We must drive this usurper out before it is too late."

Elise's eyes began to burn, but the tears did not spill onto her cheeks, just stayed there, stinging her with their salt. Oh, what did it matter who had this house? Let the Vicomte and Adolphe battle it out, and divide the tenants and servants amongst themselves. Why couldn't they just let her be? She knelt there, on the carpet, and curved herself around the body of her poor dog, wondering if she could spiral tight enough to disappear altogether.

• • •

As morning broke over the horizon, Gitta stood on the edge of the forest and waited for Elise to arrive. Dawn was probably far too early for the poor, pampered princess. Gitta wondered if Elise had ever seen a sunrise in her spoiled life.

Enyo stood waiting patiently by her side. She'd let the animal hunt in the night, and judging from the remains she'd found strewn near their little camp, the unicorn had found a vole's nest. It would satisfy her for a while, but she hoped Enyo had the opportunity for a real meal before she had to kill her. A stag, perhaps, or a nice, fat wild sow. Gitta would help, if necessary, since she knew the unicorn was not as fast as she had once been. Enyo deserved it.

Enyo lifted her head, and Gitta felt the unicorn softening in anticipation. Another unicorn hunter approached. After a moment, Gitta could hear the most horrid clomping through the underbrush, and then Elise came, dressed in the same clothes from their meeting yesterday, but with the addition of a pair of sturdier boots.

"These are most uncomfortable," Elise said abruptly. "They were my father's, and they're much too big, though I stuffed the toes with rags as you advised."

"Better this than tearing your feet to shreds on brambles," said Gitta.

The younger girl's eyes were shadowed with dark circles this morning. So this is what happened when such perfect creatures were not allowed to sleep until noon?

Enyo was already bowing before Elise. Gitta sighed and waited for the unicorn to finish her ritual. If only Enyo understood the truth of Elise's presence, she would not be so deferential. But such was the sad destiny of all her kind—helpless to control their love for maidens of the blood, overcome with adoration even as the maidens turned and slew them.

"Come," Gitta said. "We'll go practice in the spot where the hunt is to take place. You won't be able to learn quickly enough to command Enyo as I do, but I'll teach you to keep her calm and to get her into your lap as tradition requires."

Elise said nothing, just smoothed her apron over her skirt, no doubt imagining how Enyo's blood would soil her clothing. Gitta dismissed the unicorn and led Elise away.

They eventually reached the tree Gitta had chosen. It had a large trunk, and a rough pattern of bark that would make it easy enough for Gitta to scale to the lowest branches and lie in wait for the "festivities," such as they were, to begin.

"You shall sit here," she said, pointing at a patch of moss near the root. But Elise was nowhere to be seen. Gitta spun around, filtering through the unicorn's thoughts until she found the younger girl kneeling near an outcrop of greens.

"Wild asparagus!" Elise cried, holding up a bunch. "Oh, isn't it lovely!" She caught Gitta's look and straightened, stuffing the stalks into an apron pocket. "Sorry, I was distracted by the plants. I so rarely get a chance to gather wild herbs."

"You like . . . plants?" Gitta asked.

"Very much. You should see my garden." Elise returned and sat obediently at the base of the tree, arranging her skirts around herself like a queen at a picnic.

Too bad she hadn't been sent to the Order, thought Gitta. Many of her Sisters focused on herbalism in their work to make cures when the demand for the unicorn's magical Remedy outweighed the supply.

"What do I do now?" Elise asked.

"You wait," said Gitta. "Your natural abilities will draw the unicorn to you. It would help," she added, "if you tried your best to think attractive thoughts."

Elise closed her eyes and screwed up her features. Did it hurt this much, Gitta wondered, for the fool to *think*?

Judging from Enyo's indifferent response, out there in the forest, Elise's thoughts were not particularly inviting.

Gitta nearly groaned. An actual daughter of the blood on her hands, and she was still forced to treat her like any other girl. Gitta knew she could sit in the tree herself and call the unicorn to her, but Elise had the magic as well. She wanted to at least attempt to treat this hunt as something more than mere playacting.

"No," said Gitta, and Elise's eyes popped open. "You must . . . *call* her to you."

"Enyo!" cried Elise.

"No. Within yourself."

Elise looked confused. "I don't understand."

Gitta rubbed at her temples. "Do you ever—" How could she explain? After thirteen years, the magic was a second nature. "With your pug. Do you ever turn to it and wish it would come to you, and it does?"

To Gitta's surprise, Elise's eyes began to water. "No," she said. "Bisou knows his name. He—" She looked at her lap.

A moment later, the unicorn came rushing out of the woods and stopped at Elise's side.

Gitta started in surprise. Enyo had come so quickly, she'd hardly felt the change in the animal's intentions.

Elise barely moved as Enyo softly nudged her snout against the girl's arm until the unicorn could slide her head beneath it and settle down in her lap.

"There, there," murmured Elise, as tears fell onto the unicorn's mane. "*Ma petite licorne.*"

"My lady," Gitta said in wonder. "You did it."

The girl did not look up.

Gitta tasted the unicorn's thoughts. Pity, deep as a river. What a stupid beast, to pity the instrument of its destruction. Gitta scowled.

Enyo turned in Elise's lap and bleated at Gitta, then went quiet again, closing her cloudy eyes and relaxing in the girl's arms.

Gitta's brow furrowed. And then she felt a tug at the edge of her consciousness, an awareness of something stirring in the woods. It was as if the very trees breathed, their leaves spinning fast in a world gone suddenly still.

"Elise," she said softly. "Are you sure there are no unicorns in these woods?"

Elise lifted her head. "Of course. Not for decades. Used to be many, though. So many. In fact—"

But the feeling was gone. Gitta searched again, but it was as if she'd caught a note of a song too distant to hear. Perhaps it had merely been the remnants of Elise's nascent magic that had her confused. Elise's call to the unicorn had to have been a strong one, to bring Enyo there so fast.

"So," said Gitta. "That is how you will do it. And then, you must hold tight to her, for the men with their spears will make her angry."

"Angry?" Elise asked.

Gitta nodded. "Yes. She will wish to protect you. So just continue to be calm, and soothing, no matter what. I shall be hiding in the tree above in case anything happens, and at the right time, I shall shoot her, and then it will be over."

"You will shoot an arrow at us? But what if you miss?"

"I never miss."

"What if it passes through Enyo's body and kills me?" said Elise.

"I never miss," Gitta repeated, annoyed. "I would prefer not to do it at all, but your cousin insisted—"

"You didn't present him with options." Elise rose and dusted off her dress. The unicorn remained by her side. "You could have suggested we end the ceremony with the presentation of the body of a white kid, or a fawn. But instead you just stood there and drove up the price. He would not hesitate to spend my money—"

Elise hadn't presented any options, either. Gitta narrowed her eyes. "I have haggled with your kind before. The only time they ever back down is when there is money—"

"You do not want to kill the unicorn!" exclaimed Elise. "I can see it writ on your face."

Gitta turned and walked into the woods.

"Stop!" Elise came clomping through the underbrush behind her. "Sister Maria Brig—"

Gitta began to run.

•••

Who needed the ill-mannered nun anyway? Elise yanked up another weed from her flower bed, then tore off its leaves in a fit of frustration. She'd called Elise a prig. She'd called her illiterate. She'd doubted the de Commarque claim to unicorn hunting; she'd doubted Elise's own powers. She knew nothing—nothing of Elise, nothing of her family, nothing of anything except how to dress badly and eat with a knife and sharpen a sword and name a bunch of naked, pagan gods.

And Elise had it on good authority that the hunter hadn't even been sleeping in the house. Her maid had informed her that the scullery quarters had apparently not been good enough for this foreign nun and she'd taken off. Sleeping in the mud, perhaps. Would explain the smell at least.

Why should Elise bother to speak to her at all? Just get through the ceremony, give the ugly git her mark of gold, and send her on her way. Why should she even try to help the nun with her vicious, peacock-killing Enyo? Elise had problems of her own.

She moved on to the parsley beds. Since when did a commitment to God require a woman to forget herself in matters of personal grooming? So the hunter didn't need to catch a man. She should at least consider shaping her eyebrows. God created the world in beauty. He had to appreciate it in His servants.

By the time she reached the mint, Elise had worked herself into quite a froth. These beds were a mess. She'd been neglecting them too much. She'd been neglecting the entire estate while she waited for the dust to settle. First, the shock of her father's death, and then the stress of Adolphe's arrival, the Vicomte's dire predictions about her future, and the preparations for the wedding. Even now, Elise would rather be up in her room, nursing poor Bisou. She and the maid had tied up his leg in a splint, but getting him to lie still had proven to be an even bigger challenge. In the end, they'd had to bring in an old birdcage and shut him inside. He'd spent the whole night crying, growing even more agitated when the Vicomte's men had arrived and set up camp outside her door. This morning, he'd been wan and listless. He wouldn't eat and when he tried to drink, he'd vomited yellow foam all over the floor.

The only comfort of the day had been those few fleeting moments when the unicorn had laid its head in Elise's lap. Then, it had seemed as if all her cares had melted, that there was nothing but the unicorn and the smell of moss and wood and ash and earth. It was thrilling and restful all at once. And so, Elise did not want to see Enyo killed—particularly not for the pleasure of a person like Adolphe.

The unicorn hunter could rot for all Elise cared. But what of the unicorn?

She'd almost finished her work when the sound of clanging metal rang out over the garden, followed by shouts. She stood and hurried toward the courtyard and the origin of the sounds. Had a fight broken out between the Vicomte's men and Adolphe's?

When she arrived, however, it was to see members of both groups watching and jeering as two figures sparred in the courtyard. The air shimmered with dust and swords as the two people whirled about each other, their bodies clashing and retreating. Elise stopped under the arch, horrified to realize that one of the figures was the unicorn hunter—and the other was Bernard de Veyrac.

"Take that!" yelled the hunter, jabbing. Bernard lifted his sword arm, and the hunter darted in, pressing back against Bernard and blocking his arm with her body. His hand was round her chest for a moment, and then they spun apart.

The men's cheers turned vulgar.

"Italian tricks!" Bernard called back, and laughed. "Do you know this?" He swung his sword with a twist and a flick that Elise had seen him perform in many tournaments. But the hunter was again too quick and deflected his thrust with a flash of her own blade. Bernard was disarmed.

The men all shouted; in agony or triumph, Elise was not sure.

Grinning and unashamed, the nun pretended to bow like a

man. Her attempt was shoddy and rough, though that did not surprise Elise. Did she not realize what they thought of her?

Bernard also wore a grin on his face, then caught sight of his fiancé. "My darling!" he cried, striding over. "*Thou that art now the world's fresh ornament, and only herald to the gaudy spring . . .*" He bowed—the bow of a true chevalier—and kissed her fingers. "Did you see me there, brought low by a woman?"

"Indeed," said Elise, glaring at the hunter, who had miraculously grown even more dusty and sweaty. Her face was flushed, her amber-colored eyes sparkled like true gems, and beneath her shapeless tunic, her breasts rose and fell as she panted. "Quite the display."

Bernard turned to the men. "Gentlemen. My beautiful bride!"

The men let out a cheer.

Elise blushed.

"And everything a bride should be, I hear," he said softly, so only she could hear. "Your blossom is even lovelier when placed next to this bulb of garlic."

Elise giggled, which she knew Bernard found charming. "Oh, really? You seemed quite engaged by this bulb."

"Gitta?" Bernard raised his eyebrows. "She might as well be a boy."

"*Gitta?*" Was that this hunter's given name? How crude. Gitta was even now staring at her fiancé, her gaze one of almost masculine intensity. Why wasn't she the type of nun to wear a veil? Shameless.

Bernard's hand slipped to her waist. "Are you not done with the training? I grow anxious for our wedding—and our *wedding night.*"

He spoke these words out loud—too loud, as the men set about again with their catcalls. Elise's becoming blush drained from her face. "Bernard!" She slapped his hand from her stomacher. Elise was no peasant, no immodest Roman nun.

Gitta glanced at them, her expression of disdain as impertinent as ever.

Elise lifted her chin and walked away.

•••

Gitta had been on her knees for hours, but God had not seen fit to provide her with an answer. The stone floor of the chapel was cold and hard, but her penance was slight compared to the fate that would await Enyo should she not find a way to resolve this situation.

"Holy Father," she prayed, "please come to me in this hour. Please guide my hand for the benefit of Enyo, the least of your creations."

But she could not give herself over fully to her devotions, for always in the back of her mind were the words of Elise de Commarque. Gitta could have fought harder on Enyo's behalf. She could have come up with an alternative. She could have saved the unicorn's life. She could have killed it for a nobler cause than that of these foolish French and their tepid, half-forgotten wedding traditions.

And every time she put that guilt from her mind, it allowed another to rise, warm and bitter as bile: the feel of Bernard's body against her own in the courtyard that afternoon. She'd never sparred with a man before. Now she knew why.

"I beg you," she whispered, then switched to her native tongue. "*Bitte. Bitte, bitte.*"

"Gitta." The name echoed through the empty chapel, deep and commanding, and Gitta started. But it was not the voice of the Lord. No, it was something much more of this Earth. She turned to see Bernard walking down the aisle toward her.

Gitta rose from her knees, disoriented, as if woken from a dream. She was not used to being interrupted while at prayer. No one would dream of doing it in Rome. There, your only privacy was in communion with God.

"I had hoped to see you at supper," Bernard said. His dark hair was mussed, but his features were aristocratic and fine. He'd washed since their battle. "I skipped a meal with my father to find you."

"I'm sorry," Gitta replied.

He smirked. "As you should be."

Gitta was confused. What breach of etiquette had she committed now? If only she were back at the Cloisters. Or out in the wild, alone in her communion with God and unicorn.

"I looked for you in the kitchens." His tone was chiding, as if he spoke to a child. "Is this where you hide?"

"This is where I pray," she said.

He smiled as if she'd been joking. "That's right. You're a nun. A bride of Christ." He flicked his fingers at the wooden cross around Gitta's neck. "How are you enjoying that?"

"I beg your pardon, my lord?" He was standing so near. As near as he'd ever been during their match. His gaze bored into hers, his pupils wide and black, swallowing up all the color in his eyes.

He leaned close, and his voice dropped to a low murmur. "Serving the needs of Christ."

Something hot rushed through Gitta at Bernard's words. Her face and throat burned, and her throat went dry. She barely knew what he said, heard only the deep rumbles of sound from his throat. No man had ever spoken to her like this. Alone. In her ear, as if he knew some great secret in the depths of Gitta's heart.

"The way you moved today, Gitta," Bernard said, and it seemed like he was all around her, "set me on fire."

Yes, Gitta could feel this fire. Was it the heat of Hell?

"I have never known a girl like you." He *was* all around her. His arms had caged her against the altar. "I have never known a girl could *be* like you. So strong, so agile. It was extraordinary."

His hands were on her arms. His thighs brushed her own. His face was inches from hers. Gitta's skin sparked. She didn't know why her clothes were not aflame.

"You are . . ." he breathed against her, the air hot and wet and heavy between them. "You are what I always wished for. You are everything I want. And you're a girl." He pressed his mouth to hers.

The kiss turned the fire to ice in her veins, and Gitta froze. She had never been kissed, never known what it was like for a man to even look upon her with desire. So this is what it was. So this is what Elise lived for.

Gitta gagged and shoved Bernard away.

He tripped over his own feet and fell, sprawling, on the stones. "Gitta!"

"Get away from me, you pig," she said. "How dare you take such liberties with a holy woman?"

He pushed to his feet and dusted himself off. "You weren't so very holy a moment ago," he said with a sneer. "It's a wonder you can still control that unicorn, since you act like such a harlot." He grabbed her arm. "You feel it, too, don't lie."

"I have no need of lying," said Gitta. "God knows all of my failings. If I was tempted, I shall ask forgive—"

His hand came down on her other arm, trapping her there with him. "*I* won't forgive you," he insisted. "Not when I know there could be such pleasure between us. Gitta, you know who I am."

She struggled to break free.

"And now I know you. I touch you, and I feel true fire. I hold you— my soul erupts with poetry. Listen!" he cried. "*Let me not to the marriage of true minds admit impediments—*"

Gitta began to laugh. Bernard stopped and looked upon her with surprise. She wriggled out of his grasp. "You are a most unworthy man," she said, trying in vain to catch her breath. "You are . . . not only a fool, and a scoundrel, but you are a liar as well. Does your betrothed know of your faithlessness? Does she know, at least, of your thievery?"

Bernard sputtered.

"I am not as unlearned as Elise or the other girls you attempt to ensnare, sir." Gitta laughed again. "Your verse is not your own, and my body will never be yours to use as poorly." She drew her dagger. "Do not come near me again." She edged her way around him and began to back down the aisle toward the entrance to the chapel.

What a cad. And how very weak she'd been, to entertain his flattery, even for a moment. To want in that moment to know what it felt like to be desired. To be beautiful, like Elise.

She'd condemned Elise for this, but apparently she was subject to the very same weaknesses. And Elise had been trained all her life to find it complimentary, admirable. She'd been brought up for love and flattery, as Gitta had for weapons and war.

But now Gitta knew the truth. Elise de Commarque was not so very different from her. They each were far too good for swine like Bernard.

She stepped out of the chapel and ran smack into Elise.

"There you are," said the younger girl, her golden hair concealed beneath a thick woolen cloak. "I must speak to you."

...

Elise had brought a lantern, and with it, she guided Gitta to the far edge of the garden and beyond. To her left, the barn and stables, to the right, a series of low hills. Beyond lay a cluster of peasant cottages, and farther than that, the dark shadowed line of the forest.

"Where are we going, my lady?" Gitta asked as Elise led them around the side of one of the hills. Into the hill was set a crude wooden door, tied shut with a knot of rope. Elise undid the knot and motioned for Gitta to follow her down a series of earthen steps.

"These are the wine cellars," she explained, though it was probably obvious to the hunter from the rows upon rows of bottles they passed. They crept through three chambers of these, and then Elise took a path to the left, where they passed one empty room, and then the tunnel grew narrow and short. Eventually, they hit a dead end, or what looked like one. "For this next part," she said, "we must crawl."

She set down the lantern and pushed aside a great rock to reveal a dark hole in the earth. She wiggled her way through, then reached back through the hole to retrieve the lantern. She peered at Gitta on the other side. "Come through."

Gitta gave her a skeptical glance but shrugged and crawled through the tunnel, stumbling a bit as she tumbled out on the chamber floor. Elise waited, the lantern shuttered and dim, as the hunter pushed herself back up.

"What is going on?" Gitta asked. "Why have you brought me down here?"

Elise studied her carefully. "Can't you feel it? I was sure you would. I never knew what it was before. Simply a thrill, I thought, because I was doing something forbidden. Sneaking around. But today, in the forest, I felt it again. And tonight, I put it together. I realized what it was. What it has been my whole life."

Gitta shook her head. "I don't understand. What are you saying? Where are we?"

Elise lifted the lantern. "My secret place."

The walls were alive. Great dark lines swirled over the stone, delineating giant beasts and lithe human figures. Drawings of hunters chased drawings of one-horned animals around and around the inside of the cavern, tossing long spears the color of dried blood into the sides of creatures painted with broad, curved strokes. Gitta gasped as the magic rushed through her. She hadn't felt this way since the last time she'd been within the walls of her own dear Cloisters in Rome. These paintings held the same magic as the Order. This chamber held the same magic as the unicorns.

"There were once many unicorns on this land," said Elise. "And there were once many hunters."

Gitta dropped to her knees, speechless with awe. These

paintings were older than her nunnery, older than the Church itself. If she touched them, would they crumble like Egyptian scrolls?

"I have never shown anyone this before," said Elise. "Not even my father."

"How did you—"

"My grandfather's sister," Elise walked over to the largest of the unicorn drawings and held her hand up, a few inches from the paint. "She showed me when I was very young. This is our legacy. But it belongs to the women. The daughters of the blood, as you say."

"Was she a hunter?" asked Gitta. "I mean, like me?"

"She was married at fourteen to a man who beat her to death by the time she was forty," Elise replied.

"I am sorry." The nun clutched at her cross.

"It was a bad marriage." Elise shrugged. "And it was not her choice. We never have a choice, you see, Gitta. Not in our family. The best we can hope for is that our husbands are harmless. They can care for us or not, but gentle indifference is preferable to devoted mistreatment."

Gitta stared at her, her face drained of color. "Elise, your fiancé—"

"I know," Elise said softly. "You think I'm a fool, and maybe I am ignorant, but I'm not stupid. I know my fiancé is a cad whose love is fleeting, at best, and that his father sees me only as chattel. I know my cousin wishes me dead. And I know that I must cast my lot with one or the other. I have chosen life and the de Veyracs. You, who may go where you please and are answerable only to God, please do not judge me. My dog—my little Bisou—died tonight, of injuries inflicted by my cousin on a whim. I have only this cave to call my own."

The words fell into the ancient dust at their feet, and Gitta did not speak. For she had been guilty of judging this girl, of thinking her beauty and her softness meant that her life was just as sunny. She had not looked close enough at the gilt to see that the shine hid the bars of Elise's cage.

"Thank you," she said at last, and fumbled in the shadows for Elise's hand. "Thank you for showing this to me."

They stood in silence, their hands joined, and stared at the unicorns on the wall.

"You wish to save your unicorn," said Elise. "I wish this as well. Enyo should not die like Bisou. My cousin has spilled enough blood. We have several hours until the hunt. Let's form a plan."

Gita nodded. Elise sounded very determined, but her hand trembled hard against Gitta's, like a heavy bow held for far too long.

• • •

Now Gitta knew why Elise had been so quick to draw the unicorn to her side. The girl had never been trained as a unicorn hunter, but she knew the taste of the hunter's God-given magic. It was marked onto the very earth where she'd walked every day of her life. The lines on the walls were made with unicorn blood—their power reaching out through the ages to the two girls who stood in the chamber and plotted in whispers to prevent more blood from being spilled. Now Gitta knew who Elise was, beneath the powder and the stays and the springtime-colored silks. She was a warrior, just like her. She was a sister-at-arms, if not in vows, and Gitta would help her in any way she could, as any woman in the Order would step forward for the sake of another.

• • •

Before the dawn broke through the trees, Gitta released Enyo into the forest. She crouched low over the unicorn and whispered words of reassurance and love into her aged ears. *Not this time, my dear one. Not this time.*

Enyo disappeared into the darkness. Gitta turned and started hiking back to the tree where Elise and the hunters would meet for the ritual. The forest smelled wild today, as full of magic as Elise's painted caves. She carried her knife and bow, but neither helped her when she was set upon by five armed men.

They bound her head and foot and stuffed a rag in her mouth to muffle her screams as they dragged her deep into the forest.

"He said to keep her until after the ceremony," one said.

"Did he say what we could do then?" said another.

Gitta closed her eyes and reached out to Enyo in her mind. There was no response from the old *zhi*—she was either too far to hear, or she heard another call. Elise's perhaps. Had the hunt begun? Was Gitta too late?

"Is this one as good with a sword as they say?" a man said above her.

"Dunno. But good enough for Dufosset to want her out of his way."

She begged for the unicorn to save her. She prayed to God to protect His devoted daughter. She called upon every scrap of miracle or magic she'd ever known.

The reply came from the very heart of the woods.

•••

Elise de Commarque, the last daughter of her line, led a procession to the tree where Gitta had told her to wait. The aristocrats behind her carried old weapons and sang snatches of even older songs about unicorn hunts. The mood was merry and light. This was the start of a party. A wedding party.

When they arrived at the tree, Elise sat down at the base, and the hunters dispersed among the brush at the edge of the clearing, lying in wait as the maiden called the unicorn like all the stories said. Many minutes passed until the woods settled around them again, and Elise felt as if it was time.

She wore her finest gown, which was getting stained by wet leaves. Her softest slippers were already a mess of mud. Her neatly powdered hair was keeping her from smelling the woods. And the stares of the men arrayed around her, bearing spears and bows and knives trained upon the spot where she sat, was breaking her concentration.

She peered up through the leaves, hoping to catch a glimpse of Gitta. The hunter had said if Elise could not call Enyo, she'd step in and do it herself. But Gitta was truly hidden among the leaves, no doubt trying to make the experience as authentic as possible for the aristocrats who'd come to partake in a traditional unicorn hunt.

Elise took as deep a breath as she could beneath her stays. She could do this. She must.

Enyo! Her mind cried. *Come to me now!*

But there was nothing. No hint of magic flooding through her system, no flash of wilderness, of rain and rot and stone and fire. Everything was perfume and dye, stitches and stays, poetry and prattle, lyrics and lies.

Elise's hands slipped to the earth, and she stabbed her fingers into loamy moss.

And then, it was as if every man in the clearing inhaled at once. Elise opened her eyes, and Enyo was there by her side. Her clouded orbs peered deep into Elise's, and she nudged her head softly beneath the crook of Elise's arm.

"Enyo," Elise whispered. "You're here." She stroked the unicorn's mane, for once not caring about the dirt or the tangles. Enyo was warm, and real, and alive. The unicorn's heart beat softly against Elise's side. Breath from her nostrils warmed Elise's arm. Elise traced each bump and twist of the creature's long horn, then scratched at the base. Enyo sighed in pleasure.

"Are you ready?" she whispered. She drew from her pocket a wooden blade. "Play Dead."

The unicorn let out a cry and slumped against her. An instant later, an arrow flew from the woods and slammed Elise into the tree. She gasped, but could not find breath to scream. The arrow was embedded in her shoulder. Pain shot through her arm and chest, pain such as Elise had never known. The unicorn started in her arms.

"Gitta," she whispered weakly. Who had shot that arrow? Why wasn't Gitta jumping down from the tree to help her?

Adolphe leaped out from behind a bush and came running. The unicorn had ceased its feigned death throes and was licking her face. Tears streamed from her eyes as she struggled to breathe. Adolphe drew near, and she hugged the unicorn to herself, surprised she even had the strength.

"Stop, Adolphe," she said, as if she had a voice in the matter. He mustn't kill the unicorn. Elise had promised Gitta.

But Adolphe did not stop. In fact, he drew out a long, silver knife. And then she almost laughed.

Of course. He wasn't here to kill the unicorn. And he'd been the one to shoot the arrow. He *did* want her dead. This hunt had been his best chance.

Where was Gitta? Where were the de Veyracs? Was she to die alone, surrounded by men and beasts sworn to protect her?

"Now, my dear cousin," said Adolphe, leaning in so no one could see what he said. "We shall have no more disagreements between us."

"You're right," Elise replied. "We shall not." And she set the unicorn free.

Enyo knocked Adolphe onto his back and then, with a growl, plunged her horn into his chest. Adolphe's expression went from triumph to despair. His skin turned purple, and he never breathed again.

She heard a rustle from the other men, and lifted her good hand. "Stay." The Vicomte rose from his hiding place and seconded her command with a gesture to the other men. She appreciated his help, but she no longer needed it.

Elise struggled against the tree and felt the arrow break loose from the bark. She stood, bleeding, the shaft still embedded in her arm, and addressed the aristocrats in the bushes. "My friends," she said. "Adolphe Dufosset tried to murder me here where I stood, and you men—all of you *men*, and armed—weren't able to stop it. Since the death of my father, I've counted on you for protection. Today you have failed." She cast her eyes about the clearing, but the only face she could see was the Vicomte's. Not even Bernard had come forward. "I think I shall have no further need of you."

"My dear," the Vicomte said. "You're injured. It's a wonder you're not overcome. You don't know what you're saying."

"I do, my lord," said Elise. She swayed on her feet, and Enyo came to her side, standing against her until her legs stopped shaking. "I will not be getting married to your son today. Nor any day."

Now Bernard stood. "Elise! Think of what you are doing!"

Elise ignored him.

"It isn't your choice," said the Vicomte. "I have a contract."

"I have a unicorn," said Elise.

"You have more than that." Gitta stepped out of the woods. At her back were a half dozen creatures out of legend. These were not small, goat-like unicorns as Enyo was, but tall, majestic horned monsters, their bearing as elegant as stags, their coats shining whiter than chalk. Their eyes were black as they looked upon the men in the clearing, and Elise felt murder in each of their hearts.

Gitta smiled and shrugged. "You were right, Elise. There are many unicorns in this wood. But they are very hard to call."

The men cowered now as the unicorns fanned out to surround Gitta and Elise.

"I seem to have missed something quite grand," Gitta whispered to the younger girl.

Only Gitta would see a man's corpse and think that. Elise forced a smile through the pain. She raised her voice again. "I have made a decision. I am the lady of these lands. My house, my woods—you may remain at my pleasure, or leave on my command."

The Vicomte stepped forward. "Elise," he said gently. "Your father—"

"My father did not know what power I wield." Gitta was now supporting her weight, but still Elise stood on her feet and spoke to the men. "My father did not know that I could protect myself."

The unicorns, as one, turned their heads toward the Vicomte. Their horns stood out like swords.

"I think you should get used to seeing these animals on my lands, my lord," said Elise. "For they shall be here, watching, if you or any other try to collect me. I will protect my property by any means I must."

Somehow she remained conscious until the last man left.

•••

"I don't know if I can leave you," said Gitta, who sat sharpening her sword by firelight. Enyo relaxed on the hearth, her belly full of pork, a half-gnawed bone near her snout.

Elise checked her bandages. "I am healing well. And even the scar won't be so bad."

"That's not what I mean." Gitta came over and sat by Elise's side. "How do you know your own power will be enough to keep the unicorns around once I am gone? How do I know that the Vicomte won't bring an army to your door as soon as I cross the border?"

Elise shrugged. "If he does, then I will meet him. I can hire men as well as he can. And even the threat of unicorns is a deterrent. I will watch over myself from now on."

"I would have been there, if I could—," Gitta began, for the fourteenth time.

And for the fourteenth time, Elise shut her down. "It is not your fault. I didn't realize how desperate Adolphe had become. And besides, when you did come, you brought me something even better than your protection. The means by which I can create my own."

Elise glanced out the window, where she could still see the unicorns in her garden. There were more and more every day now. They came, as if awakened from some deep hibernation in the wilderness, and clustered on her lands. Let the Vicomte bring an army. She was ready.

Beside her, Gitta was silent, staring down at her roughened hands. At last she spoke. "I don't know if I can leave you," she said again. "I don't know if I want to."

"You don't have to." Elise smiled in relief. "You can leave the Order. Stay here with me, where Enyo will be able to live out her days in peace. Stay here with me, where there are real, wild unicorns. Stay here and teach me all the magic I never got the chance to learn."

Gitta looked away at the fire and said nothing. Elise peeked into Enyo's mind, and her heart sank. She saw mountain trails and endless vistas. She saw deserts and islands and dusty plains. The unicorn dreamed of travel, just like its mistress. For a moment, Elise pictured the three of them, together in those exotic places, but it would never be. Gitta would move on, and Elise would stay here, where she'd made a promise to her people.

Elise felt her friend's rough skin against her soft palm. "I don't think you need my magic," said Gitta. "You don't need any-one. Your own magic is stronger than you think."

The Spirit Jar

BY KAREN MAHONEY

What do you get when you put a vampire in an airplane thousands of miles above the Atlantic?

I swallow hard and try not to think about the punch line to *that* particular joke. It's bad enough that Theo is sending me overseas in the first place, but now I'm feeling sick—*airsick?* How would I know, I've not flown since I was a small child—and my brain is sadistically torturing me with every scenario that could possibly go wrong.

There are a lot of things that could go wrong.

At least, that's what my new roommate cheerfully told me while dropping me at the airport for my Boston to London trip.

I push aside comforting fantasies of Holly crashing her stupid motorcycle on the way back to our apartment, and decide that I may as well settle in for the flight and watch a movie. *Yeah, because a movie will take my mind off the fact that we're flying over* water *and I'm a freaking vampire.*

Crossing running water should be impossible for vampires. This is just one of the many so-called "facts" that proved to be pure myth after I was turned a decade ago. I push up the white plastic blind and look out the window, but the ocean is hidden by puffy purple clouds. Surely you can't really count the *sea* as running water. Where is it supposed to "run" to, anyway? I'd crossed plenty of rivers in the last ten years, and nothing bad had ever happened. Whoever makes this crap up really needs to get a life.

Sighing heavily, I lean my forehead against the reinforced glass. I should be reviewing the details of my destination, or maybe ensuring I know exactly what the rare book I need to "retrieve"—an ancient Arabic text—actually *looks* like. Instead, all I can think about is the fact that I'm flying through the air in a metal coffin.

I slam the cover down over the tiny window and push my sunglasses up onto the top of my head, balancing them among my annoyingly springy black curls. My blue contacts are firmly in place to hide the natural silver of my eyes. The contact lenses hurt like hell and make me feel grouchy.

Well, grouchier than normal.

I begin clicking noisily through channels on the screen attached to the back of the seat in front of me. I ignore the irritated *tutting* of the fat lady sitting by the aisle. Just let her open her mouth and say *one word*, then she'll be sorry she switched seats to come sit over here in the first place.

What did I do to deserve this? But I already know the answer to that. My Maker likes to needle me when he can, especially ever since I'd gotten home from my year-long sabbatical. It's like he is punishing me for daring to leave him. I remember the particularly wicked smile on Theo's face while he gave me the details of this crappy assignment.

Flicking past the sequel to a teen werewolf movie that did particularly well last summer, I decide on a romcom starring an actress I don't recognize. The girl is as cute as a newborn kitten and doesn't look old enough to drive the expensive car she's using to get to school. I feel old and out of touch.

This is going to be a very long flight.

• • •

I stand in a shadowed doorway around the corner from St. Martin's Lane—not far from Trafalgar Square with its fierce lions—and watch a young couple stroll past. They are holding hands and, under the gentle illumination of the old-fashioned iron lamps in the narrow, cobbled court where I'm lurking, I can see the loving expressions on their faces. Something cold twists inside of me—somewhere in my chest—and I have to swallow to get rid of the suddenly bitter taste in my mouth.

My mind wanders to the crazy time I've had since touching down at Heathrow; getting through airport security was a nightmare of epic proportions. My bad feeling about this entire trip appears to be coming true, and a growing part of me is beginning to wish I could charter some kind of boat to take me over to Ireland. Maybe I could lose myself among my dad's relatives. Perhaps they wouldn't even care that I hadn't aged a day since turning eighteen. They haven't seen me since I was a kid, anyway. How would they know the difference?

Riiight. Like Theo wouldn't send . . . *people* to bring me back. He hadn't wanted to send his "little Moth" on this particular assignment to begin with—where I'd be so far away from him—but I was fast becoming his best Retriever and this was a job that had to be dealt with quickly. It also needed to be carried out by a vampire young enough to walk in daylight, especially during the summer months, and who could travel overseas and pass for human.

Lucky me. I can't stop the sneer that curls my lip, remembering just in time to hide my fangs for the benefit of any passersby. Dammit, there are too many people around. This tiny street is supposed to be deserted after nine p.m. Sure, "Theatre Land" is just around the corner, but there's nothing open down here.

I shake my head as though I can shake off the lingering frustration, and focus my attention on the bookstore across the pedestrianized court. The steel gate is only secured with a padlock and would be easy to break, if that's the entrance I choose. But I've done my homework, running reconnaissance earlier today, and discovered an even easier way in.

At floor level there is a delivery hatch where books and other merchandise are brought into the shop. I'd spent the morning staking out the area and watching until a white van pulled up on

Charing Cross Road. Its occupant, a stocky delivery guy in blue overalls, wheeled a trolley of boxes to the hatch and dropped them through one by one.

I couldn't resist smiling to myself and wondering why people made it so easy. Of course the entrance was small, but then so am I—that's why Theo sends me on these jobs. I hadn't been able to see all the way inside the little doorway, but from what I could make out it had looked like the deliveries were thrown down a crude wooden chute and into the basement.

Perfect.

I crack my knuckles and slip through shadows pooled around the edges of the street, careful to avoid the light from the closest lamp. I sniff the air, stiffening when I detect a faint animal scent. I spot the mangy-looking fox out the corner of my eye as it pokes its nose into a trash can. Urban foxes are apparently common in London, but I am still strangely invigorated by the sight. It's like a magical encounter; a shamanic meeting with my totem animal, or something romantic like that. Our eyes meet and we exchange a long look; she's a tough cookie, this little fox, but I'm a lot tougher.

She turns tail and runs.

I crouch by the hatch and test it. Of course it's bolted from the inside—maybe with more than one set of locks—but that doesn't stop me from sitting on the ground and setting the soles of my boots against the forest green paint at the top of the hatch. I lean back on my forearms, using them for leverage, and push with both legs, trying to break the little door.

It's trickier than I thought it would be; there's nothing to hold onto. No conveniently placed lamppost or bicycle rail. My arms keep slipping backward on the cold ground, but I dig in with my elbows and kick my legs again, one final time.

The hatch crashes inward with a crack that echoes along the quiet street.

Cringing, I glance in both directions before flipping myself over and wriggling through the ragged opening on my belly. It reminds me of my favorite scene in *Star Wars* when Princess Leia uses a laser rifle to blast an entrance into the trash compactor, then throws herself through the gap without a second thought.

I heart Princess Leia. Sue me.

"Into the garbage chute, flyboy," I mutter, before tumbling down into darkness.

•••

The wooden delivery slide turns out to be badly made from shabby plywood, and I'm glad that good sense won out and I'd chosen jeans for this expedition. As it is, I still have to pull several splinters from my hands at the bottom of the makeshift chute, wincing as I wait for the tiny wounds to close up on their own.

There are some benefits to being a Creature of the Night.

I roll my eyes at my own morbid sense of humor and rub my sore palms together. I am in some kind of dispatch room. Piles of books are scattered around on the desks, and almost every inch of floor space is taken up with boxes upon boxes. A machine that looks like it might be for weighing and stamping outgoing mail is precariously balanced on a tall cabinet against one wall, while the other is covered with crooked shelves that have seen better days.

The whole place stinks of something stale and sort of musty, as though a giant wet dog has taken up residence.

I jump down from the edge of the chute and tiptoe to the doorway that leads into the shop. I'd scoped out the shop during the day, wandering among the browsing patrons and tourists but, obviously, hadn't actually been able to get inside the delivery area until now.

The door is locked, but with nothing more than bolts on the outside—top and bottom. I'd noticed that earlier.

I take a few steps back and then run at the door, aiming my flying kick toward the bottom where one of the bolts should be. There is a satisfying crunch and I feel the shock of impact all the way up both legs and into my hips. I set my shoulder against the door and heave it the rest of the way open—at least enough so I can slip through the gap. I am leaving more of a mess behind than I normally do, but that can't be helped. It's not like there'll be fingerprints that can be traced, and nobody is going to hear the noise way down here in the basement. Not to mention the fact that I'll be long gone before anyone is even aware that there's been a break-in.

Of course, I have been known to speak too soon—

Which is when I come face-to-face with a young guy who looks as shocked to see me as I am to see him. We stand staring at each other for an uncomfortable moment, under the faint yellow glow of the tiny spotlights set into the ceiling around the single display case.

He isn't very tall, though still taller than me—not exactly difficult given that I'm pretty slight. His shoulders indicate a wiry strength, though, and his hands are clenched into fists.

The boy has beautiful tanned skin and hazel eyes that are so luminous they almost appear gold. His black hair is short but messy, and it looks like it would curl if left to grow any longer. It makes me think suddenly of Theo, and how this is what his hair might be like if he ever cut it.

Irritated at myself for thinking of my Maker at a time like this, I attempt to look fierce and give this interloper my best glare. "How the hell did you get in here?"

The guy raises black brows. "I'd ask you the same question, but it seems pretty obvious how *you* got inside." He nods at the half-destroyed door to the dispatch room behind me. "Subtle."

He has an English accent that I might think was sexy under other circumstances, but I refuse to get sidetracked by the fact that he's totally cute. And young—maybe around seventeen.

It feels as though I've already lost control of this situation, and there's nothing that makes me madder than being out of control. Especially when the kid standing in front of me seems strangely composed after seeing a girl-in-black burst through the door She-Hulk style.

"You're staring," he says with a sudden grin. "Didn't your mum ever tell you it's rude to stare?"

"My mother is dead," I snap and then immediately wish I hadn't. Why am I telling this stranger something like that?

I shake my head and then sniff the air, narrowing my eyes against the sudden whiff of magic. "What are you?"

The boy is still smiling. "Why don't you come over here and find out?"

I let out an exaggerated sigh. "I don't want to hurt you, but I have work to do. Stay out of my way and this doesn't have to get unpleasant."

"If you're going to threaten me, I think it's only fair that I know who I'm dealing with. What's your name?" I have a sneaking suspicion that he might be laughing at me.

"You first," I counter.

He shrugs. "I'm Adam."

"Moth."

"Interesting name," Adam says. "Did your parents have a sense of humor?"

I bite back a sudden smile. This is crazy, but I can't stop the feeling that this guy—Adam—isn't someone I want to hurt. He seems harmless enough.

My eyes flicker to the display case. It is filled with books, but even a fleeting glance confirms that the particular tome I came to steal is gone. *Dammit!* I was only here this afternoon, and it was *right there.* Don't tell me someone bought it already—not at the price these people were selling it for. The book didn't even belong in a place like this—an occult bookstore on the back-streets of London. It should be in a freaking museum.

I look at the boy's hands and my stomach clenches. This is the first time I even notice that he's holding something. A book.

The book?

"Give it to me," I say, before I can even think about it. I don't know who he is or what he might be able to do to me, but I don't care. I need that book or I'll never get away from Theo. Each failure is cataloged; every time I don't quite achieve the impossible tasks he sets me is just one more reason for him to keep me close.

I don't let myself think of the alternative: that each success *also* ties me more securely to his side. Why would he ever let me go if I am so damn good at retrieving the items he sends me to find? If I think about that too often, I'll go crazy. I have to stay strong. The minute I let myself feel the creeping despair, I will lose myself. I will lose the part of me that is Marie—and I'll always be only Moth.

Adam raises an eyebrow. What is it about the men in my life that they all seem to know that trick? It's a weakness of mine. My mind wanders to a brief image of Jason Murdoch—all golden hair and deep brown eyes. I push it away and slam the door on it; he is my enemy, and I would do well to remember that.

I have the scars to prove it.

I wonder if the same can be said for the kid standing in front of me right now, with the amused expression tugging at his mouth and crinkling the corners of his eyes. Is *he* my enemy?

"You want this?" he says, holding up a slim leather-bound volume that has seen better days.

The door to the display case is open. The weak light from above glints on the glass and shows me Adam's reflection. I take a step back, wondering if he has noticed the fact that I don't have one. Another part of me that slowly slips away as each day passes.

"I need that book," I say, trying to sound like a tough guy but only managing petulance.

"You're telling me," he says, taking a step forward, "that we're both here for the same book? I find that a little too much of a coincidence. Don't you?"

"I don't believe in coincidences," I say, even though I've never given it a thought. It's just something to say; something that might distract him. "I only know that you're holding what I came here for. I'm not leaving without it."

Adam licks his lips. "I need this book far more than you could ever know." He looks almost regretful. "I'm afraid you're going to have to make do without this one. There are plenty more to choose from."

This can't happen, I won't let it. Rolling my shoulders and cracking my knuckles—a nervous habit that Theo has tried to *encourage* me to lose—I feel the satisfying creak of my leather jacket and set my booted feet more widely apart.

"You're not leaving with that book," I say. "Save yourself some pain and put it down. I'll let you go and we never have to give this unfortunate incident another thought."

Adam sneers. "That's very generous of you," he says, "but I think you'll find I don't scare so easy."

What a shame, I can't help thinking. And then I launch myself at him, running the few steps between us and leaping at the last possible moment to make the most of what little momentum I can build up in the restricted space.

We tumble to the ground and the book flies out of his grasp. His hands come up to try to push me off him, but I have my fists gripping the collar of his denim jacket and a knee on either side of his torso. I drag him into a sitting position and bring his face toward mine. Our noses are practically touching.

He doesn't look surprised that I'm so strong, but I don't let that phase me. I grin at him and give him a quick flash of fang— let him think he imagined it later, if he wants. He can't prove anything.

"I tried to do this nicely, Adam," I say, shaking my head as though I am genuinely sorry that things have come to this. "I don't want to hurt you, but I *will* be taking that book with me."

"What do you want with it?" His eyes are a little wide, and he's lost some of his color; his bravado seems to be drying up. Maybe he got more than just a fleeting glimpse of my fangs.

I brace my left foot on the floor and give him a shake. "That's none of your business, kid."

"I think it *is* my business if you're going to take the book I've worked so hard to find. I don't just want it—I *need* it. If you're determined to ruin my life I deserve to know why."

"'Ruin your life'?" I echo. "Aren't you being a bit melodramatic?" I can't help the frown that crosses my face. What is *with* this dude? He seems so sincere, and something about the quiet desperation in his voice is making my conscience prickle and my stomach hurt. I feel like I'm doing something terrible to him, but that's ridiculous under the circumstances. After all, we're both thieves.

His voice is suddenly much harder. "Let me go, Moth."

I shake him again, just because I can.

"Let me go," he says again, "or you'll be sorry."

"Right, kiddo," I reply, unable to resist the opportunity to bug him. "What are you going to do? Threaten me to death? Take it from me, Adam, if you're going to make threats you sure as hell better be able to follow up on them, otherwise—"

And then he just . . . disappears. My hands are left clutching empty air, and I stumble forward, partly because he's no longer there but mostly because I'm in a state of shock.

What? Where did he—?

Adam is right behind me and grabs a clump of my curls. My head is wrenched back, and my neck feels like it's about to snap. He's stronger than he looks—maybe not as strong as me, but way stronger than his skinny frame would have you believe. He certainly had *me* fooled.

This time I topple backward as he releases me and steps out of the way, moving faster than any human should move. I'm sprawled on my ass, and for a moment I don't even care about the indignity of it. I'm curious about this kid. He smells human enough, but there's something *other* about him, after all.

"That's quite a trick," I say, trying to catch my breath and keep him occupied so he doesn't think to snatch the book immediately.

It's lying just out of reach. I could stretch and snag it, but there's no way I'll be able to do it before Adam stops me.

"I told you not to take it," he says. He's not smiling anymore, no longer mocking or smirking. He doesn't look happy to have proved me wrong.

I watch him carefully, as though he's an exotic new species I've discovered. There's something fascinating about the way his eyes are shining in the half-light; now I know what people see when they catch sight of *my* eyes in all their silver glory. We are like two sides of different coins, this boy and me. He's all fire and nervous energy, and I'm ice and barely restrained power.

I sit up and rub the back of my head where I banged it on the floor. My hair is wild around my face.

"Tell me how you did that," I say, genuinely curious now.

"What," he replies, "*this?*"

And he disappears again.

Now you see me, now you don't. Just blinks out of existence and then reappears a second later, right next to the damn book. He bends and scoops it up, cradling it in his arms as though it is something truly precious—a treasure way beyond its monetary value.

I lick my lips and wonder if I could try to glamour him, but I'm wearing the damn contacts and I doubt it would do me much good even if I weren't. If he's not fully human, I have no idea if my vampiric gaze will work on him. It's not like I'm much good at it yet, anyway.

I flip onto all fours and crouch, glaring at this kid who has dared to get in the way of my mission. I have to give that book to Theo. I have to prove to him that he can trust me to do what he wants, that I'm not just waiting for any opportunity to escape him forever. No matter how much you love someone, they aren't always good for you. Theo is a beautiful drug; he's like prescription medication I genuinely needed for a while, otherwise I would have died—for real. Now I'm hooked and I can't stop.

I can survive without him. I have to try.

But maybe he can't survive without *me*. I know too little about the way things work between a Maker and the vampires he creates. Theo doesn't make many new vamps anymore. As far as I'm aware there haven't been any others in the decade since he made me. And before me? I don't know. The others in our Family tell me it has been a long time, and they were surprised that Theo turned me—especially given how young I was at the time. They still don't know *why*.

All this is whirling in my mind as I watch Adam watching me. His black hair holds blue tones under the flickering light of the display cabinet; his skin the color of pale golden sand, and his eyes almost matching. I wonder where his family came from, originally.

He is edging toward the stairs. I remember that I don't know how he got inside the store in the first place. Of course, he probably just did that handy teleportation thing. What was he? Some sort of spirit? I had to speak to Theo about this.

"Don't try to follow me," Adam says, his voice suddenly less confident. He sounds terribly alone. "I have to use the book."

Now it's my turn to look confused. "You know what it's for? How can you 'use' it, anyway? I thought it was written in Arabic."

"It is." He is backing slowly up the stairs, almost to the corner where the narrow staircase turns and heads up the final short flight onto the main floor of the shop.

"So you can read Arabic, now, as well as do impressions of Houdini?"

"I can read it well enough," he replies, stumbling on the uneven shape of the step that curves around the bend.

And there's my lucky break; that minor slip is sufficient. I suddenly burst into action, bolting up the staircase and reaching toward him. I move so quickly that everything around me seems to happen in slow motion. My hand is stretching, fingers fully extended; the book is almost in my grasp. Adam is still wobbling, one arm flailing for the banister, the other trying to tuck the book inside his jacket.

But I am fast. Faster than him. As my fingers brush the old leather of the cover and I feel the grit of almost a century on my skin, Adam disappears.

I scream with frustration—I was so close! What will I tell Theo? How will I ever track down a kid who can teleport, seemingly at will?

I stop freaking out when I realize that I am holding the book after all. Adam has gone, and the book is in my hand. I'm so surprised that I almost drop the stupid thing, juggling for a moment to retain my grip on one corner of the slim volume.

Running to the top of the stairs I gaze around the store, my night vision not necessary up here thanks to the miniature display lights lining the bookshelves at intervals. Not to mention the added illumination provided by the streetlamps outside the huge front windows.

I can't understand where he's gone. Why would Adam just . . . leave? Especially without the book he claimed to need so desperately. I'd believed him when he said how important it was. I'd actually felt *guilty*. But he flipped out the minute things got tough. Okay, so it wasn't like we were best friends after a few minutes of brawling in the basement of an occult bookshop, but he'd—

Something flies at me from the shadows, and I feel a bone-crunching impact on my right shoulder. My quick instincts save me from broken bones as I throw myself out of the way just in time. I still get walloped, but it could have been a lot worse.

Rubbing my arm and cursing because I've dropped the freaking book, I face off with Adam. Again.

So the kid *isn't* giving up. He'd simply teleported farther into the shop and waited for me to come up the stairs. It was simple enough for him to hide behind the counter cash register; there are no lights in that area, and I was distracted by his supposed "disappearance." He is holding a heavy wooden tube of some sort. It looks like a bizarre musical instrument made of bamboo. It's big, and I can certainly attest to the fact that it is *heavy*. The feeling is only just beginning to return to my right hand after Adam smashed his makeshift weapon into my shoulder.

The book is on the floor between us. Someone is going to have to make a move for it, and then the other will have an opening to attack. I eye him with irritation verging on respect, and I can't help noticing that he no longer looks afraid. He looks kind of pissed.

"I told you, I'm not leaving without the book. Why can't you just let me have it? What do *you* want it for?" His voice trembles with barely suppressed rage.

This has possibilities, I think. Maybe I can get him so angry he'll slip up. "I have to give it to my employer. It belongs in a collection overseas, not here in London."

"What collection? What are you talking about?" His fingers twitch convulsively around the wooden baton, and he raises it as though he might attack me again.

"I'm retrieving it," I say. "That's what I do. Retrieve things and return them to their rightful owners."

I watch the delicate flesh of his throat move as he swallows. "Maybe we can make a deal," he says.

This surprises me. I like deals; deals can be good, so long as I end up getting what I want out of them. "What kind of deal?"

"Let me use the book tonight, and I'll give it to you afterward. I won't need it after that."

I snort. "Right. And I have reason to believe you'll actually give it to me because . . . ?" I let the words trail off and can't help smiling at his nerve. This kid certainly has balls, I'll give him that.

"Because . . ." His face creases in frustration, and then his expression clears and turns triumphant. "Because you can come with me and keep an eye on it. If you don't let me—and the book—out of your sight, then you're not risking anything."

"How do I know you won't just pull a disappearing act again?" I don't know whether to believe him, but Adam has something intriguingly sincere about him. He's either an excellent liar or he's telling the truth.

"Well, I suppose you don't know that *I* won't disappear, but at least you'll know you won't lose the book."

I raise my eyebrows, silently encouraging him to continue.

"Why do you think I dropped the book on the stairs when I teleported? I can transport myself and anything I'm wearing—as long as the clothes are made of natural materials—but I can't take man-made objects with me."

This would make a lot of sense, except for one little problem: "The book is made of leather. That's a 'natural material.'"

He looks vaguely embarrassed. "I thought so too, but either there are other materials used in its construction, or it has some sort of magical protection on it. Maybe both."

I let my eyes leave his face for a moment and glance down at the book. It doesn't *look* very magical. I shrug and meet his almost desperate gaze again. What do I know about sacred Arabic texts? It's all Greek to me; I'm just an Irish-American girl brought up in Boston. This was my first trip out of the country since I was a child, back when we'd gone on regular trips to Ireland to visit Dad's family. Mom's had disowned her after she'd gotten pregnant with Sinéad out of wedlock and then dared to *marry* the man who was responsible. Bad enough to be a slut, worse still that she'd lived with the consequences and made a life with Rory O'Neal—a man my mother's family had considered far beneath her.

"Okay." I square my shoulders and meet his gaze. "Say I believe you. What then? What exactly do you need this thing for?"

Adam is staring at the book again. There is a muscle flickering in his smooth cheek. "I have to help my girlfriend move on," he says. His voice is almost too quiet to hear.

"Move on?" I'm confused. A crazy image of a young couple clinging together flashes into my mind. Is he having trouble shaking loose an unwanted girlfriend? Surely that can't be what all this is about.

"Her soul is trapped," he says. "I have to free her, otherwise she'll never find peace."

My mouth is suddenly dry. "Is she sick?" It sounds like maybe she's in a coma.

"No," he replies, and I realize that he is crying. "She's dead."

•••

We are sitting in a café at Victoria Station. Adam has been as good as his word and hasn't tried to disappear on me. Not yet, anyway.

I'd insisted on being the one to hold the book, just to be on the safe side. I tucked it inside my messenger bag and kept a tight hold on it as we walked along St. Martin's Lane, heading for the bus stops beyond Trafalgar Square. Before I arrived in London, I had only ever seen those four huge lions in movies; the statues are even more impressive in the "flesh." I wonder if it's true that they are called John, Paul, George, and Ringo, or if that is just one of Theo's little jokes.

The bus ride—my first ever on a double-decker—should have been more exciting, but I felt nothing but a heavy sense of melancholy. I rested my cheek against the window as I looked out at the familiar-yet-strange city streets from the top deck of the red monstrosity, and wished I was back home in Boston. I was glad when we reached our destination after the short journey, and I steered my new companion into the comforting warmth of the first coffee shop we saw.

The rain began to fall as I closed the door behind us.

I am nursing a mug of hot chocolate, and Adam is absent-mindedly stirring packets of sugar into his black coffee. I wonder how much sugar will be enough for him and begin to make bets with myself on whether he will go back to grab more of the brown paper packets. He takes a sip and doesn't even flinch.

"So tell me," I say, sticking my finger into my drink and popping a scoop of cream into my mouth. "Tell me about your girl-friend."

Adam smiles wistfully and puts down his cup. "Hasna? She's the most . . . *was* the most beautiful girl you'll ever see. I loved her the minute I saw her. She started in Year Twelve after her family moved to the area. I was assigned as her 'buddy,' and I had to show her around. We had so much in common: both of us from Moroccan families; both struggling with learning Arabic to make our fathers happy, but really just wanting to fit in with our friends."

He goes quiet for a moment, and I don't say a word. I want to ask if "Year Twelve" is the same as junior or senior year in high school, but it's like there's a magic spell on our table. We're tucked against the window with a view of a line of black cabs like giant beetles crouching outside the station.

"Meeting her was the best thing that ever happened to me," Adam says. He's not smiling any more.

This is all very moving, I want to say, *but what about the book?* Why were you stealing an ancient text from a bookstore, and why were you willing to risk getting your throat torn out by me to keep it? And how the *hell* do you do that cool disappearing trick?

I don't ask any of these things. Instead, I push away my mug of delicious but empty calories and put my hand over his. "How did she die?"

He swallows and tears well up in his eyes again. For a moment, I consider taking the book and running. Just leaving this kid and his tragic life behind—he is nothing to me. What do I care about a so-called magical book and a dead girlfriend? My shoulders slump and I stay put.

Who am I trying to fool? I'm still me; still Marie.

"Tell me," I say, giving his cold hand a squeeze. I wonder if he notices that my hands are even colder than his. I haven't taken blood in too long and already knew it was going to be a problem on this trip. Theo gave me a list of "safe donors" before I left, including the contact details of the head honcho vampire in London. Like he actually thought I'd *use* any of those lifelines?

Forget it, Theo. No way you're making me more of a monster. If I can't feed from blood banks or from my Maker, I won't feed at all. The longest I'd gone was six days, and I still remember how weak I'd been when Theo finally found me, curled up and whimpering with hunger and misery outside *Subterranean*.

I swallow and drag my mind away from those memories, not wanting to remember how Theo had force-fed me. Instead, I listen to Adam as he tells me about his lost love and why he needs Arabic magic to free her soul.

"She was murdered not far from here," he begins. "We were at the theater; I'd saved up for weeks. Hasna wanted to wait at the stage door after the performance, try to get her program autographed. We . . . took a wrong turn, somehow. I don't know what happened, but we went out of a fire exit and ended up all turned around. I took us down an alley that I thought must come out behind the theater but . . ." He shakes his head, unable to continue.

Giving him a moment to collect himself, I listen to the busy sounds of the coffee shop. There's music playing, not the usual *musak* like in my local Starbucks back home but something funkier, something I haven't heard before. The murmur of voices reaches me from the surrounding tables along with the familiar hiss of milk being steamed at the counter, just across the aisle. It's late, but people are still walking in and placing orders. I pull my china mug closer toward me, wondering how much longer the café will stay open.

Adam fixes me with those disturbing hazel-gold eyes. They are more hazel again, as though being out among the masses forces him to blend in and look like the human being that I initially took him for. He still smells 100 percent human to me, but now I know different. I want to know what he is, how he can do what he does. I've never seen anything like it, and I've seen some weird crap in my life.

He says, "It was over before I knew what was really happening.

I can move fast when I have to, and there's the whole teleportation thing . . . but even with all that, I couldn't save her. I would've done anything to save her life—even if it meant revealing my powers."

My internal bullshit detector beeps. "Wait," I say. "You mean she didn't know?"

He looks embarrassed and squirms in his seat. "We hadn't even been together a year. I was going to tell her."

I can't stop the snort that escapes me. *Sure*, I think, knowing I'm being uncharitable. A guy insisting that he was going to "tell his girl the truth." I want to shake this kid and tell him I know a thing or two about that line.

He is angry now, and I think I prefer that to the broken young man who was sitting here only moments ago. "I *was* going to tell her. You don't know anything about me, Moth." He makes my name sound like a curse. "I loved her. Hasna was my whole life."

"Keep it down, Romeo," I say, my gaze darting around the café. Adam is almost shouting, and we're drawing attention. "I'm sorry, okay? Just tell me what happened so we can put it right."

"We can't 'put it right,'" he replies, but at least he isn't yelling at me. "She's dead, I already told you that. She was murdered. It wasn't until after that I found out it wasn't quite the random act of violence that I thought it was. We were an unlucky statistic according to the police." His lips twist with disgust. "Useless bastards."

I wonder how fair it is to blame the police for not being able to deal with a supernatural crime but keep my mouth shut and wait for Adam to continue.

He tells me about the murder; about the knife in the dark and the bearded man who spoke Arabic while he sliced Hasna up like she was nothing more than meat at his dinner table. The man had been tracking Adam for a long time, attracted by his unique biology and magical heritage. And yet it was Hasna who turned out to be the victim—the human companion of a half-human boy, sacrificed in order to summon a dark spirit. Adam tells me that he couldn't move—not even to teleport—and how he had to watch his girlfriend die.

"But what *are* you?" I finally ask. I can't resist butting in anymore, and he is taking too long. "You look human."

"So do you," he counters.

I shrug. "You even smell human."

"I'm half-human. That might explain what you're sensing."

I nod slowly. "So, you're also half . . . ?"

"Djinn. On my mother's side."

"Gin?" I can't stop the sudden image of a dark green bottle of alcohol superimposed over Adam's face. "*What?*"

A slight smile lifts the corners of his mouth. "Djinn, Genie . . . you know."

Oh. I lean forward, interested despite myself. "Like in *Aladdin?*"

He rolls his eyes. "Yeah, *just* like that."

I still can't shake the Aladdin-connection and realize with a jolt of misplaced humor that I wasn't so far off with the imaginary bottle. Aren't Genies kept in bottles?

Adam frowns. "What are you thinking?"

"Nothing," I say, too quickly. I feel guilty for making light of things. This kid has lost someone he loved, and that's something I understand. I take a steadying breath and think of Mom.

Now it's his turn to lean forward. He searches my face. "I saw your teeth," he begins, voice hesitant. "Back in the shop."

"Thanks." I smile sweetly. "I try to keep them clean and shiny."

"You know what I mean. Are you . . . ?" The sentence trails off. Maybe vampires are too crazy for him to contemplate, even considering what he is and what he knows of the world.

I decide to go easy on him. "I am," I say. I glance around the café quickly, checking that nobody at a nearby table is looking our way, and show him my fangs again. They're currently in their "dormant" state, retracted as far as they will go—but they're still wicked sharp.

I sit back and give him a cheeky wink.

"Woah," he says, his golden eyes shining. "That's so cool."

I stare at him for a moment that stretches on and on. I don't understand this boy. He is unlike anyone I have ever met before. He smells human, but he is most certainly *not* human—at least, not all of him. His mother was a . . . a *Djinn*. Whatever next? I am beginning to learn that the strangeness of my life only scratches the surface of the *otherness* of all the things that make up this world. It's exhilarating and scary all at the same time.

I think I like it. I think I like *him*.

No, not in that way. He is good-looking—handsome, even, in a very clean cut sort of way. He smells delicious, it's true. But he's not—

I shake my head and focus on what Adam is saying. He's been talking for a while, and I'm forced to play catch-up; this could be important and here I am comparing him with my Maker. And if I'm going to be honest, I'm also comparing him to a guy I met just two short months ago. I don't want to think about Jason Murdoch now.

I don't want to think about Jace ever again.

Adam gives me a strange look. "Have you even heard a word I've said?"

I shrug. Well, I was half listening. "Sure. Dead girlfriend; evil magician; spirit thing; magic book. That about sum it up?"

He doesn't smile, and I can hardly blame him. I could stand to take a lesson or two in sensitivity. Humor makes for an uncomfortable shield.

"Are you going to help me or not?" Adam asks, his hazel eyes like two stones.

A magician called Bilal had killed Hasna as part of a ritual to release a particularly nasty sort of Djinn that he wanted to control. Apparently, spilling the blood of an innocent can create a portal through which *Afarit* can escape from their plane of existence and into ours.

Only things hadn't gone to plan for Bilal and the Afarit was too strong for him. It killed the magician and stole his body before escaping the scene of the crime—leaving Adam cradling the life-less body of the beautiful teenage girl he loved.

"Well, *are* you?" Adam repeats, his voice trembling with too many emotions to name. "Hasna's funeral is two days from now, but Bilal—actually, the Afarit impersonating Bilal—took her soul away in a glass jar. Will you help me to set her free?"

"I already said I would, didn't I?" I toss my hair, impatient to get moving. "Is it possible that we can . . . bring her back some-how?" I have no idea how Djinn magic works, but if a teenage boy can teleport and the bad guys can summon spirits with the blood of humans, who knows?

He shakes his head. "No, she's gone. We can't just put her soul back in her body. It doesn't work like that. When you're dead, you're dead."

I'm tempted to remind him that my existence contradicts his rather black-and-white view of mortality, but decide to cut him some slack. "Okay, so what do we need?"

"This." He opens his denim jacket and shows me the dagger in its leather sheath strapped around his ribs. *Nifty.* He gets up and heads over to the napkin stand.

I follow, pulling on my jacket with a satisfying rattle of zips. Adam grabs a fistful of salt packets and tucks them into his pocket. He hands me some more.

"Here," he says, "we'll need these."

I raise my eyebrows. "We're going to eat him? Really, Adam, you should've warned me." I flash him a grin and give him another glimpse of fang. "I would've brought floss for after."

He scowls. "Very funny. No, this is how you trap an Afarit—I'll show you. We summon it with the book and then kill it with the knife Bilal used to murder Hasna."

I'm still wondering what the salt is for when he heads out of the café, not even bothering to see if I follow.

I do.

• • •

We are in a rain-slicked alley behind the theater. Plastic bags flutter like multicolored ghosts, and the wet ground shines black under the single streetlight.

Adam is frowning at the bright light. "That's not going to help."

"You mean you don't want to be able to see what you're doing?"

His eyes meet mine. "I can see in the dark well enough."

"Oh goody," I say. "Me too."

I climb the lamppost in seconds and hang on single-handed at the top. My legs are wrapped around the heavy iron, but it's pretty slippery and not easy to maintain my grip. I have to be fast. I make a fist with my right hand, pull the leather sleeve of my jacket down with my teeth to give me a little protection, and punch out the light. There is a sad buzzing sound and then silence.

I slide down the metal pole and grin at Adam. My cheeks are flushed, and I have to remember that we are here to do something serious. He has already turned away and is crouched on the ground.

He looks up at me. "I think it was here. Where she died, I mean."

I hunker down next to him and touch his shoulder. The mood is deadly serious now, and even I know when to quit messing around. I close my eyes and reach out with my senses, trying to catch a scent—*her* scent.

I shake my head. "Too much rain." I gesture helplessly at the soaked ground. "Sorry, I can't smell anything that isn't wet weeds and dog shit."

"It has to be the *exact* spot." His voice is shaking, and I don't know what to say. "I *think* it was here. How could I forget something like that?"

Adam moves his hand a few inches to the right. "Or maybe here?"

I watch his fingers tremble and bite my lip. I hate this. I hate what I am, but if it can help him, I might as well try.

"Do you have something of hers with you? Something that will still hold her essence? What about the knife?"

He shakes his head. "I cleaned it pretty thoroughly."

I swallow. *Poor guy.* That can't have been easy for him. "Anything else?"

His eyes widen as he fastens onto my gaze. There is hope in the golden depths now, which is better than the misery they held before. "I have her charm bracelet! The clasp broke when we came outside, and I put it in my pocket. I was going to get it fixed for her."

He bows his head and takes a deep breath. Regains control.

I nod, trying to keep him focused. "Okay, good. Give it to me."

Of course, the bracelet is silver. I should've known. I almost laugh but manage to keep my mouth shut. I tug down the sleeve of my too-big jacket once more and cover my hand. "Put it here."

Adam raises an eyebrow but doesn't comment. I wonder if he knows that the silver will burn me. I wonder if he noticed the scars on my arms while we were inside the coffee shop.

Swallowing, I carefully—very carefully—raise the charm bracelet to my face. I'm not too keen on getting a bunch of silver burns on my nose. I take a cautious breath and then another. I try to separate the faint smell coming from the delicate silver chain links. I need to pinpoint that and ignore Adam's signature scent—spicy, like a hot summer sun—and the leather of my coat.

I think I have it and slide the bracelet back into his waiting hand. Adam clutches it in his fist for a moment and then pushes it back into his pocket.

"Did you get anything?"

I nod, not wanting to tell him that I'm not sure. I get on my hands and knees on the wet ground and try to trace the remnants of this girl's murder. Her blood was spilled here just three nights ago—that's what Adam said—even if it had been cleaned up; even with all this goddamn rain, I should be able to pick up something. *Anything.* Murder leaves more than just a ripple.

"Here," I say, my nose almost touching the concrete. There are stone slabs with overgrown weeds creeping out of the gaps, as though trying to drink in the rain. I point at the intersection of two large, flat stones. "Right here."

"You're sure?" Adam is almost on top of me.

"As sure as I can be," I say, not wanting to get his hopes up.

He watches me for a moment, looking as though he is about to say something else. But he closes his mouth and nods. "Okay." He pulls out the dagger. "Okay," he says again, almost a whisper that only I can hear.

I wonder what he would have done if the "exact spot" had been on stone rather than the gap between slabs, but I figure he's due a bit of luck. It's not like Adam's had it easy these past few days. I sit back and watch him work.

First, he begins opening salt packets and tipping out the contents in a rough circle around the site of the murder. It takes a lot of packets to cover the area with a thick enough layer of salt, especially because it keeps dissolving into the ground. Maybe that was why he'd given me extras.

As that thought crosses my mind, Adam nudges me and holds out his hand. "Salt."

I pass it over, grumbling as I see that one of the paper packets has split inside my pocket. I toss a handful over my shoulder for luck, and wonder if Adam will be pissed that I wasted some.

But he's not watching me at all, concentrating solely on his task. It's like he is preparing some kind of ritual. It reminds me of something from one of those old black magic movies. He pushes dark hair out of his eyes; the damp air has given him a cute curl resting on his forehead that makes him look like a half-Moroccan Superman.

Adam senses me watching him and glances up. "What?"

I sit back on my heels. "Nothing. I'm just curious."

"You've never seen magic before?" His face tells the story of his disbelief. "You're a vampire."

"So?" I feel suddenly uncomfortable under his gaze. Getting turned into one of the undead doesn't make me an automatic expert on all things paranormal.

He frowns but doesn't pursue it. "Are you ready?" he asks.

"For what?" I have no idea what to expect, and yet here I am in a deserted alleyway with a complete stranger who is trying to trap an Afarit. This is pretty weird even by my standards. I wonder if I can get away with asking Theo for a raise.

Adam has the book open in one hand and drives the blade into wet earth with the other, whispering words I don't understand. A high-pitched screeching fills the air and drives me to my knees.

I clamp my hands over my ears, but I keep my eyes wide open. That's how I see the black cloud take shape before me. It is like a plume of soot, and it smells of death. I choke on a cough, and I want to cover my mouth, but then I wouldn't be able to block my ears against the horrendous screaming.

The cloud-thing starts to take human shape, and I try to look round it—hoping to see where Adam is. For one gut-clenching moment I think that maybe he's tricked me. Has he summoned a monster and then teleported out of here, leaving me alone to face it?

But, no. He's back, appearing in front of me, the blade is in his hand. He strikes at the creature before it can take human form, but the dagger passes through it.

"What are you doing?" I shout at him, over the shrieking wind that is whirling dust into my eyes and mouth. "There's nothing to hit!"

Adam seems confused. He looks scared, which doesn't fill me with confidence. "I thought—"

But I don't get to hear what he "thought" because the next moment the black smoke becomes solid and a giant fist slams into the side of Adam's face and knocks him to the ground. The only reason his head is still on his stupid shoulders is because he managed to twist to the side, just in time.

He's still out cold, though.

Great, I think. Just perfect.

I look up at the smoke creature and wait for it to swat me like the insect I am.

But the smoke thing doesn't attack me, not right away. Instead it swirls and becomes smaller and more dense. The wind that seemed to spring from nowhere drops, just as quickly as it arrived, and I wipe dirt from my eyes. I pull out the stupid blue contacts while I'm at it and take great pleasure in tossing them away.

I watch the black cloud take the shape of a man. I watch as it coalesces and winds around and around like a miniature whirlwind, until the magician, Bilal, stands before me. He bows and then reaches out a beautifully manicured hand. "Give me the book, little vampire, and maybe I will let you return to your master."

•••

Maybe it's his use of the word "master" that makes me so angry, or maybe it is the way he so easily recognizes what I am. Adam lies quietly on the ground. I am wet and tired, and I don't know what the *hell* is going on. All I know is that Theo sent me for the book, and I am going to take it back to him. No magician or Afarit or smoke monster is going to take it away from me.

I bare my teeth and clench my fists. Maybe I can't fight a funnel of black smoke, but I *can* deal with a middle-aged guy in a suit.

The Djinn-in-human-form grins at me. Its mouth is sort of reptilian. I don't quite know where I've got that image from, but the more I think about it the more perfectly it fits. It licks its human lips. "How does it feel to be the lowest creature on the food chain, little vampire?"

"What do you know of vampires?"

"I know enough." Its voice is smooth and laced with an exotic accent that I don't recognize. "You are beginning to smell dead, did you know that?"

My stomach lurches, and I suddenly feel sick. I don't want to hear this.

It smiles a secret smile. "Your soul is too old for your body."

What am I supposed to say to that? I can only watch this strange being as it toys with me, trying to manipulate my emotions as though I'm nothing. It reminds me of how I feel when my father speaks to me.

The Afarit cocks its head to one side. "Give me the book, and perhaps I will kill you and your little friend quickly."

Another one who wants the damn book. I shake my head and give "Bilal" the finger. "Go screw yourself, Smoky."

And then it raises both hands—human-looking hands—and blasts out with a column of black smoke that lifts and carries me across the alleyway, slamming me into the fence that runs along one side.

I am on my knees with my face pressed against the rough wooden fence. I can feel a splinter work its way into my cheek, and the sharp pain shakes me out of the weird sort of coma. I am staggering to my feet, as though I'm drunk, though it has been a very long time since I was last drunk. The Afarit—if that is what it is—lunges forward before I can turn.

Something sharp hits me in the ribs, just below my heart, and the sickening sound of blade on bone makes me want to puke. I fall forward and the Afarit catches me and, almost tenderly, lays me down on the cold ground. The dagger sticks out of me and *ohmygod* it hurts; it hurts so much and I want Theo to come and take it away and make the pain stop. I can't draw breath to scream, and then I remember that I don't even need to breathe—not all the time. Not anymore. I discovered that last year, and it had taken me several weeks to get used to the idea. Of course, I do still make myself breathe. I need to at least *seem* human. That is important to me.

I lie on the floor in a growing pool of my own blood and wonder why I am thinking of this now. I feel cold—colder than I have ever been, maybe even colder than when I died. Surely the dagger can't kill me, I think. Not again.

It is getting more and more difficult to concentrate.

I try harder. The blade isn't made of silver—I know that much. Adam said it was made of iron, which would hurt the Afarit. So why is it burning between my ribs as though I will break in two at any moment? It must be magic, I think dully, trying to focus on some way I can get myself free. There must be something—I refuse to just lie here like a victim. I feel hot tears leaking out of my eyes. They roll down my temples and into my hair, and I can't stop them.

The Djinn, in the shape of the magician called Bilal, crawls on top of me and lowers his body over mine. I try to shake him off but there is no strength in my limbs; they feel like overcooked spaghetti.

The Afarit's breath is hot on my face, and I feel its neatly trimmed beard touch my cheek. I want to push it away—get it the hell *off* me—but I can't move and the dagger hurts so much. And anyway, he is almost lying on top of the hilt. He will push it even deeper into me if I struggle too much. Large, hot hands press mine against the concrete, and I can feel chunky rings digging into my fingers.

It whispers in my ear: "You stink of fear, little vampire."

Its face is pressed against mine, and I feel a flicker of wet warmth against my temple. I try to jerk away but his weight holding me down is too much. *What is it doing?* Something inside me shivers as I realize that it is *licking* me—lapping up my tears. Its tongue feels long and sharp as it collects every drop of warm, salty moisture from my face and I resolve, in that moment, to never cry again. It will remind me too much of this nightmare.

I feel sick and helpless. I want to kill this thing. Just thinking about sinking my fangs into its throat makes me feel a little better. I test my legs, trying for any sort of movement. I only need leverage, just enough to get my knee up and give this asshole something else to think about.

Bilal's face leers at me, and I wish he would get a little closer. Maybe I can bite off his goddamn nose if I let him think I'm beaten. I slump and allow him to feel the shaking in my body. Let him believe it's fear, I think savagely. Let him think I'm trembling because I'm afraid of him. I almost forget to play victim but manage to swallow the snarl that is building in my throat.

I think that maybe the creature sees murder in my eyes because it pulls back and stands over me. The pressure on the knife eases, and I take an experimental breath. The pain is turning into a dull sort of ache and I wonder if the wound is beginning to heal *around* the blade. That's probably not a good thing.

The Afarit looks like it is done playing with me for a while. I follow it with my eyes as it finds the book lying in a puddle by Adam's side. Stupid freaking book. I am tempted to burn it rather than deliver it Theo—if I actually manage to survive this and get it back from the spirit thing standing over me.

I can't help thinking of the Afarit as Bilal, even though I know that the magician is long gone. Its white teeth are gleaming as it smiles at me. "Thank you," it says in Bilal's smooth tones. "All of this unpleasantness could have been avoided if you had just given it to me in the first place." He sounds so calm, so reasonable.

I want to kill him.

I smile back. I can't help it, because my legs twitch and I am getting the feeling back in my knees. That seems like something to smile about.

Bilal's mud-spattered black shoe is close to my heavily booted foot. Close . . . *closer* . . .

I take a deep breath against the burning pain in my chest and strike with the hardest kick I can manage. Under the circumstances, I think I do a pretty good job. I hit Bilal in the ankle and he howls with shock and staggers backward. Bones might not have broken but that's got to hurt like hell.

I grip the dagger's hilt with both hands and pull. It doesn't matter that it feels as though I'm pulling out an internal organ or two, it only matters that I survive.

It only matters that I am *free*.

I fling the knife away, watching with fascination as my blood flies above me in a crimson arc. It sprays across Adam's pale cheek, several stray drops landing on his lips.

His golden eyes snap open. He wipes away the blood and licks his fingers. He grimaces at the taste and then drags himself to his feet. Adam seems to take in the situation: me on the ground, starting to pull myself to my knees. Bilal is running away with the book, escaping with the only thing that matters here. Not just for Theo, I am surprised to find myself thinking, but for Adam. For a dead girl named Hasna.

I hurt all over. It feels as though something crucial is missing from my body, and I'm afraid to look at the wound left behind by the blade. I press a hand against the ragged hole over my ribs and use the other to help me regain my balance against the fence. I am pleasantly surprised to find that I can stand.

Adam is visibly torn. He is taking a step toward me, while at the same time turning to look at the fleeing magician.

"What are you waiting for?" I shout. "Go after him!"

He responds to the command in my voice, running to the corner of the alley and moving out of my line of sight.

I am still relearning how to breathe. I hope my ribs are all in their right places, otherwise healing is going to be a bitch even with my abilities. I look up and almost scream with frustration. Adam has returned and is hovering over me, his face filled with horror and something else it takes me a moment to recognize.

"This is all my fault," he says. His eyes are wild as they swivel between me and the ground—alighting on the exact spot where Hasna died.

Of course, he thinks that I am the second girl he didn't save from the magician's knife. I swallow pain and bile and know I have to reassure him. Apart from wanting to help Adam, I can't stand being fussed over like this.

"I'm okay, you should've gone after him. It." I correct myself. It seems important that I remember the thing that stabbed me— almost in the heart—is a monster. Maybe it's even more of a monster than me? That is a bizarrely comforting thought.

He nods his head toward the end of the alley. "He went through the stage door."

"What? Why would he do that?" It was the middle of the freaking night. Unless London shows had special midnight performances, the Afarit wasn't going to achieve much in a deserted theater.

I am furious with Adam for letting the book go. *Idiot.* I want to punch him, but I am suddenly feeling weak again. I've lost a lot of blood and will need to feed, but the last thing I want to do is to have to use Theo's contacts. This job was supposed to be straight-forward, dammit. It was meant to be *easy*.

And then I fall to my knees again and wonder why every-thing is spinning. Even Adam's face is spinning around in slow circles. He crouches down with me and his golden eyes look like twin suns.

I manage to force words from my parched throat. "Why do I feel so sick?"

"Djinn magic," he replies. His hands are underneath my elbows, holding me up. "The knife was a conduit for a death spell."

"It can affect *vampires*?" I can't believe there is such magic in the world, and yet here I am on the verge of collapse.

He shrugs. "I don't know. I didn't even know there really

were vampires until today. It certainly looks like it can hurt you, even if it can't kill you."

I choke on a laugh. "Already died once."

"What can I do?" he asks.

I take a shuddering breath, trying desperately to steady myself in his arms. "What you *should* have done was stop that bastard before he got away with my book."

His eyebrow rises in response, and I could almost swear that he is smiling. "Oh, it's *your* book now, is it?" He shakes his head and the smile is gone, if it was ever there to begin with. "I couldn't leave you, Moth. Not after you trusted me."

I slump a little further. "Yeah, and look where that got me. Tossed around and stabbed." He props me up and my cheek rests on his shoulder. I take in the strange dry scent of him, and the hunger gnawing at my belly gets stronger.

Adam turns his head slightly so that his chin touches my face. "Are you going to bite me?"

"What?" I raise my head, surprise shaking me out of this half-drugged stupor. "Why do you say that?"

"You're sniffing my neck," he replies, and I can't decide if he sounds afraid or curious. I wish he *was* more afraid of me—it would be safer for him.

I sigh and drop my head again. He's so warm, even out here in the chill night air. "I guess I *do* need to feed." I don't know what to do. I should phone Theo, but that means admitting that I've failed.

I'm not ready to do that.

He nudges me so I have to pull back and look at him. Our eyes meet: gold on silver. I catch my breath; I can't help it, he is so beautiful.

He touches my cheek with warm fingertips and something inside me breaks. The tide of loneliness that I hold back, day after day, rushes through the breach, and I have to bite my tongue to stop myself from crying. *Remember what you promised*, I tell myself. No more tears. Never again.

He is stroking my face, pushing my tangled hair out of the way, and his eyes are filled with compassion beyond his years. It reminds me, just a little, of the way Theo looks at me when he is in one of his better moods. The lump in my throat expands to the size of a fist.

Adam's expression is deadly serious. "Feed from me," he says. His voice is steady and sure.

I blink and try to push him away. This isn't what I expected. I thought maybe he'd help me find one of Theo's London contacts. Or even that he might offer to steal hospital supplies with me—his Houdini superpowers would come in very handy for that—but this . . . this strangely innocent offer is a surprise.

I shiver against him and shake my head. "No, you're too young. You don't know what you're offering."

Adam puts his fingers beneath my chin and forces me to look at him. "I don't care. You got hurt because of me—let me help you."

"There are other ways you can help, Adam. You don't have to open a vein."

"I don't mind a little blood," he replies. "Djinn have a long and complicated relationship with it."

We don't have time for a history lesson on the Djinn. I frown at him and once more attempt to wriggle out of his arms, but I am weak and he is stronger than he looks. He is also determined.

"I don't want to hurt you," I tell him. I mean it, too. I didn't think I would care about him so quickly. I wish I could toughen up. All very well to be able to talk the talk, but if I can't walk the walk when it counts, then my attitude is all for shit. My image was taking a pounding right here in the back alley of a London theater. How embarrassing.

Adam shrugs out of his jacket and bares his throat. "Go on, do it." There's a challenge in his voice, but no fear that I can detect. This boy is something else.

I lick my lips and breathe him in. He smells of cinnamon and sunshine. His scent reminds me of the hot spices that drift from the Indian restaurant down the block from Holly's apartment.

My fangs extend, and the hunger grabs hold of my gut. I cry out as my whole body spasms and rips open the slowly healing gash below my chest. I snarl with helpless need and pull Adam toward me.

"Give me your wrist," I pant, barely able to get the words out. "That will be enough."

He shakes his head and puts burning hot palms on either side of my face, pulls me toward him and presses his dry mouth to mine. My fangs nick his bottom lip, and a bright bead of blood wobbles there for what feels like centuries. I watch with fascination as the dark crimson blooms and begins to flow.

My hands are in his hair, and I press against him, kissing him back, not stopping to think about the fact that he's a *lot* younger than me. Okay, on paper it's only a year. In reality? No, I really wasn't going to let that thought take hold in my head. Not when he kisses like he really knows what he's doing.

I wonder if he is thinking of Hasna.

Adam kneels on the wet ground, and I straddle him, overcome by the rich scent of his blood. It is like nothing I have ever experienced before—he tastes exotic and *other*. My body opens up with need as I wrench his head backward with both hands and plunge my teeth into his throat.

•••

We are standing outside the stage door, having followed the badly concealed trail that the Afarit left behind. It obviously *wants* to be found, an insight that doesn't sit well with me.

I cleaned as much of the blood off Adam as I could before we crept out from behind the tall buildings, and he did the same for me. Although we don't speak about what happened between us back there, the awareness is palpable. Not just awareness of the *act* but of how we both feel about it afterward.

How do I know what Adam is feeling? Because I can *feel* it. My heart beats in time with his, and I can taste his pulse on my tongue. We are connected in a way that I never imagined could happen with anyone other than Theo. I don't mean that after one random feeding we are suddenly in love. That's ridiculous. He's a half-human and I'm a vampire, not to mention the fact that he's mourning his girlfriend's death.

So, no, not love. But something else almost as strong. His blood is inside me, and it feels wicked-good. Normally, after I've fed from my Maker I feel ashamed. It's as though I've done something wrong and twisted; as though I am a monster and my desire for Theo's blood just goes to prove it. No matter how many times he tells me that it's natural to feed from the vampire who made you, I cannot allow that to be true. I worry about what that might mean.

I never let Theo feed from *me*; not since the day he turned me.

With Adam it's different. This is the first time in a decade that I don't feel suffused with shame after feeding. I glance at him through the dancing shadows, and he takes my hand in his. He is no longer as warm as he was . . . before. I have stolen some of his heat, and I feel deliciously alive. Adam told me there are legends that Djinn have fire running through their veins. After feeding on him, I can almost believe it.

I could get used to feeding on Djinn blood. My wounds have healed, and I'm glowing with the power of the sun.

Seems we have to stop the Afarit from taking the "next step." The book contains incantations that will free the creature. Adam tells me: "The Djinn love to travel. Think about it. . . As Islam spread West, so did the old legends and stories. Only, the Djinn aren't just mythical creatures after all—I'm evidence of that. My mother is a powerful Djinn; I've only met her twice in my whole life, and the first time I couldn't possibly remember. That was after she'd given birth to me and left me with my father. Dad, in turn, handed me over to an endless supply of nannies and carers while he worked overseas as an anthropologist. Afarit, however, are creatures of habit. They love their homes, and many of them live in the Middle East."

So the darkling that wears Bilal's face wants to go home. And to do that, it needs to remove the binding placed on it—a binding that holds it here on English soil. It can't travel over water until it breaks that spell.

Which is where the book comes in; the same book that Adam needs to save Hasna's soul. The same book that I must retrieve and deliver to Theo.

Adam can teleport inside the theater, but I'm not so lucky. However, what I lack in Djinn powers I more than make up for with vampire attitude and a recent intake of fresh blood. I kick down the door without a second thought and feel like Wonder Woman. I don't care whether anyone hears, though Adam looks at me with wide-eyed horror and makes exaggerated "shushing" motions.

I roll my eyes at him, crack my knuckles and stride into the darkness. I'm tired of sneaking around. There's an Afarit inside that's long past due for an ass-kicking, and I'm damn well going to be the one who delivers it.

...

Shaking off Adam's restraining hand, I push on ahead and allow my nose to guide me. My senses are supercharged right now, and I don't want to waste the additional power. I'm not afraid of anything, not with the heat of Adam's blood still warming my belly. He knows it, too, and doesn't argue with me. He seems subdued, and I wonder if it's because I've weakened him or whether he is simply thinking of Hasna.

We walk through narrow corridors and work our way into the theater itself. It is strange being here after hours; there is a magic in this place that is all its own. Not Djinn magic, but the kind of enchantment that inhabits old buildings dedicated to art. Maybe that's why the creature chose this place—there must be a ton of residual energy in the building, from its foundations to the concrete pillars and all the way up to its beautiful arched ceiling. We talk in hushed voices as though we are in a church, and there is definitely something sacred in the dusty air.

We reach the main auditorium, and I am unsurprised to find it lit by an ethereal brightness that seems to come from everywhere and nowhere. *And why not?* After all, we are chasing a spirit in possession of a human girl's soul. We left "normal" behind way back in the basement of that occult bookstore.

The old-fashioned velvet curtains are open, and the stage is empty of any kind of set or backdrop. Empty, that is, apart from a richly designed blood red carpet spread over the wooden boards.

Empty, apart from the Afarit sitting cross-legged in the center of the carpet, surrounded by a ring of stubby white candles.

My mind shows me a fleeting image of flying carpets and *Arabian Nights*. I remember fairy tales Mom used to read to me, so many years ago.

The Afarit grins at us with white teeth that shine behind Bilal's black beard. "How kind of you to join me," it says. It doesn't look surprised to see us.

Adam steps forward. He is pale but composed, and I can't help admiring his courage. "Just let Hasna go. You don't need her now."

"Foolish boy," the creature replies. "Of course I do. Her spirit allows me to walk this plane of existence. I cannot release her without killing myself."

"I could just rip your goddamn head off," I say, keeping my voice pleasant and conversational. "How do you like *them* apples?" (I've always wanted to say that.)

"I think," Bilal says, "that you are very lucky to be alive." His eyes are cunning. "If we can call what you do . . . living."

I swallow anger and keep a smile pinned to my face. "Let's see you finish the job, Ugly."

Adam glances at me from out the corner of his eye, but I pretend not to notice. He's trying to tell me something, but as far as I'm concerned the time for talking is officially over.

My fangs extend, making my gums ache. I have already fed too much tonight, but I am going to end this one way or another.

I leap up onto the stage in a single movement, stride across the carpet, and lunge at the spirit-possessed magician—

—only to bounce off a barrier that surrounds him like an invisible bubble. I fall on my butt and try to catch my breath. My hands are tingling from the impact, and it feels like one of my wrists has snapped. I test it by clenching both hands into fists. Thankfully, everything seems intact.

The only thing damaged is my pride.

I look up and see that the ceiling over the stage is painted dark blue and scattered with silver stars. Somehow, this seems appropriate.

Adam is beside me on the stage, helping me to my feet. "I tried to warn you," he whispers.

"No you didn't," I retort. I'm not really angry with him, but right now he's an easy target.

"I *did*," he says with exaggerated patience. "I gave you 'The Look.'"

"What look? I didn't see any *look*. You're just—"

"Amusing as this is, children, I am ready to complete the ritual now." The Afarit stands in an inhumanly graceful movement. The invisible shield begins to shimmer around him, kind of like a city street under intense heat—the sort of heat I have to keep out of now.

We stop quarreling and stare. The Afarit raises its right hand to the fake night sky and begins chanting in a language I don't understand. He is reading from the book and, as he continues to chant, smoke begins to rise from the aged pages. Theo once told me that not all magical books actually *contain* magic, but maybe this one does. Maybe that's why it's so important to him. I can't help wondering if the stupid thing is going to burst into flames.

Light glints off something in the Afarit's raised hand and, just for a moment, I think it is one of the rings that Bilal was wearing.

Then I see that it's a small glass jar; the sort that might hold honey under normal circumstances. Adam notices at the same time and grabs my arm.

"The spirit jar!"

He is practically crushing my bicep through the padding of my jacket. I shake him off with ease and push him behind me. "Stay back," I say, trying to sound like I know what I'm doing. "I have a plan."

Anyone who knows me knows that when Moth says she has "a plan," they should keep their heads down and stay as far away from ground zero as possible. Sadly for him, Adam *doesn't* know me, and he insists on sticking to me like freaking glue. Fine—it's his damn funeral.

I almost surprise myself with the knowledge that I really *do* have a plan. It's not a very sensible one—in fact, even based on my colorful history of crazy ideas, this one is probably the worst I've ever come up with. Still, in the last few hours I'd already been beaten, thrown around, stabbed, and *licked*. . . Tonight could surely not get any worse. I'd just have to deal with the consequences when I got home.

The Afarit places the book down gently on the floor but continues to chant all sorts of mumbo jumbo. The spirit jar is in both hands now, and I'm sure I can see something silver white swirling inside. I frown and blink my eyes, wondering if I'm imagining things. As a young vampire I have genuinely struggled with the concept of "the soul"—do I still have one? Why doesn't my reflection show up in mirrors if I *do* have a soul or spirit? But tonight I've had my perceptions shifted.

Not only can I see something in front of me that looks a

whole lot like it could be a human spirit trapped in a freaking *jar*, but back in the alley the Afarit told me my soul is "too old" for my body. This indicates that not only does the human spirit exist as a potentially separate entity, but maybe I still possess one.

I push these philosophical ponderings aside, but resolve to think on it later; this isn't the time or the place for existential angst.

Adam is pounding on the outside of the invisible shield, his eyes deepest gold and his mouth set in a grim line.

I grab his shoulder and swing him around. "Can't you just teleport through it?"

"That's the first thing I bloody well tried. It doesn't work." He shakes his head and gives the barrier a savage kick. "What's this plan of yours? We've got to hurry—the ritual must be almost over by now."

I take a slow breath, enjoying the feel of air in my lungs. I still feel strong as hell thanks to Adam's generous donation. "Have you ever tried to transport someone else?"

Confusion crosses his face. "You mean, take them with me when I teleport?"

"No, I mean send someone or something else away . . . independently of you. Without you actually being the one who teleports."

"I don't think it's possible," he says. He sounds disappointed, as though my Great Plan has already been shot down in flames.

"But you've never tried, right?" I am feeling more excited as each moment passes. This could work. I really think that this crazy-ass plan of mine could *work*.

Adam isn't convinced. "I can teleport myself and anything I'm holding or wearing that's made of natural materials. I told you that. It only works over short distances. And we found out earlier that if an object has magical protection on it, no matter what it's made from, then it won't travel." He nods at the book inside the barrier of candles.

I hold him by both arms and make him look at me. It is important that he knows I'm deadly serious. "Adam, I want you to try teleporting me inside the barrier."

"No way." He's already trying to pull away. "You could get hurt."

"What's the worst that can happen?" I flash him a grin. "Already dead, remember?"

"I said *no*—you're crazy."

"This is our only chance," I say, anger heating my face and making me wish I had the ninja skills to glamour him.

He glares at me. "You mean it's *your* only chance to get the book back for your boss."

"Adam, I don't give a rat's ass about the book any more. I want to save Hasna's soul." I am genuinely surprised to discover that I mean it, and if Adam knew what I was planning he'd know I meant it, too.

"I don't understand how my powers work," he says slowly, "but I do know that it only works on me. It has to be *my* essence that travels."

I want to slap him for being so dumb. "I just drank a whole load of your blood, you moron. I'd say that qualifies me as possessing your 'essence.'"

Comprehension dawns and his expression is suddenly clearer than I've seen it all night. "Oh," he says. Then: "Wait a minute . . . why would it work on you and not on me? I already tried to teleport and got bounced."

I shrug. "Look, this isn't a scientific experiment. It might *not* work. I just have a feeling that it will."

Because although I fed on Adam's blood—and despite the fact that an evil Djinn said I still have a soul—there's no denying the fact that I *did* die when I was eighteen years old. My very unscientific plan involves somehow "confusing" the magical barrier.

And speaking of that, I've been keeping half an eye on whatever Bilal is doing, and it doesn't look like we have any more time. The spirit jar's contents are going crazy, swirling like a tiny tornado on crack.

"Stop arguing and do it," I say, turning my back on him. The Afarit is bringing the jar to its lips. *Oh my gods*, I think. Is it going to do what it *looks* like it's going to do? My eyes focus on the spirit jar's lid; the magician's hands are slowly unscrewing it, and the creature wearing his image has finally stopped chanting. I resist the temptation to look back at Adam and instead draw the knife out of my messenger bag.

What? You think I'm not prepared? I'd remembered to grab it before we left the alley.

You never know when you might need an iron blade to kill an Afarit.

Adam has his eyes closed. Anytime now . . .

The knife still has my blood on it, which is probably why it successfully teleports through the barrier with me—I'd hoped it might (I'm not just a pretty face, you know). The world disappears, and for a second my stomach is upside down and my head is spinning and I have no idea where I am. One minute I am at Adam's side, hoping that his Djinn mojo will somehow catapult me inside the bubble, and the next I am right there next to the Afarit. Up close and personal with a killer wearing the face of a power-hungry magician.

"How—?"

I cut off its question with the dagger.

I'm not interested in trading witty repartee or gloating over how clever I am. I only want this to be *over*.

The iron blade sinks into Bilal's heart, and the creature screams. Black blood pours hot and thick onto my fist, but I ignore it and keep hold of the wooden hilt. My other hand grabs the jar before it falls to the ground, my reflexes only just quick enough to snatch it out of the air.

I have to be fast. Luckily, girls are good at multitasking.

I let go of the knife and screw the lid back onto the spirit jar.

The Afarit falls to its knees and tries to pull the blade from its chest, but I'm not finished yet. The candles are my next target—I begin kicking them over one by one. As the circle is broken, so the magic breaks and the barrier drops.

Adam practically falls on top of me. He's been waiting with his nose all but pressed against the invisible shield.

"Where is she?" he gasps. "Please . . ."

"Here, it's okay." I hand him the precious container and turn my attention to the book. *That stupid, goddamn book.* Everything began with it, and now everything is going to end with it.

I force myself to take a deep breath. I am terrified and exhilarated just thinking about what I'm about to do. Theo is going to kill me.

Oh no, I think, smiling to myself like a smartass. He already did that once.

You won't get me to admit it out loud, but I take a huge amount of guilty pleasure in picking up the only candle that's still alight. I touch the flickering flame to one of the brittle pages of that sacred Arabic text and watch it burn. I hold onto it until the last possible moment and then let it fall, still burning, to the crimson carpet.

The Afarit is crawling on the floor in agony and its eyes—Bilal's eyes—widen as it sees the bright flames consume the book: the book that we used to summon it in the first place. Adam and I step back and enjoy the drama unfolding on the stage. How appropriate that this is where we should all end up. It's the perfect final curtain call.

Black smoke begins to roll off the creature in choking waves, but it's still not dying, or disappearing—whatever is supposed to happen. I glance at Adam, wondering what I missed. He is cradling the spirit jar, and his eyes are bright with unshed tears. I swallow my own sadness at the sight, and I know what else we have to do.

But this is not my role. There's only one person who can complete this part of the ritual. I step farther back, giving him space while still keeping the dying spirit in view. We don't want any last minute surprises.

My senses are good enough that I can easily hear what Adam says to Hasna before he releases her forever. I will take those words with me wherever I go, for the rest of my very long life. I will keep them close to my heart and share them with nobody. They are not my words to give.

Adam smashes the jar and white light flies like a comet from the glittering shards. The impossible brightness hangs in the air for a moment, shivering like a swarm of beautiful fireflies or a miniature firework display especially for us.

Cool air brushes my face like a blessing, and then the light fades. I look down at the carpet, and there is nothing left; nothing but broken glass, candles scattered like strange confetti . . . and a large pile of ash.

We are silent for a couple more minutes, although I can hear Adam's soft breathing. I think we're both saying good-bye to Hasna, even though I never knew her. It seems like the right thing to do.

I take Adam's hand and lead him slowly away. I wonder what the theater employees will think when they arrive for work tomorrow, but we'll be long gone by then. I'll be on a plane across the Atlantic, on my way back home to Theo. I'll have a lot of explaining to do, but right now I just don't care.

Tonight, at least, I know that I did the right thing.

Tonight, I am still Marie O'Neal.

Lost

BY JUSTINE MUSK

1

I've always been good at finding lost things, but three weeks after a car accident dumped my best friend in a coma, I was the thing that felt lost. And nobody knew where to find me.

Except for one person.

There's an abandoned white house on Bel Air Road, two blocks up from where I live. On an afternoon in early March, I didn't know that I was going there. I thought I was taking the dog for a walk.

"C'mon, girl," I said. The little red-haired dachshund wasn't jumping around my feet or straining for the door the way she usually did when she knew we were about to do our loop up the hill to the white marble lion that sits outside the front gate of one of the mansions. I always touch the lion's paw, as if to tell him "see, we made it," and also for luck.

But it was as if Paloma knew that things weren't quite right in her world, that her mistress was still shaken from visiting Josh in the hospital. I took Vermeer calla lilies in a glass vase to put on his windowsill. I wanted them to be the first thing he saw when he woke up. (If he woke up.) The nurses all thought I was Josh's sister, because that's what his mother had told them. It was what my English teacher might call a "mythic truth"—even if it wasn't true on the outside, it felt true on the inside.

I had known Josh since kindergarten, when both of our sets of parents were still together. When we were six, we sat cross-legged in the corner of the tennis court in his backyard and pricked the tips of our little fingers with a sewing needle and squeezed out drops of blood. Then we wrapped our pinkies together and swore we'd be blood-siblings for life. Corny, I know, but what can I say. We were six.

I coaxed Paloma out the door. She shook herself, dog tags jangling, then trotted along beside me as if the lemon-colored sunlight, the flowering bushes and palms and pines and eucalyptus, the sprawling houses set behind walls and gates, were conspiring to make her feel better.

The white house came up on our right. I've always been curious about it. I've never seen anyone go in or out of it, never glimpsed a car moving through the curve of driveway flanked with drooping palm trees. The house wasn't gated off from the street, but sat exposed like a bone in the sun. You sometimes see shabby, neglected houses in Bel Air, squatting on lots that have accumulated millions of dollars of value over the decades, belonging to people who refuse to sell them even if they can't afford their upkeep, who plan to live in those houses until they die.

But nobody lived in this house. The windows were dark and blind.

Today, instead of walking past it, I paused at the lip of the driveway. Paloma took the opportunity to fling herself on her back in the grass and roll around. I listened to the chatter of birds, the roar of a nearby leaf-blower. I didn't really know what I was doing. It was like an invisible hand reached through my skin, grabbed one of my ribs, tugged me gently toward the house. *Trust your instincts*, my mother is always telling me, the implication being that if she had trusted hers she would never have married my father.

I walked up the driveway, through the pools of shade beneath the palms, up the three steps to the door. I still didn't know what I was doing. It was like something my body knew and announced to me, like when it's time to eat or go to sleep. Except now it was time to knock on the door, so I did, one rap, two raps, three, and then my hand dropped to my side and I thought, *Am I crazy? What am I doing?*

I turned around to go when a voice from inside said, "Sasha, come in."

I did not hear that. I did not hear someone say my name.

The dog was sitting on the step, cocking her narrow head at me. The wind pushed a cloud overhead, and the air darkened for a moment and then went bright again.

The door gave a clicking sound, and swung inward.

I saw white walls and a clean hardwood floor and more space than I would have expected. A man was standing in the middle of the hall. The light entering the windows behind him cast him in silhouette. Paloma gave a happy bark and jolted forward. I didn't realize my hand had slackened on the leash until the end jerked out beneath my fingers and Paloma was hurtling herself at the man. "Hello, Paloma," he said, and stooped to pick her up. She writhed in his arms and tried to lick his face.

"Excuse me," I said, "but that's my dog."

The man stepped forward. Maybe he saw the way I tensed because he was careful to keep some distance between us. "You're a little late, Sasha," he said.

The shadows fell away from him, and I could see that his eyes, even across the space that separated us, were very blue. His face did seem familiar. It was long with good cheekbones and a strong nose. He wore jeans and a long-sleeved T-shirt, and he was lean and long-limbed. I guessed him to be a few years older than me—nineteen, maybe twenty?

"We have to get started," he said.

"What are you talking about?"

"Your lessons."

"My what?"

"Sasha, don't you recognize me?"

"Who are you?"

"You know my name," he said. "Wait a moment, and it will come to you. We have an appointment, Sasha. A series of them, in fact. But we don't have a lot of time. I'll have to go back soon."

This had to be some kind of setup. He was too good-looking, for one thing. He belonged on a movie screen or the cover of a romance novel or in someone's fantasy. Maybe I'd been chosen for some kind of reality show? This was Los Angeles, after all, and every now and then you saw film trucks in the neighborhood, parked along the narrow curving roads while traffic directed around them.

I glanced around, checking for places where cameras might be viewing my every move. But the place seemed . . . truly empty, like it was just this guy, my dog, and me.

"Sasha, it's time we get started," the guy said. "It's past time."

"For all I know," I said, "you're a serial killer."

"I promise you I'm not a serial killer."

"Like you'd admit it if you were."

"You know my name," he said quietly. "Here, I'm going to write it down . . ." He suddenly had a pen and notepad in his hands—I had to blink, where had they come from?—and scrawled something down. He ripped off the top paper, folded it in half and held it out to me. "Tell me," he said quietly. "Tell me the name, my name, that I wrote down on this paper."

"I have no idea who you are." But I felt something . . . shift . . . in my brain. And suddenly I knew—knew in a way that went all through my body—that he was right, that I had met him before, and that my whole life had been leading to this moment.

"Haiden," I said.

He smiled and dropped the notepaper. It fluttered to rest on the ground with the name staring up at both of us in printed block letters:

HAIDEN.

2

So I stood there for I don't know how much longer, the guy—
Haiden—looking at me with those preternatural blue eyes. Part
of me was still thinking: reality show. Kind of clinging to the idea.
But then I felt that invisible hand tug my rib again.

Trust your instincts. So I stepped across the threshold and into
the hallway.

And I swear I felt the air *shimmer*, as if part of reality had
rearranged itself around me. *If he does turn out to be a serial killer*, I
thought, *I'm going to feel really, really stupid.*

I followed him into a long sunken room with a stone fireplace
in the corner. The only piece of furniture was a table in the middle. There was a bowl of fruit on it. Apples. They had the kind of
dewy, rounded perfection you only see in magazines.

"What are we doing?" I asked. Paloma trailed behind us, her
toenails clicking off the hardwood. "What do you mean by
'lessons'?" Absently I reached out for the fruit on the table. I was
picking out an apple when Haiden barked, "Don't!"

The apple dropped from my hand, rolled across the table.

"Don't eat that," Haiden said, "don't eat any of that fruit
until you're absolutely sure and ready. Do you understand me?"

"Until I'm ready for what?"

Haiden watched me for a moment. Then, ignoring my question, he said, "What if I told you there was another realm that ran
alongside this one?" Haiden had something in his hands—like
the pen and notepad, it had just somehow appeared there—and
he approached me with it.

It was a black scrap of fabric. A blindfold.

"I'm going to teach you how to see and feel and communicate with it. I'm going to teach you a kind of clairvoyance.
Clairsensing."

"You're seriously going to put that thing on me?"

"It's the first exercise," he said patiently. Then he said,
"Sasha, are we going to do this or not?"

"My dog likes you," I said, "and my dog never likes anybody."

"Dogs and I understand each other."

I liked the idea of another realm. It reminded me of the stories I used to write when I was a little kid, back when I had this idea that I wanted to be a novelist.

Maybe that's why I let him blindfold me. I liked his voice, and his vaguely European accent, and the rich warm sense of his presence beside me. His hands, as he fastened the blindfold, were gentle.

"The point of this," he explained to me, "is to demonstrate that you already know everything you need to know. It's all living there deep inside you. What you need to do is focus inward. You need to clear away all the distractions—all the things you *think* you know—all the things people told you when you were little and didn't know not to believe them. In a way, you're not learning so much as *un*learning."

"Cool," I said.

I mean, what else was there to say?

"I painted an X on the floor," Haiden said, "and it's your task to find it. I want you to use your inner sense of direction. I want you to feel your way toward it."

I imagined how ridiculous this would look on a reality show: me stumbling around with a blindfold trying to find some secret X as this awesome-looking actor chattered on about unlearning. I pictured the kids at school howling laughter at me in the hallways. But I also remembered the way Paloma had gone right up to him, no hesitation, and the way his name had surfaced in my brain like that.

He was right. I had met him before. I didn't understand it, but in that moment I didn't have to. All I had to do was find the X. That was what mattered.

I could feel that gentle tug inside me, leading me across the room. I stepped slowly, the blindfold dark and silky on my eyes.

When the sensation of tugging stopped, I stopped too. I lifted my hands to the blindfold and slipped it off and turned to look at Haiden. He was standing beside the table holding the apple that I had dropped. Paloma was on her haunches beside him, as if she was his dog, not mine.

Traitor, I thought.

"So?" I said.

"Look down," Haiden said.

He crunched into the apple.

I was standing right on the middle of the X.

3

I wasn't sure what that proved. My mind went into gymnastics trying to fit this into a rational explanation. Maybe I had agreed to do a reality show and then someone had put me under hypnosis? Maybe this was all some kind of subliminal programming? But that seemed just as nuts as Haiden's talk about "another realm."

For the rest of the "lesson" Haiden had me stare into a candle flame. "This is to help you develop your focus and concentration," he said. "You need a clear mind in order to see clearly." He gave me the candle to take home. He told me to practice meditating with it for half an hour every day. That was my homework.

And then the lesson was over, and Paloma and I were out on the street again. If it wasn't for the candle in my hand I would have thought the whole thing some kind of hallucination, a waking dream. Especially when I checked my watch and saw that, from the time I entered the house until now, exactly two minutes had passed. In the presence of Haiden in the abandoned white house, time, it seemed, had stood still.

4

That night, my mother was rushing around to get ready for her date with this Silicon Valley mogul dude who was totally all wrong for her, except my mother hadn't figured that out yet. Her instincts can be slow to kick in. "Have you seen my black Chanel clutch?" she asked, popping her head into my bedroom. "I can't find it anywhere—"

I thought for a moment, then felt an image of it surface in my mind, much like Haiden's name had done. "It's in the top left-hand corner of the hall closet," I said, "beneath a balled-up sweater."

She looked at me for a moment and shook her blond head. "You're amazing," she said, and blew me a kiss. Then I heard her clatter down the stairs.

It hadn't occurred to her to ask what I was doing, standing in the middle of my bedroom and looking around me. I felt like an alien dropped in from another planet trying to put together clues about the locals.

The candle in its little brass holder sat on my desk. The session with Haiden had left me with a calm settled feeling. My room felt different, like it belonged to someone who resembled me but wasn't . . . me. There were posters on the walls of bands I no longer listened to. The rhinestone-studded cover for my iPhone seemed childish and stupid. There were application forms on my desk from colleges that I realized, in a sudden blazing flash, I didn't even want to go to. I had decided I was going to be a lawyer. Now I found myself wondering why. Because I was good at English lit, because I liked to read and write, because it was so much more practical than trying to be a writer, which was a crazy ambition anyway? Because I wanted to earn lots of money and wear cool power suits? Because it was a good answer to give people when they asked you what you were going to be when you grew up (assuming you ever did)?

Haiden's words hummed through my brain.

You need a clear mind in order to see clearly.

My life was filled with a lot of noise, a lot of bright lights, a lot of daily drama that, in the end, didn't add up to much. My grades were slipping because I found it harder and harder to keep still, to

absorb what the teachers said in class or to complete my homework. Now, though, with my mother gone and the house quiet
and lonely and the image of Haiden's flame still bright in my
mind, and the memory of Haiden's voice still warm in my ear, I
sat down at my desk and pulled out my textbooks and immersed
myself in work. Hours slipped by and I barely noticed. Suddenly
I was caught up. I pushed back my chair with a rich feeling of satisfaction. Then I noticed the candle. . . .

I hadn't done Haiden's homework yet.

I found the silver lighter I used to sneak cigarettes on the
back balcony, lit the candle, and stared into the flame for maybe
half a minute. Except then I started feeling stupid. It was just a
candle, for crying out loud. I could imagine my friend Ashley
rolling her eyes at me. I blew it out and went to call her instead.

5

That week I found a lost cat I recognized from posters pinned on
telephone poles around the neighborhood and returned her to her
owner. Ashley lost her cell phone and I helped her remember that
she had left it behind at King's Cross Café, where the manager
was waiting for her to reclaim it.

"I'm good at finding lost things," I once said to Josh, "it's like
a talent or something."

"No," he told me, a little mischievously. "Lost things are
good at finding *you*."

His condition was unchanging. His room filled with flowers
and little stuffed animals and get-well cards. I visited him almost
every day and pulled the chair up beside his hospital bed and
talked about everything and nothing. I imagined that he could
hear me, deep down in his slumber, and that any moment he
might stir and open his eyes and say, where am I? like in the
movies.

But it didn't happen.

I told him—and only him—about the episode with Haiden in

the abandoned white house on Bel Air Road. "It seems more and more surreal all the time," I said. "Maybe I dreamed it. Maybe I went temporarily insane and imagined the whole thing. But I keep thinking about him."

I didn't mean to say this last bit, it just kind of slipped out. In class, or walking the hallways, or hanging out with Ashley and Steven and the others in the parking lot after final bell, I would flash on Haiden's eyes, his light golden skin, the shape of his shoulders. I would imagine his breath in my ear or on my neck. I remembered what it was like to stand close to him.

Every time I walked past the white house I went up to the door and looked in the windows. Everything was locked-down, shuttered, and silent. "It's like it never happened," I said to Josh, "except I can't shake this conviction that it did, it really did, and Haiden is real. He's not just a figment of my overheated imagination."

I touched Josh's hand. I remembered the blood-ceremony we did when we were kids, how serious we were. I laced my fingers through his and confessed, "I really want to see him again, but how can I even make that happen? I don't know anything about him."

And it was as if Josh's voice spoke inside my head:

Do your homework, stupid.

That night I lit the candle and did the meditation exercise exactly as Haiden had shown me. I did it every day in the week following. On Saturday morning I woke up to the feeling of that invisible hand on my rib, gently tugging.

I knew where it wanted me to go, and who would be waiting for me there.

6

Haiden said, "Now I need to teach you how to see."

When Haiden opened the door, the little dog ran into his arms again, and he picked her up and rubbed her behind the ears.

It was as if they'd known each other forever. He smiled at me, and my heart did a quick little salsa in my chest. I wasn't sure I could talk without stammering, so I just smiled and followed him into the sunken room with the table and the bowl of fruit.

We did the candle meditation exercise again. Haiden made a gesture with his hand and suddenly the room went dark, even though afternoon sunshine should have been leaking around the edges of the blinds. I said, "Do you use . . . I mean is this . . ." I couldn't believe I was even asking this. I took a breath and tried again. "This is about magic, right? You're teaching me magic?"

"You could maybe call it that," he said. He tipped his head at me, and his eyes crinkled at the corners. It was a look that made me feel warm inside. I had the feeling, again, that I had met him before. "I'm teaching you to see what most people can't. Give me your hand."

He had elegant hands with long tapered fingers. His skin was smooth and cool. "I want you to do this . . ." He swept my hand through the air. ". . . and I want you to clear your mind and concentrate on what you see."

After about fifteen minutes of this, I said, "I don't see anything."

"Try again. Keep trying."

"But this is stupid!"

"Sasha," he said, "you have to be patient. I know it doesn't feel like you're getting anywhere, but your brain . . ." He touched my temple. " . . . is making new connections, laying down new neural circuitry. But it takes a bit of time and practice, practice, practice."

"But what am I supposed to be looking for?"

"Don't worry," he said. "You'll see."

When I shot him a dubious look, he added, "You will."

Then Paloma and I were on the street again, blinking in sudden light. I checked my watch. I had been with Haiden for what felt like hours, but only two minutes had passed.

7

I may not have known what I was looking for, but I looked for it that night and every night following. All I saw was my hand waving through the air. Maybe I was crazy. Every day I walked Paloma past the abandoned white house and knocked on the door and looked in the windows.

Haiden was nowhere around.

Then one afternoon when I was visiting Josh, I moved my hand across his. I saw golden trails of light stream from my fingertips, hover in the air for several seconds, then fade. My breath stopped.

I swept my hand through the air and the same golden light traced the passage of my fingers. I couldn't believe it. "Look at that, Josh," I cried out, "look at that!" Josh slept on, lost in his coma, as I played the light above him.

8

"It's astral energy," Haiden explained to me when I saw him at the house one day later.

"Astral energy?"

"Every living thing generates it. And once you can see that, you can see . . ." He thought for a moment, then said, "Watch."

He closed his eyes and let his head hang. I had the urge to reach out and brush the dark hair from his forehead. As I watched, he seemed to . . . divide. A second version of Haiden slipped out from the first, until it was standing beside him in the same pose, arms limp, head hanging. A feeling like cold electricity passed through me, and I could feel the prickling of goose bumps rising from my skin.

I couldn't speak. The second version of Haiden had a shimmer to its body, reminding me of the surface of a sunlit lake.

It lifted its head and opened its eyes.

Then it was gone.

The real Haiden said, "You saw that, didn't you?" There was

a kind of urgency in his tone, as if nothing could be more important. "You saw that very clearly?"

My throat felt dry. I ran my tongue across my lips and said, "What . . . what was that? What did you do?"

"That was my astral projection. My soul projection."

"You looked like your own ghost."

"Ghosts are a slightly different form of energy," Haiden said, and I didn't know what to say to that. I had never believed in ghosts, but the whole world was now slanting and tilting around me. If, in that moment, a portal opened in midair and a unicorn came dancing through it, I would not have been surprised. "Astral projection is the art of sending your soul from your body."

"Will I be able to do that? Will you teach—"

"No," Haiden said sharply, cutting the air with his hand. "It's dangerous. Your body is left empty and vulnerable, and your soul could get lost and not be able to find its way back. The only time your soul should ever leave your body is when you die."

"But you did it," I said.

"Only for a moment. And I am . . ." Haiden smiled a little, turning his hands palms up. "I'm not a regular guy."

I took a breath. "Then what are you?"

Haiden blinked a little, as if the question had taken him by surprise.

"There's something different about you," I said. Stating the obvious.

"There's something different about you, too," Haiden said. "That's why I'm here. That's why *you're* here."

"Do you do this all the time? I mean, do you just appear in random places and teach things like . . . astral energy . . . to teenage girls with dachshunds?"

"I don't just appear in 'random places.' I came here specifically for you."

"Why?"

"Because I need you."

He put his hand on the back of my neck and gently drew me to him.

He kissed me, softly, on the lips.

Then he murmured, "Session's over for today. Go home."

9

It happened two days later. I walked Paloma up the hill to the stone lion that sat outside the mansion at the top part of our loop. I reached out to touch the lion's paw the way I always did—

—when I saw the teenager suspended in the air.

His toes rested on the top of the fence. He seemed to be sitting, except there was nothing to sit on but air. He had blond curly hair and tanned skin, dressed in jeans and a blue hooded sweatshirt. Paloma whined and pulled back on the leash. I only stared, and kept staring.

" . . . Ricky? Is that you?"

He moved his head. I couldn't tell if he'd heard me or not. But I was sure it was Ricky Newman, even though I hadn't seen him since his family moved to Arizona in eighth grade. My mother and Ricky's mother were good friends. They'd forced Ricky and me to play together as kids, although a real friendship between us had never happened.

"Ricky?" I said again.

He stood up and walked along the fence like a gymnast on a balance beam. Then he drifted down through the air to the road. He turned his face to me, although I couldn't tell if he was actually seeing me or not. I could only note his troubled expression.

The words rose up through my body, from some deep place of knowing that I didn't consciously understand. "That way," I said, and felt my arm lift, pointing to the right. "You need to go that way." I was pointing off the road, into a cluster of hedges and bright bougainvillea.

An expression of peace settled over Ricky's face, and he walked off in that direction. He didn't leave any footprints in the gravel. He didn't make any sound at all. Sunlight shafted over him—and then through him—and his form seemed to shimmer and dance as it dissolved into the hedges.

And then he was gone.

At dinner that night, my mother said, "Terrible news. Ricky Newman, remember him?"

I'd been pushing pieces of chicken around my plate. I had no appetite. At the mention of Ricky's name I looked up and said, perhaps a little too sharply, "What happened to him?"

"He died," my mother said. "Earlier today."

"He died," I said blankly.

I felt numb. There was the surreal, impossible knowledge that someone my own age had died, someone I'd known, but there was also the matter of Ricky's astral projection, soul projection, or whatever it was that I had encountered earlier. My mind touched on the implications, and shied away. I wasn't ready to go there.

"An asthma attack," my mother went on. "He didn't have his inhaler with him, and by the time . . ."

But I couldn't listen to the rest. I was pulling on my leather jacket. "I have to go somewhere," I muttered.

"Sasha—"

"I won't be long."

And I was out of there.

10

"Haiden!"

The white house seemed as abandoned as always, but this time I wasn't having it.

"Haiden!" I banged on the door. I walked around and banged on the shuttered windows. "Haiden!" Where did he come from? Where did he go when our sessions were over? *Who was he?* Unanswered questions filled my mouth like ash.

"Sasha."

I whirled.

"Sasha, stop yelling, you'll disturb the neighborhood."

He was standing beneath one of the palms, his face and body carved in shadow.

"I don't care," I said. "Something happened today . . . and I need to know . . . ." I could feel my voice falter. I cleared my throat and tried again. "I need answers."

He tilted his head.

I told him what had happened with Ricky. "And then I found out that he died! Did I do that? Am I responsible for that in some way?" I was thinking about what he had told me the other day, about how easy it is for someone's . . . soul . . . to get lost and never find its way back to its body. I had told Ricky what direction to go in, I had even pointed, as if I'd known anything at all about what I was doing.

Had he lost himself, had he . . . died . . . because of me?

Haiden seemed absorbed in his own thoughts. "So it's already happening," I heard him mutter. "I didn't expect it this soon—"

"What's happening?"

"Your gift has begun to truly manifest." Haiden spread his hands. "Ricky was lost, Sasha. You showed him the direction he needed to travel to pass from this world into the next. This kind of thing will happen again. Other lost souls will find you—they'll be drawn to you—and you will help them find their way."

"That's why you've been . . . teaching me? That's what you've been teaching me?"

Haiden nodded.

My knees felt watery. I stumbled. "You've been teaching me to communicate with the souls of dead people." I sat down—"collapse" is probably the better word—on the doorstep.

"Not all of them are dead." Before I could respond to that, he said quietly, "There's more." He sat on the step beside me. "In order to continue your education, I need you to come with me."

"Come with you?"

"I live," Haiden said, "in that other realm I once mentioned. Sometimes known as the Underworld. I kind of . . . rule it, actually."

And something clicked in my head. My voice dull with the shock of it. I said, "You mean . . . Hades? You're, like, that guy Hades?"

"That's one of my names."

"You're the freaking god of the Underworld!"

"If I had a job title," Haiden allowed, "that would probably be it."

I could only stare at him. Is that why he had always seemed familiar to me? Memory seemed to be moving around, dislodging the blocked parts: I was a little girl, and he was a crossing guard with vivid blue eyes smiling at me as I trooped across the street. I was ten, and downtown with my mother, and he was a handsome stranger who asked us for the time. I was fourteen, and working at a fast food restaurant, and he was a customer ordering a cheeseburger and fries. And those were only the moments, the encounters, I could remember.

Suddenly I knew that he had always been there, in my life, crossing paths every now and again while I grew up, and he remained the same. He didn't age. He was constant and unchanging. I was fifteen, and he was the good Samaritan who helped my friend's hissing black cat out of a tree, even as it flattened against the branch and took swats at his head. "What's your name?" I had asked in gratitude and now, clear as a streak of birdsong, in my memory I heard him say, "Haiden."

"Sasha," he was saying now, "I've made mistakes in the past that I would never make again. I want you . . . I need you . . . to come to my kingdom with me. To be at my side. To be my Queen. There are so many lost ones whom you could help, the same way you did Ricky—"

The words burst out of me. "Why can't you help them?"

"Because you bring the two worlds together," Haiden said, "in a way that I can't. You are one of them—the lost—in a way that I will never be. Trust me, Sasha, I've gone over this in my head. I try to understand it all over again every time you and I go through this, life after life after life—"

"I have to go," I said suddenly. "This is way too weird."

"Sasha, I would never force you to do anything. If you come with me, it will be of your own free will."

"I have to go."

He didn't reach out for me or stop me or follow me. I strode away from him, beneath the palms, down the curve of driveway, then ran the rest of the way home.

11

In the blur of days that passed I read up on Hades . . . on Haiden. Except the patient, gentle, blue-eyed teacher I knew didn't square up with the fearsome god of the myths. He seemed best known for the story involving Persephone, the young maiden he fell in love with and took to the Underworld. When she begged him to return to her own world, he let her go—except first, he gave her a pomegranate. She ate half of it, including the six seeds that would forever bind her to the Underworld—and to Hades— for six months of every year.

I remembered reaching for the bowl of fruit on the table, and the way Haiden had snapped, "Don't!"

I remembered the softness of his voice and the sadness in his eyes when he said, "I've made mistakes in the past. If you come with me, it will be of your own free will."

12

My friend Ashley and I went up to Malibu that weekend after I visited Josh. Ashley's father had a house on the beach, and Ashley thought I needed some time in the sun. "You're starting to look really pale," she complained.

At dinner Ashley's father talked about the movie he was making and bickered with Ashley's mother about computer games. Afterward Ashley and I watched a couple of DVDs and drank wine and talked late into the night. When I made my way up the stairs and down the hall to one of the guest bedrooms, I knew I wouldn't be able to sleep. There was a piercing ache in my chest, as if someone had run a blade through it.

The only person who could make that ache go away was Haiden, and yet I had been avoiding the abandoned white house on Bel Air Road and trying not to think of him at all.

God of the Underworld. For crying out loud.

Why couldn't I have fallen for some nice normal boy at my school? Every so often I'd catch myself touching my lips, tracing their outline, remembering Haiden's kiss. But I didn't want to deal with lost people, dead people. I didn't want to sit at some guy's side in the Underworld. I wanted what other people had, or what I believed other people had, even if I didn't know any of them. I wanted happy and normal.

I didn't want to be Persephone. What had happened to her, anyway, that Haiden had to come looking for me? Maybe she had moved on. Maybe the myth wasn't accurate—it was a myth, after all. Or maybe she was a kind of metaphor for other girls—girls like me—who maybe had some Persephone in them. "Life after life after life," Haiden had said. Maybe there were a bunch of us Persephones, trailing down through the ages, and every so often Haiden had to come find us.

I changed into my pajamas and threw open the French doors so I could listen to the ocean while I slept. I went out on the balcony. The water glimmered a midnight blue, waves spilling along the private beach.

Someone was walking through the sand.

At first I thought it was Ashley's father, but the figure was too tall and slender. Then my heart kicked and I thought—*Haiden*. But it wasn't him either.

The figure moved into the glow of the security lights. I saw the longish, tousled brown hair, and the shimmer of his body, the way the light seemed to sift right through him.

"Josh!" I yelled. "Josh!"

He paused, and for a moment I thought he heard me and was going to look in my direction. But no. He was simply standing there, the light falling over him, the half-moon high overhead, the waves sliding to his feet and sliding away again.

He wasn't leaving any footprints in the sand.

I ran out of the guest room. I clambered down the stairs. I spent a few moments trying to find the door that opened onto the beach. And then I was outside, the salt spray in my face, screaming, "Josh!"

He turned to look at me.

"Don't be dead." I was half sobbing. "Please don't be dead."

He smiled.

And I felt it, that deep sense of knowing that came from inside me but also somewhere beyond me. It felt as cold and ancient as the stars. It moved through my body and I felt my arm lift. I was pointing out into the water. "That way," I said. I tasted salt on my lips, from the ocean but also my own tears. "That way." Josh smiled again. His lips moved—I think he said *thank you*—and he turned away from me and started gliding into the water. His form dissolved into the waves and he was gone.

I fell to my knees in the sand.

I don't remember returning to the guest room, but at some point I must have. I must have crawled into bed and fallen asleep. Because bright light streamed into my room and Ashley's voice was in my ear: "Sasha, Sasha, wake up! You have to wake up!"

"Go away," I muttered. I didn't want the day to start, because I knew what it would bring me: the news that Josh was dead.

"Josh is awake," Ashley said. "He's out of his coma and asking for you!"

13

Three days later I went back to the little white house. I left
Paloma at home.

I called out Haiden's name. No answer.

But the door was unlocked and opened easily.

I walked down the hall to the sunken living room where my
lessons had taken place. I listened to the sound of my breath and
the rap of my footsteps and the faint strains of birdsong filtering
in from outside.

The table was still in the middle of the room.

The bowl of fruit was still on it.

I knew I was alone . . . and yet I could feel Haiden's presence.
He was somewhere close. He was waiting to see what I would do,
why I had come here.

I wanted to tell him about Josh. I wanted to describe the
warm glow of love in my chest when I saw him, awake and alive,
sitting up in the hospital bed and poking at the remains of his
lunch.

"Sasha," he said when he saw me. "I'm back!"

"You're back." I was laughing.

And I wanted to tell Haiden what Josh had said to me, after
we'd cycled through our first rounds of conversation, talking
about everything and nothing. Then a pause settled over us, and
Josh looked at me with his calm, level gaze that was familiar and
strange at the same time.

"Do you know what it's like to be lost?" he said to me.

"Everybody gets lost."

"I mean . . . really lost." His eyes searched my face. "So lost
you don't know if you'll ever find your way back . . . or forward.
You don't know where you are. You don't know where you're supposed to be. It's like the universe misplaced you and then forgot
you ever existed."

"It sounds terrible," I said, "and lonely."

Josh touched my wrist. "But you were there." His voice was

a rasp. "You were there," he said again, a touch of awe in his voice, "and you found me."

I've always been good at finding lost things.

Now, in the abandoned white house that no longer felt so . . . abandoned, I sifted through the mess of apples until I found the one pomegranate, hiding at the bottom of the bowl. I'd brought a knife for this purpose. I sliced the fruit open and picked out six seeds.

I would live in my world and be a writer, and I would also live in Haiden's world and be Persephone. I swallowed the seeds one after the other.

"Haiden," I said, "Haiden."

I could feel him somewhere close, and drawing closer. I was ready. I stood there and waited.

The Spy Who Never Grew Up

BY SARAH REES BRENNAN

There is a magic shore where children used to beach their coracles every night.

The children have stopped coming now, and their little boats are tipped over on their sides, like the abandoned shells of nuts eaten long ago. The dark sea rushes up to the pale beach and just touches the crafts, making them rattle together with a sound like bones.

You and I cannot reach that shore again. We've forgotten everything. Even the sound of the waves and the mermaids singing.

But the men in Her Majesty's Secret Service can go anywhere.

•••

The submarine drifted to a stop not far from the island, its periscope breaking the surface of the water like the lifted nose of an inquisitive pointer dog. After a few minutes, a man emerged from the submarine and got into a boat, one not at all like the children's boats arrayed on the shore.

When the boat sliced through water to white sand, the man stepped out of it.

They had given him a number and taken away his name. Unfortunately for him, his number was 69.

This was a subject of many tasteless jokes in the Service, but nobody would have known that from 69's serious face and his extremely dapper black suit.

He took a few purposeful steps along the shore to the forest, then looked down. Under his feet, and under a layer of the black grease of age and filth, were pebbles like jewels and children's toys and human bones.

There was a barely perceptible shift in the air before his face, but the men and women in Her Majesty's Secret Service are extremely highly trained. 69 looked up.

The boy before him was beautiful in a slightly terrible way, like a kiss with no innocence in it.

More to the point, he was holding a sword as if he knew how to use it, and floating about a yard above the ground.

"Dark and sinister suit," said the boy. "Have at thee."

"I am afraid I do not have time to indulge you," 69 said. "I am here on a mission from her Majesty."

"Ah," said the boy, tilting his chin. "I know it well."

"I beg your pardon?"

"The Majesty," the boy said, waving his sword vaguely. "Belonging to . . . Her. I know all about it."

"Her Majesty *the Queen*," 69 said, with a trifle more emphasis than was necessary.

"I knew that," the boy informed him.

"She feels that the Service has a need for a man—"

The boy hissed like a vampire exposed to sunlight, lifting his free arm as if to protect himself from the word. *Man.*

"Excuse me. A *boy* of your special talents," 69 said smoothly. He had been raised in diplomatic circles.

The boy spun around in a circle, like a ballerina with a sword in zero gravity.

"My talents are special! So awfully special!"

"Indeed," said 69. His countenance remained unchanged. 69 was very highly trained, and also a gifted amateur poker player. "And the Queen needs—someone of such talents for a job."

The boy started to laugh, a high lovely laugh that wavered between a baby's gurgle and the peal of bells. It did not sound quite sane.

"A job?" he asked. "Make a *man* of me, will you? Oh no, oh no. You sailed your boat to the wrong shore." He made a quick, deadly gesture with his small sword to the island around them, the dark stones and trees with branches like bared claws. "This is no place for men."

"So I see," said 69. "And I see there is nobody here who would be brave enough to risk all for her Her Majesty's sake: nobody who is enough of a patriot to die for their country."

Peter was not entirely sure what a "patriot" was, but he would have scorned to betray this fact. He did not even acknowledge it to himself, really: Peter's thoughts always move like a stone on water, skipping and skimming along the surface until they hit a certain spot.

69 had turned toward the sea, but he was not entirely surprised when a sword landed, light as a very sharp butterfly's wing, on his shoulder.

He turned back to meet the sight of the lovely, terrible smile.

"To die for your country," said Peter. "Would that be an awfully big adventure?"

•••

The party was a very glamorous affair, with chandeliers like elaborate ice sculptures and ice sculptures like elaborate chandeliers. This created an effect of very tasteful strobe lights playing on the discreet black clothing of the guests.

A suspiciously nondescript man paused on his voyage over the glowing floor to speak to a lady. She was wearing a dress more daring than any of the party dresses around her, and very striking lipstick.

They were, of course, both spies.

"Who are you hunting today?"

"Oh, the English, of course," said the lady. She did not turn her *T*s into *Z*s except when playing certain roles, but her faint accent was nevertheless very Russian. "Look at their latest golden boy."

She laid a certain emphasis on the word *boy*.

Let us play *I Spy*, and follow the spies' line of vision to the bar where a boy was leaning. He wore a black suit like every other suit in the room, tailored to discreet perfection.

The look was rather spoiled by the knotted dead leaf he was wearing as a bowtie.

The Russian spy detached from her companion and came over to the bar, slinking like a panther in an evening gown. Which is to say, with some suggestion that the evening gown might be torn off at any moment.

She offered the boy her hand. "I don't believe I've had the pleasure."

The lady noted his wary look, and told herself that no matter how young he seemed, he was obviously a true professional. She was not to know this was how Peter regarded all grown-ups.

"Ivana," she murmured, which I must tell you was a fib.

"The name's Pan," said Peter, who I must admit was showing off. "Peter Pan."

Neither of them was really on their best behavior. Spies rarely are.

"What will you have?" asked the bartender.

"Martini," said Ivana. "Shaken, not stirred."

"Milk," said Peter. "Warm, not hot."

The bartender and Ivana both gave Peter rather doubtful looks. Peter has been receiving such looks for more years than he could ever count, and he looked disdainfully back.

"Come now," Ivana said, and reached for Peter's arm. "I think we can do better than that. After all, you're almost a man."

Peter's eyes narrowed. "*No. I am not.*"

She was very clever, that Russian spy who was not really called Ivana. She instantly saw she had made a mistake.

"I meant to suggest that this affair must be boring you. After all, it really isn't up to the excitement that a boy of your . . . many talents must be used to."

Peter looked more favorably upon her. "I do have many talents. Thousands, really. Millions of talents. Nobody has ever had as many talents as I!"

"I don't doubt it."

"I keep them in a box," said Peter, and looked briefly puzzled when Ivana laughed and then triumphant as he decided he had meant all the time to make a splendid joke.

He beamed at her, and Ivana reared back.

She quickly collected herself, however. Remember, she was very well-trained.

"I imagine you have done many things," Ivana murmured. "Such as the affair of Lady Carlisle's necklace in the embassy?"

"Oh that! Yes, I took it! I flew in under cover of darkness and stole it."

Ivana blinked. "You did?"

"I am a master thief," Peter said with some satisfaction.

"It was my understanding that the English were the ones who got the necklace back," Ivana said slowly.

"Oh yes," Peter told her. "I fought the dastardly thieves single-handed and restored the jewels to their rightful owner! I remember now."

"I see," said Ivana.

• • •

The spies in Her Majesty's Secret Service have long been renowned for their discretion. To protect their country, some have been known to spin a deft tale. Some have died rather than speak. Some, even under torture, have preserved a perfect British silence.

No spy but Pan has ever confessed to everything.

Ivana the Russian was getting a bit of a migraine. She rather wished Peter would take a breath between highly incriminating confessions.

"The Taj Mahal," she began.

"I killed him," Peter said. "He was a tyrant."

"It is a *building*," Ivana informed him with a certain amount of hauteur.

Peter, occupied with relating the details of the epic battle he had fought, chose to ignore her. They were sitting at a small table in low light, away from the bar. Ivana had quite a row of martini glasses lined up before her. Peter was working on his seventeenth glass of warm milk.

"And what about the documents regarding that invention the Americans were making such a fuss about last week?" said Ivana, who had abandoned diplomacy and cunning around the time of martini number nine.

"I have those," Peter told her complacently, and Ivana was heaving another irritated sigh when Peter added, "Upstairs in my room. I have them hidden in the nightstand. I'm meant to hand them over to the Queen tonight, but my helpers needed to rest, so here I am at this boring party."

Ivana hesitated. "I should very much like to see them." She paused and then smiled a coaxing smile. "It would be so thrilling to see proof of how clever you are, Peter!"

"It would be very thrilling for you," Peter agreed.

"And I would be terribly grateful."

"How grateful?" Peter asked.

Ivana looked slightly startled. "Very grateful indeed."

Peter's eyes brightened. "Do you know any bedtime stories?"

"My dear boy," said Ivana, not missing a beat. "Hundreds."

Since Ivana really was very clever, and Peter could be extremely heedless, she might very well have got her hands on the American documents that night. Except that Peter, careless as always, had forgotten to mention one small detail.

His helpers were indeed resting. Pan's elite team of killer fairies was having a little nap in the nightstand, right on top of the documents.

"Troops, troops!" Peter bawled over all the yelling. "Attention! Attention! That means you, Ninja Star! Stop kicking her in the earlobe right now!"

Ninja Star was his best fairy and was the captain whenever Peter was on a solo mission or got bored and wandered off. There was no denying zie had a temper.

"You should be ashamed of yourselves," said Peter severely because he knew that discipline was vital. Then he became bored with his role as stern commander, spun and levitated three feet in the air.

It was probably for the best. It hadn't seemed to him like Ivana knew any bedtime stories at all.

Ivana made the discreet decision not to try and get up. She watched with wide eyes as the boy rocketed out of the window, a silhouette in the moonlight, with the fairies following him like a host of tiny stars.

Given the new evidence, Ivana was going to have to reevaluate some of Peter's claims. With his ability to fly and his tiny helpers, a good many more of the missions he boasted about might be true.

And many of his stories *were* true, especially the wildest ones, because Peter often had strange and terrible adventures.

Which ones, we will never know. Peter does not even know himself.

Still, I think we—and Ivana—may be reasonably sure that Peter never fought a duel to the death with the Taj Mahal.

...

Her Majesty, by the Grace of God, of the United Kingdom of Great Britain and Northern Ireland and of Her Other Realms and Territories Queen, Head of the Commonwealth, Defender of the Faith, was quite vexed.

She had been forced by abject pleading, several resignations, and (in one unfortunate case) an incarceration in a secure mental facility, to receive Pan's reports herself.

It was, however, growing extremely late. She had been up all day meeting with tedious ministers and an enormously dreary duchess, and she found her eyes traveling too often to the sack that lay at her butler's feet.

I hesitate to tell a lady's secrets, but she was wearing a dressing gown. It was sky blue and patterned with tiny silver crowns.

She was also wearing fluffy bunny slippers. The bunnies had crowns too.

"If I might be so bold, your Majesty," said her butler, who was called both Dawson and Night Shadow. He was a judo master and weapons expert, and his butlering was exceptional. "The boy is late."

"The boy is always late. I gave him a watch once."

"How did he lose it?" asked Dawson.

"He *claimed*," the Queen said in the magnificently noncommittal voice that made statesmen blush and prime ministers recall other engagements, "to have choked a mutant shark to death with it."

Dawson bowed his head.

Hurtling through the purple sky of London, streamers of light thrown across it by the city, through the wide windows of Buckingham Palace, came a boy. Fairies danced around him, wreathing his wild hair like a crown made of lightning.

Peter touched down lightly on the carpet, presented a roll of documents to Her Majesty, and swept her a superb bow.

The Queen graciously inclined her head and unrolled the documents on her tea tray.

"The device illustrated in these documents actually expands mass," she said absently. "Which would be most useful in the right hands—curing world hunger and the like—but since it seems to have been invented by the *wrong* hands—"

Since this was boring adult stuff, Peter wandered about the room and danced up and down the velvet curtains, from the floor to the curtain rungs and back again. The Queen glanced up from an intricate plan of weaponry.

"Exemplary work as always, Mr. Pan." The Queen glanced up from the diagrams Peter had brought her.

"Yes, I am exemplary," Peter crowed.

He went pinwheeling across the solemn crenellated dome of the Queen's bedroom ceiling. The Queen cleared her throat to indicate that aerodynamic acrobatics in the presence of royalty were frowned on.

Peter plummeted neatly onto the hearthrug and bowed again, as if he took the royal throat-clearing for applause.

"You must know," said the Queen, "I would be happier with a more traditional means of payment for your services."

Peter tilted his head to one side. There was a cold watchful light in his eyes now, like the glint children imagine they see after bedtime, when the night-light has been turned off and shadows and shivers start creeping into bed with them.

Peter has been peeping through windows for a very long time.

"Do you mean 'money'?" he asked, pronouncing the word as if it was in a foreign language. "What use do I have for money, grown-up? If I want something on Neverland, I kill for it. If I want something here, I steal it. There is only one thing I want that you can give me. I want my mother!"

The Queen inclined her head again, this time less graciously. She had made many terrible decisions in her time. Her Majesty always, always pays her debts.

"There she is."

The eyes of the Queen, Peter, and Night Shadow aka Dawson the butler, all turned to the sack at Dawson's feet. We can see now that there is a slight shifting of the rough material, as if something is breathing beneath.

Peter looked uncertain. "They never used to come in sacks," he said. "They used to be happy to see me."

The Queen, who had had a lot of ruling to do that day, and for the last sixty years, lost patience. She turned away from the boy and the moving sack, back to her own plans.

"As I am certain you've noticed, Mr. Pan," she said. "Times have changed."

...

"Second to the right, and straight on till morning," are not real directions, though Peter thought they were. The truth was that by now the path to Neverland knew Peter by heart and was always drawing him home, like a compass point to true north or a ghost to the place he was murdered.

Peter flew with an easy grace, even with the sack in his hand. Sometimes he tossed it about with the fairies, just for sport, but Peter thought he was being most responsible. He made clear that any fairy who dropped the sack would have to answer to Ninja Star.

It was a piece of great good luck that the bag only started squirming and making loud, distressed sounds as they were flying over Neverland. The sack had been quiet so long, Peter had forgotten what was in it, and was startled enough that he dropped it.

Ninja Star and the team flew very quickly to catch it, but only succeeded in slowing it down, so the sack fairly tumbled to the stones and bones below.

Ashley Horowitz, daughter of Karen, daughter of Tracy, daughter of Margaret, daughter of Jane, daughter of Wendy, came out of the sack rolling, and pepper-sprayed Peter in the face.

For a moment she thought she must have made a terrible mistake. There she was on the island of nightmares—even worse than Grandma had described it—but the boy before her could not possibly be Pan the destroyer, Pan the thief in the night. He was sitting on the blackened shore and weeping in bewildered pain, as if he was terribly young and crying for the very first time.

"Boy," began Ashley. "Why are you—"

Then she remembered: that was how he got you. She took a

step back and lifted her pepper spray in steady hands.

"Stay back," she said. "Or I'll make you cry harder."

When he rose to his feet, she knew it was him. Pan. He was not exactly as her grandmother had described him either: he was worse. He was as beautiful as her grandmother had said—as fascinating as a snake's golden eyes to a bird—but he was that thing he never was, never could be. He was . . . older.

She was older, too. She was past the age when he was meant to be exactly her size, and now here he was looking down at her. The bones of his wild, lovely face had stronger, sterner angles than in the pictures. His body had more muscle and was more easily weighted to the earth. He was not a little boy anymore.

It was horrible to see those curling, crowing lips part, to show he still had all his baby teeth.

"Pan," said Ashley.

Peter smiled more widely, his tiny teeth like little pearls gleaming in his changing face. "Mother."

He advanced and Ashley backed up, wielding her pepper spray like a weapon.

"My name is Ashley. And I'm not your mother!"

"There was a bargain made," said Peter.

Quick as a flash, he drew and thrust. At the touch of his blade, the pepper spray flew out of Ashley's grasp and into the dark seas beyond.

"My great-grandmother," said Ashley, starting a little uncertainly and then gaining strength as she spoke. Margaret had been nothing but old family history to her, a story in a book. But so had *he*. "Margaret. She went mad."

Peter tilted his head, his eyes blank. "Margaret?"

"She used to scream your name," said Ashley. "My grandma used to hear her through the walls screaming for you. And you don't remember her?"

"Well, if you're going to get all sniffy about it, I'll say that I'm sorry," said Peter, with the air of one making a great concession.

"Tracy," said Ashley. "Margaret. Jane. Wendy!"

Peter drew in his lip a little, startled and hurt, as if it was the very first time he had ever been hurt, although the tears from his last bout were still wet on his cheeks.

"Wendy."

It made sense that he would remember her. She had been the first.

Ashley drew in a deep breath.

"I don't want to be here," she said flatly. "I demand to go home."

She turned and walked away into the forests of the Neverland.

...

Neverland was both like and unlike her grandmother's stories, and the pictures in the book. It was unmistakably the same place, but it was changed like Peter himself: the trees naked as skeletons, no ships on the horizon. There was a quality about the silent darkness that Ashley recognized from being a little girl, too scared even to get out of bed and reach the light switch. The whole island was like a huge bedroom for a scared child, in which morning would not come again.

The silence was broken by some terrible rustles and slithers. Ashley turned fast at the sound and found Peter gliding beside her, a few feet off the ground.

"Those are the wild beasts," he said. "Don't go too far away from me. They'll kill you if they can. They're starving."

"Where are the—the Native Americans?" Ashley asked.

Peter gave her a blank look.

"Tiger Lily, I mean, and the others," Ashley said, summoning up the name from the book.

"Most of them died," Peter replied. "The others went away."

Her grandmother had made sure she always had pepper spray under her pillow. Ashley wished now that Grandma Tracy had told her to always dress for an abduction. Bare feet and glittery pink pajamas were not exactly ideal for a trek through Neverland.

She kept walking, though, until they came to Marooners' Rock. The rock was just the same. The lagoon stretched around it, black and viscous, like tar with ghosts moving in it.

It took Ashley a moment to realize that the gray shapes, their ragged fins dragging the surface, their hair like clogged seaweed, were the mermaids who used to toss bubbles to each other and sing. Peter flew over to hover above the lagoon like a huge dragonfly.

"What—" Ashley said, and stood rubbing the gooseflesh out of her own arms. "What happened here?"

"There was a Lost Boy who came back," Peter said distantly. "He had—he was a—"

Peter choked trying to say the words "grown-up" with the same trouble other people had talking about death.

"He thought there was a profit to be made of the Neverland," Peter said. "He learned too late that he was wrong."

Peter twisted in midair until he was floating on his back, kicking at a breeze. A mermaid reached up out of the waters to touch his heel: her fingers were withered and gray.

"But the island changed before that," Peter admitted. "Children's dreams were changing."

That was what Grandma Tracy had seen, the spring Peter had come for her. That was what had scared her so badly. The beginning of *this*.

"I knew that I wasn't wanted," said Peter. "Windows have been barred against me before. I didn't come for the next girl, did I?"

"Yep, thanks for not kidnapping my mom," said Ashley. "Big of you."

Peter came to settle on Marooners' Rock, sitting near where Ashley stood. The mermaids swarmed in the waters about his feet like goldfish wanting to be fed.

"I knew I wasn't wanted," he said. "But . . . I still need a mother."

He leaned trustingly against Ashley's legs. Ashley, who was a kind-hearted girl, resisted the impulse to push him into the lagoon.

"Times have changed, Peter. A lot fewer girls dream of being mothers. Some of them want adventures of their own."

You will have to forgive Ashley. She did not know Peter very well yet.

She began to know him better when he tilted his head back to grin up at her. His curly hair was against her knee, and his smile was a devil's.

If Satan had all his baby teeth, that is.

"You want an adventure?"

"Peter," said Ashley, with commendable, but much belated, caution. "Peter, noooooo!"

I would not have you think Ashley screamed out of fear. In fact, she screamed because Peter had seized her up and was flying with her through the trees.

Hang gliding is a bit alarming at the best of times. When your hang glider is a flying boy criminal, it is most unnerving indeed.

They zoomed over the trees of Neverland, wind rushing in their ears. Ashley soon ran out of breath to scream.

"Fly!" Peter yelled encouragingly. "Fly, fly! All you have to do is think happy thoughts!"

He began to let her go when a furious tinkle from Ninja Star, like a dinner bell in a panic, gave him pause.

"What's the fairy saying?"

"Oh," Peter said airily, "zie says that if I don't blow fairy dust on you, you will plummet to your death."

"Plummet to my death!"

"I think you're being most unfair," Peter said to Ashley sternly. "I cannot be expected to remember every little thing."

He detached an arm from around her—I confess she

screamed again—and reached out for Ninja Star, who he shook expertly over Ashley's head like a top chef with a saltshaker.

"Suspended in midair with a boy pouring glitter on me," Ashley muttered. "I was really looking forward to being old enough to get into nightclubs. Now? Not so much."

"Nonsense, being old isn't any fun, everyone knows that," said Peter briskly. "Quick, happy thoughts!"

"Peter Pan in jail for kidnap and assault!" Ashley yelled. "Peter Pan gets a twenty-year sentence! No! Ever so much more than twenty!"

Peter dropped her.

He managed to catch her before she dashed out her brains and broke every bone in her body on the rocks below, but it was a very near thing.

"You idiot!" Ashley screamed, grabbing hold of his shoulders and shaking him. "I nearly died!"

Peter made play with his eyebrows. "Well, yes," he said. "That happens with adventures."

• • •

The tree house was very cold at night, and Ashley could hear the mermaids howling like wolves in the moonlight. Peter seemed to drop off instantly to sleep, but Ashley had no plans to escape her captor. For one thing, she had no idea how to get back from Neverland, and for another, she had no desire to have her head bitten off by a wild beast. She huddled under a blanket of flowers and leaves, and tried to sleep.

In the morning Ninja Star woke her by tinkling about her head like a glittery mobile alarm clock. Ashley thought longingly of home, and flyswatters.

Upon further study of Ninja Star, who was a violent blue color and covered in scars, Ashley decided she probably wouldn't dare.

"Zie wants to know if you would like to train with zir team," Peter translated in gentlemanly fashion.

Ashley's brow furrowed. "She—"

"*Zie*," Peter said. "Ninja Star is intersex. That's what zie prefers."

A line from the book floated through Ashley's head: *the mauve ones are boys and the white ones are girls, and the blue ones are just little sillies who are not sure what they are.*

Ashley wondered why she'd never noticed that line before. She also noted that Ninja Star looked pretty sure of what zie was.

She was right. Fairies, as you and I both know, only ever feel one feeling at a time. Ninja Star spent 99 percent of zir time feeling fierce.

"Why is—um, zie—called Ninja Star?"

Peter looked rather shocked at Ashley's ignorance. "Because zie is the best ninja, of course."

Ashley chose her next words with care. "Are . . . *all* your fairies ninjas, Peter?"

"Naturally," said Peter with a lofty air.

Ashley was left with a dilemma. On one hand, these were the survivors of Neverland, the battle-scarred companions of Peter Pan, fierce and deadly warriors. On the other, they were about three inches high and glittery.

"I'd be very honored to train with you," she told the blue blur that was Ninja Star.

From then on Ashley trained most mornings with the ninja fairies on the shore. She tried her best, but I confess sometimes Ninja Star despaired: she was so big and clumsy, it was hard to teach her to be stealthy like the ninja. And, of course, not being able to fly, Ashley could not perform the ninjas' very best trick— aggressive skydiving at the enemy's eyeballs.

Nevertheless, it cheered Ashley up. She was a girl who liked to keep busy.

She was also growing more used to Peter. He had a way about him, it must be admitted. If Peter awake fails to charm, Peter asleep is a heartbreaker.

On the third night in the tree house he woke Ashley, crying and shaking in his sleep. Ashley remembered his dreams—the sore shaking dreams of a boy who had lived through a hundred child-hoods and a thousand lost, dark memories—not from her grand-mother's stories but from Wendy's book. Wendy had loved him.

He had more dark memories now than in Wendy's day, and he was older, at last. Ashley could not hold him, but she did her best. She stroked his wild curling hair until he was quiet.

"What did you dream last night?" she asked the next day.

"Dream?" said Peter, and laughed a blithe sweet laugh. "I have so many adventures when I'm awake, I never have to dream!"

"You dreamed something last night," Ashley persisted, fol-lowing him. He was playing a game of leapfrog from one toadstool to the other. You would think they might break under Peter's weight, but they never did.

Peter spun on his toadstool, and Ashley found herself staring down the length of his blade.

"No, Ashley lady," he said. "I never dream."

Ashley stepped back. Peter sheathed his sword and per-formed a cartwheel in midair.

"What adventure shall we have today? Do you want to—"

"No, I don't," said Ashley. "I've told you. I don't want to be your mother, and I don't care for Neverland!"

She turned on her heel and then found Peter hovering before her. He was very irritating that way.

"Oh well," he said. "Why didn't you say so? Would you like to go on one of my missions for the Queen?"

I am afraid to tell you that Ashley was not what you might call a trusting soul. She did not believe a word of Peter's tale about being a spy for Her Majesty's government.

In her defense, Peter did tell the Taj Mahal story.

Of course she did not believe him, but she did see an oppor-tunity.

"If I go with you on this adventure," she said, with great cunning. "Shall we play a game? Shall we have a bet, between us?"

Peter's eyes lit. "Yes!"

"Great," said Ashley. "If I don't like this adventure, and if, after it, I still want to go home—you have to take me."

. . .

Meeting the Queen of England is an important event in a girl's life. The social niceties should be observed. Little things like using the correct fork, dropping a deep enough curtsy, and not breaking into the royal boudoir while wearing pink pajamas.

Ashley found herself rather embarrassed before she realized that the Queen was responsible for her kidnap.

"Doesn't that strike you as a bit of a terrible thing to do?" she demanded, cutting her off as the Queen briefed Peter about a new mission.

The Queen had taken the break-in with great aplomb, sitting up in bed and reaching for her spectacles with one hand while waving away her killer butler with the other. A little thing like being accused of a criminal act was hardly going to faze her.

"My dear child, I do a hundred terrible things before breakfast, that is the role of the monarchy." She directed her spectacles toward Peter again. "Do you understand the situation, Mr. Pan? I would like you to apprehend the person who has invented this device to multiply the mass of objects by ten."

"You can rely on me with absolute confidence!" said Peter, who was perched on the edge of a priceless Ming vase.

The Queen rubbed her royal brow. "May I stress that 'apprehend' means 'bring to me,' Mr. Pan? We need this person's brain in her head, rather than—I pick this example purely at random—impaled on one of the clock hands of Big Ben."

Peter rolled his eyes in protest at this senseless rule.

"I am forced to trust in your discretion, Mr. Pan," the Queen said. "Remember that the fate of the free world rests in your hands."

It was very unfortunate that at that precise moment Peter aimed an idle kick and shattered the Ming vase into a thousand pieces.

"Oh my God, you—you . . . Your Majesty," exclaimed Ashley, not quite outraged enough to insult royalty. "I beg your pardon. But are you insane? The fate of a boiled egg shouldn't rest in his hands! Isn't there some other agent you can send?"

"Another agent with the power of flight and little helper ninjas?" the Queen asked, her brows lifting above the frames of her spectacles. "I regret to say, no. Please close the window on your way out, Mr. Pan: last time there was a shocking draught."

• • •

"So will we have to stake out the town?" asked Ashley, who was beginning to get enthusiastic about being a spy. Being personally given a mission by the Queen of England is very motivating. "To see which house is the crazed inventor's—oh!"

Do not be alarmed. Peter has not dropped Ashley out of the sky at the last minute. Ashley had made it clear she did not think that was a hilarious game.

She had merely spotted the small picturesque village of Litford by the Sea, which had thatched cottages and rambling manors, cobbled byways and streams under wood bridges. And on top of a hill near the town was a gaunt black structure with fiery windows. It looked like a castle of nightmares, a place an old pirate went to retire and gnaw on booty and bones.

It looked like something out of Neverland.

"Seems to me we've tracked the varlet to his lair!" Peter crowed.

"Peter, doesn't this seem a little weird to you?"

Peter stared at her, all guileless eyes and crazy smile curling around those little pearl teeth, his dead leaf bowtie fluttering in the wind.

"Weird?"

"Ah," said Ashley. "Never mind."

It struck Ashley that this was something Peter and the ninjas just accepted: the macabre and fantastical, all the trappings of Neverland. Ashley was the only one who could see the difference between what should be real and what should not be: she had some power here.

It pains me to confess Ashley had little poetry in her soul. She would have preferred titanium body armor.

The castle floors were largely made of big flagstones. Ashley's bare feet ached for the carpets of home, or even the forest floors of Neverland.

The castle echoed with the creak of machinery, the pop and sizzle of flames, and the sound of screams. This place reeked of pure, storybook evil.

Ashley kept thinking of a particular name in the story.

Hook.

"The villain never really dies," she murmured as she crept after Peter. Her ninja training made her light on her feet, so it was really a shame that Peter and the fairies showed her up by gliding silently a few inches off the ground.

She was distracted from these dark musings by three mad scientists. Ashley could tell they were scientists by the lab coats, and that they were mad by the maniacal laughter.

Peter drew his sword and killed two of them. Ashley gave the other a kick in the kneecap, and then he went down. The fairies finished him off.

"Now we put on these evil lab coats and make our way into the heart of the evil fortress," Peter commanded.

Ashley put on her lab coat doubtfully. It was really quite evil-looking. The name tag read DR STRANGE FEELINGS OF CONFUSION AND RAGE.

She was also extremely uncertain about two barefoot kids trying to pass themselves off as scientists, no matter how mad said scientists happened to be. It would never work.

When she heard steps barging down an appropriately echoing stairwell, she thought frantically of how the spies on TV would act to distract attention from what they were doing.

So as the next set of mad scientists approached, she whirled, pushed Peter up against the wall, and kissed him on the mouth.

She had her eyes shut, but she could feel his mouth open in amazement. For a moment the world was still and peaceful, the hard angle of his jaw against her fingers, her senses flooded with the taste of berries and the smell of leaves.

When the scientists had passed, Ashley leaned back. The world remained peaceful for a moment, the wild lights in Peter's eyes gone golden and a little hazy.

"Peter," Ashley asked softly, "Do you know what that was?"

"Of course," Peter said, much affronted. "A thimble."

"No," said Ashley, staring. "That was a kiss."

"It was a thimble!"

"Didn't it strike you as a little different from other thimbles you've had in the past?"

Peter looked shifty.

"Well, yes."

"Ha!"

"It was my first thimble with tongue," Peter told her with dignity.

Ashley fixed him with a look of unutterable despair and then stalked down the stairs toward the grim creaking of dread machines, her evil lab coat trailing in her wake.

The fairies and Peter followed her, Ninja Star making a belligerent ringing sound as they went.

"Ninja Star please, how can you be so inappropriate!" said Peter, deeply shocked.

"What'd she say?"

"I refuse to tell you!"

"Heh," said Ashley, making the wise decision that being amused was better than being driven to madness. "You're a bit old-fashioned, aren't you?"

"I am not old anything," Peter snapped.

And so bickering at the top of their lungs, our spies stumbled into the evil at the heart of the fortress.

There was a large chair, of course, looming almost like a throne. It stood on a dais, shrouded in shadow.

There was someone sitting in it.

Ashley's voice died in her throat, and her heart beat like a child's fists on a door, begging to get out. All the fears of her nursery got together and whispered.

Hook.

The figure in the chair leaned forward. "Peter?"

It was a golden-haired girl, plump and beautifully dressed.

Even taking into account the natural distortion of legends over time, Ashley felt this could not possibly be Captain Hook.

She looked to Peter for help, but Peter was looking perfectly blank.

"It's me, Peter," said the girl. "Only—I'm bigger now."

Ashley's world tilted a little, the story changing beyond all recognition. The Queen's documents showed a machine that increased an object's size ten times.

Not just an object. Anything.

The machine had not been created for an evil purpose, not at first. But who knew what terrible mixture of science and magic had worked together to enlarge a creature who could only feel one thing at a time—and fix her like that forever, full of rage and hate.

Creating a villain out of a fairy.

Ashley whispered, "Tinker Bell."

• • •

"Doesn't ring a bell," said Peter. "Sorry."

Tinker Bell went purple with rage. Under the circumstances,

Ashley felt she could hardly blame her.

"Perhaps you're thinking of a different Peter," Peter continued helpfully. "Though it would be hard to mistake me for another boy. There is nobody quite like me!"

"This is no time for crowing," Ashley said out of the corner of her mouth.

"He'd have to be really amazingly wonderful," Peter went on and then Ashley kicked him in the ankle.

Peter looked surprised and annoyed.

"Peter," Ashley said firmly. "We're on a mission. Now I don't think she'll attack you" —though looking at Tinker Bell's enraged face, she was not altogether certain about that—"so I'll get her to attack me."

"I wouldn't dream of it," Peter said. "I am the spy here. I'll run her through."

"The Queen said she was to be brought back for questioning! And if we can change her back, make her less inclined to be, well, you know, evil—"

Peter looked around at the high Gothic windows and the white cat in Tinker Bell's lap.

"I do see your point."

He looked around further and espied a machine that looked a little bit like the offspring of a telescope and a giant spider. "I say, Ashley. I think I've come up with a brilliant plan!"

"Have you indeed," said Ashley, very dry.

"You'll never guess."

"I'm not so sure of that, Peter."

Peter began to sidle with rather obvious stealth toward the contraption.

"What are you doing?" Tinker Bell asked sharply.

Ashley took a hasty step forward. "Why did you want to be big, Tinker Bell?"

Tinker Bell blushed under the fading purple of her rage. "I forget."

Ashley took another step. Tinker Bell's gaze followed her. "I don't think you do."

"Well," said Tinker Bell, and shrugged. "It just didn't seem important afterward, you know. I mean—I realized, Peter *is* quite ridiculous."

"I quite agree," said Ashley. "Of course, so is world domination."

The white cat was rather abruptly tipped out of Tinker Bell's lap as she stood up. "You take that back!" she exclaimed, and in her fury, her voice was like the ringing of bells.

"I will not," said Ashley. "Jealous other woman, doing it all for love, evil overlord bent on world domination? Don't you ever get tired of being a cliché, Tinker Bell? Don't you ever just— Now, Peter, now!"

For Ashley had broken off in the middle of her sentence and delivered a roundhouse kick to Tinker Bell's stomach. Tinker Bell fell directly into the path of the machine Peter had just turned on.

In some ways it was a pity. It had been shaping up to be rather a good speech.

Ninja Star approved very much, however. Ashley even received some compliments from the other fairies about her style.

Tinker Bell, the evil genius; Tinker Bell the fairy transformed, was captured in a ray of light and diminished once more, her stolen inches glowing and falling away. It was terrible at first, Tinker Bell's face locked in a snarl. But then it was different suddenly: like a snake shedding a skin, or a butterfly emerging from a chrysalis.

When the light of the machine faded, Tinker Bell was small and shining once again.

Ashley stood staring, fascinated. Ninja Star took the initiative and imprisoned Tinker Bell in an empty crisp packet.

"I did it!" Peter crowed, and very nearly hit his head on the ceiling of the evil lair, soaring in triumph.

•••

The Queen took being presented with the tiniest evil genius in the world very well. She commended both Peter and Ashley, which left Ashley rather dazed for a while until Peter's crowing annoyed her again.

"Oh Peter, do be quiet," she said crossly, as they flew over Big Ben, badly startling a family of pigeons. "I think it's rather sad. She did it for love, after all."

"Did she?" asked Peter, rather bored. "Who did she love then?"

Ashley gave him a withering glance.

"Well, it's no use looking at me like that," Peter told her, injured. "How am I supposed to know? I've never seen the fairy before in my life!"

And no matter how she argued, he stuck to that.

Ashley finally sighed in exasperation and gave up. "You know, considering her, and Tiger Lily, and Wendy . . . for someone determined never to grow up, you're a bit of a playboy."

Peter frowned, and then his brow smoothed. "It's true that I am a *boy*," he said. "And I love to play!"

Ashley forbore from slapping him upside the head. He might have dropped her.

"What game shall we play next?" Peter inquired eagerly. "I'm sure that with a bit of perseverance, we can get you flying."

"Peter."

"A little bit of falling hundreds of feet onto bare rock never hurt anybody."

"Peter."

"You just need to think some absolutely scrumptious thoughts."

"Peter," Ashley said. "I prefer to keep my feet on the ground."

She looked at the city of London, sprawled huge and glittering far beyond her dangling toes.

"And," she continued. "I know you haven't forgotten our bargain. I want to go home."

Peter is many things: one of them, when reminded, is a boy of his word. He is too proud not to be.

He flew Ashley back to her window. It was lucky that Ashley, as a rather spoiled only child, had a balcony where he could deposit her. Had he flown her into her bedroom, he would have woken her parents, who were, of course, in there waiting for her.

They had also alerted the police for miles around, but the Queen dealt with that later.

Peter stood on empty air about a foot away from the balcony, his head tilted insouciantly back, arms crossed over his chest.

"You'll grow up," he threw out at Ashley, as if it was the direst threat imaginable.

"You bet," Ashley said. "You might, too."

There was a moment of stillness. Ashley remembered that instant of quiet at the evil fortress, and remembered him dreaming and weeping in Neverland.

"Not yet, Ashley lady," said Peter. "Not yet."

"You can't stay on that island forever."

"Maybe not," Peter told her. "I used to live in Kensington Gardens with the fairies. Dreams change. But there's always another game."

Ashley raised an eyebrow. "The spy thing?"

Peter beamed at her, beautiful and terrible, young and sweet. The monster her grandmother had feared, with all his first teeth.

"You must admit, Ashley," he said. "I am perfectly splendid at it."

"You're all right," Ashley said grudgingly.

"You assisted me quite creditably," Peter told her grandly.

I do not think it will surprise you when I mention that Ashley was not overwhelmed by this tribute.

"I don't suppose . . . ," said Peter.

"What?"

Peter smiled his most fascinating smile. "You might want to come on another mission with me?"

Ashley studied the horizon. She shouldn't. He was a creature of nightmares as well as dreams, and he had kidnapped her, scared her grandmother, driven her great-grandmother mad.

Her great-great-great-grandmother had loved him, left him, and lived.

"I'll think about it," Ashley said.

Peter crowed and launched himself into the sky, perfectly and blissfully happy, the bright triumphant sound trailing after him back to the balcony where Ashley stood.

She squared her shoulders and opened the doors that would lead to her parents.

Knowing Peter, the next time he came might be many years later. He might be coming for *her* daughter. In which case, Ashley was not going to bother with the pepper spray. She was going to make her child sleep with a Taser.

Of course, Peter had no sense of time, and he might get bored and decide to arrive next week.

Ashley went into the house smiling slightly. She would have to look into acquiring that Taser as soon as possible.

Across a sky painted with the neon lights of a changing city, headed toward an island being destroyed as dreams grew dark, flew Peter Pan, who never grows up, except now and again—from the fairies' baby in Kensington Gardens to the boy who ruled Neverland to the greatest spy in the Queen's Secret Service.

Times change.

There is always another game.

You don't have to grow up yet.

Dungeons of Langeais

A Hush, Hush Story

BY BECCA FITZPATRICK

Loire Valley, France
1769

It was a vividly black night, the late October moon suffocated by cloud cover, but the road leading up to the Château de Langeais was anything but sleepy. Gravel popped under the spindly wheels of the post chaise, and over the shriek of wind, the sound of the coachman's whip cracked all four horses into a desperate race. A sharp turn rattled the coach up on two wheels, only to jar it back on all four at the next moment.

Inside, Chauncey Langeais's hands flew to the walls. He would have slid the window open and barked at his driver, but he'd ordered the man to drive as fast as possible—faster, even. Chauncey's eyes roved to his lap, and from there to his long legs. He snorted with disgust at the picture he presented: his clothes were soiled and torn. A white linen shirt, strapped around his thigh for a bandage, was soaked through with blood. Every muscle in his body cried out in protest. He was trembling with pain and, alone in the carriage, had given up trying to hide it.

Pressing his elbows into the tops of his knees, he bent his head and clasped his hands behind his neck. He sat that way until the pain returned, proving once again that no manner of shifting or stretching would bring relief. Tugging at his neck cloth, he estimated the minutes until he would be home and able to shut his doors on a long night. Of course, there was no way to shut out the fiery dread in the pit of his stomach telling him nothing could prevent time from marching forward.

Cheshvan.

The Jewish month began tomorrow at midnight and with it, the brutal ritual Chauncey underwent every year of giving up control of his body for an entire fortnight. He braced himself for the great clench of anger that always followed any thought of Cheshvan or the dark angel who would come to possess him. He'd spent a huge portion of the past two hundred years hunting for a way to undo what had been done. The task had consumed him. He'd pushed large sums of money into the pockets of Paris mystics and gypsy fortune-tellers, looking for hope, then for a loophole, and in the end, finding he was nothing but a swindled fool. They'd all nodded sagely, swearing the day would come when Chauncey would find peace. If he hadn't already outlived them all, he'd have stretched their necks one by one.

But the disappointment had taught Chauncey a valuable lesson. The angel had stripped him to nothing. There was no hope, no loophole. He only had revenge, and it had grown inside him like one lone seed in a forest burned to ash. He breathed softly through his teeth, letting cold, savage anger swell inside him. It was time the angel learned a lesson. And Chauncey would go to any lengths to teach it to him.

One gaudy tiered fountain streaked past the coach window, then another. Chauncey drew himself up to see his château, candles guttering in the diamond-paned windows. The coachman slowed the horses with a jolt that ordinarily would have escaped Chauncey's attention. Tonight, he gritted his teeth in pain.

Without waiting for the coachman, Chauncey opened the door with the heel of his boot and swung out awkwardly, unfolding himself to full height. The coachman, who barely came to the top of Chauncey's rib cage, yanked off his threadbare hat and alternately bowed and scuttled backward, tripping over his feet as if he were facing a monster, not a man. Chauncey watched him, frowning a little. He tried to remember how long the coachman had been in his service, and if he'd reached the point where it was becoming painfully obvious that, with each passing year, Chauncey didn't seem to age. He'd sworn fealty to the angel at eighteen, freezing him at that age for eternity, and while his manner, speech, and dress made him appear a few years older, it could only go so far. He might be mistaken for twenty-five, but that was the limit.

He made a distracted mental note to dismiss the coachman at the new year. Then, swatting away the plumes of dust stirred up by the horses, he limped along the flagstones trailing up to the château.

Chauncey gave the massive fortress an appreciative once-over. No earthly temptation could look as inviting as it did at that moment. But he couldn't relax just yet. He had no desire to spend the night haunted by the knowledge that in just over twenty-four hours, it would all begin again. The horrible, maddening sensation—the control of his body peeling away and falling into the hands of the angel. No, before sleep, he needed to think carefully through all the information he'd gathered on this latest trip to Angers.

...

Washed, bandaged, and freshly clothed, Chauncey eased into the chair stationed behind his desk in the library, and tipped his head back, closing his eyes, drinking in the sensation of stillness. He motioned blindly for Boswell, who stood at the door, to bring him up a bottle from the cellar.

"A particular year, Your Grace?"

"1565." *For irony's sake.* Chauncey kneaded both fists into his eyes. He had spent two hundred years wishing he could walk backward through time to that year and alter the final hours of that night. He could recall the finest details. The drill of rain, cold and relentless. The smell of mildew, pine, and ice. The wet slate headstones protruding like crooked teeth from the ground. The angel. The frightening loss he'd felt as he'd realized he couldn't command his own feet to run. The invisible hot poker jabbing every corner of his body. Even his own rational mind had turned on him, letting him believe the pain was real, never guessing it was simply one of the angel's mind tricks.

Your oath of fealty, the angel had said. *Swear it.*

Chauncey did not want to remember what happened next. He let out a groan. He'd been a fool. He hadn't understood the significance of what he'd been ordered to give. The angel had deceived him, tortured him, blinded him, taken away his will to speak for himself. Chauncey had given his oath to end a phantom pain. A few spoken words that had proved to be his undoing. *Lord, I become your man.*

He flung his arm across the desktop, sending ink bottles and a glass paperweight crashing to the floor. "Damn him!"

There was a disturbance in the shadows along the far wall.

Chauncey's body went taut. "Who's there?" he demanded, hoarse with rage.

He expected a sputtered apology from one of the servants, but instead a polished and feminine voice spoke.

"Back in town, Chauncey? And you hadn't thought to pay me a visit?"

Chauncey breathed deeply through his nose and squared his shoulders. He tried to place the voice, thinking he should know it, but at present it escaped him. "You should have spoken up," he said more composedly. "I would have had Boswell bring an extra glass with the wine."

"I didn't come here for a drink."

Then what? he thought. "How did you get inside? Boswell?" But he couldn't believe the butler would leave a strange woman inside Chauncey's personal library unaccompanied. Not if he valued his employment.

"My key."

Well, hell.

He dragged his hands down his face and attempted to sit again, but a sharp pain in his leg cut the movement short. "I never got that back, did I?" he said at last, finding it unfortunate that of all the things his memory could have failed him on tonight, Elyce wasn't one of them.

They'd met in a hotel de passe; she was a dancer, the most exotic and venomous creature he'd ever seen. She couldn't have been more than seventeen, which led him to believe she was a runaway. He'd wrapped his cloak around her and escorted her back to his home with less than a dozen words of introduction between them. She'd stayed at the château . . . what? Eight weeks? Their affair had ended abruptly.

Elyce had revisited him often in the weeks following their breakup, demanding payment for something (a gown she insisted she'd left that he'd never returned, reimbursement for the carriages that had moved her belongings from the château, and eventually, just because), and he'd indulged her, secretly finding pleasure in her titillating company. Finally she'd disappeared altogether, and he'd seen nothing of her in two years.

Until now.

She picked up the glass paperweight off the floor and studied it with a bored expression. "I need money."

He snorted in amusement. Always right to the point—particularly that point.

She slid him a look. "I want twice as much as last time."

Now he laughed outright. "Twice? By God, what do you do with it all?"

"When should I expect it?"

Chauncey cringed as he stepped around the desk to blow out one of the lamps, which was inflicting a headache. "If you'd been this demanding when we were together, I might have respected you more." She'd always been demanding; he was saying it now to take the upper hand in their banter. In a certain twisted way that he didn't care to analyze, he enjoyed sparring with her. She was pushy, self-serving, and manipulative, but above all, entertaining.

She was a mirror of himself.

"Give me the money, and I'll be on my way," she said, running her finger along the top of a gilded frame and inspecting the dust. She was the picture of ease, all right, but she couldn't look him in the eye.

Chauncey walked to the fireplace mantle and leaned into it; a favorite position of his for deep contemplation, though now he was propped against it for support. He tried to hide that fact. The last thing he needed was to fuel the curiosity burning in her eyes. He didn't care to be reminded of the humiliating circumstances that had put his body in its present shape.

An image of chasing a carriage down the boulevards of Angers flashed up from his memory. He'd bounded onto the back of the carriage in an effort not to lose Jolie Abrams, the young woman he'd been following all night, but had lost his footing when his cloak became tangled in the wheels. He'd been dragged behind the carriage a good distance, and when he'd finally rolled free, he'd been half trampled by an oncoming horse.

Elyce cleared her voice. "Chauncey?" It sounded more like an impatient order than a polite reminder that she was waiting.

But Chauncey hadn't fully shaken the memory. He'd spent a full week in Angers, searching out the seedier parts of the city where the angel was known to play cards in gambling houses or box in the streets—a modern alternative to dueling that was spreading across the whole of Europe. There was good money in it—if you could win. Chauncey had no doubt that the angel, with his arsenal of mind tricks, could.

It was while spying on the angel at one of these matches that Chauncey first laid eyes on Jolie Abrams. She might have been disguised in peasants' clothes, her dark brown hair unpinned and loose, her pouty mouth laughing and downing cheap ale, but

Chauncey wasn't fooled. This woman had attended the ballet, the opera. Underneath the shabby clothes, her skin was clean and perfumed. She was a nobleman's daughter. In the middle of his amused inspection of her, he saw it. A secret glance between her and the angel. The look of lovers.

His first impulse had been to kill her directly. Anything the angel valued, Chauncey longed to dash to pieces. But for reasons he wasn't altogether sure of, he'd followed her. Watched her. He hadn't headed back to the château until he'd lost her in the carriage. The entire trip home, he'd reshaped this startling revelation. The angel valued something physical. Something Chauncey could get his hands on.

How could he use this to his advantage?

"Do you mean to keep me waiting all night?" Elyce folded her arms and drew herself up a little taller. She lifted an eyebrow, or maybe both; half her face was turned away from the light and hidden in shadow.

Chauncey merely looked at her, willing her to shut up so he could think. What if . . . what if he locked Jolie Abrams away in the château? The idea took him by surprise. He was a duc, the Lord of Langeais, a gentleman. He'd as soon plow his own fields than take a lady hostage. And yet there the idea was, rolling forward. The château had a myriad of towers, convoluted corridors, and . . . dungeons. Let the angel try and find her. Chauncey sneered.

As a child, his stepfather had warned him of the fate of those who wandered beneath the château without a guide, and Chauncey had thought the tales the scare tactic of a man who relied on fear to discipline. Then, during one secret exploration of the musky tunnels beneath the kitchen, Chauncey stumbled across skeletal remains. The rats had scattered from under the bones at the sight of his torch, leaving Chauncey standing alone with the dead. He'd made it a point from that day on to keep to the above-ground parts of the château.

"You'll get your money," he told Elyce at long last. He looked over his shoulder at her. "Once you do something for me," he said slowly.

Elyce tossed her hair back and jutted her chin. "Pardon?"

He nearly smiled. She was indignant. Heaven forbid she had to earn her keep. "Jolie Abrams," he said, the idea of kidnapping flexing inside him.

Elyce narrowed her eyes. "Who?"

He turned, giving her his full attention. "The lover of an enemy," he murmured, eying Elyce with newfound interest. If the angel caught scent of him, all would be lost. Which meant he needed a proxy. Someone capable of moving unnoticed under the watchful eye of the angel. Someone capable of securing Jolie Abrams's trust. A woman.

"Then I feel sorry for her. You're hardly one to treat your enemies kindly. I'll expect my money by the end of tomorrow. Good night, Chauncey." She turned, bustling away in a dress that was too lavish to be anything but a Coste original, and had, no doubt, been funded by his pockets.

Chauncey clenched the silver candlestick he'd been absently stroking and hurled it through the air at her.

She must have heard the candlestick scrape against the mantle; she half turned and ducked under the hurled object, tripping backward into the sofa. Her whole expression blanched. She was scarcely breathing, and Chauncey smiled at the fine tremble vibrating through her.

He cocked his eyebrows in silent inquiry.

Shall we start again? he spoke to her mind, using one of the great and terrible powers that came with being the bastard son of a dark angel. He'd never met his real father, but his opinion of him was fixed in contempt. However, the powers he'd inherited from him were not altogether loathsome.

He watched a flick of confusion seize Elyce's face as she grappled with the idea that he'd spoken to her thoughts. It was quickly replaced by denial. Surely he couldn't have. It was impossible. She'd imagined it. It was a typical boring response that only irritated him further.

"Don't be such a bully, Chauncey," she said at last. "I'm not afraid of getting my hands a little dirty. What did you have in mind?"

She was trying hard to sound inconvenienced, but Chauncey could tell that underneath the well-practiced layers of her expression, she was more than a little worried of his answer. Of *him*. Her boldness had always been a cover for her fear.

"I want Jolie Abrams brought here. Before tomorrow night. You'll have to hurry; she lives in Angers."

"You want me to bring her here?" She blinked at him. "Why not just send a carriage for her?"

Send a carriage. Oh, certainly. With the family crest of Langeais blazed across the door. If that didn't alert the angel, he didn't know what would. "Tell her lies, make her promises, I don't care. Just make sure she's here before midnight."

"And her lover?"

Chauncey made a disgusted gesture.

"Does he have a name?" Elyce pressed.

Chauncey nearly snorted. She wanted to know if the man was of stature and wealth. She'd turn on Chauncey for a generous sum. Elyce's loyalties always went to the highest bidder.

"No," was all Chauncey said, an image of the angel's face darkening his mind.

"Surely he has a name, Chauncey." She took a bold step toward him, laying her hand on his sleeve.

Chauncey retracted, locking his hands behind his back. "Meddling doesn't become you, love."

"I'm not your love." She covered the frustration in her voice by injecting a new level of spite into it. "Do you have your eye on her, then? This *Jolie*. Do you wish her to be . . ." She trailed off, but Chauncey was perceptive enough to finish her sentence.

Do you wish her to replace me?

He smiled to himself. Ten seconds ago Elyce had despised him, but now that she feared he'd found someone to fill her void, she was suffocating in her own jealousy. She hadn't completely hardened her heart to him, then.

"I could find him, you know," Elyce said. "I could, and then what would you do? Kidnapping? They'd send you to prison!"

"I never said anything of kidnapping," Chauncey said quietly.

"Oh but I know *you*, Chauncey."

He grabbed her chin, wrenching her face up to meet his eyes. He was about to say something, but realized the rough gesture was more threatening than words. Let her fill the silence by imagining the worst.

She tossed her head to the side and stumbled back a step. Then she hurried toward the door, stopping at the threshold.

"After this, I'm through with you."

"Delivering the girl will earn you half the money."

She stared, momentarily dumbfounded. "*Half?*" she echoed, eyes flashing.

"Keeping an eye on her here at the château and making sure she doesn't die under my roof will earn you the other half." He didn't want to bring down the full wrath of the angel—he merely wanted a bargaining chip. "I'll pay in full when the job is finished."

He saw her balk at the idea of a dozen consecutive days of labor. As if she had no concept of what he went through for the same period of time every year. And would again, unless he brought the angel to his knees.

"No," she said.

Chauncey took a seat on the sofa's armrest. He meant to speak pleasantly, but an undercurrent of warning slipped into his voice. "I doubt I need to remind you how I've come to your aid in the past. What do you think, *love*, will become of your future without me?"

"This is the last time," she snapped.

He folded his hands loosely in his lap. "Always slinking back, begging for money. Always swearing this time it's the last."

"This time it is!"

He made a face of mock belief, which he could tell only infuriated her further. She might let him have the final word tonight, but it wouldn't last. She'd come around sooner rather than later to trump him. He was already looking forward to it. She was a fiery nymph, standing before him in cream velvet that melted seamlessly into her translucent skin and pale hair. Only her icy blue eyes stood out. He found himself on the verge of being spellbound by her all over again. "Do we have an agreement?"

"Beware, Chauncey. I'm not a woman to be toyed with." At that, she whirled back around, marching past Boswell, who jumped to life from his station just outside the door and jogged after her to try and reach the château's doors first. He lost. The doors slammed, reverberating through the halls.

Chauncey smiled, despite the headache splitting his skull. He hated surprises, but Elyce's unexpected visit tonight, well, he couldn't have planned it better himself.

He'd be very surprised if Jolie Abrams wasn't sitting prettily in this very room tomorrow evening.

•••

The following evening, Chauncey was in his bed chamber, his valet dressing him in green velvet breeches and a matching waistcoat, when Boswell entered.

"Miss Cunningham and Miss Abrams are waiting in the library, Your Grace."

"I'll be down in a minute."

Boswell coughed uneasily into his fist. "Miss Abrams is in a state of *sleep*." He put a funny intonation on the word.

Chauncey turned to face his butler. "She's sleeping in my library?"

"Heavily drugged, My Lord."

Chauncey broke into a grin. Elyce drugged her? The nymph was even more imaginative than he remembered.

"Miss Cunningham said Miss Abrams offered resistance. Myself and two other servants carried her in. She's dead to the world, pardon the expression."

Chauncey thought on this a moment. He hadn't expected her to arrive drugged, but it was of little consequence. She was here. His eyes swept to the window. The moon was high, the stars taunting in their brightness; midnight sneaked closer with every passing second. He'd planned on relishing the deep, lurid satisfaction that came from hearing Jolie scream as he dragged her deeper into the labyrinthine tunnels, damp with standing water, musty from the catacombs, but there wasn't time to let the sedative wear off. He needed to get her into the bowels of the château before he left to meet the angel in the cemetery. There was much still to do: he had to map the way. He had to prepare provisions to last her a fortnight, just in case. He had to instruct Boswell and the other servants to stay away from the château. He wanted no one around to unwillingly help the angel—

Suddenly his impatience faded away. Knowing he was not the only one unable to control his own destiny tonight caused him a sudden wave of satisfaction.

In the kitchen, Chauncey lit a torch and opened the heavy door leading down to the cellar. The tunnels were still very much a mystery to him, despite all the years he'd lived in the château. He'd gone down once or twice since his last excursion as a child, and only to prove to himself he could—he was a grown man now, and not afraid of the invented monsters of his childhood.

He thrust the torch into the darkness of the stairwell, light gleaming on the gray walls. His boots rang out against each stone step. At the bottom, he fixed the torch into a wall bracket. There was one other bracket on the far side of the cellar, but as far as he knew, it was the last. There had been no need for brackets in the tunnels beyond, as nobody but prisoners and their guides had ventured there.

Chauncey had four large spools of thread in a leather satchel slung over his shoulder, and he pulled out the first. He tied one end to the banister, tugging on it several times to confirm it was secure. The hairs on his neck prickled at the thought of losing his way in the tunnels. His stepfather had joked that there was only one direction to the tunnels—in. Reminded of this, Chauncey gave one last jerk on the thread. Satisfied it would hold, he picked up the torch and set off into the devil's mouth, unraveling the spool as he went, mapping his way with a web of thread.

•••

Even in the smoky near-black cell, lying awkwardly on the dirt floor, Jolie Abrams was pretty. She was unconventionally tall for a woman, but Chauncey was hardly one to be critical of height. Her peasant clothes were gone, replaced by peacock green silk, and her wavy brown hair was pinned up, giving him an unobstructed view of her cheekbones and oval face. She had obscenely long eyelashes and a splattering of freckles that he somehow intuitively knew caused her to throw her hands up every time she faced the looking glass. A gold locket adorned her neck.

Chauncey growled at the locket, using his thumb to push it open. To his surprise, it wasn't the angel's face painted inside, but another woman. She resembled Jolie too much to be anything other than a sister. He closed the locket, feeling suddenly foolish at prying into her most intimate belongings.

He inspected the cell. A cot in the corner and a silver tray of food on a table, out of reach of the rodents. He suddenly wished he'd brought something to make her more comfortable. Extra blankets at the very least. She was a lady, and proper treatment of the opposite sex had been ingrained in him by tutors as far back as he could remember. Which probably explained why he chose farm maidens or dancers, like Elyce, who sought a wealthy patron, not a husband—when he wanted a woman at all.

He eyed the manacles hanging from the walls, but saw no need for them. The cell door was as thick as the tree it had been cut from; Jolie would have to scratch at it with her fingernails for a thousand years to carve a way out. A pair of mice scurried along the wall as he waved the torch into the deeper shadows. He chased them under the door and scraped their droppings off the heels of his boots.

Jolie stirred at his feet, letting go of a sleepy troubled sigh. She was on her side, lying on dirt made colder by late October. Frosty puffs of air smoked from her lips.

"Who are you?" she said between her teeth, her voice a hiss of anger. Her upturned shoulder rose and fell with every breath. "What do you want from me?"

He felt the need to tell her this was the angel's fault, but the truth was, he could have let her go. He could let her walk out right now. He could order one of his coachmen to drive her home. She would return to her safe comfortable life, while he spent the next fortnight in agony.

"You're going to be staying here for a while," he said. "I'll see that you're comfortable, with enough food and water—"

"Comfortable? *Comfortable?*" She sat up and flung a fist of dirt at him.

Chauncey was slow to brush the dirt off his shirt. He was a brute, was he? A mindless savage? What did she think of the angel? That he was *better?*

If Chauncey was a tyrant, the angel was ten times more the devil. He held Chauncey's body hostage *every year!* And it wasn't like Chauncey could run away during those dozen days and nights, or block out what he saw. No. For a whole fortnight he was trapped in a body that didn't feel like his own, forced to watch every despicable act the angel put him through. The angel gambled *his* money. Drank *his* wine. Commanded *his* servants. Romanced *his* women.

Two years ago, he'd suffered in raging silence as the angel seduced Elyce, treating her to what she pronounced were "the most magical fourteen days" of her life. Chauncey had ordered her out of his presence the moment Cheshvan ended. He still remembered the confusion and fury in her eyes. He didn't tell her he wasn't responsible for her fortnight of blissful *magic*.

"You don't have the decency to tell me what this is about?" Jolie's cheeks were fully flushed, every word that came from her mouth stabbing Chauncey like a needle. Her eyes raked his tailored clothing, and Chauncey read her thoughts.

A gentleman in dress, but not in action.

What gentleman would kidnap a lady and hold her prisoner? He swelled with humiliation, but he also had the angel to think about. Chauncey wasn't going to let the angel possess him again. The thought goaded him past reason.

Jolie cocked her head to one side, the light of recognition filling her eyes. "You . . . you were at the fight. In Angers. The other night. I saw you." He could practically hear her thoughts trying to pull sense from her words.

"I have business with the angel." He smiled faintly, in spite of himself.

"Who?"

Chauncey's smile deepened. "He didn't tell you?"

"Tell me what?" she said testily.

"Your lover isn't a man. More like an animal, I'd say."

The first glimpse of wariness shadowed her face.

"He's one of the banished angels. That's right, love. An *angel*. Don't believe me? Get a good look at his back. Wing scars." Oh, he was enjoying this.

"He—told me he was flogged."

Chauncey tipped his head back and laughed.

She was on her knees, her hands balled into fists. "He told me it happened while he was in the army!"

"Did he now?" he said, then let himself out of the dungeon

room. He'd planted the seed. The angel wouldn't find his sweet-heart quite so ignorant at their next meeting. If she agreed to meet him at all.

He pulled the door shut hard, locking it with the drop of an iron bar. He heard her on the other side, beating the door and shouting profanities. He heard the tray of food clash against the door, and growled. Now he'd have to leave the thread intact so Elyce could deliver a second tray.

He groped blindly for the thread, feeling his way out. Each step felt heavier, and each breath took more work. *Cheshvan*. Mid-night was all too close. He felt its approach echo in every sinew. Chauncey redoubled his efforts, walking more quickly, fearing what would happen if he didn't reach the cemetery in time.

...

Rain pattered down on the darkening countryside surrounding Château de Langeais, but Chauncey crossed the courtyard to the stables unaware of the mud slinging on his boots. He wore no hat; his hair clung to his face, wet and disheveled. He knew without proof his eyes reflected the blackened sky above.

He ducked under the roof of the stables, breathing irregu-larly. He could feel Cheshvan upon him, crushing him. He could feel control of his body peeling away. He had to meet the angel by midnight, or the pain would spike to become unbearable. Part of his oath was to turn his body over freely. The first year, Chauncey had gone to meet the angel, having no idea what was in store. The second year, wiser and hardened, he'd forced the angel to come to him. Chauncey had passed out from the pain before the angel had even arrived. There were still lines down the walls of the château where he'd raked his fingernails in agony.

The one-eyed groom limped out of the shadows, frowning.

Bracing his hand on a beam, Chauncey gave a terse nod in the direction of the stalls. He hoped the groom was smart enough to interpret his gesture. He was breathing with difficulty and had no desire for speech.

The groom blinked his good eye. "But it's nearly midnight, Your Grace."

"Horse." His voice sounded rough, strained.

"It will take a minute, m'lord. I—I wasn't expecting you. That is to say, it's rather late—"

"I haven't got a minute," Chauncey snapped.

A bolt of lightning crackled through the sky. The groom lifted his eye and quickly crossed himself. Chauncey glowered at him. The insolent man was still standing in place, fearing God more than him.

Chauncey sank suddenly to one knee, panting. The ground was spinning. He felt bile surging up his throat. The pain was so bright it clawed from the inside out.

The groom cautioned a step forward. "M'lord?"

"Horse!" he choked, thinking he would have wrung the groom's neck if it were in reach.

Minutes later, Chauncey rode from the stables, whipping a gelding to breakneck speed. He headed straight for the forest, feeling the groom's good eye follow him to the edge of the trees. Feeling the groom's fear lie thick on his back.

···

The angel was on time. He sat on an ornate headstone in the rustic cemetery sheltered deep in the forest. His hands were clasped between his knees, his dark eyes watchful but not nervous. His hair was damp with rain, and despite the chill in the air, his shirt was open at the neck. His mouth curved up on one side, a pirate's smile, easy and ruthless at once.

"Where is she?" the angel asked.

Chauncey flinched. Did he mean Jolie? This wasn't how he'd planned their conversation. He'd anticipated being the one to tell the angel that Jolie Abrams was locked away somewhere between here and Paris, with limited food, and unless the angel cooperated, she would inevitably die. He'd left Jolie with more than enough food, but didn't allow himself to think on it, fearing the angel had some way of deciphering his mind. "Good luck finding her in time," he replied, almost calm.

"I'm going to ask once more," the angel said quietly. "Where is she?"

Chauncey sneered. "I hope . . . she's not afraid of rats?"

A muscle in the angel's jaw jumped. "Her, for my word not to possess you?"

Adrenaline itched under Chauncey's skin. Was he asking? Agreeing to bargain? Could it be that simple? Chauncey had anticipated some kind of struggle.

Chauncey shook his head. "I don't trust your word. Release me from my oath. You'll never take possession of my body during Cheshvan again. Anything less, and the girl dies. I've heard starvation can be quite painful." Chauncey raised his eyebrows, as if asking the angel's opinion on the subject.

The angel's eyes were so black, the night seemed to pale in comparison. Chauncey held that gaze with wariness stirring in his stomach. Had he spoken too soon? Had he asked too much? But it was his body, his life!

"Your final offer?"

"Yes, it's my final offer," Chauncey growled impatiently. Was the angel backing out? Was he so depraved he'd let the girl die? Chauncey felt midnight squeezing down on him, the pain twisting every ounce of patience and sanity from him. He clenched his teeth, swearing he would kill the angel if he laughed at him for this humiliating twitching and jerking. *Hurry up and make a decision!*

The possession happened all too fast. Chauncey was slammed up against a tree with no way to escape. He ordered his legs to run, but it was as if a great wall of ice separated his mind from his body. He tried to move his head, to see where the angel was, but his stomach sickened with the truth.

It was happening all over again. The angel was not there. The angel was inside him.

Here comes the struggle, Chauncey thought.

The angel slammed Chauncey's body against the tree a second time, stunning him. Another time, and another, and another, until Chauncey felt blood trickling down his face. His shoulder throbbed. He felt bruises sprouting all along the battered side of his body. He wanted to scream for the angel to stop, but his voice wasn't his to command.

Next, the angel shoved Chauncey's fist into the tree. There was a ghastly crunch, and Chauncey saw bone protruding from his skin. He howled, but it was a silent sound, trapped inside him. He knew what was coming next and tried to brace himself for the hot torment. The angel forced Chauncey to kick the tree, over and over, until the bones in his foot snapped and Chauncey felt himself wilting in shock. He screamed and blubbered, but it was ripped from him. He was nothing but reason and feeling. He couldn't act; he was only to be acted upon.

Just as quickly as he'd lost control, he was breathing on his own again. He lay crumpled on the ground and instantly cradled his broken hand against his chest. The angel stood over him. He gave a significant look at the tree, now painted with Chauncey's blood.

"I'll never tell you where she is!" Chauncey spat.

Chauncey felt the dizzying torment of the wound on his thigh being ripped open. The angel was in control again, using Chancey's hands to whip his leg with a branch. The wound opened, and blood blossomed across his velvet breeches. Chauncey's temples throbbed with panic, the smell of terror leaking from his skin.

Do not talk! Do not talk! he shouted at himself through the whir of terror shaking him. *Do not let him win!*

Chauncey collapsed, swimming in and out of consciousness; one half of him yearned for the darkness of slumber, the other half feared the loss of control. What if he revealed Jolie's location in his sleep? He couldn't. He couldn't . . .

With his cheek cushioned by icy dirt, Chauncey's eyes fluttered. He thought he saw the angel jogging away. Chauncey tried to smile. Going to search the countryside for Jolie, was he? His mouth formed the words *good luck*, but they stayed on his lips. Through his haze, Chauncey knew this was a pivotal moment. The angel had to possess him now, or never. The time frame was one hour. The angel had never missed his window in the past, but now . . .

But this time . . .

Even if the angel correctly guessed Jolie's whereabouts, by the time he went to the château and back, it would be too late.

He'd miss this Cheshvan . . .

Chauncy's eyes rolled back in his head. He had been through this kind of pain many times before. He wouldn't die, but he'd lose a great deal of blood, and would sleep—even as long as a week or two, depending on the severity of his wounds—while his body slowly stitched itself back together and became whole once again.

• • •

Chauncey woke in the cemetery. He was slumped against a headstone, the cold slate seeping through the back of his shirt. Between the slits of his eyes, the world was black and silver. A few snowflakes drifted down, melting as they hit his breeches, his shirt, his bare hands. He turned his hands over, back and forth, staring at them, nearly weeping that they were in his power. He dragged himself upright and knew it was over. He didn't know how long he'd slept, but the icy morning and transformed scenery made him guess several days. He'd escaped Cheshvan. He'd defied the angel. A certain stone that had hung inside him all these years cracked, turning to dust. If he could do it once, he could do it again.

He grinned at the trees, not caring that his clothes were torn and soiled with blood, or that he reeked of his own unwashed body. He dragged his hands down his face, blinking at the morning. Everything was fresh. He breathed in the intoxicating scent of the forest, held it, let it go. For the first time in his life he stood mesmerized by the harsh beauty of the world slowly freezing. He spun circles until his mind reeled, whooping and shouting with joy, and when dizziness overtook him, he fell back in the half-frozen mud, laughing.

He lay that way for quite some time, basking in the forest—which no longer felt like his enemy—feeling immeasurably happy, until his eyes flew open.

Jolie. The château. The dungeons.

His feet were already carrying him in a run.

...

Chauncey could not remember the way.

Gripping the torch, he splashed through the water pooling at the bottom of the tunnels, swallowing his boots.

"Jolie!"

His voice echoed like a disembodied spirit's.

With an impatient grunt he forged ahead, letting the spool unravel in his free hand. He came to an intersection, turned left, and a length of thread caught him in the navel, bringing him up short. He'd already come this way. He was creating a web of circles. Around and around, nearer or farther from Jolie, he didn't know. He leaned back against the wall, squeezing his eyes shut, breathing heavily. He had to think. He had to remember. If he could just push aside the darkness and remember the maze.

"Jolie!" he yelled again.

He wondered if she would answer. He was the tyrant who had locked her away. She could be down this tunnel, or the next, listening, but hiding in fear.

"Don't die on me," he muttered.

The angel. He couldn't stop thinking about the angel.

Hang Cheshvan! The angel would launch a full-scale war if Jolie died down here. How long had it been? Days and days, but how much beyond that? He'd sent the servants away, and there was no one to ask. And where the hell was Elyce? He was paying her to keep watch. Had the food lasted? Had Jolie stayed warm enough? He'd woken in the cemetery frozen solid, the weather far colder than he'd expected with winter still weeks away. He should have planned better. If only he'd had more time!

Chauncey turned and turned again, crashing through the tunnels. He came around a bend, and there it was. The door stood at the end of the passageway. The iron bar was still in place, locking Jolie inside. He flung off the bar and threw the door wide. Rats scuttled lazily into the shadows. Two silver trays were overturned on the floor, but the food was gone, replaced by a thick covering of rodent droppings.

Chauncey saw the body on the cot, but his brain was muddled, unable to make sense of it. He blinked as if he weren't seeing properly. The girl was covered in a thin layer of frost. Her cynical blue eyes were open, frozen in a stare.

Elyce was dead.

Chauncey's hand flexed on the doorframe. He saw himself as a nine-year-old boy, standing in the cellar beneath the kitchen, stumbling upon death.

"No," he said. He blinked again. "No."

His legs pushed him toward Elyce. He stood over her, unable to stop staring. He couldn't seem to see her as she really was, rather as she was supposed to be.

Alive.

A flood of memories broke through his mental dam. He didn't believe in *love* at first sight. He didn't believe in love. It was the religion of fools. But the first time he saw Elyce, for one fraction in time, he'd doubted everything he knew. Dancing in a way that outshone the common girls, she stole the stage. Every coin in the room

flowed her way. She took something ordinary and made it lucrative. She ruled her own destiny.

Not once in his life had Chauncey felt understood, but in the weeks Elyce had stayed with him here at the château, the deep gap that had always separated him from the rest of the world narrowed. They were the same, he and Elyce. Calculating, manipulative, and cynical, yes. But also driven, hungry, and uncompromising. He didn't love her in the way other men loved their women; he loved her in the only way he could—for not leaving him alone in a world that understood him even less than he understood it.

The only reason he'd cast her out of the château was because of the angel. He couldn't stand in the same room with her and not hear those words.

The most magical days of my life . . .

He'd hated Elyce for those words, but his anger was misdirected. All blame fell on the angel.

Lowering himself onto the cot, he pressed Elyce's hand to his face. His emotions flapped inside him like birds dashing against a glass cage. Who did he have now? He was utterly alone. Utterly misunderstood.

Chauncey jolted to a stand, believing he sensed the angel nearby. His posture was guarded, but the walls outside the cell shimmered not with the angel's shadow, but with the spirits of the dead. Chauncey could feel them, trapped and wandering. His body convulsed at the thought of them surrounding him, and he backed further into the cell.

"Elyce!" he hissed. Down here in the dungeons, he felt certain that death was very far away, and very near at the same time. "Can you hear me? Did the angel do this? Did *he*?"

The door to the cell swung shut. Chauncey heard the iron bar drop into place, locking him inside.

He crossed to the door in two strides. "Who's there?" he demanded.

There was no answer.

"Elyce?" He didn't believe in ghosts. On the other hand, what else could it be? "It was the angel, he killed you," he said. "I had nothing to do with this." He glanced back at her body on the cot to make sure it was still there. He'd heard stories of corpses rising from the grave to drink the blood of the living. In the dungeons, he ruled nothing out.

"Talking with the dead, Duke? Keep it up, and people are going to question your sanity."

Chauncey stiffened at the voice on the far side of the door. He made a guttural sound of hatred. "*You.*"

"I hope you like rats," the angel said quietly.

"Not a wise move, angel. These are my dungeons. You've trespassed on my land. I could have you hanged." Even as Chauncey said it, he realized how worthless the threat was.

"Hanged? With what? All this thread?"

Chauncey felt his nostrils flare.

"Then I'd better take it on my way out." The angel's voice started to fade.

Panic seized Chauncey's throat. "Open the door you insolent fool! I am the Duc de Langeais, and *this is my château*!"

Silence.

Chauncey slammed a fist against the door. The angel thought he was clever, did he? Well, he'd just laid the groundwork for his own destruction!

Slicing his palm open on his riding spurs, Chauncey shook out a few drops of blood. He swore an oath to bring the angel to his knees. He would be relentless. Ruthless. Jolie would grow old and die, but there would be other women.

Chauncey would wait patiently.

Behind the Red Door
BY CAITLIN KITTREDGE

"Down in the willow garden where me and my love did meet
There we sat a-courting
My love fell off to sleep
I had a bottle of burgundy wine which my true love did not know
And there I poisoned that dear little girl down by the banks below."
—Unknown

1. July

The first time Jo Ryan found the red door into Ash House, it was a hot, still day in the middle of July, the kind of day when nothing moved, not even the air.

She was with Ani and Deirdre, Ani's girlfriend. They'd bought red slushies from the 7-Eleven on Chestnut Street and were sitting on the hill behind Ani's grandmother's barn, mixing the slushies with vodka. Deirdre had a clove, which she wasn't smoking because it was creeping up on ninety degrees. All of them were sticky with red sugar and sweat.

"My dad wants me to get a job," Ani said. "He said I could work for Mrs. Highsmith until school starts."

"Cleaning houses?" Deirdre flicked ash into the grass. Matted and green, it was past Jo's ankles. She dug her bare toes into the cool earth at the roots.

"What's wrong with that?" Ani demanded. Ani and Deirdre loved to argue more than the old married couples who summered in Coffin Hollow to escape New York. Jo added another half inch of vodka to her slushie.

"It's just so . . ." Deirdre sighed and stubbed out the clove. "God, Ani. Why don't we just go live with my sister in New York? This town is like something out of a horror movie."

Jo felt sweat drops creep down her back, in time with the buzzing insects in the field beyond. "It's hotter in New York," she said.

"See? I don't want to sleep on your sister's floor all summer," Ani said. "Besides, New York is expensive, and I'm paying my own way after next year."

Deirdre rolled her eyes. She was a summer girl, bringing the sweat and smoke of the city with her every June 20th since Ani and Jo were in sixth grade. She'd been the first one in black boots, the first one to cut the necks out of her brother's T-shirts and wear them over a skirt from her old prep school. The first girl Ani ever kissed.

"I'm done with watching the cows fart," Deirdre said. "Let's go see if my brother has some pot."

"You said you'd give me a ride to practice," Ani said, when Deirdre stood up and brushed grass off her butt. "And that you'd talk to Thom about the shirt designs for the gig on Saturday. I hate how you get when you drive around baked."

Deirdre was pretty, Jo supposed, but when her face got that way, all off-balance, like a toddler about to pitch a fit, she was a doll who'd come out of the mold wrong. "Shit," was all she said, before she slumped back down.

Ani sucked more of her vodka cherry slushie through her straw. "What should we do?"

Jo looked down the valley. The field ended at a barbwire fence. Beyond that was overgrown, except for a slate roof poking through the trees. It vibrated in the sunlight, spreading an ache behind her eyes. Like a drop of quicksilver on green glass, the roof blurred her vision. The buzzing of the insects grew louder than PA feedback at one of their shows.

"We could go look around Ash House." The words came into

her mind like raindrops, spoke from her mouth like ripples. It wasn't her idea, but it was in her brain like a seed.

"Yeah," Deirdre said. "And when we're done maybe we can tip over some cows and smash a mailbox. God, Jo. You are such a hillbilly sometimes."

Ani gave Deirdre a hard punch on the shoulder. "Shut up. It's not like we have anything better to do."

"I gave you a better idea," Deirdre said. "Go back to my house. At least my room has an AC."

Jo stood up and pulled her boots back on. Deirdre and Ani kept arguing. All they did was argue and hook up, when Deirdre wasn't baked or locked in her room, drawing her creepy pen-and-ink pictures. Bleeding women, vampires, men with raven heads, and children with fish tails. Deirdre's drawings bothered Jo somewhere low in her stomach, like when her mother had been drinking back in Providence, and dating the guy who liked to open Jo's door and look at her when he thought she was asleep.

". . . And I'm not going to poke around that place and break my damn neck," Deirdre's voice rose. "Besides . . ." her voice slid into that mean, petty register that always reminded Jo of a blade going into something soft. "You know it's haunted as shit, right? They hanged a guy in the front yard, vigilante style, old Wild West shit. Like, a hundred people have died in there, I bet."

"That's just kid stories," Ani said. She'd had more of the red drink than anyone. Her plastic mini-mart cup was almost empty, and her words were slower than the heat.

"There's nothin' in there. Rats and spiders maybe."

Deirdre's eyes narrowed. "I dare you to go in. Put a mark on one of the upstairs windows."

Ani looked sick. Ani hated spiders, had as long as Jo had known her.

"Forget it," Ani said. "Let's stay here. Jo and I have to get to practice soon anyway."

Deirdre opened her mouth to say something else, shrill and

nasty as a New York taxi, and Jo spoke instead. "I'll do it."

Deirdre stretched, her skinny arms flexing under her tattoos. She'd drawn them herself—an angel with black wings on one arm, a goat-legged satyr on the other, prone girls blond and brunette at their feet, the blood from their wounds running down her arms in dark red ink. "Well," she said, "you may be a hillbilly, but at least you're not a pussy."

"Jo, this is stupid," Ani muttered.

"Yeah, probably," Jo said. She was walking down the hill, though, her boots sinking into the high grass. The barrier between Ani's property and Ash House was a rusted fence, and she stepped on it to get over. It wasn't like anyone was going to yell at her for letting the livestock out. Ash House had been abandoned for years, probably since the forties, which was when Ani's grandmother had moved to the farm to marry Ani's grandfather when he got back from France.

The house appeared and disappeared, peeping through the apple trees and scrub oaks.

The undergrowth wasn't just grass. Blackberry vines scraped along Jo's bare legs, drawing blood. Wild roses coated her with pollen and scent, petals sticking to her skin.

She'd look like hell when she came back out. Her Stiff Little Fingers shirt was damp all along the spine, and she peeled it off, going down to her bra. Hell, it was more than Deirdre wore, most summer days.

The orchard ended, fewer and fewer trees, and Jo was no longer walking through brush but a long-forgotten lawn, Queen Anne's lace and daisies brushing the blood from her thighs.

Ash House was all at once no longer a mirage but solid, tall and black, nearly blotting out the relentless sun. Jo stopped, standing in the tall grass, and wiped sweat off the back of her neck with her shirt.

Ani and Deirdre were probably watching her. She'd be a tiny white figure in the green. The little girl lost. That is, if Deirdre hadn't gotten bored and gone back to picking fights with Ani or taken her busted-ass Dodge Dart and gone home to smoke pot, which was how Deirdre's temper tantrums usually ended.

Jo had liked it much better when only Ani would have been watching her from the top of the hill.

Ash House waited, while all around her the insects hummed, air vibrating with their song, sweat and dirt pressing against Jo's skin.

All of the broken windows stared at her, the biggest insect of all, refracting a thousand tiny, shirtless Jos back into the wilderness beyond the panes.

She picked her way along a pitted path, bricks strewn across the lawn, some upright like tiny headstones, some buried in overgrown grass. Big, shaggy bushes that she guessed had once been topiary animals cluttered the lawn. She could still see a leg and a head, a tail. She'd come up on Ash House from the rear, and when she set foot on the sagging wraparound porch, boards cracked like rifle shots.

The back door was nailed over with plywood, a NO TRESPASSING sign turned to metal lace still attached to the center.

Jo picked her way along the side of the house. It was covered in dead leaves and spider webs, but she didn't see any of the usual stuff—the beer bottles, food wrappers, used condoms—that usually drifted up around an old abandoned place. The town cemetery, most of which was disused and ancient, was littered with the stuff. Ani and Deirdre had hooked up on one of the cool, flat granite sarcophagi that sat above ground in the far corner, back by the woods.

The far edge of the same woods crowded Ash House, at this angle blocking her view of the hill. All she could see were twisted trunks, scrub, and glossy green leaves like beetle shells.

The front of Ash House looked down a winding drive. Once, it had been white abalone shell, but now weeds had erupted, turning it into a ribbon of wildflowers and green amid the vines and brush. A bridge at the foot of the drive forded the Acushket River, here just a narrow stream with steep banks and a current that could knock your legs out. The Acushket ran down and widened and powered mills to the south, but here it was just background to the insects and the whispering leaves.

The roof of the porch was sky blue, paint peeling in long fingers, hanging almost down to Jo's face like Spanish moss.

The door of Ash House was twice as wide as Jo, and it was red. Iron pulls looped through snarling gargoyle mouths in place of knobs.

The door stood open. Not much. Just enough to invite someone in.

Jo put a hand on the door, slid a foot over the threshold. There were dead leaves on the floor inside, and in advance of her footsteps, things scuttled into the shadows.

Before she could think too hard about it, she gave the door a hard shove and let it propel her inside. The hinges shrieked, echoed off the high ceiling, and then everything went silent.

The insects outside stopped humming. The things in the shadow stopped moving. The only sounds were Jo's own heart and the Acushket, rushing through the iron pilings that held up the bridge, and on over the rocks.

Jo made it six steps into Ash House that day. She had decided to go up the sweeping front stairs, banisters like the winding river outside, carpet rotted like winter moss, and signal Ani and Deirdre from the round stained glass window that rose at the first landing. It was pink and green glass, light like underwater wavering through it, and it was remarkably intact. Like the rest of Ash House, nature had its way, but the local kids didn't seem to know the place existed.

She walked the six steps, to the center of the entryway. The leaves crunched under her boots, hissing across the tile floor. There was a picture there, but it was too filthy to make out.

When she looked up, there was a shape in front of the window. Tall and thin, at first she took it for another shadow. Then she saw the eyes and the teeth, the dark jacket and tie, the white shirt with black space floating above it. The light bent where it shot through the shape, and hit the floor in front of Jo. The shape cast no shadow.

Jo didn't distinctly remember running from Ash House, skipping the steps, and thrashing through the grass to the bridge. Deirdre and Ani eventually found her walking down Route 7. She wasn't hot, even though the sun bounced off the asphalt and made everything shimmer. Jo couldn't get warm until they'd dropped her off at home, and she'd watched the Dart's tail lights disappear into the gathering twilight.

2. August

Jo woke up to music. It wasn't music-box music, or the thump and hum of the world stuff or old-school jazz her mother usually played while she was in her studio. This was loud. Loud enough that it rattled the screen in her open bedroom window.

She rolled out of bed and peeked outside. The Ryan house was one of a pair on a dead-end street. There had been three houses, but the one on the far left had burned down in the 1970s, when Jo's mom lived in the Ryan house with Grandpa Paul and Grandma Leigh. There was just a chimney now, and a vacant lot.

The three driveways were close together, three lines of shell and sand. In the neighbor's driveway, a car was parked, stereo blasting.

It was easily the ugliest car Jo had ever seen—the color of a rotten pumpkin where it wasn't just bubbled primer and rust, the bumper strapped on with plastic zip-ties, the windshield spattered with dead bugs.

Square and lopsided, like an aging pit bull, it crouched facing the street, daring anyone to get too close. She wondered where it had come from—if it ran, she'd be amazed. Unfortunately, there was nothing wrong with the radio.

Jo pulled on shorts and a tank top and walked outside barefoot. Her mom was locked in the back room with the air conditioner, which she needed to cool her computer system. She'd picked up some design work for some big animated movie coming out at Christmas, and she was working nonstop, drawing and rendering a pair of adorable space aliens so that they could be inhabited by the voices of celebrities.

"Hey!" Jo shouted. She could see a pair of legs, and part of a torso, ensconced in the car's innards. It kind of looked like the car was eating them. "Hey!" she shouted again. She left her porch and crossed the driveway. The song was something old, that you'd hear on an 8-track. *Old black water, keep on rolling.*

Jo winced as a piece of shell bit into her foot, and thumped on the hood. "Hey!"

The body inside the car jerked upward, slamming his skull into the underside of the hood. "OW!"

Jo drew back. "Oh man," she said. "Sorry about that." She wasn't entirely. The guy reached inside the window and turned down the stereo.

"I know you," he said. "You're Mel's kid."

Jo realized she knew him, too. "You're the Powells' son."

He grabbed a rag and swiped at his hands, then picked up a beer from the shadow of the car and took a long pull. "Guilty."

"How do you know my mom?" Jo said. She didn't think Melanie Ryan, with her smart black clothes and wire-rimmed glasses and her four years of sobriety, would have anything to do with their next-door neighbors beyond yelling at Mrs. Powell to bring her crop of small, yappy dogs inside when it got late. She didn't think she'd ever seen Mr. Powell. Maybe there wasn't one.

"I trimmed her roses and did the lawn a few times last summer," the guy said. Jo knew his name was something short, like something a tough guy in a black-and-white movie would be called.

The guy stuck out his hand. "Drew."

"Jo," said Jo. Drew's hand left a long smear of grease on her palm, picking out all the flaws, all the calluses from playing bass with Ani, and the thin line where she'd cut her hand on a rusty lawn chair as a kid.

"So why'd you come over here?" Drew leaned against the car and finished off the beer. "You lonely?"

"What?" Jo's voice rose a little more than she would have liked. "No! I mean . . . the music. It woke me up."

He actually smirked at her. "It's eleven in the morning."

Jo narrowed her eyes. "Night owl."

"Fair enough," said Drew Powell, and turned his music back up. Jo supposed she could try to go back to sleep until Ani came to get her for practice, but she'd woken up twisted in her sheets, sweating even though the day wasn't humid.

She dreamed a lot, and in the dreams were things that sent her shooting into wakefulness. They were dark shapes standing in front of stained glass, things with dark faces whispering at her from piles of leaves. Thorns the size of her little finger wrapped around pale, naked thighs.

Jo went back to the screened part of the porch and pulled on a pair of sneakers. She got her cell phone and her army surplus pack, which was stuffed with her wallet and her lyrics notebook, a flashlight, and an umbrella. Melanie believed in being prepared, and it was easier to lug the stuff around then get chewed out.

She thought for a second and then went into the kitchen drawer and added Mel's camping knife. Not a lame little Swiss Army knife like you could buy at a grocery store—Mel's had a three-inch blade and attachments to open cans and saw through rope.

Grabbing a bottle of water, Jo was back out the door, ignoring Drew Powell even though he stopped working on his eyesore of a car again and stared at her.

It was at least three miles to Ani's grandmother's farm, and she was soaked by the time she got there, the water bottle depleted. *Great plan, Jo*, she thought. *You're going to die on the way back*.

Ash House peered at her over the treetops again, and now its slate roof, gables sharp as razor blades, didn't seem at all mysterious or inviting.

She circled the wilderness of the orchard, though, and repeated her walk up the drive. The red door still stood open. Her footprints were still in the tile of the front hall.

When she stepped into the house, the oppressive silence almost smothered her. She almost couldn't make herself look up at the landing. A few panes were gone in the stained glass now, like someone had picked the petals off a flower. Pink glass crunched under her feet when she made herself go up the stairs, stand in the spot where she'd seen the shadow.

Nothing there. Nothing to spook her except a lot of cobwebs and a really, really dead bird that had clearly flown into the house some years ago and made its final resting place on the sill.

Jo blew out a puff of the stale house air and felt like the world's biggest idiot. She'd actually been scared, standing down there in the entry. *Known* something was watching her, when it wasn't anything except a reflection.

Letting light and shadow fool you wasn't very punk rock. Jo wiped sweat off her face and watched it fall to the filthy floor.

Another set of footprints sat in the dust, next to the scuffs of her shoes. Precise, pointed toe and square heel. No scuffs. Standing still.

The sun snuffed out behind a high bank of anvil-shaped thunderheads, bloody pink through the lens of the window. A puff of wind blew the red door wide, hinges shrieking.

A voice spoke into Jo's left ear, very close and clear. "*Who are you?*"

Jo took a step, tangled her feet, and went down hard. The same hand Drew Powell had covered in grease twisted under her, sharp and hot as driving a nail through her palm.

When she looked up, she saw the shape. Saw it wasn't a shape, but a figure. The weak, yellow stormlight spilling from outside passed through him, and dust motes danced from her fall, silvered as if they were falling through a projector light.

The figure stretched out his hand. "*Don't be afraid.*"

Thunder cracked the heavens open. Rain cascaded from the sky, a thousand leaks sprouting in the ceiling of Ash House.

Jo managed to get up. She thought the figure might have reached for her, his hand drifting through the fabric of her tank top. His face, she noticed with that snapshot clarity that comes with panic, was very young, close to her age. Hair dark as ink swept back in a style at least seventy years out of date. Dapper suit and tie.

And dead. Dead, dead, dead.

Jo didn't know how the thought came to her that the boy on the stairs was dead. Not a hallucination or heatstroke, but a departed. When it did come, though, she ran. Ran from the house through the wide open door, out into the thunderstorm that rolled from one side of the hollow to the other, into rain that was colder than putting ice cubes on bare skin. Ran until she couldn't go any further, and collapsed under the Route 7 overpass, which was where Drew Powell found her after the rain stopped, when he came rattling along in his barely functioning '71 Nova. He took her with him to buy belts and a new air filter and then drove her home.

He never asked what she was doing on the road in the first place.

3. September

Jo hadn't intended to start her junior year with her arm in a sling, but at least it got her out of PE for a few weeks. By the time Drew had gotten her home that afternoon, her hand was twice its normal size, and she couldn't bend her wrist without her eyes watering.

The doctor had diagnosed two broken fingers and a severe sprain. Jo told her mother she fell doing a stage dive. Mel muttered something about that Deirdre girl and bad influences, and drove her to the urgent care clinic in Pittsfield.

She didn't tell Drew her "ghost story," as Ani insisted on calling it. Jo would have argued that just because she saw a boy the light cut straight through, who appeared out of nowhere, that didn't make the boy a ghost. Even if that ugly coffin-heavy word had dropped into her head when they "touched." *Dead*.

At least it gave Ani something to talk about, and it was better than her endless chatter about Deirdre, who was back at her pretentious private art school in New York.

Ani should be the one in a private school, Jo thought. Ani was talented—the drawing, the guitar playing, singing, anything she turned her hands and voice to. Jo had never been jealous of it until Deirdre showed up. Before her, they were Ani and Jo— Jo got decent grades and wrote songs, Ani got detention and wrote the music.

During the free period that should have been PE, she wandered behind the outbuilding that housed the mowers and the thing that painted lines on the football field. Smokers went there, and occasionally you came upon a couple who just couldn't hold it together until final bell.

She thought it would be deserted, and maybe she could nap in the sun. The dreams were worse and sleeping at home wasn't happening that often.

She never should have gone back in that house. She saw it almost every night in her dreams—but not ruined, like it really was, but whole and inhabited, every window glowing with yellow lamplight. Apple trees thrashing in wind, shedding their ripe, red crop all over the ground. And the thorns, winding around and around her legs, blood running over her skin and slicking across her thighs.

Drew Powell leaned against the shed when she came around

the corner. His hair was a little longer now, the high-and-tight he'd come home with mussed on top. Drew had been in military school all of last year. Jo figured that was a polite way of saying juvie—Drew didn't look like structure and marching were his thing.

"Hey," he said. He was smoking the end of a cigarette, holding it pinched tight between two fingers like James Dean.

Jo gave him a nod, crouched against the wall, and tilted her face into the sun.

"You didn't tell me you broke your hand doing B&E," Drew said. Jo cracked her eye open.

"It's not B&E if the door's open."

Drew threw his cigarette down and stomped on it. "Why poke around that place? Nothing there."

Jo bit her tongue. Oh, there was something there. Just not what Drew was thinking of. "It was a dare," she said.

"Oh yeah?" Drew perked up, and he slid down to sit next to her. "You do that a lot? Truth or dare?"

Jo shook her head. She knew he was fishing for her to say something so he'd know whether she was a slut or not, whether the vintage Cure shirt and short imitation-leather skirt and ripped up tights meant she gave it up, or if she just wasn't into American Eagle and pastels, like the rest of the girls at Hawthorn High. Drew Powell wasn't the most subtle guy who'd ever hit on her.

"Just the one time," she said. "And I broke my hand, so there you go."

She stood up. She might as well go try and squint at her homework until next period. Besides, if faculty caught her out here with Drew, who clearly didn't have an excuse to be wandering hither and yon and sparking up cigarettes, she'd get bounced to detention, and she could put off having *that* conversation with Mel forever.

"My brother went down there once," Drew said. "He said it

was pretty crazy inside."

"He on a dare too?" Jo shouldered her bag. She'd thrown out her backpack—she couldn't get the smell out, the musty, dirty graveyard smell of dry rot and small, dead animals it had picked up in Ash House. The new bag was made of recycled seat belts, and she'd let Ani spray-paint some designs on it.

"Nah, him and his buddies were drinking after graduation," Drew said. "They got wasted and decided to go have a séance. There was a murder there, you know."

"Sure," Jo said, wondering if it was the same one Deirdre had been babbling about. But she didn't ask. Being too interested would give Drew his in. "I should be going. I have calc seventh period."

"Or we could go get some beer and ride out to the quarry," Drew said. He suggested it the same way other guys would suggest soda and slices at O'Reilly's Pizza Explosion. "I rebuilt the engine on the Nova. It's smooth. And I cleaned it out some since I gave you that first ride."

"No thanks," Jo said. She felt as if she were in a PSA—say no to drugs, skipping school, and guys with blue eyes and Chevy Novas.

Drew shrugged. "Your loss."

Jo left, because what could you say to that? She was going to study in the student lounge, but she went to the library instead, and spent the last thirty minutes of the period reading about Ephraim Day, who planted the ash trees that gave Ash House its name. His son Nicholas, and Nicholas's intended bride, Abigail Worth, who drowned in the Acushket in 1902, on a perfectly clear and sunny day. A piece from the historical society, years later, suggested that the poor, desperate girl might have thrown herself into the current. But no one knew. Would never know.

It was a good story, but it wasn't murder, and it wasn't what made Jo go sprinting to the girl's room with a wave of panicked nausea.

The picture of Nicholas Day was a picture of the boy on the stairs.

Jo guessed Ani was right. She had a ghost story. Even if she didn't want it.

4. October

Jo and Ani used to tell ghost stories, when they were ten or eleven, mash-ups of stories told to them by Ani's older siblings to make the girls leave the grown-ups alone, the weird kid superstitions that get passed around, and slasher movies they'd watched on cable when Mel thought they were asleep.

Their favorite was the Hookman—largely because it gave Jo a chance to recite, dramatically, "And there . . . on the handle . . . was a HOOK!" while their friends shrieked and hid in their sleeping bags.

Plus, it started with older kids making out, something Jo and Ani were deeply committed to researching.

The Hookman had been a real person, an escaped lunatic or, if Jo was telling the story, escaped serial killer who'd lost his hand to a combine harvester. That detail always got an "Ewwww."

Nicholas Day wasn't that kind of ghost. He was real. A ghost who'd showed himself to her, and talked to her, and left Jo with baggy blue crescents under her eyes from the dreams he sent swirling through her mind like luminescent fish on a current.

The trees around Ash House were all leafless, and she could see it clearly from the road. Spiny, black, skeletal porch rails like fingers trying to hold a bundle of sticks together.

In Jo's new bag was a candle, a Ouija board, and a couple of the pumpkin cookies she'd baked with Ani, before Ani went to New York to spend Halloween with Deirdre. They were going to dress as two of the seven Greek muses, and walk in the Greenwich Village parade. Unsurprisingly, Deirdre was Melpomene, the Muse of Tragedy.

Hallow's Eve was the day when the space between the living

and the dead was smallest. Ani's grandmother had told them that. The dead stood at arm's length, just out of reach, unless you had the tools. Ani's grandmother always had the best stories.

Jo considered, before she opened the red door, that maybe she didn't want to talk to Nicholas Day.

But she had to. Had to see him. Had to make sure it was real, and that she wasn't just crazy or totally sleep deprived in that unfun, *Fight Club* way.

She brushed aside the dead leaves on the foyer floor, and knelt. The tile was cold through her jeans, and she zipped her coat up to her chin.

One of Ani's lighters had found its way into her bag, and she snapped it against the candle. It wasn't anything special, just a scented pillar she'd lifted from her mother's room. The candle guttered in the wind, and then the door slammed shut, gusts howling around the outside of Ash House.

Jo put the Ouija board on the floor in front of her, and the little plastic shoe-shaped thing on the board.

This wouldn't work, she thought.

This *couldn't* work.

If it were this easy, people would be talking to ghosts every day.

Still, she breathed in, the cold musty air of the closed-up house, and spoke. "Nicholas Day."

The candle flickered and went out, smoke fleeing into the draft, twisting back on itself in the sliver of moon that came through the pink and green window.

"Shit!" Jo flicked the lighter once, twice, three times before she got a flame, and her shaking fingers knocked over the candle as she tried to light it.

It rolled away, and when it stopped it lay before a pair of black, pointed men's shoes.

"*Yes?*" Nicholas Day said to her. "*What is it?*"

In the moonlight, he was nearly whole. Hair darker than

black feathers swept back from a narrow forehead. Dark, straight brows topped dark, piercing eyes. A sharp chin tilted down at Jo, where she crouched, lighter cupped in her hands. She couldn't have moved, not for anything in the world.

Nicholas Day put his hands in his pockets. Watching him move wasn't like watching a person move. He flowed, from one point to the next, like ink suspended in water.

"*I saw you before. In the summertime, when the roses were blooming.*"

"Yeah," Jo said. Her voice was no bigger than a breath. Her throat felt curiously itchy, as if seeing the ghost had compressed everything in her body, sight and breath, down into a single point. All she could see was Nicholas Day, the young face above the serious black old-fashioned suit. "That was me."

"*Why did you come here?*" he asked.

Jo swallowed hard, over the lump in her throat. "It was a dare. Then, I wanted to see if I was crazy."

"*You don't seem mad to me,*" Nicholas said. He crouched, on the same level as her. "*What's your name?*"

"Jo," she whispered. "Jo Ryan."

"*Jo.*" Nicholas made a face, those stone white features rearranging themselves like living clay. "*Is that for Joanna or Josephine?*"

The lighter burned her hand, and Jo dropped it. The darkness wasn't absolute, just creeping around the edges of the room. Nicholas was the brightest thing in it. "It's Josephine," she said.

"*Then I shall call you Josephine,*" Nicholas said. He stretched out a hand, sleeve pulling back to show a white cuff precise as a paper fold, a cufflink of black stone bordered in silver, and twin scars on his wrist, running the long way.

"Can I . . . touch you?" Jo asked. This close, she could feel the cold coming off him. Not like the air outside, but a deep, glacial cold that breathed and drifted across her skin.

"*If you wish,*" Nicholas said. "*If you believe I'm real.*"

Jo lifted her fingers, stopped before they met the tips of his. "But you're not real. Are you?"

"*I'm real*," Nicholas said, and his flesh met hers. It felt like plunging her hand into ice, and velvet, and pins and needles. It didn't feel like skin.

"*See, real*," Nicholas told her. "*Simply dead.*"

5. November

At the top of Ash House, there sat a cupola with just enough room for one girl and one ghost to share the space, along with half a dozen doves and drifting falls of cobwebs.

Below was snow, patchy, showing the dark ground beneath near the river. Jo blew on her fingers through her gloves, tapping them together to keep warm.

"I died in these clothes," Nicholas said. "I wish I could change them. You're so bright. Girls nowadays wear so many colors."

Jo had come every day for a week. Slowly, Nicholas had showed her Ash House. She went through the red door, and she stayed until it was almost too dark to find her way back down the drive and across the bridge. She would have stayed longer if she could.

Nicholas was more solid now. She had a theory it had to do with her really *seeing* him, all the details of his face and his thin, elegant hands that drifted through the cobwebs hanging from the eaves, brothers in white, spidery and insubstantial.

The question came out before she had time to think about it. "How did you die?"

Nicholas smiled sadly. He didn't look like anyone who'd be alive now, in the twenty-first century. He looked like something from an old movie or a faded portrait come to life. His eyes were even more striking in daylight, obsidian holes that saw everything and let nothing escape. "My love drowned in the river. It was after the new year. The ice was melting, and the current was swollen."

He drew back the sleeve of his jacket, and then his shirt. "I used a razor. I couldn't bear life without her."

His voice, too, was no longer a powdery, echoey thing that bounced off the ceiling of the rooms below and scared the hell out of Jo when it whispered over her shoulder.

"That's awful," she said. Nicholas reached out, and a cold spot blossomed on her cheek.

"I've been alone for a long time. It wasn't the escape I hoped it would be."

"Are you like. . . stuck here?" Jo gestured around. "In Ash House? Or can you fly off anywhere you please?" It would be nice, she thought. No grades, no mother, no sleepless nights. No Ani asking her to read the latest text from Deirdre and analyze what it meant and no Drew sneering at her from across the parking lot where he sat on the hood of his stupid Nova.

"I'm bound to the place I died," Nicholas said. "I think most of us are. The dead. I can only leave if . . ." He coughed, and looked away, to where an eighteen-wheeler rumbled past on Route 7.

"If what?" Jo said.

"It's only a theory, you understand," Nicholas said. "But if I were to have a living . . . well, an escort. Someone who desired me to come home with them. I think I could go then. I could haunt a person and not a place."

Haunt. Such an ugly word. A tombstone word. Jo shifted. Her feet were numb, and the rest of her was starting to freeze. The sun was an orange halo below the horizon.

"I have to go," she said. "My mother has been getting on my ass about homework. And I have rehearsal tonight with the band. We're playing in Lee at the end of the month. A real all-ages show. It's a big deal." For Ani, anyway. Lately, her bass felt like a rock in her fist, and her fingers could barely pluck the strings.

"Josephine." Nicholas touched her again, closing his marble-ice fingers around her wrist. "Don't go."

"I should," Jo sighed. "I'll come by tomorrow, though. It's Friday. I can stay later." She could just lie to Ani, and her mother. She'd rather listen to Nicholas anyway. How many people had a person to tell them firsthand about life in 1902?

"Then let me give you a parting gift," Nicholas said. He closed the space between them and pressed his lips against Jo's. It was like kissing velvet and swallowing snowflakes caught on the tongue and it was her pulse throbbing in her ears and a million other things, until her lip pricked and she pulled away, feeling the crack and tasting the droplet of her own blood on her tongue. Her lips had gone chapped and numb.

Nicholas backed away. "I so wish it wasn't this way, Josephine. For the first time in a really long time."

"Me too," Jo whispered. The sun was gone now, the sky silver as the tinge on Nicholas's skin. She slipped through the trap door without saying anything else and started home. She crossed the bridge, listening to the water rush along under and over the cracks in the ice. River ice was rippled, in the shape of waves and current, and staring down in the twilight Jo could almost imagine a hundred faces staring back at her from under the ice. The burbling water turned to voices, the wind in the bare trees to screams.

She didn't know why, but she was gripping the rail and leaning over, staring back at those frozen, open-mouthed ice women in the river. Trying to make out the voice that whispered, *Black water, cold water, come on in.*

A murder of crows landed in the snow-heavy wild rosebushes on the bank, seemingly impervious to the thorns, and started cawing. Their cries blended with the wind and the water, and Jo felt her foot press against the rickety rungs of the bridge rail.

Black water, the voice soothed. *Cold water, down deep below the current.*

Jo wanted to stop, already felt like she was drowning as her lungs sucked in great gulps of frigid New England air. But she couldn't move, in any direction but forward. Over the rail. The weight of her body could crack the ice. She'd go below it. Down into the black water.

A tunnel of light swept over her, and the sound of a snarling eight-cylinder engine cut out all others. "Jo?" Drew got out of the car and jogged toward her. "Jo!"

His hand on the back of her jacket was big and solid, and he yanked her off the rail. "What the hell are you doing all the way out here?" Drew panted. Jo looked back at the ice and the river.

The light was gone. The faces were only ice floes.

On the bank, the crows took flight, disappearing into the last vestiges of the sun.

"Come on," Drew said, hand firmly on her back, guiding her. "I'm gonna drive you home."

His car was warm, so warm that Jo's hands and cheeks stung at the change. She huddled against the passenger door. She wanted to go back to Ash House, climb to the cupola, listen to Nicholas tell her stories until she could erase that horrible voice from her mind.

Crackly old rock blared at her instead, a cigarette-voiced singer and glassy, plinking guitar. *I put a spell on you. Because you're mine.*

"You're a weird chick," Drew said. "Don't take that the wrong way. I always figured your friend Ani for the freak, but you take it to another level."

"You wouldn't understand," Jo mumbled at him. Drew leaned over, in that businesslike way he did everything, and laid the back of his hand against her cheek. He smelled like cheap smokes and engine grease. Jo felt bile rise in her throat.

"Jesus," Drew said. "You're freezing." He looked at the road, depressed the Nova's lighter, lit a cigarette from a pack he'd shoved between the windshield and the dash, looked back at Jo. "Were you gonna off yourself?"

That pulled her out of her thoughts a little. "What?" Jo said.

"You were on the bridge," Drew said. "This time of year, you'd be out in about thirty seconds in that water. Just sink right down. Like a stone. You gonna kill yourself, Jo?"

"Don't be dramatic," Jo sighed. "I thought I saw something under the ice."

"Yeah?" Drew glanced at her, back at the tunnel before them that the Nova's headlights cut along the wilderness at the edges of the road. "Like what?"

Jo leaned her head against the window. She could almost fall asleep with the radio and the close smell of Drew's cigarette and the gentle vibration of the Nova beneath her. If it wasn't for the dreams waiting for her when she did.

"Nothing you need to know about," she said, and didn't speak again until Drew dumped her at the foot of her driveway and unceremoniously peeled out again into the night, taillights winking out like small candles in a vast, black sky.

6. December

On Christmas Eve, Jo had the worst dream yet. Ani was on break visiting Deirdre, Drew had moved his work on his idiotmobile into the garage for the winter, and Jo had spent most of break at Ash House. She'd hidden a stash of granola bars, candles, and a Mylar running blanket in the kitchen, high up in a cabinet where animals couldn't get at it.

Not that many animals came to Ash House. Nick said they didn't like being around the dead. Jo had taken to looking up tidbits on microfiche at the library, or searching on Wikipedia, for things for them to talk about. Phonographs rather than radios, the elaborate yards-long dresses the girls wore, how Ash House had the first electric light in Coffin Hollow—anywhere in western Massachusetts, really, except the county seat.

When Nick wasn't covering her hands, her neck, her arms, and every inch of skin she could stand to be exposed in slow, velvety kisses, that is.

He couldn't be *there* enough to manage a try at her clothes, but he touched her hair, and he whispered poetry. He'd taken her down to the music room, where an ancient piano stood. It clanked like a carnival when Jo played it, but for Nick it was always in tune. He played what he said was Brahms and Beethoven and other slow, sad pieces, his sure fingers flowing up and down the ivory.

Nick was well-read, as young men of his generation were supposed to be. He knew Yeats, Blake, all of the old magical, apocalyptic poetry that Jo could imagine scribbled on sheets of vellum, strewn across a room lit by gaslight.

Mel had insisted they do Christmas dinner, even though neither of them had enjoyed it since before Mel had gone to AA and moved them to Coffin Hollow, when Jo was in middle school. Jo figured after five years, she should get a pass from candied yams and Mel freaking out over how long to cook a turkey, but Mel put her foot down.

"If I didn't know you weren't that damn stupid, I'd think you were on drugs," she told Jo. "Now get your ass in that kitchen and pretend you like me for a couple of hours. It's Christmas, dammit."

Jo thought about detailing just how many times she'd smoked pot with Ani since the band started, and how many times at gigs older guys or club owners had offered her everything from LSD on fake postage stamps to what she could only assume was really good cocaine, from a little platinum vial that looked like a skull.

But she got her ass in the kitchen. She figured a woman Nick would like would at least know how to cook.

She should have been in a tryptophan coma, out for the count until Christmas morning, when Mel would have a mimosa with sparkling cider rather than champagne, and she'd have a hot chocolate and they'd exchange gifts before Mel went back to work. The production company she'd done the designs for had

hired her as a full-time animator for their next summer block-
buster, and she was hard at work making cute, chubby dogs and
gerbils sit up and talk.

But instead, she was back in the dream, and it was so real she
could taste the smoke, see the thorns embedded in her calves and
thighs, hear the wavering scream that rose from somewhere close
by.

A girl stood on the bank of the Acushket, and Jo knew it was
a dream because it was summer, river wild and blue as it flowed,
banks choked with brambles and wild roses. Her dress was white,
whiter than the foam that rode the top of the current, and it
swirled in the wind, along with hair the color of fire.

Jo knew she herself was bare, standing in the wilderness
while Ash House burned behind her. Thorny vines crawled up
her legs, her arms, twisted around until she felt like her skin was
burning too.

The girl looked back at Jo and said, "Drown."

Jo woke up in the silver light of before dawn. Christmas
morning, and there was no snow falling. Ice covered everything,
and made it gleam like the entire world was frozen for good.

She got her boots, jeans, a jacket, and slipped outside. She'd
lost weight, and everything flapped around her when the wind
caught her clothes. The dream was hard to shake. It was as if she
really were bleeding from the hundred wounds, slipping under
the surface until she'd be pale and dead as Nicholas.

He was in the music room when she reached Ash House,
playing the piano. He smiled when he saw her. "You came."

Jo could touch him now, and he smoothed her sleep-tossed
hair from her face before he put his lips on her forehead. She was
so cold already she didn't feel the change. "Did you have Christmas already?" he inquired. Jo shook her head.

"I had the most horrible dream. I was at the river and I . . ."
She felt the flush prickle her cheeks with warm blood, and she
looked at her boots. "I was naked and these thorns . . . there was a

girl." She didn't realize Nicholas was holding her hands until he pulled her close. "She wanted me to go into the river and drown."

"Shh," Nicholas said. "It will be all right."

"I woke up and I ..." Jo thought she must be crying, as a crystallized flake slid down her cheek. This close to Nicholas, vapor froze and fell out of the air. "I wanted you there," she whispered.

"I wish that were possible, love," Nicholas said. "I wish I could go home with you."

Jo pulled back, hands on his chest. His jacket really was velvet, and she could feel the satin lapel now, the crisp linen of his shirt. He was almost there ... almost real. "I've been thinking," she said. "Maybe if I gave you permission ... if we went together ..."

Nicholas's eyes narrowed. "You'd want that? You want to be with me?"

"I do," Jo said. She put her head back against his chest. "I want to be with you."

"Then come," Nicholas said. "The worst that can happen is I'll disappear, back to Ash House. I've been trapped here for so long anyway, it will hardly matter."

Jo took off her glove, so she could feel his hand. "I need you, Nick," she said.

He smiled down at her. "I know."

They walked from the music room and down the grand hall and into the entry. The red door stood open, and Jo tightened her hand on his. If they could just cross the threshold ... If Nick was with her, the dreams would stop. She knew they'd stop.

"You look so beautiful," Nick whispered. "You're so delicate, Josephine." He brushed his free hand down her cheek. "Promise me you won't ever forget," he said. "Even if I vanish into vapor. Promise me, Josephine, that you will never forget me."

Jo watched her breath turn to steam as the cold of outside crept across the threshold. "Never," she said.

She stepped across the threshold, and Nicholas held her hand. They walked down the drive, across the bridge with the river ice below cracking like gunshots, and down Route 7. They walked home, into Jo's house, past the Christmas tree and the gifts, past Mel's call of "Jo? Jo, where the hell have you been?," and into her room.

Nick pulled her to him, pressed her lips to his, and for the first time he began to feel warm against Jo's skin. She dropped her jacket, her gloves, the flannel shirt she'd pulled over her tank top. She tangled her hands in Nick's hair, felt water clinging there. Her fingers traced the scars on his arm. She could *feel* the scars for the first time.

His hands traveled under the hem of her shirt, raising gooseflesh on her abdomen. His lips caressed her ear. "Josephine . . ."

"Jo!" Mel shouted. "Ani is here! Get downstairs!"

Ani . . . That broke Jo away from Nick's ardent caress. "I have to . . ." She fought a giggle at his comical pout. "I have to go. That's my best friend."

"I'll come," Nick said. "She can't see me. Nor your mother."

"I'll just be a minute," Jo said, and slipped out, hoping she wasn't flushed or disheveled. She remembered to kick off her boots before Mel got even more pissed off about her tracking mud and ice everywhere.

"Ani?" she said, at the sight of her friend standing in the foyer. Her hair was bright candy-apple red, shorn in a pixie cut. "Wow. Hey."

"Hey," Ani said. "Deirdre and I broke up. I wish I could light that bitch's Dodge Dart on fire, but instead I'm here, and I'm going to drown my sorrows in Christmas cookies and pie. Yes, it's ten a.m. Don't you judge me."

"It's good to see you," Jo said carefully. She didn't have time to listen to the no-doubt epic tale of Deirdre and Ani, no more to be. Nick was waiting.

"So, join me?" Ani said. She looked Jo up and down as she descended the stairs, and her eyes widened. "Jesus, Jo. You look like shit."

"What is that supposed to mean?" Jo snapped. She was beautiful. She was thin and delicate, and she was the best she'd ever been.

"I mean, you look like you're living in a POW camp," Ani said. "Oh shit, are you anorexic? How did I not notice this?" She grabbed Jo's hands. "I know I've been a shit friend lately, dude. I was really messed up over Deirdre, and I'm really sorry. But this . . . " She looked down at their twined fingers. "Jo, you're freezing."

"It's cold," Jo said. Ani's eyes widened again, all pupil.

"No, it isn't," she said. "I'm sweating bullets, and this isn't even my warm coat." She pulled off her vintage army jacket and scarf, and pulled Jo's face into her hands. "This isn't some cheerleader eating disorder. What the hell is wrong with you?"

"Jo," Mel said, and there was a snap in her voice like a switch. "I need you to take this extra pie over to the Powells'. I'd do it, but I have an emergency conference call with L.A. in about two minutes."

Her mother was in sweats and slippers, hair pulled back in a messy bun. She held out the pie to Jo. "When you get back, maybe you'd like to tell me where you were."

"Not particularly," Jo said, snatching the dish and her coat. Ani followed her, running to keep up.

"*What* is going on? You and your mom are like the only functional parent/child relationship I know of."

"Ani, just leave me alone!" Jo shouted. "You're so incredibly nosy it drives me insane!"

Ani drew up, like someone had hit her in the face. "Oh, eat me," she said. "You haven't been normal since the summer. I don't know if it's drugs or some secret boyfriend or what, but you're being an utter dick. You used to be my best friend, Jo, and I *need* you, so piss off with your dysfunction. I'm going home."

She left. Jo wanted to run back upstairs, cradle herself in Nick's arms, have him kiss the top of her head and say everything

was fine, fine, just fine, love. Instead she stomped up the Powells'
steps and jabbed at the doorbell. After what seemed like an hour,
Drew opened the door.

"Well, happy freaking holidays," he said, looking her over.
"That a pie?"

Jo shoved it at him. "It's from my mom."

"Nice," he said. "My mom has been listening to Perry Como
all morning. I'm about seven seconds from getting my dad's shotgun out of the safe and killing either her CD player or myself.
Care to join me?"

"I have to get home..." Jo started, but then Mrs. Powell was at
the door, taking the pie, cooing thanks, ushering her in. She was
wearing a Patriots sweatshirt and perfect makeup, a sprig of fake
holly in her helmet-like hairdo. The diametric opposite of Mel.

"So, Jo, your mother tells me you're quite a student," she
trilled, cutting into the pie. She tapped a cigarette out of the pack
with her other hand—the same brand Drew smoked, Jo
noticed—and paused to light it, flicking ash into a tray shaped
like a sleeping cat. "Maybe you could tutor my son here sometime, so he doesn't end up in vo-tech and covered in grease for
the rest of his life."

"Jesus Christ, Mom," Drew complained. Mrs. Powell swat-
ted him on the head.

"None of that. Your mother tells me you're very interested in
history, Jo. What are you studying now?"

Jo wanted to turn around and run. She could feel Nick calling
to her, the feel and smell and chill of him tugging at her, wanted
more than anything to feel him against her whole body, pressing
into her like the thorns in her dream.

"Ash House," she lied. "The history of Ash House. It's an
independent study project."

"Ash House." Mrs. Powell shivered and tapped ash off her
cigarette. "That place gives me the creeps. I lost a girlfriend there
in high school, you know."

"Here we go," Drew muttered. "This is a really long story, FYI, Jo."

"Hush, boy," she said, waving a hand at him. "There were six of us, and we got to playing truth or dare, and she and I were to walk across the bridge on the rail."

"I have to . . ." Jo tried. Her stomach was boiling, the acid eating at her insides, even though she hadn't eaten anything since a few bites of Mel's turkey the night before.

"We fell in, probably because we were drunk off our kettles on cheap bourbon," said Mrs. Powell. "Judy . . . Judy Templeton, that was her name. . . she hit her head and drowned. At least that's what the coroner said."

Jo smelled a sweetish scent rolling off of Drew's mother, and realized for the first time that if she wasn't drunk, she was doing a good job getting there.

"When I was in the water," Mrs. Powell continued, "I felt as if something . . . something was almost, pulling me down. Not a root or a rock, but something strong, like . . . well, like a hand. And I heard this voice while I was under the water. Whispering about black water, drowning. Anyway." She shivered again. "Grim old place. 'Course, we were only there because of what happened to that girl back in '58."

Pins made of ice pricked Jo up and down her spine. "What girl?"

"You know." Mrs. Powell waved a hand. "Effie Walker. Kids called her Pepper, on account of she had this fabulous red hair . . ."

"*Mother*," Drew sighed. "Wrong holiday for this shit."

"Relax, dear, I won't embarrass you in front of your cute little friend much longer," Mrs. Powell said. Drew mimed shooting himself in the head behind his mother's back.

"What about her?" Jo said, voice coming out loud and high.

"She had a fella," Mrs. Powell said. "Real mysterious. Theory is he got her knocked up, dumped her, or something like that. Anyway, she walked into the Acushket down at Ash House with rocks in her pockets, even though nobody ever saw her with the boy and her sister and mother swore she wasn't in a family way. Just decided one day to up and end it. That bend in the river's had a lot of accidents. They need to put up a guardrail there."

It was as if the river had come to her, had filled up Jo's ears with rushing water. She couldn't hear what Drew was saying, nor the smarmy carols pouring from the Powells' stereo. Couldn't think of anything but the dream, the girl with flaming hair at the river's edge. Thorns in her skin. Ice filling up her lungs as she stared into the black current.

Her stomach twisted, and the next thing Jo knew, she was staring into the face of Effie Walker. Her hair had been carefully curled once, but now it hung lank against her cheeks, and her makeup ran down her face in rivulets. She wasn't the only one. Judy Templeton, cutoff shorts and platform sandals and a ripped-up Journey shirt, sodden and clinging to her petite body. Both of them, sunken-cheeked and hollow-eyed, starved white fingers reaching for something they could never catch hold of.

And Abigail Worth, who leaned down and whispered in Jo's ear in the language of black water.

You set him free. Do you even realize what you've done?

Jo couldn't speak, couldn't even breathe. She could feel again, and her joints ached. Her bones pushed against her skin, and she wasn't cold now but burning up, and if there had been anything in her stomach, she would have spewed up on Drew's scuffed leather army boots.

"I'll get her home," he said. "Don't worry about it."

Outside, staring up at her lit window, Jo clutched at Drew. "I can't go home."

He stopped in the driveway, didn't argue with her. "Where can you go?"

A shadow flicked in front of Jo's curtains, the size of a tall thin spirit. Watching her. "Ani's," she said, thinking of the only place she could. "Take me to Ani's."

Drew backed the Nova out of the garage while she shivered. She could feel Nick's eyes on her.

You set him free.

Not just his intended had died at Ash House, been consumed by the river. He'd lied. He'd lied to her, and she'd walked him across the threshold, set him free. To do what?

Jo jumped into the passenger side of the car, slamming and locking the door, as if it would do some good. She caught her face in the door mirror and almost vomited again. Her eyes were sunk into her skull, and her hair was dull and tangled. Her cheekbones stuck out like razor blades, and her lips were chapped. She could see every vein under the skin.

"You okay?" Drew asked. Jo managed a nod, curling her knees up to her chest.

"For now. Just drive."

Drew drove and got her to Ani's grandmother's place in record time. Ani's dad was an EMT, and he'd drawn the dubious honor of being the one to patch up family scrapes and drunken bar brawls on Christmas Day.

"Jo?" Ani dashed out of the house wearing nothing but a thermal shirt she'd cut the collar out of and jeans hastily stuffed into boots.

"You know what's wrong with her?" Drew said. "Because I sure as hell don't."

Jo knew she was going to fall over soon, but Ani was there, and Drew, and they held her up. "Jesus," Ani said. "I knew she was thin, but she's . . . Christ, she's *bones.*"

"Listen," Drew said. "I gotta get back, before my mom finds the rest of the holiday cheer and drunk-dials my dad up at the state pen. I'd just as soon not have that conversation."

His voice was a radio broadcast from some far-off country, fading in and out on waves of static and whispers from the ether.

"I . . . I'm sorry," Jo tried. "I'm sorry, Ani . . ."

"Shit, man," Ani said. "Don't worry about that now. Just

come inside with me, okay?"

Ani helped her inside, and while Ani's grandmother made her hot tea, she told Ani the truth. "I think he's . . . he's evil," Jo said quietly. "Abigail said . . . And now I let him out. . . ."

Ani's grandmother sat at the table with them. "Now you've got to fix it."

Jo looked up at her. Everything blurred and gently vibrated around the edges. She half wondered if she was still dreaming. "You don't think I'm crazy?"

"Seen stranger things in my life," Ani's grandmother said. "Hauntings and worse. What you're callin' evil is ghost sickness. When the dead get under your skin, bleeding your life so they can cling to theirs for another minute or two. Makes you sick, makes you hungry, makes you do anything to keep them."

"Makes you dream," Jo murmured. She'd ignored the warnings. Abigail and the others had tried to tell her, with the dreams. Tried to tell her that she'd pine and eventually die for Nicholas Day, by her own hand or his, just as they had.

"Dream, ayuh," Ani's grandmother agreed. She reached under her plaid shirt, unhooked a silver necklace, a simple flat disc stamped with a symbol made of straight lines. "This should keep him off you for now, but the question remains, missy—what are you gonna do about your ghost?"

Jo accepted the necklace. When it slipped against her skin, the spot the silver touched warmed, just a little. Her vision cleared, too, and all at once she was simply massively tired. "I don't know what I'll do," she said honestly.

"You better figure that out sooner rather than later," Ani's grandmother told her. "He already made three girls so sick and sad they joined him in that house forever. Don't you go down that path."

"No," Jo said, pressing the silver down into her skin with her palm. "I won't." She thought of Nick's touch, of his taste, and even though she knew he was only ashes in her mouth, she still craved him. "I'll try," Jo amended.

Ani took her up to the guestroom, and she really slept for the first time in months. She woke at the creak of the rocking chair in the corner of her attic room, saw the black-shod foot pushing back and forth across worn board, *scritch-scritch. Creak-creak.*

"You said you'd never leave," Nicholas told her. Jo gasped, grabbing at the necklace. Nick flickered, like he was a faulty TV channel.

"What do you think you're doing with that, Josephine?"

Jo found her voice, though it was small as the puff of air her breath made in the suddenly frozen air. "Stopping you."

"Abigail thought she could stop me," Nick said. "She loved me, but her head was mixed up. She ran from me. She cut her legs on the wild roses on the riverbank. I held her, until she stopped moving. Her hair was so beautiful under the water."

"They hung you," Jo said. "In your own front yard. You didn't kill yourself."

Nick nodded, steepling his fingers, and then he was up, pressing her into the mattress, hands on her bare arms. "They all loved me, Josephine, but I never loved any of them as much as I love you." Lips against her forehead, searing with the black mark of frostbite. "And I'm never letting you go," Nick whispered against her ear. "I'm going to haunt you until the day you die, Josephine Ryan. Be it sooner, or later. Die soon enough, and you can join me on this cold dark road. We can run on forever, like the river."

He vanished like smoke in a howling wind, and Jo was left shivering, until she kicked back the blankets and fumbled for her shoes. She went to wake up Ani. Nicholas wouldn't stop. Wouldn't stop when he'd killed Abigail, wouldn't stop when he'd tormented Effie into drowning or pulled Judy down to be beside him forever.

Jo knew what she had to do.

The lights were out when Ani pulled into Jo's dead-end

street, both her mother's and the Powells'. Ani touched her wrist. "You sure you're okay?"

"Yeah," Jo murmured. Ani couldn't be a part of what had to happen next. Jo didn't want her to become one of the staring girls, the girls by the river.

She waved until Ani pulled away, but instead of going inside, she went into the garage and filled up her bag until it was almost too heavy to shoulder. Snow started, light crystalline flakes falling from the sky, turning the road silver as she walked.

By the time Jo reached the junction of Route 7, a full-blown blizzard swirled around her, wind turning the road into a tunnel of ice and snow.

Ash House rose out of the snow, crouched above the river like a sleeping thing, waiting for spring to wake up and be hungry again.

Ani's grandmother had told them that the dead were bound to the place or thing they'd held most dear in life. Her. And Ash House. The scene of all Nicholas's sins.

Jo pushed open the red door. She listened to the wind howl around the eaves, as if it would like to tear off the roof. She stripped off her gloves and closed her hand around the necklace. It wasn't cold, but warm from her skin just under her coat.

She jerked, and the chain broke. It was seconds, mere heartbeats, until Nicholas appeared before her.

"I told you," he said. "I'm yours now, Josephine. I'll follow you no matter where you go. No matter where you try to hide." His hand trailed over her cheek, left a cold teardrop. "I'll find you. I'm glad you know that now."

"I do know," Jo said. "But look where we are." She kicked over the gas can Mel kept in the garage for emergencies—for storms, like this one. It spilled across the floor, melting the snow in its path, soaking through the rotten wood and tile.

Nicholas smiled at her. Once so full of promise, now it was like a knife. "It doesn't matter where we are, Jo. Just that we're together."

"It does, though," Jo said. "You're home, Nicholas. On the same soil you died." She pulled out Drew's lighter, which had found its way into her pocket when he left her at Ani's. The wheel sparked on the first try. "They hanged you right out there," Jo said. "On the oak tree in the yard. After you killed her. You said it yourself—you held her under and drowned her. The girl you *loved.*"

"Doesn't matter," Nicholas said. "Everything I did was for love. It can be forgiven." He touched her again, her hair, her cheek, her hand. "You can't let me go, Josephine. You and I are together now. You can't be free, even if you burn yourself up."

"I'm not the one burning," Jo said. She cocked her arm and tossed the lighter. She wasn't ready for the noise as the gasoline ignited—all of the air sucked out of her lungs, and her ears popped as a column of orange flame erupted in the center of the floor. "I'm burning this. This house!" she shouted. "You know what you love, Nicholas? Yourself! And this goddamn house!"

Nicholas grabbed her by the wrists. "You'll never leave me. You know it."

Jo jerked away from him. She made it to the porch when he grabbed her again, by the hair, whipping her off her feet. They rolled over and over, down into the snow and the brambles beneath.

Nicholas was on her, ripping away her scarf and her coat, letting in the cold. Behind them, windows exploded in Ash House as the wind fed the fire.

Jo rolled away from his searching, claw like hands and stumbled toward the bridge. She had to get to the bridge. Cross the running stream, like in Ani's grandmother's stories. If she could just get over the bridge, she'd be all right. At least, she repeated that to herself as she stumbled through the blizzard, through the bracken, guided only by the roar of the fire and the heat on her back.

She didn't get to the river. He found her again, through the swirling snow and screaming wind, in the half-daylight the blaze inside Ash House cast across the river.

Jo fell, and felt her ankle twist the wrong way. Her exposed skin was blue-white in the predawn, ice frosting it. Nicholas put his hands on her neck. "She ran from me too, Josephine. But she loved me, even as she denied me. And so do you. You'll die for me. In the end, they all do."

Jo met his eyes. He was solid now, solid as person. But he was cold. And his eyes were what they had always been—dead man's eyes, staring a hole in her soul.

"I don't . . ." Jo managed under his grasp. Nicholas's face slackened.

"What?"

Jo reached out for an icy, frozen tangle of thorns near her face, as Nicholas pressed her into the wild rose bushes, covered over with snow and frost. She pricked her thumb, tangled the vines around her fingers, watched the blood run down her wrist. Clawed at Nicholas with her free hand. Saw the marks on his arm for what they were, not razor cuts but nail marks, the last grasp of a desperate, drowning girl who hadn't seen him, really seen, until it was far too late.

She felt her blood run down, into the earth, soaking through the roots and stones and into the riverbed, born on the water, far far away from here, as the last of her air leaked out.

The girls came when Jo knew she was dying. Black stars sparkled at the edges of her vision. Nicholas filled up the rest. Her chest was heavy, a stone where her lungs should be. And the cold. The cold was inside her. Her bones were ice. Her blood was snowflakes.

The first, redheaded Effie, put a hand on Nicholas's shoulder. "No more," she said. Then Judy Templeton, and lastly, his own love, Abigail. She was still dripping wet, still bore the marks of Nicholas's hands on her neck.

"You held me," she said. "So tenderly. Under the black water. Until it filled me up. Until I became the water." She turned his face to her, so their noses were nearly touching. "For that, I thank you. I live in the river, Nicholas. You ended me, but I live in the river, and it's not a bad life."

"I live in the fire," Effie said. "I live in every sad soul who passes by on the bridge. I burn for every one of them."

"I live in the rocks," said Judy. "I'm the weight on your soul, Nicholas Day. The weight of everyone you took before their time."

They looked down at Jo. "You're not one of us," said Abigail. "You are not the ice. You are not the wind or the cold." Through her translucent form, Ash House gave a roar, a last death rattle as the roof caved in.

"Go," Effie said. "Go back to the world. You brought him home."

"Yes," echoed Abigail. "And home is where his heart shall stay."

"*No*," Nicholas screamed, as the three girls bore him up and away. "No, she took me away! I won't go back!"

He turned his eyes on Jo. "Please, Josephine. Nobody can love you like me."

Jo rubbed her bloody hand across her freed throat. "My name," she rasped, a voice like ashes, not her own, "is not Josephine."

Nicholas and the three moved backward, on a current of their own making, until they stood in the red door, framed by the fire. Things leaped and danced in the flames, screamed and wailed, until the wind gave one last push and the house collapsed on itself, eating its own innards in a jet of flame that shot into the silvering sky.

Jo stood, and watched, blood dropping into the snow, and she watched the spot where Nicholas had last stood. She watched until the Coffin Hollow volunteer fire department came crawling down Route 7 in the blizzard, and watched until an EMT—Ani's father, as it turned out—brought her to the ambulance. She watched, but she never saw Nicholas Day or any of the girls again.

7. Epilogue—January

Jo never said a word, and no one ever asked her beyond a cursory question how Ash House had burned. Ani came and sat with her in the ER and asked if Jo could forgive her for telling her father her best friend was fixing to do something stupid.

Ani's grandmother patted her bandaged hand when she came by to return the necklace. "You hold on to that, child. You're going to need it more than I ever did."

Jo asked why, and Ani's grandmother sighed, and lit one of her rancid cigarettes. "You think just everyone goes around attracting the dead, honey? Ain't so. You've got an eye that sees into that shadow place, and unless you want to be deviled all your days—you keep that thing on."

They went back to school, where nobody questioned that Jo had cut her hand on a broken glass in her own home.

Drew Powell came up to her their second week back. "You have my lighter," he said.

"Not anymore," Jo said. "Trust me, it went to a good cause."

He reached out and lifted the necklace from her clavicle with his finger. Jo realized this was the first time she and Drew had ever touched. "Interesting," he said. Jo shrugged.

"It's broken. The clasp." She twisted the chain to show where she'd affixed the two ends with a paper clip.

"I could fix it for you," Drew said. "And maybe you can tell me why my mom had a nervous breakdown the day after Christmas, and told me that her friend from high school forgave her for not getting her out of the river."

"I couldn't tell you," Jo said. She wanted to pull away, but Drew's eyes caught her, while he tilted his head.

"Can't, or won't?"

"Drew," she said. "Some things are just better off staying buried."

He considered for a second. "You want a ride home?"

Jo smiled. "Yeah. I'd like that."

"Come on, then," Drew said. He smiled back at her. Jo realized this was the first time she'd seen Drew Powell smile. His smile was crooked and half-mast, like a bend in a country road. Nothing like a knife.

January thaw turned the roads to mud while Drew took the turns too fast, throwing up a fantail of earth and ice. Birds chittered from the bare trees, and on Route 7, the Acushket burbled under the ice, whispering in the language of black water. Jo reached over, turned up the radio, and drowned them out.

Wash away my troubles, wash away my pain, with the rain in Shambala. . . .

Drew didn't slow down when they passed the bridge and the burned relic of Ash House, and Jo was glad. She nodded when Drew offered her a cigarette, and rolled down the window so she could put her hand out and feel the wind.

The trees would get green and the river ice would melt, and she and Ani would apply to all the same colleges and probably end up going to different ones. But not too far away. Spring would come. She'd spend time getting to know Drew Powell, whose eyes were gray and clear and hid nothing, and whose hands felt like nothing but warmth and calluses.

And soon, all along the banks of the river that had once hidden Nicholas Day's terrible secret, the wild roses would bloom.

Hare Moon

BY CARRIE RYAN

It's because the paths are forbidden that Tabitha always finds her way to them. She's tired of being trapped behind the village fences, tired of being told what to do all the time. She wasn't made for a life like this: sedate, rule-following. Boring.

The first time she opens the gate it's on a dare to herself. To see if she's just a dreamer or if she's someone who can follow through on her promises. She wants to know that she's more than just desires—she's action.

She'd like to believe she isn't terrified. That she doesn't approach the gate and hesitate. Look through the rusty metal links at the brambles and brush obscuring the path and tremble.

That the dead along the fence don't frighten her, their cracked and broken fingers reaching, always reaching and the moans calling for her.

It's the sound of them that gets to her, the way they invade every part of her life. She hears them in her sleep, in her day-dreams, during chores and services. She hears them when she's praying to God.

And on the path there's no escaping the Unconsecrated. They shuffle along the fences on either side of her, pushing and pulling and grating and needing. She's never known need like that in her life. Doesn't understand it.

But all the same she wants it.

Tabitha knows there are rules and rules are meant to be fol-lowed. Every morning she attends services and every evening she recites her prayers. She gives deference to her parents, cares for her younger siblings and completes chores without complaint. Well, without too much complaint.

During the winter months she does as she's asked and smiles and demurs to the eligible young men her age, waiting for a husband to choose her.

They never do.

She's okay with this because it isn't the young men who call to her at night. It's the Forest of Hands and Teeth. It's the whisper of the trees that there's a bigger life outside the fences. That there's still a world that's bigger and braver than any she could ever comprehend and all she has to do is find the strength to go after it.

At night she writhes in her bed listening to it. Wanting it. Needing it until it causes her cheeks to burn red and tears to run from her eyes. And in the morning she slows her steps as she passes by the gate in the middle of an errand. She promises herself that tomorrow she will sneak through it. Tomorrow the world will be hers.

...

Tomorrow she does pass through the gate. Just enough to know that no siren will wail at her departure. That no one will notice her absence.

...

In her dreams and when she's awake, again and again she crosses through the gate. She's timed the Guardian patrol just right so that she knows when to slip away, when to sprint down the path with a lightness of freedom unlike she's ever known. It consumes her.

Sometimes she tells herself she won't ever come home. Yet she always does. Because there are rules and she's a good girl. But not so "good" that her skin doesn't start to feel tight and itch as if her body's shrinking and the only thing that will release the compression of it is to escape to the path.

So she does, pushing farther and farther into the Forest. She learns to ignore the Unconsecrated who follow her every step, learns to listen instead to the way the wind tickles its way through leaves overhead and to the chirp and whir of birds.

The sun feels brighter and the shade cooler in the Forest and she starts to wonder why it's off limits. She likes that she doesn't have to think what's next when she's on the path: it's just one step and then another and the fences keep her moving straight ahead.

One day, she walks far enough to find a second gate, and she stands for a long time staring at it, wondering if she should go through or if it's a sign that she's wandered too far.

She sets her hand on the metal latch, feeling a pattern of rusty prickles against her fingers. She still hasn't decided what to do when a voice calls out to her. "You're here," it says.

Startled, she runs her gaze through the Forest and down the path and finds a pair of eyes looking back at her. A young man approaches the gate from the other side.

Not expecting anyone else to be on the path, especially a stranger, it takes a moment for her to find her voice. "I am," she responds because to show her confusion and shock would make her appear weak. Tabitha never likes to appear weak. "Are you expecting me?" she asks because she's suddenly not sure whether she's awake or asleep.

She notices that the young man has his sleeves rolled up and his forearms are exposed. She's seen forearms before, of course, but there's something different about his. Something so informal and intimate about the sloppiness of the sleeves rolled up to his elbows, as if she could push a finger underneath the fabric and tempt the sensitive skin there.

The sun glows off the blond hair covering his arms. His fingers look long and tan, curled slightly as he stops on the other side of the gate. "Not especially, but I'm glad you're here," he says. She looks up from his arms to his face.

He's smiling at her, eyes slightly crinkled because the sun is at her back. "I think," she tilts her head and ponders for a moment because she doesn't like to be rash with her words. "I think I am too." She grins at him.

She learns that his name it Patrick and that he comes from another village in the Forest.

"I didn't know there were other villages in the Forest," she admits, and he explains the system of the paths and gates, the tangle of their order.

She tries not to let him see what this knowledge does to her, how it makes her blood pump furiously through her body. Growing up, she'd been told they were all that was left. Her village the only survivors of the Return.

She was told it was her sole and sacred duty to continue the path of humanity.

"Quite a few of the villages are gone," Patrick explains. "But there are enough left that we'll survive."

Neither of them opens the gate between them and, as she walks home in the late afternoon, Tabitha's head explodes with the newly learned reality of her world. It's as if she's spent her life kneeling on the ground, staring at a rock, and suddenly she's standing, staring at a field full of stones.

She wonders what it would be like to fly. To see the entire world at once. She runs through the Forest, arms out, with fingers almost—but not quite—brushing the metal links of the old fences. She realizes that the world might be hers to know after all.

...

They agree to meet at the same gate on the second afternoon after the full moon each month. Tabitha spends the between days lost in dreams. Her mother starts to scold her for burning dinner. Her younger brother skins his knee one day when she's not paying attention. She barely remembers the words to the prayers she's asked to recite at services.

But she's alive. And she wants to grab everyone around her

and scream that there's a world that's more important than any of these daily toils. Yet she doesn't say a word because she fears them locking the gates. Locking her from the path, and from Patrick.

•••

The first two times they meet again, neither opens the gate. They stay on their respective sides and tell stories. She rolls onto her back on the path and stares up through the canopy of leaves and watches how the sun caresses each one as Patrick tells her about his dreams.

Sometimes she closes her eyes and wonders what it would be like to walk through the gate and run away with him. And sometimes she imagines bringing him home with her and claiming him as hers.

At the end of their third meeting, he laces his fingers through the links of the gate and she laces her fingers through his and they sit that way for an afternoon, feeling each others' pulse fighting.

He brings her a gift at their next meeting: a worn book with pages as soft as feathers. She's astonished at how small it is, how compact. The only books she's ever seen are copies of the Scripture in her village, thick heavy tomes with paper like onionskin.

"It's my sister's favorite," he tells her. "I thought you might like it too."

She reads the little book three times before their next meeting, trying to understand what it means. It's about a house and a woman and her husband who, she discovers, may have drowned his first wife. It's lush and dangerous and makes her body pound and pulse.

"Why would a man be so cruel to his wives?" she asks Patrick after the next full moon.

He looks at her with his head tilted. "It's just a story," he says. "It's just made-up. It's fiction."

She nods but she's frowning because she still doesn't understand what that means and he pulls her into his arms to ease her worries.

In the winter she tells him about Brethlaw, the celebration of life and marriage at her village. He opens the gate and she walks through it, and now they tangle together under blankets surrounded by snow that floats through the air and melts against their skin.

He traces his finger down the spine of her back, weaving between her bones. "Would you leave your world for me?" he asks.

"I might," she tells him. She wonders how the world ever fell apart with this much love in it.

•••

Her parents are unhappy with her. She's not focusing, they tell her. They remind her that if she doesn't find a husband soon she may be left with no option but to join the Sisterhood like her friends Ruth and Ami. And where this might have been an effective threat to her in the past, she just swallows back smiles because she knows there is no man or God for her other than Patrick.

•••

Patrick's not at their meeting spot. It's the first time he's been missing, and Tabitha wraps her arms around her body and paces little circles in the freezing rain. She walks through the gate and sprints down the path wondering if he's hurt or lost, but there's no sign of him.

She goes home confused and a little empty. Where before she felt too big for her skin when she walked around her village, now she feels too small. Her body doesn't work the way it should—she's clumsy, tripping when she walks. Nothing is right anymore.

The next month she checks the moon, making sure she knows

exactly when it's at its fullest. She's so anxious to go to Patrick two days later that she's not as careful as she should be. One of the Guardians sees her placing her hand on the gate to the path.

He takes her to the Cathedral, and the Sisters whisper in a tight little knot while her parents stand to the side white faced and silent. No one will marry her now, they know. She's a dreamer, and dreamers need to be broken to the will of the Sisterhood.

Her parents don't object when the Sisters proclaim Tabitha as one of theirs. She puts on the black tunic and combs her hair from her face into a severe bun. She stands with the other two newest Sisters, Ruth and Ami, and listens to the enumeration of her duties. She bows her head and recites the prayers but that is not where her mind and heart are. They're on the path, waiting.

•••

She spends the next month planning her escape. Soon, she can't sleep anymore, and she's memorized every detail of her room. She's tired of the stone walls, stone floor, tiny window looking past the graveyard at the dead roaming the fences. She thinks she might understand a little now why they moan.

She thinks she might understand the pain of such intense desire. It brings tears to her eyes that never seem to go away.

She starts to wander through the Cathedral in the darkness of the too early morning hours. She counts the number of windows, she counts the number of benches and cushions and even stones in the floor. Anything to stop thinking about pregnant moons and Patrick and the feel of him trailing a hot finger down her spine.

She's tracing her finger along a crooked crack in the wall, remembering the feel of his skin against hers, when the crack dips behind a curtain and she follows it. There's a door there, and she doesn't hesitate before pushing it open and revealing a long hallway. She wanders down it to another door, this one thick and banded with metal.

It's dark and she has no candle and it's late, and Tabitha spends a long while staring at that door before she turns around and goes back to bed. The moans of the Unconsecrated whisper her into the deepest sleep she's felt for ages.

The next night she doesn't even change into her sleeping gown, but instead waits in her black tunic for the Cathedral to fall silent. She takes the candle and flint from beside her bed and goes straight to the curtain in the sanctuary, her heart pounding so hard that her fingers shake from the force.

She sneaks down the hallway, her footsteps disturbing a thin layer of dust, and this time she doesn't pause before going through the metal-banded door. It leads her down a set of stairs, the air growing dank and thick enough that the light from her candle barely penetrates it.

She's in a basement, and it smells like dirt, tastes like the wet rot of fall. Rows of wooden racks march through the large room, some cradling old grimy bottles but most just barely withstanding entropy. There are no other doors and no windows, no escape from the heady mustiness.

Along one wall hangs a curtain, and Tabitha already knows this trick. She pulls it aside and finds another door, but this one is locked. She tries every way she knows how, but the door won't open, and eventually she gives up and goes back to bed, but this time she cannot sleep.

Soon, to Tabitha, the locked door behind the curtain in the basement becomes like the gate blocking the path. She knows she must go through it. And as with the gate, she makes her plan carefully.

She offers to take on the chores assigned to Ruth and Ami, cleaning rooms and scrubbing walls and floors, using them as an excuse to rifle through drawers and cabinets. She finds dozens of keys and she tries them all, but none of them work.

This time when the moon is full she thinks about abandoning Patrick in the Forest. It's been months since she's seen him and she's angry and hurt and broken. Sometimes she'll pull his book out from under a loose stone in the wall, and she'll flip through the pages, wondering if all men are so cruel; if love is like a spring blossom that builds and bursts in a bright hot color and then wilts and dies, never to return.

Two days later, she spends the afternoon torn. She finds herself walking toward the gate and then turning back. She doesn't know what's right. She doesn't want to give up the hope of him, but she's not sure she's ready to deal with the pain of him either.

It frustrates her that he occupies so much of her mind. Even when she tries to think of other things during the day, he invades her dreams at night, and she wakes up sweaty and alone. The second night after the fullest moon is no exception. She crawls from her bed and carries her candle to the gate and walks the path through the Forest to their meeting spot.

The tiny flame of the candle barely penetrates past the fences bordering the path, and it throws cruel shadows across the Unconsecrated who follow her. Their eyes seem more hollow, their cheeks sharper, their teeth and tongues black maws.

Moans surround her, peel away her flesh until she feels bare and raw. The Unconsecrated bang against the fence, claw for her so hard their fingers snap and bones protrude gleaming and sharp. She can't sprint because the candle will go out, and so she's forced to walk slowly, unable to outrun the death on either side of her.

The gate is as it always is: impassive and sturdy. As she expected, the path on the other side is empty. She stands in the darkness surrounded by the agony of existence and tries to decide what to do next. Go back? Go forward? Curl up on the path and let time take its toll?

Her shoulders crumble, her fingers going limp and dropping the candle. Just before the flame sputters out against the damp earth, she catches the reflection of something lying on the ground.

The moon is fat but waning, and she doesn't bother relighting the candle before opening the gate. In the middle of the path is a small basket covered by a scrap of material.

She pulls it back to find a spray of wilted flowers, their petals black in the darkness. Nestled amid the limp leaves rests a scrap of paper, and it takes her three strikes of the flint until her candle is bright enough to read the words.

"My Tabby," she whispers aloud to the dead around her. "My family has grown sick, and my father is on the verge of death. I couldn't bear to leave my mother and sister so soon. Forgive my absences. Please forgive me. I have missed you like the shore misses the touch of waves. I promise that nothing will keep me from you after the hare moon. Hopefully you remain mine as I remain yours. Always, my love, Patrick."

She presses the words to her lips, hoping for a taste of his skin on the paper. She holds her hand against her chest, wanting to rip out her heart and leave it in this basket among the wilted flowers for him. Because she now understands that it belongs to him and always will.

...

Tabitha keeps the note on her person at all times, tucked between the bindings for her breasts and her heart. She doesn't care that the sweat of the day blurs his words, she needs them against her. She needs to remember the feel of him.

She continues her search for the key in a fever and daze. Her skin often feels flushed, and she finds herself in the middle of mundane tasks staring off into space. She's late for services more than once and as punishment is tasked with the duty of the Midnight Office and Matins for which she spends several hours alone in the darkest time of night on her knees in the sanctuary.

Her eyes begin to look a bit hollow, the bones in her cheeks a little sharper, and her jaw more defined. There are confusing moments when she thinks she almost feels the comforting heat of God when she's in her deepest prayers and she stumbles to her bed with thoughts muddled and hazy.

She's so lost in the conundrum of her thoughts one afternoon that she doesn't realize at first what it means when she comes across a large key while dusting the shelves and stacking papers on the desk of the oldest Sister's chambers.

She holds it in her hands, feeling its weight, running her fingers along the blunt lines of its teeth. Something warms in her chest, loosens along the small of her back. She slips the key into the binding around her breasts, with Patrick's letter, and spends the rest of the day itching for the time to pray.

•••

She's standing in the middle of the Cathedral, staring at the altar and trying to decide if she believes in prayer when a little girl comes and stands next to her. The girl's name is Anne, and Tabitha recognizes her as a friend of her little brother's.

Anne stands next to Tabitha quietly for a moment, and then she shyly looks up at her. "Are you praying?" she asks.

Tabitha thinks about this for a moment and answers, "I don't know."

The girl looks puzzled. "Why don't you know?"

"Because I don't know what to believe in right now," she answers.

The little girl takes a short breath and then shoves her slightly damp hand into Tabitha's, squeezing her fingers. "I know what to believe," she says. "My mother told me and her mother told her."

"What's that?" Tabitha asks.

The little girl scrunches her face. "You won't get me in trouble for saying?"

Tabitha shakes her head.

The little girl motions for Tabitha to bend down, and she obliges, getting on her knees so that she's face-to-face with the child. The girl leans forward, her dark hair falling against Tabitha's cheeks. "My mother says there's a world outside the fences. She told me about the ocean, and when I get older, I'm going to find it. If you want, you can go with me."

The little girl pulls back, her eyes shining and her little body almost trembling with energy. Tabitha thinks about telling her that it's true, that there's something greater beyond their gate. That she's touched the very edge of it. But when she opens her mouth, nothing comes out.

...

Tabitha starts the Midnight Office early and races through the words, baldly reciting them hot and fast without thought to their meaning or significance. After the last Amen, she slips from the pews past the altar and toward the secret door.

She's just pulling back the curtain when she hears the whisper of feet over stones. "I thought we would keep you company tonight," Ruth says, carrying a candle into the sanctuary, a yawning Ami at her heels. They pause when they see Tabitha and the hidden door.

Tabitha's heart beats fast and wild. There's a certain thrill, she realizes, in getting caught. "I finished early," she says.

Her two friends drift closer. "What's that?" Ruth asks.

Ami tugs on her sleeve. "It's not our place to know if they haven't told us," she says. The whites of her eyes almost glow in the darkness.

"Where does it go?" Ruth asks Tabitha.

Tabitha grasps the key tight in her hand, dull teeth digging against her palm. "I don't know," she says because in truth she doesn't know what's past the door in the basement.

"Ruth?" Ami's whine is tinged with anxiety. She glances over her shoulder as if expecting someone to come upon them at any moment.

"You're going to explore it?" Ruth asks. Tabitha recognizes the hint of thrill in her voice. Knows that Ruth is like her—that she craves the knowing.

Tabitha raises her chin. "I am."

"Ruth," Ami is now close to panic, scrabbling at her friend's arm. Ruth looks between them, and Tabitha knows the moment she makes up her mind because her shoulders sag a little. She places a hand over Ami's.

"We'll pray for you," Ruth says. Ami sags with relief. "And will make sure no one asks about your absence."

Tabitha nods. "Thank you," she says, thankful to be left alone but more grateful to know her friends will be looking out for her.

Ruth tugs Ami toward the rail, and together they kneel. Tabitha slips through the door and, before the curtain falls back into place, she sees Ami's head bowed low and Ruth's glittering eyes following Tabitha's movements with a lusty resignation.

•••

The basement is the same as before: dark, damp, fecund. She slides back the curtain and pulls out the key. The lock on the door doesn't even protest or groan, just slips away revealing a long low tunnel.

There's a thrill in her chest like the first time she opened the secret gate between her and Patrick. On a small table just past the door, she finds a stash of old candles, but she ignores them, cupping her hand around the tiny flame she brought with her and pushing into the darkness.

She can tell she's underground, the walls slick with moss and sweat, the floor a hard-packed dirt. Her steps are slow and hesitant not because she's afraid, which she is a little, but because it is rare for there to be something new in her life.

Rare for her to have a feeling she's never experienced or a thought she's never shared. She assumed she knew this village and this life and everything about it, and now she's found something new, and she wants to make it last, not gobble it up like the tart treats of the Harvest Celebration.

Down the low tunnels she finds a series of doors, most of

them with locks that her key won't budge. But one door opens easily after she twists away metal bars that hold it closed into the stone wall. Inside, the glow of her candle illuminates a low bed piled with mildewed blankets and a rotted mat on the floor.

Against the far wall sits a rickety table with a thick book resting on top. She knows even in the dimness that the book is a copy of the Scripture, and she's about to return to the hallway and her explorations when something about it calls to her.

She wonders if this is what it was like for the prophets she's learned so much about, this pull and tug toward some offering of a truth. She places a hand on the book, thick dust sliding smooth under her fingers.

With a reverence and deference she's never before felt, she opens the cover. The printed text is as she expects, as she's seen before. But what she doesn't expect is the cramped handwriting covering the margins. She sets down her candle and leans closer to the page, reading the first line: *In the beginning, we did not know the extent of it.*

She immediately recognizes the writing for what it is: a history of the village beginning at the Return. She carries the book to the bed, arranges the blankets around her, and reads. When her candle burns out, she gets another from the table by the door.

Time ceases to exist for Tabitha in that room. All that matters is the words, the memories. The horrifying facts of her world. Memories and stories she'd never even known about the brutality of the pre-Return existence. The sacrifices those who'd come before her had made to keep her village safe.

It feels as though the words slide from the page and eat their way under her skin, infecting her with a fever that causes her head to pound and her blood to burn.

She begins to understand the precariousness of their existence. The delicate balance of what knowledge to pass down to the general populace of the village and what to keep locked up safe in the Sisterhood.

And she learns the reason the paths are forbidden. She reads about the bandits who attacked the village in the early years. About the men who would leave and never return, who would alert the outside world to the village's existence, who would incite a fresh wave of refugees that overwhelmed the village's resources.

There were times the infected from other villages would try to invade. There was a year when her village almost perished because a small child had wandered from the Forest and turned Unconsecrated in the middle of the night, sparking infection that raged.

In a desperate act, those who'd come before her closed off the paths. Sent word that their village was infected and broken, would never survive. They started to tell the next generation that they were all that was left. They killed any who dared to tip this delicate balance.

They did it out of love. Out of loyalty. Out of a desire to continue the existence of humanity in the service of God. They did it with a passion of conviction.

This, Tabitha realizes, is what she inherited. This is what she jeopardizes every time she steps into the Forest.

As she closes the book, Sister Tabitha understands that she has to decide what she will stand for: her own selfish desire for love or devotion to her village and the people within it.

...

Tabitha has just stepped back into the sanctuary, weak and trembling, her face pale, when the oldest Sister comes upon her. "You're late for the Midnight Office," she scolds. "Your face is streaked with dirt and hair uncombed. This is no way to come before God."

In the past Tabitha would have seethed inside for being treated like a child, but tonight she merely nods and walks stiffly to her room. She'd been in the tunnel chamber almost an entire day, and her eyes burn dry and painful.

She washes her face and plaits her hair and returns to the

sanctuary half-asleep for the midnight prayers. It's hard not to weave on her knees, not to rest her head against the altar railing and slip from the world.

Ruth and Ami join her. Ami keeps her head bowed, her fingers laced so tight that her knuckles blaze white, but Ruth looks Tabitha straight in the eye. "We covered for you," she says.

Tabitha nods. "Thank you."

"What did you find?" Ruth asks. Ami closes her eyes tight, mumbling prayers as if to drown out everything around her.

Tabitha thinks of the Scripture with the journal written in the margins. She thinks of the burden of the knowledge and wonders what it would be like to share it. To seek counsel of someone else.

She thinks of telling Patrick. Of lying in the spring grass with his fingers tangled in her hair.

"A basement," Tabitha says truthfully. "Old dusty bottles and broken shelves." She turns her attention to the altar and the cross though she still feels Ruth's heavy gaze.

"That's it?" Ruth sounds disappointed, deflated.

Tabitha nods and joins in Ami's mumbling prayers, reciting the words without thinking or hearing or feeling them. In her mind she's begging God to tell her what to do—what choice to make.

...

Tabitha sneaks back to the room underground whenever she can, each time with a growing sense of dread and apprehension rather than excitement and joy. She sits on the old bed surrounded with the taste of mildew, and she stares at the book lying on its rickety table.

There hasn't been an entry recorded in it for seven years— since the last oldest Sister passed on in her sleep. She wonders if the Sister simply forgot to mention the book to her successor or if its loss was more purposeful. If maybe the Sister meant for the village to forget its past and start anew.

Tabitha understands that this determination rests in her hands now. She's suddenly become the keeper of her village, and she must decide whether to accept or demur.

Thus agitated, Tabitha paces down the long dark hallway past the rows of locked doors, past the tiny room with its bed and book and rot. She stops at the end of the tunnel farthest from the Cathedral basement and sits on a narrow set of steps carved into the earth.

Above her, set horizontal to the ceiling, is another locked door. Another taunting gate. She's tired of these damn secrets, tired of them pulsing in her dreams. She pulls useless keys from her pockets and shoves them into the lock, but none of them will turn.

She trembles with the rage of it and storms back to the basement, ripping apart one of the old empty shelves until she has a pile of dry splintered wood cradled in her arms. For good measure, she swipes a few candles from the table just inside the door and piles it all haphazardly under the lock on the door at the other end of the tunnel.

She strikes her flint, letting sparks fly until everything begins to smoke darkly. Eventually the wood catches, and the flames lick the old wood around the lock on the door. She stumbles back down the tunnel seeking fresh air and watches it, her eyes burning and her lungs protesting while heat sears her face.

She's never been one for patience, and when she thinks the fire's done enough damage, and when she starts to fear that the smoke might be leaching itself too far down the tunnel, she wraps one of the moldy blankets around her arms and scatters the charcoaled wood, stomping it out with her feet.

Not even caring that the steps are burning hot and that stray embers sear against her skin, she kicks at the lock with her feet until it breaks free.

Fresh air storms in through the opening, bathing her face with its pure sunlight. It's like an epiphany, this rising from the ashes and into an outside world.

She crouches in a tiny clearing, nothing but soft clover spread around her, white flowers woven through it. An old fence circles around her, woven through with blooming vines that make Tabitha feel like she's stepped into another world.

She flings herself out into the grass, feeling the caress of the soft earth against her burned face and fingers. A shard of bright sunlight streaks through the trees, falling on her face, traces of smoke and ash sparkling around her. And for a few moments, nothing exists in her world except her breath and blood and pounding heart and belief that she's been reborn here for something important: something greater than herself.

• • •

The hare moon is pregnant in the sky. Tabitha watches it from her little clearing in the woods. She doesn't care that the dead have sensed her and wandered from the Forest to trace their fingers along the old links of the fence. She sits cross-legged, old pilfered tools that she's used to repair the door to the tunnel scattered around her.

She has two days to decide what to do about Patrick. The words from the journal about duty rattle around in her head, but her body remembers the feel of his fingers weaving around her spine.

She prays to God, but He's silent. She searches for guidance, but the Forest only moans.

• • •

Two days later her hands tremble so badly she has to replait her hair several times before it will lay flat along her back. Her face is scrubbed clean, her tunic freshly washed, and she pretends to gather wildflowers from the cemetery while she waits for the Guardian patrols to rotate off so that she can sneak through the gate and down the path.

It's an achingly beautiful spring day, one whose soft air whispers into Tabitha's ears about love, and she smiles as she listens. It's been too many months since she's seen Patrick, and as she makes her way to him, her body almost vibrates with excitement and anticipation.

In her arms she carries the basket he'd left for her, this time with fresh flowers hiding a change of clothes underneath. Pressed against her breast is his letter.

If he asks her to leave her world for him, she will say yes.

She practices saying it as she walks: "Yes, yes, yes, yes!" She smiles and blushes and twirls each time she utters the word.

When she arrives at the gate, he's not there, and she has a moment of uncertainty. She sets the basket on the ground and then picks it up again. She runs her hands over her tunic, smoothing out nonexistent wrinkles. She holds her breath and blows it out and tugs on her braid and paces.

The dead catch up with her and rake at the fences, and they do nothing to calm her agitation. She grabs a stick from the ground and pokes at them, trying to force them away but, of course, they don't notice or care or move. Not when she flays their skin. Not when she destroys their eyes with a sharp squish, despising the idea that they're somehow looking at her and judging her.

She's about to scream in frustration, and she closes her eyes and inhales deep, trying to find a way to calm the mortified burn of her skin. She's standing just like that, strong and tall in the middle of the path with her fists clenched when Patrick finds her.

"Tabitha," he says, his voice sounding dryer than she remembered, like the bark of a dew-starved tree.

She smiles, of course she smiles, the world suddenly lilting into place. When she turns to him, he's nothing as she remembered and the same all at once. The blurred bits of her memory sharpening into focus: his eyes a deeper green, his lips fuller, his skin that much more lush and warm.

"My Patrick," she cries out, racing to him.

It isn't until he fumbles with the gate that she sees he's not alone and her steps falter. She tilts her head, looking at the little boy stretching on his toes to grasp Patrick's fingers.

"Patrick?" she asks. She's thrown off by his recent absence, by him being late. By the child.

Patrick looks between the two of them. He pulls the boy in front of him and grasps his fingers around his shoulders. Tabitha doesn't notice just how tight his grip is on the child.

"My brother," Patrick says. She can tell he's trying not to sound hesitant.

"I . . ." She doesn't know how to finish the statement.

"I need your help, Tabby," Patrick says, and she hears the misery in his voice. He falls to his knees and crawls to her. He wraps his arms around her waist and presses his face into her abdomen. Her hands go to his head, slip into his hair, but her eyes are still on the little boy who just stands there. Watching.

Patrick is telling her how he missed her. How he loves her and didn't know what to do when she wasn't there before. How so much has gone wrong and his father has died. She nods and tells him she understands and how sorry she is for the loss of his father but really she's waiting for him to explain the boy. She feels the muscles in her cheeks straining and twitching, an aching pain beginning to radiate through her mouth.

He tips his head back, his cheeks damp. "I need to ask you something, my Tabby-cat," he says, and she trembles, waiting for the words he's whispered to her every night in her dreams—*run away with me*. To leave everything she's known behind.

She's waiting for him to unlock the world for her.

"My brother's sick," he tells her.

She looks at the child, eyes wide. "Infected?" she breathes before she can stop herself.

Patrick shakes his head adamantly and tugs on her hands, demanding her attention. "Your village, they have medicine. They can fix him."

She struggles away from him, but he won't let go. He crawls after her on his knees.

"Please, Tabitha, please," he says. "We don't know medicine the way your village does."

She jerks her hands until she's free and stumbles away.

"I thought you were going to ask me to leave with you," she says, her forehead crinkled.

"There's nowhere for me to take you," he says.

"But you talked about the world. The life outside the Forest." The bindings around her breasts are pulling too tight, squeezing her so that it's difficult to breathe. The little boy's just standing there. Staring at her.

Patrick shakes his head. "I have to make my brother well first. I promised my mother I would take care of him. It was the last thing she asked of me before pushing me out of our village."

A bright exquisite grief begins to wail inside her. She presses her lips together, doing everything she can to swallow the growing agony. She turns and stumbles away from Patrick. She wishes she had something to sag against, something to support her, because she's not quite sure her legs will hold. But there's nothing: just fences lined with the dead, waiting for any chance to sink their teeth into her.

"How did your father die?" her voice is defeated.

Patrick slowly walks toward her, she can feel when he's just behind her. When he inhales, his chest brushes against her back and she closes her eyes, aching for him to take his finger and weave it around her spine.

"He was infected," he says softly.

She clears her throat. She will not sound weak. "How?" she asks.

"Someone from another village. They'd checked her over when she arrived but she'd hidden the bite by cutting off her own finger. They thought it was under control after my father was ill but . . ."

Tabitha winces. "But your brother? And you?" She thinks about the book in the basement, the words of her village twisted around the words of God. It's the way her world has always been.

"He's not infected, Tabby," Patrick says. "Nor am I. I promise."

"The rest of your village?" She clenches her fists and prays to God that *please just this once let the answer be what she needs it to be.* She's been a loyal believer for so long, all she asks is for this one small token in return.

"Chaos," he says simply. "My mother shoved my brother into my arms and told me to save him. I ran to you."

She clenches her teeth to stop from crying out.

She turns to face him. "Do you love me?" she asks.

His expression softens, and his lips part. "More than anything," he says, tracing the back of his fingers down her face.

She feels the tears in her eyes. She doesn't want to give up on the dream of running away with him. She doesn't want to turn back to her village and its claustrophobic fences and rules.

But Patrick has asked for her help, and she loves him. "Then I will help you," she says.

...

As planned, Patrick and his brother stay on the path until darkness falls and wraps itself thickly around the village. Tabitha spends the hours kneeling in the sanctuary. Her lips tremble as she prays, the words feeling hollow in her heart.

When she's sure no one will see them, Tabitha leads Patrick and his brother into the Cathedral. The boy's eyes are wide, astounded by the warren of hallways, the soaring sanctuary, and the dominance belief plays in her world. She takes them to her room and leaves them there.

"I have duties," she says. She doesn't know why it's so hard for her to meet Patrick's eyes. Maybe it's because he's sitting on the bed. *Her* bed where she's dreamt of him and thought of his fingertips sliding along the back of her calves to her knees.

She shivers and looks down at her hands. If the boy weren't there . . . Would Patrick touch her like that when she returned?

"We'll be okay," Patrick says. His little brother sits next to him on the bed, silent.

"I'll try to bring food," she says. Patrick nods. It feels strange and wrong for him to be here, in the Cathedral with its sharp stone walls and ceilings, rather than on the path with the air and the leaves and the light and the freedom.

Tabitha walks to Midnight Office, welcoming the silence of thoughts.

•••

Tonight she's slow with her prayers. Ami and Ruth kneel beside her, their heads bowed, but she sees them glance at her and then each other. She knows they sense something is wrong, but she keeps her fingers twined tight and her lips moving in praise of God and doesn't allow them the chance to interrupt.

When she goes back to her room there's a promise of morning in the air, the sweetness of grass and dew. She slips open the door, and Patrick's asleep under her blankets.

The hare moon is still in the sky somewhere, allowing her to see his face. She stands for a bit, the moans of the Unconsecrated threading through the fences as she stares. He sleeps with his lips parted, one hand thrown out to the side as if waiting for her to slip her fingers into them.

It's like he cares for nothing. Has no fears.

Tabitha knows she sleeps curled around herself in a small ball, protecting herself from the world.

He opens his eyes, sees her.

She inhales at the intensity of his gaze. Something inside her flutters, warms, spreads. He doesn't say anything as he slips from underneath the covers, the thin sheet trailing over his chest and down across his hips.

He's wearing nothing. She swallows.

Her voice is a panicked squeak. "Your brother—"

"Is in the room next door. It looked vacant, dusty. Never used."

She nods her head. No one's stayed in that room so long as she's been here. He comes closer. She swallows again. She's still not looking directly at him, and he raises a fingertip.

He starts at her thumb, trailing his touch around her wrist, up the inside of her arm and across her elbow. Along her upper arm so that his knuckles brush against her bound breasts.

She's not sure what breathing is anymore. What heat is.

His fingertips dance over her collarbone, slip just lightly under the hem of her tunic, over her chest. His skin is sleep-warm, his eyelids heavy.

"My Tabby-cat," he says, lowering his face to where her neck meets her shoulder. Every part of her is alive and waiting for that first touch of lips to skin. When it happens she opens her mouth, her body unable to contain air any longer.

He kisses the line of her jaw and along her cheekbone. Into her ear he murmurs, "My love."

She stands there, eyes closed, wound up so tight she doesn't understand how his next touch won't cause her to explode and end the world.

She wants to raise her hand and touch him. To wrap her fingers around his muscles and feel them twitch at her touch. She wants to make him catch his breath. She wants to make him feel as full of need and desire as she does at this moment.

His lips are just skimming hers. She breathes him into her, and he breathes her into him, and she wonders if anything can be more intimate than this: this sharing of breath that is life.

He slips a hand behind her neck, into her hair, untangling her bun. His fingertips dig into her scalp, and she can feel that he is wound tight, like her. That in the next moment he will pull her mouth to his and his to hers and they'll ignite. She'll crack and open and be nothing but pure light energy, her soul bursting into the world to burn with his.

The scream is high pitched and long and so unexpected that it takes Tabitha and Patrick too many heartbeats to understand what's happening.

In the hallway roars a commotion and banging and then the door flies open. "Tabitha," Ruth comes racing in, blood trailing down her arm. She's too far into the room before she realizes what she's barged in on. Before she sees the naked young man with his hands threaded around Tabitha.

Ruth pauses and, in that moment, a tiny body struggles out of the darkness at her. It's Patrick's brother, his lips dripping blood and fingers digging into the Sister's knee as he bites at her calf.

Tabitha screams. Footsteps pound down the hallway, and before she can warn anyone away, Ami careens into the room. Patrick's brother switches targets, pawing at the newcomer.

Ruth stands there, sobbing, and Ami dissolves into panic just as fast, trying to fling her body to dislodge the Unconsecrated child but managing only to tangle herself in her tunic—allowing him access to her ankle. More footsteps in the hallway. The boy drops Ami and looks straight at Tabitha. He stumbles toward her and Patrick rears back.

Tabitha doesn't think. She just acts. She snatches the boy by his arm, twisting him to keep his teeth from her. With all of her force, she flings him across the room. He slams into the wall. Bones crunch, and Patrick shouts.

"Out!" Tabitha screams at everyone. Patrick tries to approach his brother who lies crumpled on the floor, little mewling moans dribbling from his lips. The boy starts to crawl toward them, his fingertips shredding and snapping against the stone floor as he tries to gain traction.

Tabitha pushes the two infected Sisters from the room and grabs Patrick's arm, tugging him behind her.

He grips her hand as she slams the door. "I didn't know," he says. "I didn't know," he says again as if repeating it over and over again will still the confusion inside.

...

Tabitha sits in the corner of a cramped room while the rest of the Sisters figure out what to do next. Ruth and Ami are in the infirmary. They're being given their last rights and will be put down soon. "We'll tell the village it was a bout of food poisoning," the oldest Sister, and therefore their de facto leader, says. Everyone else murmurs in stunned agreement, but Tabitha stays silent.

"Now about the infected child," the head Sister says. As if she's leading some sort of meeting with an agenda.

Patrick's brother is still in Tabitha's room. She knows he's made it to the door because she thinks she can hear him scratching against it. Tiny moans floating through the hallways. Patrick's been tied to a bed in another room. Tabitha's sure they gagged him or else she'd be able to hear him shouting for his brother, screaming that he didn't know.

She presses her lips tight together. She's very aware that everyone around her struggles not to look at her. She's trying to figure out what she believes. She's trying to decide if it matters.

She knows she asked him directly if his brother was infected and he said no. She doesn't know if he was lying. She closes her eyes, remembering the earnest panic of his expression as she pulled him from the room.

Tabitha thinks about the book in the tunnel room. About how long this village has lasted being cut off. How she's the one that endangered them.

Ruth and Ami, her only two friends in the Sisterhood, will be dead soon. Her family could have died as well. *Everyone* in the village could have become infected.

"Someone will have to take care of the child," the oldest Sister says.

Tabitha rubs a hand over her face, shifting in her chair. It's all her fault. Whether Patrick lied to her or not, she was the one to bring the infected child into the village. The little boy is her responsibility. Just as Patrick's fate belongs to her as well.

It would be so much easier if she knew Patrick lied to her. If she could believe that he knew all along his brother was infected. But she knows her heart, and her heart knows his, and this is how she is sure that Patrick tells the truth when he says he didn't know.

And yet it doesn't matter that she believes him: belief is irrelevant in the face of fact. He brought the infection. She allowed it to happen.

"I will take care of the infected child," she says softly. She looks at the other women in the room—really looks at them. At how soft some of them appear. How old and tired. How they devote their lives to God and leave nothing for themselves.

How unlike Tabitha. She who lusted. She who put desire for a man before God. She who almost brought down her village.

"And the older brother?" the head Sister asks. For the first time Tabitha realizes the hesitation in her voice. She realizes how weak this woman is to be in charge of not just the Cathedral, but the fate of the village. She wonders if any of the rest of them know of the journal downstairs, know of the legacy of their survival.

Tabitha thinks about taking Patrick's hand and leading him down the path and away from the village. Of banishing herself and him together. She smiles, letting the dream roll warm and round in her mind.

"He I will take care of as well," Tabitha says.

"About the circumstances in which the older boy was found ... ," the head Sister begins to say, leaving an opening for Tabitha to fill in the blank.

Tabitha stands and squares her shoulders. She keeps her chin level and voice even as she says. "It is none of your concern." She sweeps toward the door, black tunic floating around her ankles.

She waits for the head Sister to challenge her, to maintain her authority and dress Tabitha down in front of her peers for what she's allowed to happen. But the old woman is silent.

"What will you do?" one of the other Sisters asks, as if this was some sort of democracy where everyone can voice a thought.

She pauses in the doorway, examining them, meeting their eyes one by one. Establishing her control. "I will do what is necessary," Sister Tabitha responds.

•••

The boy is small and broken and weak. His moans are those of a newborn kitten. Tabitha steps into her room and walks toward the window easily avoiding his reach. He starts to pull himself across the floor toward her, and she stands and stares at the Unconsecrated outside past the fences.

So much useless death. Such a waste.

When the boy is closer Tabitha kneels and cups his cheeks in her hands. He tries to squirm, tries to twist and turn so that he can taste her. "May God show mercy on us both," she whispers before snapping his neck and bashing his small fragile head against the stone floor.

For a while she looks at him. If only Patrick had asked her to go away with him. If only they'd been on the path when the boy turned, he could have infected them both. They could have woken up dead, entwined together forever.

•••

As she unties Patrick's ropes she avoids his eyes.

But he grabs her and makes her look at him. "I didn't know he was infected," he says, his voice hoarse and lips dry. "My mother gave him to me, told me to take him away. I never knew."

Tabitha nods. "I believe you," she says. And it's true.

"I would never lie to you, Tabby. I love you too much."

She nods again. She understands this as well.

She tells him they put his brother in a special room—a safe place where Patrick could say good-bye. Then, she tells him, she will lead him back into the Forest and away from the village and together they will find a way to live and love beyond this constricted world.

He doesn't question as she pulls him down the stairs into the basement, nor when she pulls aside the curtain and unlocks the hidden door. He follows her blindly as she leads him down the dark tunnel. She stops at the stairs climbing from the ground at the far end.

They face each other and Tabitha inhales deep, the scent of him mingling with the smell of old smoke and rot. She closes her eyes, trying to sear it into her memory. Slowly, she runs a hand up his arm, along his collarbone and around his neck until her fingers dig into his hair.

She thinks about the kiss they almost—but never—shared and she wonders if his lips could have been a part of her, if they could have left this world before his infected brother Returned— if their love had been pure, maybe they'd have been able to stop time.

"I will love you always," she says, pulling his lips to hers.

Through her kiss she tries to explain everything that words cannot. About love and duty and God and need and choices and memory and history. She wants him to taste her and understand her. In that kiss is everything she was and could be, all that she's giving up in her life.

She needs to take this part of him with her because it's the only way she can go back to the life she needs to live. To her duty to village and God.

When she pulls away she's crying and Patrick reaches up to her cheek and catches a tear on his finger. He doesn't realize she's saying good-bye to him. "I will love you always," he says, and she smiles, sad and aching.

She gestures for him to go up the stairs first, and he pushes open the door. Before he disappears above ground she presses her lips to her fingers and her fingers against his spine, and then he's gone and she closes and locks the door behind him.

She huddles on the top step and listens to him bang and call for her and then to the sound of the moans. She tears at her clothes and her body, raking her nails against her flesh hoping to let the agony pulsing inside her escape, but nothing can dull the torment.

•••

Her hand shakes as she dips the pen into ink and holds it above the page. The printed words are impossible to decipher, tears trembling from her eyes and her body racked with sobs. And then she writes: *There is always a choice. It is what makes us human. It is what separates us from the Unconsecrated. But that does not mean that choice cannot turn men into monsters. I have chosen survival over life.*

•••

In her life, Tabitha has felt consuming desire only once—on those too short days with Patrick in the Forest. She watches him along the fences with the others now, at the way he grabs at the metal links and pleads and begs. She touches the old note from him, tucked against her breast under the cross she wears around her neck.

A part of her likes to believe that he's different from the others, that he doesn't moan for anyone but her. That he spends his days and nights trying to return to her.

He is always there for her, always waiting. The most constant companion anyone could pray for. One of these days she will return to him. She will feel that desire again, that need beyond human comprehension, and they will be together forever.

Familiar

BY MICHELLE ROWEN

"That one."

The witch followed the direction of my pointing finger, which singled out a tiny, tawny-colored striped kitten sitting in the far corner of the pen. She frowned with disapproval.

"Wouldn't you rather have one of the others, Brenda? They're more playful. That little runt looks half-dead. I'm not even sure why my apprentice put it in the mix today."

I shrugged. "I guess half-dead runts appeal to me. My mother said I could pick whichever one I wanted."

"Your mother also said she's wanted you to do this for almost a year now."

"What can I say? I've been busy."

I tried to ignore the icy glare my flippant comment inspired. When it came to witch manners, I figured I was lacking. Not that I really cared. It's not like my powers were any big deal. Not compared to my mother's.

"Go pick out your familiar so you can start your real training."

"But I don't want to be a witch."

"You can't change what you already are."

We'd had this discussion every Monday for nearly a whole year, ever since I turned sixteen. But when you don't really want to do something, it's hard to feign interest. Basically, I just wanted to be normal. I didn't want to go into the "family business," as it were.

Maybe I should have gone to live with my dad after the divorce. Normal high school, normal friends, normal life. I just wished I knew for sure what the right answer was. A little bit of perfect clarity would really come in handy every now and then.

Like this—picking out my "familiar." A familiar is a witch's pet, an animal that becomes her constant companion and is supposed to help her do magic and bring protection and good luck. Frankly, I could use all the luck I could get. My mom was a high-level, respected witch in our neighborhood coven, but me? I could barely do a decent card trick. Mom said it's because I don't practice very much, but I had other things to do. More important things. At least, that's what I kept telling myself.

But to get her off my back for a while, I agreed to go to Hocus Pocus, a magic shop that supplies all sorts of witchy paraphernalia—including potential familiars. There were cats, ferrets, snakes, rats, even a couple of bats. No puppies, though. I really would have preferred a puppy.

I wasn't much of a cat person. But, in my opinion, it was way better than a snake.

The kitten hissed as Mrs. Timmons picked it up by the scruff of its neck.

"Interesting," she said. "It's wearing a little rhinestone collar. Denise must have put it on earlier. I'll include it with the price since it suits him."

"Great," I said, not really listening to her. Instead I swept my gaze over the interior of the shop. I'd been there loads of times before with my mom as she picked up her supplies. The place always creeped me out with its musty, dusty interior and cluttered shelves holding everything from carved wooden boxes to crystal balls of all shapes and sizes to herbs and spices for potion-making to what looked like a dried-up severed monkey's paw on a shelf directly to my right.

I grimaced. *Poor monkey.*

"Here you go," Mrs. Timmons said, and her face cracked into a thousand wrinkles as she forced a smile that was not even slightly genuine. She didn't like me very much. I once heard her call me a troublemaker. She handed me an open shoebox that weighed next to nothing even with the tiny kitten sitting inside. "I know your mother already has a feline familiar, so I won't worry about food and litter."

"No. Don't worry."

"You'll have to give it a name. Just concentrate and it'll come to you. Remember, there's power in names, so be sure it's the right one."

"Power in names. Got it." I resisted the urge to roll my eyes. "Do I need to pay anything right now?"

"No. I'll bill your mother's account."

"Okay, then, bye. Thanks." I turned to leave.

"Wait!" Mrs. Timmons grabbed my arm. "One last thing."

"What?"

"The bond."

"The—"

"It's important it be done right away. As long as you're certain this kitten is your chosen familiar . . ."

"Couldn't be more positive if I tried." I glanced at the clock on the wall that read seven o'clock. How long was this going to take?

Mrs. Timmons grabbed my wrist tightly and reached into the box to touch the kitten. "I bond you together as Brenda Collins, apprentice witch, and her loyal and obedient familiar."

"And what does—*ahh*!" I gasped as an electric bolt of pain jolted through me so fast I barely had time to register it.

"Ow! Damn it!"

I frowned at the sound of the pained male voice. Who said that?

"Now you can go." Mrs. Timmons wiped her forehead with the back of her hand and gave me a weary look. "Give my regards to your mother."

"Yeah, I'll do that."

I was out of there before she changed her mind and turned me into a toad, or something. Mission accomplished. I hoped this would be enough to get Mom off my back for a while longer. I mean, the cat had to grow up before it could be any real use to me. How long did I have? A few months, maybe?

I'd take what I could get.

"Now I have a kitten," I mumbled, holding the shoebox close to my chest as I walked home in the dusky light of early evening. It was only a half-mile to my house from the store. "At least you're cute enough. Kind of antisocial, but cute. Sort of like me, without the cute part."

"I think you're cute."

I stopped walking and looked over my shoulder. No one was there. I continued on walking, figuring it was just my imagination. My positive affirmations bubbling to the surface. Mom always told me not to put myself down. Maybe I was starting to get it.

"I have no idea what to call you," I said. "Mrs. Timmons said just to concentrate and it would come to me."

"The name's Owen."

"I don't like that name at all," I told my imagination. "I want something way cooler than Owen."

My imagination swore under its breath. *"Wait a minute, you can read my thoughts? How the hell can you do that?"*

I was about to answer my imagination when I noticed that someone was standing in my way. Two men, actually, both well over six feet tall with broad chests and shoulders like football players, blocking what little light there was on the horizon. I stopped walking and looked at them nervously.

"We need that," one of them said.

"I don't have any money," I stammered. "Like, maybe five bucks total."

"Keep your money, we just want what's in the box."

I looked down at the box holding the kitten. The kitten itself eyed me curiously for a moment before the box was pulled completely out of my hands. The kitten jumped out, and one of the men grabbed for it.

"*Hands off,*" my imagination—which I was now thinking wasn't my imagination at all—snarled.

The kitten arched its back and hissed, swiping a tiny paw in the man's direction.

"Aw, isn't that adorable?" one of the men said sarcastically to the other. "Little Owen's showing his big, scary claws. *Kids.* Pain in the ass, if you ask me."

Before I could say anything, do anything, something crazy happened. And, growing up in a house with a magic-using witch as a mother, that was saying something.

The kitten grew before my very eyes.

Instead of a tiny striped kitten standing between me and the men, there was now a huge tiger who had to be five hundred pounds or more.

It growled, baring long sharp teeth and flicked a glance at me.

"*Stay back. Werewolves are dangerous even in human form.*"

Werewolves? I staggered back a step, almost falling over.

"Come on," one of the men said, although he was backing up a step at a time. "We don't want a fight, Owen. Not here, not now. Just give us what we're after, and nobody has to get hurt."

What they got was another fierce growl as the huge tiger moved toward them. Without another word, they turned and ran, the tiger stalking after them.

Had they called the tiger *Owen*?

I looked with shock down at the discarded shoebox that had contained a tiny kitten only minutes ago. Next to it was the sparkling collar the kitten had been wearing around its neck—*rhinestone*, Mrs. Timmons had said. I reached down and picked it up, looking at it closer. I didn't know jewelry, but it didn't really look like cheap knock-off rhinestone jewelry to me. And it didn't look like a collar for a pet. It looked like a bracelet with a broken clasp. A *diamond* bracelet.

Another growl from the huge wildcat now loose in the city made me instinctively turn around and start running for my house. I didn't think I'd ever moved so fast in my life. Keeping the bracelet on me made me nervous so I decided to quickly hide it under a Dumpster in an alleyway I passed on my way home. I'd come back for it in the daylight when every shadow didn't seem as if it was ready to pounce.

"Hey honey," Mom said, distracted since she was on the phone when I blew through the front door. "How did it go at Hocus Pocus? Did you find a familiar?"

"I don't know," I said when I'd found my voice. It came out really shaky. "I'll have to go back tomorrow. I have homework. Talk to you later."

I ran upstairs and shut my bedroom door, trying to put what had happened out of my mind forever.

...

There was a small striped kitten sitting on my chest, looking at me, when I woke up the next morning. It cocked its head to the side.

"You're finally awake. I've been waiting forever. Where's the bracelet, Brenda?"

I heard the voice in my head, the same voice from last night. I pushed the kitten away from me and scrambled out of the bed and got tangled up in the sheets and my baggy pajamas. My legs felt shaky.

"Wh-what do you want from me?"

The kitten watched me carefully. *"The bracelet. Like I just said."*

"How come I can hear you?"

"Good question. I figure it's because that old witch did her abracadabra thing last night. I'm your familiar now, remember? Who knew that would actually mean something? But at least it helped me find you again. You're like a homing beacon for me now." He didn't sound terribly happy about that.

The familiar/witch bonding spell.

"You turned into a tiger last night." My mouth felt very dry.

"And you're lucky I did. You have no idea how dangerous those werewolves were."

"Werewolves? Wh-what did they want?"

"See? We've come back to the subject of the bracelet again. It's what they want. It's what I want. So why don't you hand it over so I can go on my merry way and leave you to your normal life?"

"Brenda!" Mom called from the hallway outside my closed door. "You up?"

I tensed. "Yeah."

"Breakfast is almost ready. I made blueberry pancakes."

I gulped. "Super. Just a moment."

"I'll bring you up some orange juice to start."

"No, that's not really—" But I heard the footsteps on the stairs, indicating she'd already headed back down to the kitchen. Great. Today of all days my mother decides she wants to hand-deliver me some vitamin C.

I blew out a long breath. It didn't matter. It wasn't as if I was hiding anything other than a little kitten in my—

I turned around and nearly screamed, stopping myself only by clamping my hands over my mouth.

The kitten was gone. In its place was not a tiger this time, but a boy with tawny-colored hair and dark blue eyes. He was bare-chested and had my sheets pulled up to his waist. I had the sinking feeling that was all he was wearing.

"Comfortable," he said, pressing on the mattress. "I could get used to this. Haven't had a bed for a while. Being on the run has a tendency to mess up your sleeping patterns."

He said it flippantly, but there was a strange slide of emotion through his eyes. Something like envy and a little sadness.

I pried my hands off my mouth for a moment. "You're a shifter."

I'd never met a shapeshifter before, but I'd heard plenty of stories about them. Most of those stories made me positive I wanted to stay very far away from them.

"Good guess. What was your first clue? The fact that I can shift form? Brilliant deduction, Brenda."

"Don't call me that."

"It's your name, isn't it?"

"Yes, but . . . but I need you to go away."

"My name's Owen, whether or not you think it's cool enough for you. My mom—may she rest in peace—thought it was pretty cool seventeen years ago, so it's good enough for me. So, it looks like we're all bonded together now. I have this strange compulsion to be close to you. So annoying." He actually rolled his eyes. "Witches. Honestly. Think they rule the world."

I wrung my hands. "If you're a shifter, you can't be my familiar."

"The spell that shopkeeper put on us seems to challenge that theory." He placed his hand casually over his stomach, and my gaze followed. Owen was fairly gorgeous, actually, with a thin but muscular body. He looked like a runner. I could even count his abs. You know, if I wanted to.

And I didn't.

"You need to get out of my bed right now." Words I'd never actually spoken together in that sequence.

"Sure thing, boss." He began to move and the sheets started to slip over his bare left hip. I turned my back to him so I wouldn't see anything else.

"No, wait! Stop, just stop. Just change form again."

"Back to my kitten? Or the tiger? Or I can be a full-sized regular cat—that's the best for staying incognito. Perhaps a Puma would be fun, though. Or a leopard. Choose your kitty-cat, Brenda."

"Just the kitten is fine!" There was an edge of hysteria in my voice as I heard the stairs creak. My mother was coming up with my orange juice. I turned and looked at Owen. "Please change back!"

"Because if mommy dearest sees me here like this . . ." His lips curled. "That would probably look bad for you, wouldn't it? She'd think her darling daughter is a naughty little witch?"

"Yes!"

"So I'm guessing you don't have a lot of guys sneaking into your bed in the middle of the night?"

Even though I was freaking out, I had enough time to send him a withering glare. "That's none of your beeswax."

"You *didn't* just say beeswax. You couldn't have." He laughed and the sound was low and throaty. "That's so completely adorable I could seriously die."

My cheeks were blazing with heat. I always said the lamest things when I was nervous. "Change! Now!" It was more of a frantic whisper than a shout.

His smile faded as if it had never been there in the first place. "I want the bracelet."

"Okay, okay. I'll get it for you, but it's not here."

"You hid it somewhere else?"

"Yes!"

The door opened the next moment, and my mother walked in carrying a small glass of orange juice. I nearly passed out. When she saw Owen, there was no way I could ever possibly explain having a naked boy lying in my bed. I'd be grounded till I was thirty. There was no possible—

"Oh!" she exclaimed. "How adorable! But I thought you said you didn't get anything last night."

I whipped around to see that the boy in my bed was gone, replaced by a tiny, striped kitten. A tiny, striped, *purring* kitten.

"No, uh, you must have heard me wrong. I got one, obviously." I frantically waved my hand at the kitten. "But I don't have any supplies for it yet."

Still holding the juice glass, she picked the kitten up in her other hand and nuzzled it against her face. "So precious. Excellent choice, Brenda. I approve. Does it have a name?"

"Yes, it's, uh, Owen. And it's a he."

"This means you're excited to start your training in magic?" Before I could say anything, she continued, "I know you've resisted, thinking you don't have the natural talent, but I know you do. You've already shown it in the few lessons we've done. You simply need to believe in yourself. And now that you have this darling little friend to help you, I think the sky's the limit, Brenda. I really do."

My mother was nothing if not encouraging. I couldn't help but feel guilty for constantly making up reasons why I couldn't study witchcraft along with my regular high school classes.

"I don't know if I can say I'm excited," I said honestly. "But I'll give it a try."

She smiled and handed me the juice and gently put the kitten back down on the bed. "It's a start."

So I'd devote myself to learning to be a witch. If I failed, then she couldn't very well hold it against me. Fine. It was decided. No more excuses.

However, I had an excuse for today. I needed to get the bracelet for Owen so he could get out of my life. And Mrs. Timmons thought *I* was a troublemaker. Right.

Mom left my room and I saw, out of the corner of my eye that Owen turned back into his human form and was still in my bed.

"I need clothes," he said.

I didn't turn to look at him full-on, but I knew he was right. He couldn't very well wear my bed sheets all day, could he?

"My brother's in college right now, but he's got a closet full of clothes here. I'll get something for you."

"You're so accommodating."

"I get the bracelet, and you leave me alone right?"

"I get the bracelet, I deliver the bracelet to the person expecting it, and then we need to get this bonding spell between us removed."

"I don't feel anything," I said honestly.

"That makes one of us."

"What do you mean?"

He sighed. "It means that because of this spell I feel this need to be close to you. And I have this crazy sense that I . . . *belong* to you, and only you. And I don't think I like that very much."

When I turned to look at him to see if he was messing with me, he'd already changed back into a kitten.

•••

Behind the house, Owen changed into an old pair of my brother's jeans, Reeboks, and a blue T-shirt, before we set off for the alley where I'd stashed the bracelet last night. Then I had to get to school.

"So, *Brenda*," he said my name as if taste-testing it. "You're a witch-in-training, are you?"

I glanced at him sideways. "You could say that."

"Can you do magic?"

"That's kind of the point, isn't it?"

"But can you?"

"Not really."

"Why not?"

"Because of the 'in training' part. I need to practice."

"Like playing the piano."

"Sort of. Only completely different." I nervously crossed my arms, feeling the weight of my backpack pull at the shoulder straps. "And you're a weretiger? Werecat?"

"Just *shifter* is fine."

"I thought you might be a werewolf."

"No. Werewolves are a breed unto themselves." There was a sneer in his voice. No love lost there. "They can only shift into one form. I can be any size or kind of cat I want to be."

Even though I found it unsettling, I couldn't help but be slightly impressed. "Shifters like you and werewolves fight like cats and dogs. Seems kind of appropriate."

"My pack and theirs don't get along and never will."

"And you don't want them to get the bracelet."

"Nope. They got wind of me having it, and they've been tracking me for days. I was fine inside the magic store since everything inside was protected with a magical ward."

"You were hiding out in there?"

He nodded. "The owner had no idea. I just sneaked in and made myself at home. Not bad. Lousy food, but not bad. That woman who gave me to you? She seems like a bitch on the surface, but she's actually really nice when there's nobody there but the animals." He sighed. "Thought I was okay for a while, but then *you* had to single me out."

"'Half-dead runt,'" I repeated what Mrs. Timmons had said about him.

"It's a look I was trying to perfect. Who knew that was your type?"

My type. I suppose you could say that.

He didn't look like a runt at the moment. In fact, he was almost a whole foot taller than me, so that put him at a few inches over six feet. He wasn't hugely muscular, but he was solid and lean. My brother's clothes didn't fit him perfectly, but they looked pretty good, all things considered.

"Yes?" he asked, making me realize that I was openly checking him out.

I cleared my throat. "Nothing."

Owen swore under his breath, his eyes now on the sidewalk ahead of us. I looked with alarm at what had caused this reaction. Someone stood there, leaning against the fence next to the sidewalk as if waiting for our approach.

He was tall, lean, with tawny-colored hair a lot like Owen's. Only this guy was easily a few years older.

"Brother," he said, and a wide grin spread over his face. "Long time no see."

I jumped when I felt Owen's hand on the small of my back, and he leaned toward me to whisper, "Play along, please, or this is going to go badly."

He then pulled me fully against him until I was pressed against his hip, his hand sliding around to my side. "Jeremy."

"Is that any greeting for me?"

"Sorry, I guess after our last brotherly chat I'm not really feeling the love."

Jeremy spread his hands. "It had to be done, you know that."

"Right." There was a tightness in Owen's voice.

"Who's she?" Jeremy nodded at me.

"This is Brenda," Owen said. "She's . . . my girlfriend."

I raised my eyebrows with surprise. *Girlfriend?*

"She's a witch," Jeremy said. "I can sense it."

"Your point?"

"No point." Jeremy drew closer, his gaze assessing me from feet to face. "So you're dating my little brother, are you?"

Play along. Owen had nearly begged me a moment ago.

"I . . . am. Yes, that's right."

"Pretty little thing." He grinned. "Owen has good taste. Who knew?"

"Listen, Brenda, I'll catch up with you in a sec, okay?" Owen said, leaning closer. "Just go on ahead. I need to talk to my brother alone for a minute."

"Okay, I'll just—" But I couldn't finish my sentence because Owen kissed me, taking my breath completely away. His lips felt soft, but a bit demanding, as if he wanted some sort of response from me. I kissed him back, confused by what was going on, confused by how good this felt.

Owen pulled back from me after a moment, and there was confusion on his face as well, his brows drawn together. I touched my mouth with my fingertips.

Good kiss. Very, *very* good kiss. By the look on his face, I think he might have agreed with me.

"Get a room," Jeremy said dryly.

Owen gave me a gentle shove to propel me a little down the sidewalk. I "played along" and started walking away.

One thing I did learn when it came to using my so-called natural witchcraft was how to eavesdrop at a distance. And, yes, I had paid attention to that lesson since it helped me to listen in to my parent's hushed arguments just before they separated. It eased my mind a little that they weren't divorcing because of me. Although, it didn't ease my mind *that* much. Divorce sucked, but at least my parents seemed much happier now. Good friends, but lousy spouses. That was how they put it.

I walked without looking backward, but I focused on tapping into that eavesdropping ability.

"I hear you've acquired a little something shiny," Jeremy said. I was at least fifty feet away by now, but I could hear him as clearly as if I was still standing beside Owen.

"Who told you that?"

"A little bird." There was a smile in Jeremy's voice. "You think that will appeal to Stan's sensibilities, do you?"

"Come on." There was a catch of emotion in Owen's words now. "You know how badly I want back in the pack. I don't understand why you're not helping me."

"Because I don't want you there. Mom was the only one who thought you had a home there. And now that she's gone—"

"Yeah, I know. You never wanted me around in the first place. Do you honestly think I'd be competition to you? I'm not interested in being alpha—"

"When Stan dies, *I'm* alpha," Jeremy said, and there was a growl to his voice. "And after me, you're next in line and that would cause problems."

"I wouldn't fight you for it."

"That's just a chance I don't want to take. Because you know what? You'd lose. And I'd rather not have to kill my own brother if I can help it." He was quiet for a moment. "But I will if I have to."

Owen exhaled shakily. "I don't have anyone I can depend on out here. Without the pack, I have no family. I have nothing."

"Yeah, well, I guess that's fitting." Jeremy's voice was cold. "You *are* nothing. Mom told me you were a mistake she wished she hadn't made when she cheated on Stan. It's time you accepted that and stopped trying to buy your way back in with stolen jewelry. You're almost eighteen. Time to find your own life and get the hell away from mine."

I wondered if it had something to do with the bonding spell, but I could actually feel Owen's emotions then. His brother's words were like a physical blow to him.

I couldn't help but hurt for him. I didn't know much about him at all, but I didn't need to. He was in trouble. He'd been kicked out of his shifter pack—his "family"—after his mother's death. Maybe she was the only one who protected him from the brother who just flat-out didn't want him around. Some brother. My own brother was a thousand miles away at college right now, but I knew—despite our many differences and disagreements— that he'd do anything for me.

"I'm still going to Stan, and you can't stop me," Owen said after a moment. His voice had grown stronger. He wasn't backing down. "He'll listen to me. The bracelet is only to buy enough time to explain things to him. He won't refuse. The thing's worth a lot of money, and I know he likes money. He'll see that it's what Mom would have wanted."

"Stan's my dad, not yours. All you are is an unwanted little bastard. Now why don't you go back to your pretty little witch girlfriend, consider yourself lucky that somebody wants to be around you, and stay the hell out of my life and out of my pack."

Again, there was that sharp twist of pain I felt coming from Owen. His brother's words hurt him deeply and made him feel completely and utterly alone. I kept walking, but I realized I was now crying. I wiped the tears off my cheeks.

I stopped eavesdropping, cutting it off as if mentally hanging up a phone. I walked and walked before I looked over my shoulder. Owen wasn't anywhere to be seen.

I didn't stop till I got to school. I didn't see Owen again, although for the rest of the day it was as if I could still feel his grief—the grief of a boy I barely knew but felt a deep magical bond with whether I liked it or not.

My heart ached for him.

•••

"Morning."

I pried my eyes open the next day to be greeted with a total déjà vu. There was a tawny-striped cat looking at me. A larger, older version of the kitten from yesterday.

"You," I said.

"In the fur."

"Where did you go yesterday? I thought you were going to catch up to me but you never did."

"Sorry. Had a couple things I needed to take care of after talking to my brother."

"That's vague."

"It is, isn't it?"

"I got more clothes for you." I nodded over at a stack of folded clothes on a chair I'd grabbed from my brother's closet.

"Cool. Thanks. Your mom already left. It's Saturday so she said she was letting you sleep in. She talks to herself a lot?"

"All the time. It's bizarre." Although, not as bizarre as having a conversation with a cat. Luckily Mom had barely been around yesterday after school so I didn't have to explain what had happened to my familiar that seemingly had vanished into thin air.

He was back. I wasn't sure how I felt about that.

"I'm going to change and, uh, get changed," Owen said. *"Consider yourself warned."*

I quickly turned over and sat up so my back was to him. Through our connection, I could actually sense when he shifted form back to human. Then I heard the soft sound of rustling material as he grabbed something to wear off the pile and got dressed.

"So we're all alone," he said after a moment. "No mommy to barge in on us and find out the little secret you've been hiding from her."

I stood up and finally turned around. He stood on the other side of my small peach-colored bedroom wearing a new pair of jeans. He hadn't put on a shirt yet. His skin was tanned as if he'd just come back from vacation in the sunny south. He pulled a white T-shirt on over his head, covering up everything I was gawking at.

"Your brother is a jerk," I said.

He looked at me with confusion before his dark blue eyes narrowed. "You were listening? What is that, some kind of a witch trick?"

"A simple one, actually, which is the only reason why I could do it since I suck at magic. If it's your pack you should be allowed to go back without having to jump through hoops."

"I don't do hoops."

"It's just an expression."

"Like 'none of my beeswax' was just an expression?"

"Sort of." I looked at him sharply and realized he was smiling. "What's so funny?"

"You are. Why the hell do you care about me?"

I frowned. "It's probably because of the bonding spell."

"So you're admitting that you care about me."

I just looked at him, afraid to answer that. What was I admitting? I didn't want to admit anything, but the truth was kind of obvious. I *did* care about Owen. I cared about what happened to him, and I felt the pain he felt when he was rejected by his brother.

And it wasn't just because he was inarguably gorgeous. I just . . . liked him.

I blamed the bonding spell entirely. I never fell for a guy after only knowing him only a day.

Well, *hardly* ever.

"I guess I just don't want you to get hurt," I said honestly.

He drew closer and brushed my long dark hair back over my shoulder. I suddenly felt very aware that I was wearing a pair of pajamas that had tiny smiley faces all over them. I felt like a little girl even though I was only a month away from my seventeenth birthday.

But I *wasn't* a little girl. Despite the PJs.

"Thank you," he said simply. "And I'm sorry I had to kiss you like that yesterday. I needed Jeremy to believe you were my girlfriend. I don't think he'd understand if I told him I was actually your *familiar*. I don't even understand that."

"It's okay, I didn't mind."

He raised an eyebrow. "You didn't?"

My cheeks warmed. "Let's just forget it happened, okay?"

"Not so sure I can."

"Why not?"

"Because I want to kiss you again."

He drew me closer to him. His hands were on my shoulders, and my hands were pressed against his firm chest so that I could feel his rapid heartbeat. His warm breath glanced against my cheek as he lowered his mouth to mine.

The phone rang. I jerked away from Owen, pulled out of whatever spell I'd just sank into and grabbed for the phone on my nightstand.

"What? I mean, hello?"

"You. Me. Shopping. Noon. Yes or no?"

My best friend Sandy often spoke in bullet points.

I glanced at the clock. It was a little after nine. I flicked a glance at Owen and realized I wished Sandy hadn't called to interrupt our potential second kiss.

Dangerous kitty-cat.

I quickly calculated what had to be done. Owen wanted his bracelet. Then he wanted to deliver it to Stan, his stepfather, as payment for letting him back into the pack, even though his brother was still a major obstacle there. I assumed that whatever Stan said was gospel for the pack. If he agreed that Owen was back in, then all was well with the world.

Then we needed to have our bonding spell removed. I had no idea what I was going to say to Mrs. Timmons, but I'd cross that bridge when I came to it.

"Noon sounds doable."

"I need new socks," Sandy said. "Are you up for the challenge?"

I turned away from Owen. The sight of him was very distracting. "Socks. Exciting stuff."

"They disappear. And I can't even blame magic for it."

"Socks are obviously the source of all evil."

"We'll have lunch in the food court first. Then sock hunting. Mike's joining us. Is that okay?"

"Totally fine with me."

Mike was Sandy's new boyfriend. A senior. She'd introduced us the other day. Nice guy. Now he was automatically part of our little group of misfits through his association with my best friend.

Sandy was also a witch-in-training with two overbearing magic-using parents. It was nice to have something in common that we could complain to each other about. Didn't mean we couldn't have fun, too.

I wondered what she's think of my current situation with Owen. She probably wouldn't believe that he was technically my witch's familiar at the moment. Nothing interesting usually happened to me. And Owen—well, he was very interesting.

After ending the call, I looked at Owen. He waited patiently over by the door.

"I need a minute to get ready," I said. "*Alone.*"

"No problem."

"Um, Owen? Do you want some breakfast or something?"

A smile stretched his face, making him better looking if that was even possible. "Breakfast sounds really good. Almost as good as 'or something.'"

He slipped out of the room and closed the door before he could see just how red I was able to turn.

•••

Two bowls of cornflakes later—I never claimed to be a great chef—we were out of the house and on the same route we were taking yesterday morning.

"Look, Brenda," Owen said after a couple of minutes. He stopped walking and turned to me. "I know this has been a real nightmare. I appreciate your help."

"My help? I stole your bracelet."

A smile played at his lips. "I didn't exactly come by it honestly myself, although if it helps, I stole it from a horrible rich woman who killed a litter of kittens by drowning them when her Persian got knocked up."

I shuddered at the horrible thought. "It represents a lot more than a few expensive diamonds to you, doesn't it?"

"It does."

"I know I shouldn't have listened in yesterday, but I did. And I'm worried that what you're doing is going to end up getting you in trouble."

There. I said it. It was none of my business, but I said it anyway.

"Because of my brother?" he asked stiffly.

"Yes."

His jaw set. "Let me worry about Jeremy, okay?"

I racked my brain for a good answer to his difficult situation. "What if you don't go back to your pack? What if you find a new home and a new, uh, pack? Just start fresh somewhere else?"

His expression shadowed. "Because it's not that easy. You

don't understand. That bracelet that you've got stashed somewhere is my only answer."

"I totally disagree."

"You don't know my situation. Overhearing one conversation
isn't enough to make you an expert on me."

I faltered. "Maybe not."

He raised an eyebrow. "Just like my knowing that you're afraid
to embrace your magical potential is only *part* of who you are."

I felt a sharp and sudden stab of anger at the accusation. "I'm
not afraid."

"Could have fooled me."

"Just because I'm not interested in doing something doesn't
mean that I'm afraid."

Owen shrugged. "If you say so."

I crossed my arms and studied him for a moment. "You're trying to change the subject."

"From what *you* were talking about, you mean." He blew out
a breath. "All I want is the bracelet. There's nothing else in this
town I'm interested in. And the kiss? Don't read too much into it.
It was more to fool my brother than anything else."

I'd be hurt more by his words if I didn't remember what he'd
said to me only forty minutes ago.

"I want to kiss you again."

Maybe he was lying. Maybe he thought I was easy and just
wanted a distraction to get his mind off his troubles.

The smiley-faced PJs *were* rather fetching, now that I thought
about it.

I mean, what did I think this was between us? Something
real? Something that had the potential to be something more?

I was such an idiot. All I was to Owen was a flashing arrow
pointing him to where his shiny diamond bracelet was—his one-
way ticket back into a shifter pack that he was too stupid to see
didn't even want him around.

And I wasn't *scared* about learning magic. I wasn't afraid that

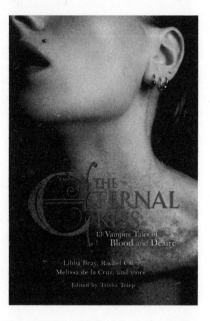

"That's right. And in turn you can give us some inside information about Stan and your big brother's secrets. You don't owe them a damn thing anymore. Not your presence, your loyalty, or anything else."

"And you're willing to do this out of the goodness of your heart, are you?"

"That bracelet you have should help the goodness of my heart a little bit. I know you were going to use it to buy your way back into your pack. Now you can use it to buy your way into mine."

"Two for one deal," Owen said.

"Today only."

"There's a small problem."

The thug raised an eyebrow. "What?"

"I don't know where the bracelet is."

The man nodded. "I find that hard to believe. Caught a glimpse of it only a moment ago. Gave it to your new girlfriend, did you? How sweet."

He grabbed my arm and pulled up my sleeve. The bracelet circled my wrist, where it had been since leaving the house earlier.

Owen's mouth dropped open with shock at the sight. "Brenda—"

"I got it yesterday after school," I said. "Fixed the clasp last night."

"Why didn't you tell me?"

"I was going to." I bit my lip and felt the sting of tears threatening to fall. I wanted to give it back to him. And I was going to. This walk to the alley was only to buy some time. But I wanted to talk to him first, tell him that I felt going back to his pack was a mistake and wouldn't get him what he was seeking. You shouldn't have to buy your way into your family. Love couldn't be bought.

The thug unfastened the bracelet and dangled it from his

index finger. "Nice. At least a couple hundred grand, I'd esti-
mate."

"At least," Owen agreed reluctantly. "So you have it. Now
what?"

"I want something else, too." The man raised an eyebrow
and nodded toward me. "The girl."

Owen flicked a glance at me. "What are you talking about?"

"She's part of your entry fee. Give her to me, and we have a
deal."

Every part of my body went cold. I looked at Owen, but
couldn't see any expression on his face at the moment other than
anger. I had a feeling it was directed at me for keeping the location of the bracelet a secret until now.

"There's a problem," he said. "She's not really mine to give."

The thug chuckled. "Oh, come on. You know that doesn't
really matter. All I want to know is if you're going to give me a
problem about it."

I held my breath, waiting for his reply.

"You can have the girl," Owen said flatly. "But you can't have
the bracelet."

I gasped. "Owen!"

He didn't look at me. The guy laughed out loud and held out
the bracelet. "You prefer the jewelry to the girl? Interesting."

Owen shrugged. "What can I say? I know what real value is.
Girlfriends are a dime a dozen."

"You're a funny kid. Cold-hearted. You'll make a killer addition to my pack."

Owen grinned and took a few steps closer. "You think?"

"Definitely. Tell you what, kid. You can sell the bracelet for
me. I'll split the proceeds with you eighty-twenty."

"Sixty-forty," Owen said.

"Seventy-thirty. You want it?" The thug held it out. "If we
have a deal, you can have it."

"Sounds perfect." Owen was only a couple feet away, and he

reached out to touch the bracelet, flicking it with his index finger so it sparkled in the sunshine.

Then he knocked the gun out of the man's other hand. It skittered across the pavement.

A split second later, he'd shifted to tiger form and pounced, taking the thug to the ground hard enough to knock him unconscious.

Even though I was shocked beyond words by what had just happened so quickly, I could barely register it. I reached into my shallow pool of magical knowledge and threw out the first thing I could think of. A confusion spell. It wasn't much, but it was enough. The werewolves turned around in circles for a moment, not knowing which way was up or down. Two of them lost their balance and fell to the ground.

I stared at them for a moment, dumbfounded. *Wow, it worked. Who knew?*

"*Come on, Brenda!*" I heard Owen's voice in my head. "*Run!*" I ran.

The tiger bounded after me as I ran out of the alleyway and kept running for three blocks before I slowed to catch my breath. A glance over my shoulder showed Owen, again in human form, but now wearing tattered clothing, following closely behind me.

"Don't stop!" He grabbed my arm and pulled me along with him until we found a safe place to hide, slipping into someone's backyard behind a tall fence. My heart slammed against my rib cage, and I looked at him with confusion. He looked as if he was about to say something, but I spoke first.

"Why didn't you grab the bracelet before you ran out of the alley?" I asked.

He stared at me for a moment before he started to laugh. "After what just happened, that's what you want to know? Why didn't I grab the bracelet?"

"Well? It's all you've been wanting for two days."

"I thought so. But I was wrong. That bracelet hasn't brought

me anything but bad luck. Hopefully it'll be enough to keep the werewolves off my back—and yours—now that they have it."

"But your pack—"

"Forget my pack." He looked down at the ground. "It's time I moved on. This just proves it once and for all."

"But he was going to give the bracelet back to you."

He raised his gaze to mine, a look of incredulity on his face. "Yeah, in exchange for you. No way that was going to happen. He's lucky he got knocked out first, since I was in the mood to tear him apart. Must be the bonding spell. I feel a fierce need to protect you, no matter what."

In a few moments, he'd made the decision that would shape his future. Without the bracelet, he wasn't going back to his pack. And it was mainly because he didn't want me to get hurt.

Don't get me wrong, I definitely appreciated the gesture more than I could say. But it was a major deal. *Major*.

"Owen—"

"And look at you with the witchcraft going on. I thought you said you sucked at it."

"I do suck at it."

He raised an eyebrow. "Just imagine what you could do if you studied hard like your mom wants you to." He pulled at his ripped shirt in an attempt to straighten it out. "And you know what you need in order to do that, right?"

"What I need?" I frowned. "A nap so I can get over my near-death experience?"

"No. Well, maybe, but not right now. You need a proper familiar. And to get that we need to have this spell removed. I may be many things, but I'd make a lousy witch's pet."

I smiled despite myself. "Have to agree with you there."

"Then let's not waste any more time. We'll go to Hocus Pocus right now."

He held his hand out to me.

After only a moment's hesitation, I took it.

"And that's why you need to remove the bonding spell," I finished. My words had tumbled out of my mouth since we'd arrived at the magic shop. We had Mrs. Timmons alone in the back room and were explaining everything.

I just hoped it made some kind of sense.

She pursed her lips, rocking back on her heels as she studied me and Owen one at a time.

"Let me get this straight, young man," she finally said. "You broke into my store and fooled me into believing you were a cat. You said nothing about this. And you ate my food and used my protection wards to save yourself from those who wished ill on you."

Owen stood very rigid next to me. "Yes. Yes, ma'am. That's pretty much it."

She pushed her glasses down on her nose and came closer to him. "How old are you, boy?"

"I'm seventeen."

"Why aren't you in school?"

"I was in school. But I had to leave."

"High school diploma?"

"Not yet."

"You're a senior?"

"I was."

"It's currently seven months before graduation, according to my calendar. And now you have no home. No family. No pack."

He stared at her defiantly before the expression faded, and he nodded once. "Yes, ma'am."

"Call me Vera."

He frowned. "Excuse me?"

"I don't like ma'am. It makes me feel old. And having a seventeen-year-old boy staying in my spare room and eating my food will make me feel old enough as it is."

Owen and I exchanged a confused glance.

"What are you talking about?" I asked.

Mrs. Timmons huffed. "Well, I would think that's obvious. Owen has no place to stay, no family to claim him. So, *I'll* claim him. He can live here and finish up school with you. Unless you have a better solution, young lady. Do you?"

"No, I don't." My heart pounded loud in my ears. "That sounds pretty good to me, actually. What do you think, Owen?"

I had a feeling he wouldn't be interested. If it wasn't for his shifter pack, he would probably take off. Backpack across the country. I had no idea what might happen to him then. All I knew was I probably wouldn't see him again.

That thought made me very unhappy.

"What do I think?" Owen repeated, his forehead creased as if a million thoughts were coursing through his mind. "I think that's the best idea I've heard in a very long time. Thank you so much . . . *Vera*."

I couldn't help but hear the gratitude and emotion that thickened his words.

Mrs. Timmons pushed her glasses back up her nose and nodded once. "Then it's decided. I haven't had anyone here for a long time. It's ten years since my Franklin left for college, but his room is still the way he left it, and you're welcome to it and the clothes there, too."

"So you don't have a problem with me being a shifter?" he asked.

"If I had a problem, I wouldn't have suggested this. You don't need a litter box, do you?"

"Well, no. Of course not."

"Then there's no problem." Finally a smile spread across her wrinkled face. She reached up and patted his cheek. "Now, I have a shop to run. Let's break this bonding spell and then get back to our regularly scheduled lives, shall we?" She looked at me. "And Brenda . . ."

I straightened up automatically under her sharp gaze. "Yes?"

"You'll have to pick out another familiar. I don't suppose

Owen will be much use to you there anymore."

He still looked shocked by what had just happened—the opportunity to live here with Mrs. Timmons and go to high school to get his diploma.

"I guess you're right," I said.

Owen didn't say anything.

After the spell was broken, which took about three seconds total, I left Owen to check out his new bedroom and slipped out of the store. I was going to be late to meet Sandy at the mall.

I tried to ignore the big lump that had formed in my throat. When Mrs. Timmons broke the spell I hadn't felt anything change, other than the immediate twinge of pain. But it was over. Owen was no longer my familiar. He'd never really been my familiar in the first place. How could he be? He was a boy, not a cat. It didn't matter what form he was able to shift into. It didn't change the fact that he had his own life that definitely didn't have to include me anymore.

"Brenda!"

I heard him shout behind me, and I froze, wiping at the tear that was sliding unceremoniously down my cheek.

I turned slowly to see him walking quickly to catch up to me. "What?"

"Why did you take off without saying anything to me?"

"I didn't want to get in the way. Also, I have to meet Sandy at the mall like I said I would."

"Oh." He cleared his throat. "I just wanted to thank you for all your help."

"You mean helping you lose your bracelet and your chance at getting back into your pack?"

His lips twitched into a small smile. "My pack was lost to me when my mom died. I just didn't want to accept it. I don't want to be anywhere I'm not wanted anymore. I don't want to force any-one to want me in their life if they aren't interested in having me around."

"Your brother's a jerk."

"Yeah, you said that before. And it's true. Maybe he'll realize that one day, too, but I won't be there when it happens." He raked a hand through his tawny-colored hair. "Look, there's a bit of a problem."

I looked at him with surprise. "What?"

"It's the bonding spell."

"Mrs. Timmons removed it."

"I know, but I'm not sure she did it right."

"What are you talking about?"

"I feel the same as I did before," he said softly, approaching me so he was only standing a few inches away. I didn't pull away when he slid his fingers into my hair and swept it off my shoulder.

"Which way is that?" I asked, looking up at him.

"Like I belong to you." He smiled. "And that's kind of hard to ignore."

A breath caught in my throat. "Well, I don't think that has very much to do with the spell."

"Why not?"

"Because the bonding spell would make a witch's familiar feel like he belonged to the witch, right?"

"Right."

"The thing is—I feel like I belong to you too."

"So it's a mutual problem we seem to be having here." He nodded. "And what do you think we should do about it?"

I slid my hands up over his chest to his shoulders. "I'm thinking . . . nothing. Nothing at all."

"That sounds like an excellent plan." He bent forward and kissed me.

My heart swelled and felt like it was going to burst. I was crazy about Owen. I didn't care if I'd known him two days or two years, it wouldn't change a thing about how I felt.

After a long moment he pulled back a little from me. "So now what, little witch?"

"Now?" I reached down and took his hand in mine. "I need to introduce you to some people."

"Who?"

I grinned at him. "My pack of misfits. Consider yourself the newest member."

His dark blue eyes filled with happiness. "Sounds good to me."

That made two of us.

Fearless

BY RACHEL VINCENT

"Sabine, look at me."

Not likely. But staring out the car window wasn't much better. All I could see was the building—long, low, and squat with tall windows arranged in pairs. Better than correctional custody, but not by much.

The brick-backed sign to the right of the sidewalk read "Holser House," but that was a lie. "This isn't a house."

"Sabine . . ."

"Houses have yards. This is a parking lot."

May as well have a barbed wire fence or a metal detector at the door; the effect would have been the same. Everyone knew about Holser House, and the Holser girls. Whores, junkies, and thieves in training, biding their time till they turned eighteen and were officially booted from the Texas Youth Commission with a sealed record and a prayer.

"It's only for six months." Navarro insisted, and I rolled my eyes at his optimism. Six months was the minimum stay, the maximum to be determined by the director. "Better than the alternative, right? You can wear your own clothes and go to public school when the semester starts. And when you turn sixteen, they'll let you get a job, if you've been playing nice."

But I would only be there when I turned sixteen if I decided *not* to play nice. So much for optimism.

Finally, I turned to look at him, my fingers curling around the door handle. "Can I go in alone, or am I still under escort?"

He gave me a strict, parole officer frown. "There's paper

work . . ."

There was always paperwork. You know you don't really exist when you're known by a case number, instead of a name.

"Sabine, do *not* run away from Holser. This isn't prison, but you're still in state custody. Running away is considered escape, and you do *not* need an escape charge. Next time it'll be Ron Jackson."

The Ron Jackson State Juvenile Correctional Complex. Navarro says it makes the detention center look like kindergarten, and four days in juvenile detention was plenty of time for me to remember that I hated orange jumpsuits and institutional food.

"I didn't run away." I'd just missed curfew. By seven hours. Evidently a grievous violation of my parole, even without the additional status offense—underage drinking.

"David reported you missing."

That's because David was a dick. "Whatever."

Navarro sighed. "Look, Sabine, I'm trying to help you. I had to call in a favor to get you placed here. They don't usually take violent offenders."

"I'm not violent." But Navarro only frowned. We'd agreed to disagree on that one.

"If you don't take this seriously, there's nothing else I can do for you."

He wanted to help me. He might even have believed me if I'd explained about missing curfew. That Jenny was out of town, and I didn't want to be alone with David because he might decide to do more than look, and if that happened, I'd have to hurt him. Then I'd be in Ron Jackson for sure. With the *actual* violent offenders.

Because even if Navarro believed me, the rest of the system wouldn't. They'd never take the word of the troubled teen parolee over the upstanding foster father.

"Promise me you'll stay here. Just ride it out for a few months, then you can go home."

Assuming the Harpers would take me back. Not that I cared

about them, but a new foster home meant a new school, and then I couldn't see Nash. But I refused to follow that line of thought.

"Promise me, Sabine."

I looked up, meeting his dark-eyed gaze, studying him for the millionth time. "Why do you care? For real. You'll still draw a paycheck even if I puke up my well-balanced, state-mandated group dinner."

Navarro sighed again, and the weight of the world slipped a bit on his shoulders. "I don't want to see you waste your life."

It was a lie, yet very close to the truth. He wasn't afraid I'd never reach my full potential, but that he would fail me. Or one of his other girls. That he would drop the ball, and one of us would wind up dead.

Oddly enough, his was a fear I'd never felt the need to exploit. At least, not while I was the one benefiting from his efforts.

"You ready?" Navarro asked.

I opened the door and stepped out of the car. Fort Worth was sweltering, even at ten a.m. on an early June morning. Navarro slammed his door and circled to the back of the car, where he popped the trunk and lifted out my two suitcases. I took one, then followed him inside.

Holser House felt sterile and blessedly cool after the blinding heat outside, and my sweat quickly gave way to chill bumps. When my eyes adjusted, a long white hallway came into focus, the tight throat of the beast that had swallowed me whole.

It would choke on me, sooner or later. Just like the holding houses, foster homes, and the detention center. I was indigestible by the Texas Youth Commission and social services. Eventually, they all realized something was off about me. Fortunately most humans lacked the ability to interpret that feeling of *wrongness*.

At the end of the hall, I saw a waiting room-style couch, and the corner of a chair. The room flashed with the bluish white glow of a TV screen. Though if anyone was actually watching it, I

couldn't tell.

"In here." Navarro extended one arm toward a door on the left. He led the way without touching me, like all well-trained employees of the state. Care from a distance. From across that vast gulf where lawsuits breed.

The office was lit by fluorescents and the glow of a computer screen, while the window was tightly covered against the Texas heat. A large woman sat behind the desk, but she stood when we entered. The nameplate on her desk read, "Anna-Rosa Gomez, Director."

"Cristofer, you're early!"

Navarro smiled and shook her hand. "We could come back later, if you want . . ."

"Of course not. This must be Ms. Campbell?"

Good guess. Might have something to do with the edge of my file, which was sticking out from under the pile on her desk, where she'd probably slid it as we'd walked in the door.

Navarro nodded and gestured for me to shake the plump hand the director held out.

I studied Gomez first, taking in dark eyes, the firm line of her jaw, and the patient, steady hand waiting to grip mine. She looked decent enough. But you can never really know a person until you've seen what scares them.

I set my bag down and took her hand reluctantly, bracing myself for the sensory onslaught.

A white wall. A tall amorphous shadow. The darkness coalesces as I cower, lost in her terror. The silhouette becomes a man with a tightly clenched fist. The shadow arm rises, and I recoil. I know this horror. It has dozens of variations, and I've felt them all.

The fist swings, and I flinch. Shadows have no substance, yet the first blow breaks my rib. I scream, awash in pain. The second blow fractures my skull. The hits keep coming, bruising and breaking me, but there are no words. No explanation, because I don't deserve one. He is mad, and I am there. That's all the logic there is.

Then there is only darkness.

Time moved forward again, but I could only stare at the director with her hand clenched in mine, her fingers warm against my suddenly chilled skin. "Sabine, are you okay?" she asked, wariness peeking from beneath her mask of concern. I'd made her uncomfortable two minutes into our relationship. Might be a new record but probably not for long.

The things that make most people's blood run cold make mine burn with anticipation. They light a fire deep in my soul, which can only be quenched by a deep drink of their fear, left vulnerable during the dream phase of sleep. But Gomez wouldn't want to know that. She couldn't understand it, even if I told her.

"Yeah. I'm good." But *she* wasn't. She was terrified he'd beat her to death next time, if he ever got paroled. She was right.

I pulled my hand from hers and dropped my gaze to keep her from seeing the lingering horror in my eyes. The reflection of her own fear. If she thought something was wrong with me, she might change her mind about taking me, and there were no other residence spots open. It was Holser Not-Really-A House or Ron Jackson, and I would *not* go to jail.

Not just for breaking curfew.

"Sit down," Gomez said, sinking into her own seat. I dropped onto one of the two chairs facing her desk, one foot on the cushion, hugging my own knee. Navarro sat next to me. "I have your file here somewhere . . ."

"On the bottom," I said, and Navarro glared at me. I ignored him.

"Yes, thank you." Gomez opened the folder and scanned the first page. "Says here you pleaded guilty to breaking and entering four months ago . . ."

"I didn't break," I insisted. "I just entered."

"Sabine . . ." Navarro warned, and I rolled my eyes. The details might not matter to them, but they mattered to me.

"Look, the back door was open, and I only went in to grab

Tucker's bat." Unfortunately, the state of Texas considered that proof of my intent to commit a crime. And they were absolutely right.

Navarro sat up straight, looking like he'd like to throttle me. "Remember what we said about your right to remain silent? That applies even when you're not currently under arrest. Ms. Gomez has all the facts she needs."

I shrugged. "She has the facts, but she doesn't have the truth. Don't you think she should know what really happened, if I'm gonna live in her 'house'?" Especially considering she'd never really know what I *was*. Neither of them would. They'd probably never heard of a *mara*.

Navarro sighed, then waved one hand in a "be my guest" gesture.

I glanced at Gomez. "What else does it say in there?"

She studied the file again. "You pleaded guilty to misdemeanor vandalism."

It was originally *felony* vandalism, but the prosecutor gave me a break. I was a first-time offender.

"It says you beat in someone's taillights, fender, and rear passenger side window with a baseball bat, resulting in more than two thousand dollars in damages." Gomez looked up at me with one brow raised. "Isn't that a little cliché for someone as smart as you're supposed to be?"

What, did she have my test scores in there too? I shrugged. "I'm fifteen. I have limited resources. Besides, I used *his* bat. That's, like, poetic justice, right?"

Her brow rose even higher. "Justice for what?"

"Tucker . . ." In my head, I spelled his name with a capital F instead of a T. ". . . gave me a ride home from school that day, but he pulled over half a mile from my house and said I couldn't get out unless I worked off the gas money he'd wasted on me." The prick had unzipped his pants and tried to shove my head into his lap.

"And how did you handle that?" Gomez closed the file and

crossed her arms on her desk, focused on me now. She was good. She should have been a social worker.

"I punched him in the junk, then ran all the way home while he puked."

I thought I saw a flicker of satisfaction on her face before the director remembered she was supposed to be firm and generally disapproving. "Did you report him?"

"I fight my own battles."

"So you went back that night for his car . . . ?"

I nodded, though actually, I'd gone back to give him a nightmare he'd never forget. But he wasn't home. Fortunately, both his bat and his vehicle were. "That car was his weapon, and someone had to disarm him. I was doing society a favor."

Navarro groaned. Evidently I wasn't showing enough remorse.

Gomez cleared her throat and tapped her pen on my file folder. "You know, we have a system in place to deal with people like Tucker. But it can't work if the crime isn't reported." She sat straighter and opened the file again. "It sounds like taking justice into your own hands was your first mistake."

No, my first mistake was getting caught.

"But clearly not your last." She spread her arms to indicate all of Holser House, and my presence in it. "You got probation on breaking and entering, and misdemeanor vandalism, which you violated last week with a missed curfew and underage consumption of alcohol."

I'd also taken twenty bucks from David's wallet, to pay for my drinks, but suddenly it seemed like a good time to exercise my right to remain silent.

"You should know that missing curfew here constitutes an escape from state custody and will result in an additional charge against you. And likely a bed at Ron Jackson."

"So I hear." I dropped my leg and sat up, glancing around at the plaques on her walls. "Are we done?"

"Your foster mother has already signed the necessary forms." And she'd left before I even got there. Not a good sign. "Mr. Navarro and I have some additional paperwork to complete, but you're welcome to look around while we do that. I'll give you the official tour when we're done."

I stood and was halfway to the door when Navarro called my name. "Sabine . . ." I turned, but what he wanted to say was clear in his expression. *Don't screw this up. This is your last chance.*

• • •

The living room—they probably called it the "common room"—was big and mercilessly bright. There were several stiff-looking couches and waiting room chairs, most facing an old-fashioned TV—the kind with a thick, curved screen—tuned to a Spanish-language soap opera.

I stood in the doorway, watching. Trying to convince myself that this was home, at least for the next several months. Group meals, shared chores, full accountability. *I can do this.* Like there was any other choice.

But on the bright side, with twenty beds, lights out would be a virtual buffet. So many nightmares to gorge on, and with this many people to share the burden of my appetite, they'd never connect the bad dreams with my arrival.

At least not consciously.

Maybe I should have violated probation sooner. I'd practically starved with only David and Jenny to feed from.

"Marina, if you don't turn off this Latina drama shit, I'm gonna throw that TV out the window, and you with it." A tall, heavy girl about my age walked into view and dropped onto one of the couches on her knees, shoving her hands between the cushions. She had huge brown eyes, smooth dark skin, and deep hollows beneath sharp cheekbones. "Where's the damn remote? I can't take any more of this Speedy Gonzales babble . . ."

"That's Sharise's drama," a second girl insisted in a thick

Latino accent, just outside my field of vision. "My show went off."

"Both of ya'll shut up," a third voice—obviously Sharise—snapped. "I'm tryin' to learn Spanish."

"You're not gonna learn to say nothin' from this crap but 'I'm pregnant' and 'I'm dyin.'" The first girl paused in her search and glanced over her shoulder at Sharise. "But you're gonna need to know those anyway, right? That, and 'I need another hit.'"

"Whatever," Sharise said, and couch springs squealed. "I'm done with that."

"Hey!" the first girl interrupted, and I looked up to find her staring at me, now holding the missing remote control. "You the new girl?"

"Yeah." I'd been caught; might as well own it.

"Well, look at this. We got another white girl, even paler than BethAnne. Looks like crime finally found the suburbs."

I wasn't sure what to say to that, so I kept my mouth shut.

More springs squealed on my right, and I turned to find two more girls watching me from the second couch. "Hey, I'm Sharise, and this is Marina." The girl who stood and offered me her hand was older than me—maybe seventeen?—and looked exhausted. Used up, but not shut down. She was shorter, skinnier, and darker-skinned than the first girl. I braced myself for new fears as I took her hand.

But all I got was a vague whisper of discomfort, like a chill up my spine.

Sharise didn't live in fear. She held her personal terrors close to her heart, buried too deep to be read with the first casual contact. I respected that, but not enough to give her a pass. Secret fears always made the heartiest meals.

Sharise shook my hand, then glanced over my shoulder at the girl still holding the remote. "That's Elesha. She's mean, but she's just coverin' her own insecurity."

"Yeah, and Sharise thinks she's gonna be a psychiatrist, if she hasn't already fried her brain."

"See?" Sharise lifted her brows and shot a scowl over my shoulder. "Mean as a snake."

"I just say it like it is," Elesha insisted, dropping the remote to the center cushion. "What's your name?"

"Sabine."

Elesha snorted. "You even got a white girl name," she said, and I shrugged. "What'd you do?"

I didn't have to say, and Gomez wasn't allowed to. But acting like I had a secret would only make people more determined to figure me out. "Missed curfew and found a bottle of Jack."

"That's it?" Elesha looked skeptical.

I shrugged and sat on the arm of the couch. "I was already on probation."

Before they could pry any deeper, I heard footsteps behind me and turned to find Gomez leading Navarro out of her office, one hand on his arm. He stopped in the hall. "Sabine?"

"What?"

"Wednesday at four." Every week like clockwork, I met with my parole officer when most girls my age were watching television or not doing homework.

I nodded. Then I grabbed my bags from Gomez's office while she walked him to his car. When she returned, she gave me an assessing look, then nodded like she'd just made her mind up about something. "Okay, let's get you settled in."

Gomez squeaked her way down the hall in rubber-soled shoes, and I followed with both bags. She showed me offices belonging to the assistant director and the events coordinator.

Next came the meeting room, for all the rehab classes and group sessions. The sign hanging on the door read: SUBSTANCE ABUSE TREATMENT AND PREVENTION EDUCATION. I peeked through the window. Most of the girls looked bored.

Past the common room was the cafeteria, which—Gomez explained—doubled as the classroom for the girls who lacked the privilege points to go to school. Her short, thick heels clacked as

she marched into a kitchen and small serving area. "Our full-time cook has Tuesdays and Thursdays off, but you'll meet her tomorrow. Penny is our relief cook."

Penny waved as she worked a commercial-size can opener around the edge of a huge can of tomato sauce.

I nodded, then followed Gomez back through the kitchen and around the corner. "We have twenty beds for girls between the ages of thirteen to seventeen. The older girls are on this wing; the younger ones are down there." She turned to point behind us, at an identical hall. "Each wing has a community bathroom. There's no door, obviously, and they're pretty closely monitored by the techs."

One of whom was visible through the bathroom doorway, wearing slacks, a blouse, and an ID tag hanging around her neck.

"This is your room." Gomez opened the last door on the left—notably missing a lock.

The room was sparse. A bed, a dresser, a built-in desk, and a window. I set my suitcases down and headed straight for the window, hoping to find the grass that was missing from the front "yard." There was a small, dry patch of green, sprinkled with concrete picnic tables, squeezed in next to a basketball court and an open recreation area. The whole thing was surrounded by a tall chain-link fence.

Easily climbable. I made a mental note.

"You can wear your own clothes, so long as you stick to the dress code. Jeans and plain T-shirts. Sweats are okay, when it gets cold. Athletic socks and shoes. If you lose privileges, you wear the issued tees and sweats."

"What about phone calls?" I leaned against the desk, trying not to be overwhelmed. *It's better than the detention center*. And probably *way* better than Ron Jackson.

"You can call the people on your approved list, unless you've lost privileges. You'll need a calling card for long distance."

Shit. The approved list would include only David and Jenny,

Navarro, and my court-appointed lawyer, who was about as useful as the gum on the bottom of my shoe.

The only person I actually wanted to talk to wouldn't be on the list. *Nash.* I couldn't handle six months with no contact. I'd lose my mind. Or my temper. Or both.

"No matter what you hear, you're currently our only violent offender," Gomez said, recapturing my attention.

I frowned up at her. "I'm not violent."

She raised one of those arched brows at me. "You gave a car a baseball bat–makeover."

"Yeah, but I didn't make *Tucker* over." Which was what I would have done in his nightmare, if he'd been there, to mess with.

"Your file says you broke a girl's jaw with a lunch tray in the detention center."

I rolled my eyes. "She tripped me and called me a white trash whore. I came up swinging."

"You put her in the hospital."

"She put *herself* in the hospital. I was just defending myself."

Gomez narrowed her eyes at me. "Sabine, if you defend your-self so vehemently around here, I *will* let them lock you up. These girls aren't dangerous. Most of them just took a wrong turn in life, and they're getting themselves back on track. Holser is the best halfway house in the state, and I won't let you ruin our record."

"I'm not looking for trouble." I held her gaze, letting her see the truth in my eyes; there'd be plenty to hide from her soon enough.

"Good," she said, one hand on my doorknob. "Cristofer thinks you're special. Worth the effort. I hope he's right."

Me too.

She pulled the door closed as she left the room, and I sank onto the bed. *Welcome to Holser Hell.*

●●●

I lay on my bed in the dark, in a tee and baggy gray shorts. Staring

at the ceiling. Missing Nash. It was hard not to think about him at night, when there was nothing to distract me from his absence. I could feel him squeezing my hand. His lips warm on mine. I could hear his voice in my head, warning me not to let myself get too hungry. Promising he'd be there when I got out. Telling me he loved me.

No one else had ever said that to me. Ever.

But those bits of him were figments. Memories at best. I'd lost him, at least for a while, and I couldn't even see him in my sleep because I can't dream. Maybe that's normal for a *mara*, but I don't know; I've never met another one.

The closest I can come to dreaming is feeding from someone else's nightmare. I need that, like I need food and water. Or maybe more like I need air.

Hunger gnawed at me—a ravenous beast chewing me up from the inside. I hadn't fed much in the detention center because so many of the kids there were drugged. Their sleep was unnatural, thus beyond my ability to manipulate, and if I couldn't mold their dreams into nightmares, I couldn't feed from them.

The same could be true at Holser, but I hadn't seen many meds handed out, so I clung to the hope of a nightly all-you-can-eat as the one bright spot in an otherwise gloomy sentence. Because Nash was right—I'd lose control if I got too hungry.

Lights out for the last group of girls—those with the most privilege points—was at ten o'clock. My alarm clock, casting a weak crimson glow over the small room, read 12:13.

I rolled over and stared at the wall, silently feeling out the rooms around mine. I can sense sleep like a rat smells cheese, even when he can't see it. Most of the girls near me were out cold, and so far, their slumbers felt natural. Organic. Delicious.

It was time.

I closed my eyes, mentally drawing energy into the center of my body. It coiled there, pulsing slowly, cold and sluggish from hunger, but eager to be used. Then that energy gradually

stretched into my limbs, mimicking my body structure. I stood and felt this energy-me separate from my physical form—the metaphysical equivalent of dislocating a joint, only it didn't hurt. It felt satisfying, like stretching first thing in the morning.

The energy-me crossed the room. My footsteps made no sound. My form had no substance. No one would see me, even standing right next to me. I turned to look at the bed, where the physical me still lay, eyes closed, one hand resting on my stomach, breathing steadily.

Privately, I call this part Sleepwalking, because while part of me was up walking around, my physical form seemed to be sleeping. That's exactly what anyone who saw me lying in bed would think. They'd notice how peaceful I looked, and how innocent.

The irony of that thought gave me a small, secret smile.

My Sleepwalking form enjoyed a freedom my physical body could never experience, but there were some weird limits, most of which I'd discovered through trial and error.

Not like Nash. He was no more human than I was—but his mom and brother were around to teach him stuff and answer questions. I had only instinct, and ignorance on a cosmic scale. Kinda tragic, if you think about it.

So I don't think about it. I think about the stuff I *do* know.

Like Sleepwalking physics, I thought, stepping into the dim hallway without opening my door. I could Sleepwalk through doors, climb through closed windows or boarded up holes in walls, and through anything else that might serve as an entrance or exit for my physical body. But I couldn't fall through floors or walk through solid walls. My Sleepwalking-self slammed into them just like my physical form would have.

It made no sense. But then, very little of my life did.

The hallway was empty and quiet, but I could hear the night-shift tech watching TV in the common room. She would make rounds, checking all the beds and bathrooms, but with any luck, in a nonsecure facility, nights would be pretty low-key.

The room next to mine belonged to a girl named BethAnne. During dinner, my fingers had brushed hers when we'd both reached for a saltshaker, and I'd slid into her fear as easily as sinking into a tub full of hot water.

Sometimes fears exposed secrets, a glimpse of the memories they were based on. Other times, especially in little kids, they were a fleeting terror inspired by a scary movie or a dark closet. But BethAnne's fear had the gritty feel of real pain—a satisfying meal, as opposed to a quick snack.

I glanced down the empty hall again, then stepped through her door into a room just like mine. BethAnne slept on one side, her knees tucked up to her stomach. I knelt by her bed. Her face was inches from mine, and if I'd had a physical presence, her breath would have stirred my hair.

I ran one finger over her cheek, and *that* I could feel—warm and soft and bumpy from a mild breakout. I could feel her in my bodiless Sleepwalking form because she was dreaming, and I was pretty sure she could feel me too, though how she'd interpret my touch in her sleep was anyone's guess.

But she wouldn't wake up while I was touching her. No one ever had. I was part sedative, part leech, and all bad dream—literally. And I wouldn't even have known that much, if not for Nash's mother.

You're a mara, she'd explained the night he'd brought me to her in tears. *One of several breeds of parasitic empath. My generation would call you a Nightmare. You can read people's fears, and when they sleep, you guide their dreams to cultivate that fear. Then you feed from it.*

She was right, though I could never have explained it so well on my own. For years, I'd done what my body wanted—what it *needed*—with no understanding of what was actually happening. Of what I really was. I'd only known that when people touched me, they saw their worst fears reflected in my eyes, and it scared them. *I* scared them.

Hell, for all I knew, that's why I'd been abandoned on a

church doorstep when I was no more than two, by the social worker's best guess. No one knew my birthday or my real name. For all practical purposes, I was born that afternoon, in social services, to the woman who named me after the heroine in a romance novel and the label on a can of her favorite soup.

But she didn't keep me. No one kept me for more than a few months at a time. I made them uncomfortable. When I was around, fear floated in the air like dust moats in sunlight. Floorboards creaked louder, goose bumps grew fatter, and the dark felt darker than ever before.

Obviously, I don't make a lot of friends. But when people go to sleep, I know them better than anyone. I see things they wouldn't show their best friends. Hear things they wouldn't whisper to their therapists. Sometimes I know things they don't even know about themselves. Buried memories. Forgotten trauma. The quiet terror slowly rotting away at their souls.

I gave their terror life. I gave it form and purpose, carefully weaving borrowed images to create a dream tapestry, sticky as spider's silk and a million times stronger. They struggled pointlessly against my carefully braided dream threads while I rode their fear, gorging on it to nourish my own soul until the hunger ebbed—at least for a while.

In their nightmares, I had power, and for those few moments—precious because they were so brief—I felt sated. Full. In the most hedonistic, pleasure-filled sense of the word.

Just thinking about it made my hunger swell, a cold-blooded beast demanding warmth and nourishment. Tonight, BethAnne would be both.

She sighed beneath my caressing finger, and I laid my palm flat on the side of her face, treasuring her warmth. I slid my hand over her jaw and down her throat to her shoulder. Then I pushed.

BethAnne rolled onto her back with a soft grunt. Her forehead furrowed, but her eyes didn't open. I pulled the covers back and knelt on one side of the mattress. She was helpless, and prac-

tically plump with energy she didn't even need, while I was cold and starving. *It's not wrong*, some stubborn voice in my head insisted. *It's survival. She'll live, and this way, so will you.*

I slid my leg over her stomach and straddled her on the bed. Her tee was soft against my thighs, her skin warm through the material, in contrast to the cold hunger chilling me from the inside.

My eyes closed, and I scooted forward until I felt her rib cage beneath me. Her breath hitched, struggling beneath my weight. But I wasn't heavy enough to truly suffocate her, and I would only take as much energy as I needed.

I leaned forward and touched her face. Warm cheeks, warmer neck. The physical contact I needed to establish a mental connection.

Then the world shifted, and I saw what she saw. I wasn't truly in her dream, but I was in firm control of it. The wizard behind the curtain of her subconscious.

BethAnne sat on a beach in the sun, sculpting a sandcastle with the handle of a broken plastic fork. She glanced up and smiled at a man in a folding lawn chair, then carefully scraped sand from the side of a turret. The man had no face, and I'd been in enough dreams to interpret that one—BethAnne had never met her father, but her subconscious hoped he was the kind of man who'd set aside an entire day just to watch her on the beach. To be with her.

So peaceful. So hopeful. So . . . completely useless to me. Peace and hope are cute. But fear is my medium. It's the vibrant paint on the canvas of my life, the only color bright enough to mean anything. To truly feel.

With it, I could paint her dream into a nightmare . . .

I started with something simple. The next time BethAnne turned to look at her blank-faced father, he was gone. So was his chair. I was proud of that little detail; it said that he hadn't merely left her—he'd never really been there in the first place.

Next, the sand melted beneath her feet, flattening and hardening into featureless gray concrete, gritty against her bare legs.

BethAnne stood, frightened by the abrupt changes. That's when I dropped the rest of the nightmare around her, as sudden and disjointed as any natural dream.

I dried up the ocean, giddy with power in my dream-state kingdom. Then, when BethAnne whirled again, bars slammed into the ground in front of her, clanging like a prison cell door. Three more bar walls dropped on her other sides, and she was trapped. Caught. Alone.

BethAnne tried to shake the bars, but they didn't move. She yelled, but her throat made no sound. She was locked up—cut off from the world. This was the fear she'd shown me. Total isolation. Being gone and forgotten, like she'd never existed in the first place.

She was afraid now—the real BethAnne trembled beneath me on her mattress, so small and scared—but I needed more. There is a well of true terror in everyone's heart, and she was hiding hers from me instinctively.

No fair holding back. I wanted it all.

The Sleepwalking-me leaned forward and stared down at BethAnne in her bed. Her eyes were squeezed shut, her fists clenching the sheet at her sides.

I closed my eyes again and swiped an eraser over my mental whiteboard. In her dream, the concrete beach disappeared, along with the dry ocean bed. But the bars remained, and BethAnne could see nothing beyond them but a yawning black abyss. I'd left her no sign that the rest of the world still existed.

She opened her mouth for a scream, and I gave back her voice. But the blackness devoured it the moment the sound flowed past the bars. No one would hear her. No one would see her. She could scream and cry and bang on the window all day, but . . .

Wait. A window?

And that's when I saw through the cracks and into that well

she'd tried to keep from me. I fell into its depths and landed in the middle of her *true* nightmare—the remembered terror I'd somehow recreated for her with no conscious thought. I was on autopilot, gorging on her fear without noticing the changes until they'd gone too far.

BethAnne whimpered.

A basement, pitch dark, but for the pitiful streetlight shining through a narrow, filthy window at the top of one wall. A child version of BethAnne sat in the stretched rectangle of dirty light, tiny arms hugging her knees. Something skittered in the corner, and BethAnne sobbed. Her empty stomach growled and cramped. Her tongue felt thick and dry. She'd wet herself the day before.

The stairs were lost in darkness, and the door at the top was locked from the outside. With a padlock. BethAnne had gotten out of the house once when her mommy went out, and someone called social services. Mommy wasn't taking any chances this time. She had to keep her daughter safe from nosy strangers with cell phones. Safe from anything until Mommy came back with food and water, smiling and playing the hero. And when she did, BethAnne would love her and hug her and cling to her shining salvation. So what if her savior was also her jailer?

But what if her mommy didn't come back this time? What if no one ever heard BethAnne again?

Beneath me, her heart beat faster. Too fast. She was sweating now, and her pulse was irregular.

Too much. Too far. What kind of sick-ass parent would do that to a kid? No wonder BethAnne kept that one buried.

Maybe I was better off without a mom.

I opened my eyes and withdrew from her dream, and without my will to support it, BethAnne's nightmare collapsed like a house of cards. I was done with her. Just like some restaurants are too dirty to eat at, some fears are too filthy to consume, for fear of planting rot in my own soul.

Her breathing slowed, and I slid off her chest. BethAnne rolled onto her side. She pulled her knees up to her chest and

tucked one hand beneath her cheek. Silent tears streaked her face, but she breathed deeply now, without my weight to constrict her lungs. She looked so vulnerable—a larger version of the girl huddling in the basement—and suddenly I wished I'd chosen someone else to feed from on my first night at Holser. Someone a little less damaged.

I was warm and full, nearly glutted, but the meal sat heavy on my soul, like bad fish in my gut. There was nothing left to do but lie awake in my bed and wait for morning. And try to forget BethAnne's basement, and the fact that I—a walking Nightmare—had been outplayed by the memory of an ordinary, human nightmare of a mother.

...

Morning couldn't come fast enough. It never did. You'd think I'd be used to that, after fifteen years of lying awake in bed—I only seem to need three to four hours of sleep—but it never gets easier to fill the empty hours before dawn.

And I'd learned quickly not to ever, *ever* wake anyone else up.

But by quarter to six in the morning, I'd had all the nighttime I could take. By six fifteen, I was showered, dried, dressed, brushed, and scowling at the locked cafeteria door.

"I don't serve breakfast until seven thirty," a voice said from behind me, and I turned to find a blue-eyed woman in khakis and a green button-down shirt. An official laminate ID hung around her neck, reading KATE GREER. "Most of the girls aren't even awake this early in the summer."

"I'm not most of the girls." But I was starving for actual food, now that my more exotic hunger had been temporarily satisfied.

"Then you must be Sabine," Greer said, and I nodded. "Well, Sabine, how 'bout this: I'll let you eat now, if you help me serve breakfast afterward."

"Yeah, I guess." First served, plus I wouldn't have to pretend

not to notice the others avoiding me as they ate.

"Great. It'll fulfill your chore requirement for today too. Follow me." Greer pulled a pink coiled key chain from her pocket and unlocked the door, then led the way through the dining room into the kitchen, where the combined scents of bacon, butter, and syrup were enough to make my head swim.

"Why is the food ready, if you don't serve it for another hour?" I asked, staring at the serving line, where steam rose from slits in aluminum foil covered buffet trays.

"Because I feed the day staff before their shift starts."

"That's really cool of you." And probably not a requirement of her position.

"I don't mind. Help yourself." She pointed to a stack of plastic trays at one end of the serving line. So I did.

I scarfed pancakes, bacon, and juice while the day-shift techs and staff members wandered in alone or in pairs.

None of them sat near me. A couple smiled—I'd seen them the day before—but when my gaze met theirs, they looked away and hurried past my table. My creepy factor was strongest after a good meal, and I'd fed well the night before.

Kate Greer was the only staff member, so far, who didn't seem in a hurry to get rid of me. After I ate, she gave me an apron and a pair of tongs. "You do bacon, and I'll handle the pancakes. If they want seconds, they have to wait until everyone else has eaten. Got it?"

I nodded just as the first residents pushed through the double doors into the cafeteria. But twenty minutes later, when everyone had been served, Greer's pile of pancakes had dwindled to a single stack of five, but my bacon tray was still full. I'd only served two girls. All the others had passed me by after one glance.

"That's weird." Greer frowned as I covered the full tray. "Bacon's usually a hit. Now what am I going to do with all this?"

I had no answer, so I hung up my apron and crossed the cafeteria in silence, avoiding eye contact while I was still so warm and

full—and obviously sending out creepy-vibes—from BethAnne's nightmare.

It wouldn't take long for Greer to notice that no one was eating whatever I was dishing out. I'd have to find a more solitary house chore and wait to eat with the general population, no matter how loud my impatient stomach complained.

At least the nighttime self-serve is plentiful.

Or so I thought . . .

•••

I spent most of my second day at Holser House alone in my room, avoiding people so they couldn't avoid me. That night, I was still pretty full—or at least not starving—from BethAnne's nightmare, so I decided not to feed, hoping people would find me a little less spooky the next day. It turns out solitude is a lot easier to deal with when foster parents are the only people trying to ignore you. Though I would never have admitted it, being alone in a house full of girls my own age . . . well, that kind of sucked.

And it made me miss Nash even more. He and his family were the only ones I'd ever met who didn't mind me hanging around—probably because they weren't human either. Knowing *why* I was creepy had gone a long way toward helping them get over it.

Unfortunately, revealing my species to the rest of Holser wasn't an option. But skipping one meal wouldn't kill me, right? I'd gone longer than that plenty of times. So that night, I put in my earbuds and listened to the iPod David had given me while I waited to fall asleep on an empty stomach.

The next day was Saturday. Visiting day. From ten a.m. on, there were strangers everywhere I turned. Or at least, that's what it felt like, though once I started counting, I realized only about a dozen of the girls had company.

I wasn't one of them. Not that I'd expected to be. Jenny was pissed that I'd gotten arrested again, and David wouldn't come

see me without her. Not after I'd pulled a no-show on his watch.

So I decided to scout out a suitable meal for that night from among the girls who didn't have visitors. I tried the common room first, but the only two girls there were talking to parents, one of whom had brought along a kid brother, evidently glued to a PSP.

The cafeteria was the same, only worse. Several more fractured family units were spread out around different tables, alternately talking, arguing, and sitting in uncomfortable silence. Another point in favor of me not having a real family.

My only other option was the backyard. None of the visitors wanted to leave the air-conditioning for the broiling Texas heat, so all three picnic tables were occupied by Holser residents. The only girl I knew by name was Sharise, who sat alone at the shaded end of a concrete picnic table.

I dropped onto the bench across from her. "Hey."

Sharise looked up from a game of Solitaire and met my gaze, unflinchingly. "Hey."

She hadn't picked up her cards and run—definitely a good sign. My growing hunger would make it harder for me to read her fear, but easier for her to tolerate my presence. "No company today?"

"Or any other day." She flipped over a red five and stacked it on a black six. "No one left to come see me 'cept my sister, and she can't drive yet. What about you?"

Had she just asked me a personal question? That was new. "Same. Minus the sister."

Sharise nodded like she understood. "You in foster care?"

Wow. Two questions in a row. That was practically a conversation! "I was." I shrugged, trying not to look shocked as I squinted into the blinding sun. "Not sure anymore."

Jenny probably wouldn't let David take me back. I was pretty sure she'd gone out of town that night to get away from me anyway, even if she didn't even really understand her own motivation. She hadn't been sleeping very well lately—plagued with

nightmares of one miscarriage after another, caused by the fear that she'd condemned her husband to a childless life. Well, caused by that, and by *me*.

What she didn't know was that David's worst fear was actually being saddled with an infant. He'd been having trouble sleeping lately too . . .

"So, how long does this family love-fest last?" I asked, glancing around at the other residents who'd chosen the heat over the Visitor's Day commotion inside.

"Till five. But everyone with enough privilege points gets to check out for dinner."

Dinner out? Something told me I wouldn't be so lucky. Fortunately, so far the food at Holser was much better than I'd expected.

I was oddly reluctant to end the unexpected conversation with Sharise, which would definitely happen once I touched her. But my other hunger had to be satisfied too . . .

"Hey, you can use this two on that red three." I leaned across the table and pulled a card from Sharise's hand, letting my fingers brush hers in the process. I'd gotten very little from her before, but this time I got absolutely nothing. Not a single whiff of fear. Not even the brief spine chill I'd read from her the first time. All I felt from her now was a thick, smoggy kind of peace and acceptance of her past crimes and her conscious decision to move past them.

Sharise stared at me like I'd just snatched a bite of food from her fork. "I got it." She plucked the card from my hand and played it, then went on with her game without another glance in my direction. Pointedly ignoring me. *I* might not have freaked her out, but my interference in her Solitaire game was definitely unwelcome.

"Sorry," I mumbled, and stood and wandered away from her table, as confused by her complete lack of fear as I was disappointed to have lost her company. Sharise seemed cool enough—

she was certainly nicer than anyone else I'd met at Holser. But making friends with her, if that was even possible for me, would have been like getting to know my hamburger right before lunch.

At least, that's what I told myself.

Speaking of human hamburgers, I still hadn't found a meal . . .

Across the yard, a girl I didn't know sat on another concrete bench, while a second girl, perched on the table behind her, braided long strands of her hair. I accidentally-on-purpose bumped their table as I passed and knocked a bag of tiny, neon colored rubber bands to the ground.

"Sorry." I knelt to pick them up, and when I handed them to the girl on the bench, our hands touched. I looked into her eyes and felt . . . nothing. No fear. I saw only patience and a weathered acceptance of Holser House and the part it played in her rehabilitation.

Really? Patience? Acceptance? And no fear?

"What's your problem?" The girl asked, without any real venom. That's when I realized I was frowning at her, still holding the bag of rubber bands while she tried to pull them from my grip.

"Sorry," I said, for the second time in as many minutes. I backed away from the table and into the shade of one of the few trees on the property.

I might not be the poster child for normality, but I'd looked into the eyes of at least a hundred girls my own age in the last couple of years and had seen fears ranging in severity from the stereotypical dread of being dumped in public to the shy, quiet girl's terror that her brother would lose his temper again and beat her to death in her own room. I'd also felt all kinds of paranoia, insecurity, and rage. But I'd rarely *ever* felt simple, overwhelming patience and acceptance from a normal teenage girl. Much less two in a row. Two parolees, who should—logically—have more to fear and resent than your average high school kid.

In fact, the only time I'd ever felt anything like what I was

getting from Sharise and the other girl was when . . .

"Sabine?"

I glanced up to see a tech I didn't recognize holding a clipboard and squinting out at the yard from the doorway.

"Yeah?"

"Your brother's here to see you. He's in the common room." Then she stepped back inside and let the door slam shut behind her.

Brother? Then I smiled. *Nash* . . .

Sharise raised one brow at me as I pulled open the back door, but I only shrugged. She knew I had no family, but she wouldn't tell anyone. She was feeling too peaceful to start any trouble. I happened to know that for a fact.

It took all of my dwindling self-control not to race down the hall, but I didn't want to look too eager. I mean, how happy would a girl really be to see her own brother?

I stopped in the common room doorway, and there he was. He turned when he heard my footsteps, and his hazel eyes lit up, one side of his mouth curled into a half-smile.

"Hey, *sis.*"

I almost laughed out loud. My relationship to Nash could in no way be described as 'sisterly.' I made myself take the next few steps one at a time, and then I merely wrapped my arms around him, instead of running to jump into his arms.

He squeezed me tight and whispered into my ear. "You don't seem very happy to see your only brother."

I whispered back, "I might be, if I had one."

"I'm kind of glad you don't. He probably wouldn't like what I'm thinking about his sister right now."

I grinned as he let me go, then glanced around to find the two separate groups of visitors watching us curiously. "Come on." I started to grab Nash's hand and then stopped myself and tugged on his short sleeve instead. I wasn't sure whether we were allowed to have visitors in our rooms, but I *was* certain that if we got caught, no

one at Holser would ever mistake Nash for my brother again.

Still, a few minutes alone with him would be worth the risk.

From my room, I glanced up and down the hall to make sure no one was looking and then closed the door and turned to face Nash. He was there in an instant, in my arms again for a real greeting this time. "Damn, I missed you. School sucks when you're gone."

I grinned and pulled him closer. "School sucks anyway."

"Well, it's worse now." He kissed me like I was the only source of oxygen in the room—like he'd die without me—and something in my chest ached so fiercely I thought my lungs would pop. I hadn't felt right since I'd last tasted him five days ago, four hours before the cops picked me up outside the mall, drunk and very, very disorderly.

And I wouldn't feel right again once he left. I *never* felt right without Nash. He was the only person in the world who wasn't afraid of me, or repulsed by what he saw in my eyes. He wanted me, even knowing what I was. Even knowing what I had to do to survive. He *loved* me.

And I loved him more than I had ever, in my entire life, loved a single living soul.

When I finally pulled back—more for lack of air than anything else—Nash smiled at me, but didn't let go. "So, I guess you think you're badass now, huh? An ex-con parole violator?"

"Whatever. I probably would have gotten probation again, if I hadn't broken that girl's jaw while I was waiting for my court date."

His brows rose, but he didn't look truly surprised. "You broke somebody's jaw?"

I shrugged. "She had it coming."

"You should join the football team," he said, and I laughed.

"You just wanna tackle me."

His gaze smoldered. "We don't need pads and helmets for that."

"No, but we might need a door that actually locks. Speaking of security measures, how'd you get in here, *brother?*"

Nash smiled and sank into the only chair in the room. "I have a way with words."

"The understatement of the millennium . . ." I straddled him in the chair and stared down into his eyes, trying to convince myself that he was real. That he was actually there, in the flesh, beneath me. If I could have a dream, that would be it. "So, what? You just showed up at the door and Influenced your way in?"

"Nah." His grin deepened. "I called first and got myself put on your approved visitors list. *Then* I showed up at the door . . ."

"Your Influence works over the phone?" Nash was a *bean sidhe*—or banshee, to the uninitiated—the little known male of the species. The females were more famous in folklore, because of the girlie, nerve-shredding screech they let loose when they sensed someone near death, but the male *bean sidhe*'s ability is actually much more powerful. And convenient. With nothing more than the sweet, seductive sound of his voice—his Influence—Nash could convince just about anyone to do just about anything. The best part? They thought they actually *wanted* to do whatever he talked them into. It was like hypnosis, only better.

Unfortunately, the effect wore off almost as soon as he stopped talking. So if we were caught, he could probably talk us out of serious trouble *for the moment*, but later, I'd no doubt get written up and lose some privileges.

But Nash was still worth it.

"Apparently. Tod didn't think it would work over the phone, but I never pass up a chance to prove him wrong."

"He knows where you are? Is he gonna tell your mom?" It was a good hour's drive from Nash's house to Holser, and he'd only had his license for a month.

"Nah, but he'll probably use it against me next time he wants to get out of mowing the lawn." He smiled and ran his hands up

my sides. "So how happy are you to see me? I'm guessing this place really sucks?"

"Extremely, on both counts." I kissed him again. His hands roamed upward, but I pushed them back down reluctantly. "We'll only have a few minutes alone."

He scowled. "This place *does* suck. At least the eating's probably . . . plentiful though, right?"

I frowned. "More like pitiful, if today's any indication."

"What does that mean?"

I climbed off his lap and sat on the edge of the bed to get comfortable. "Thursday night, I visited the girl next door—who is screwed up beyond belief, FYI—and had a pretty heavy meal. Last night, I abstained. But then today, I was looking for something appetizing outside right before you got here, and I found . . . nothing."

"Nothing good?"

"Nothing at all. No fear, no panic, not even a taste of chronic discomfort. They're all . . . content."

"Wait. *All* of them?" Nash scooted the chair forward until his knees hit the mattress between mine.

I shrugged. "The two I tried, anyway."

"Well, that's hardly the entire population. Still, what are the chances of two in a row? This is a halfway house, not a birthday party. If the residents were shiny, happy people, they wouldn't be here." He caught my frown and amended. "Present company excluded."

Yet we both knew I was neither shiny nor particularly happy, at least when *he* wasn't around. "According to the director, I'm the only hardened criminal—most of the others are here for possession with intent or truancy. But yeah, there should be some major fear in here. Or at least regret or anger. But I'm getting nothing but peace and acceptance. It's creepy."

"Are you feeling okay? Getting enough sleep?" Nash asked. I rolled my eyes, and he shrugged. "Okay, *any* sleep?"

"Nash, I don't think it's me. I think it's them. I think something's wrong with them."

"How do you know?"

"It's just a hunch, but this place doesn't feel right. I've been here for two and a half days now and haven't heard a single person yell. No one's arguing over chores or showers or food or the phone. No one's arguing about anything. They're all just . . . getting along."

"But isn't that a good thing? You know, rehabilitation and all?"

"They aren't rehabilitated. They're lobotomized. Or at least, neutered."

"Bina, how do you neuter *people?* And *girls*, at that?"

"I don't know, but that's what's happened. They've lost their balls. And you can't tell me they never had any, 'cause if you've never caused any trouble, you don't end up here in the first place."

"Well, *you* certainly haven't been neutered. Or lobotomized."

"Yeah, I seem to be the exception. And the only other thing I'm the exception to is humanity."

"You think you're immune to whatever's wrong with them because you're a *mara?*"

I shrugged again. "I'm kinda thinkin' out loud here. But yeah."

"Okay, but what if you're wrong? What if whatever's wrong here is only affecting *you?* Throwing off your empathy?"

"I guess that's possible." Especially once I thought about it. "They don't seem very scared of me. At least, not today . . ."

"We need a test. Try it on me. Read my fears."

"Nash, that's not a good idea." We'd been down that road; it ended on the edge of a very steep cliff, and I wasn't sure either of us would survive the fall.

"Just try it. I can take it. You know that."

Yeah, I knew. That was one of the reasons Nash and I were

perfect for each other. I could read his fears—could even feed from them, if I absolutely had to—but because he wasn't human, he could stop me whenever he wanted. I literally couldn't hurt him, which was all I could ever have asked for in a boyfriend. Though he was so much more.

And while he could certainly use his Influence on me, I could feel what he was doing because I wasn't human. With a little practice—at his suggestion—I'd learned to break his hold on my willpower. Which meant he couldn't hurt me either.

We were both weird and scary. When I was being truly honest with myself, I had to admit we were monsters, both manipulating people for our own benefit. But we were a *matched set* of monsters. We balanced each other out. Kept each other in check.

Nash and I were made for one another.

"Okay, are you ready?" I asked, hesitantly.

He nodded, and his eyes took on this weird look they sometimes got—like the colors in them weren't quite steady—and he grinned. "Yeah, but make it fun, Bina."

I returned his grin with a sultry one of my own. "Fun" was the least I could do.

As one of several kinds of empaths, I can typically read people's general emotional state at a glance, no matter what they're trying to hide. But it usually takes some small amount of physical contact for me to accurately read someone's fears—to get the nitty gritty details. With everyone else, that contact had to be subtle and small to keep from completely freaking them out.

With Nash, I got to be truly hands-on.

I climbed onto the chair with him again and kissed him, long and deep. His mouth opened against mine, and my tongue met his. Dimly, I felt his hands on my hips, anchoring me on his lap, but then all that faded into the background in a single instant.

I saw his deepest fear in that moment, and it looked like . . . me.

Huh? Nash was afraid of me? That was new. And weird.

In his mind—or maybe somewhere deeper and darker, wherever fear truly lives—I lay on his bed, in his room, in only my Cowboys tee and underwear. I remembered that night.

But why would he be scared of that?

As I watched, he lay on the bed next to me, wearing nothing but a pair of jeans. I remembered that too. He was so warm, and he'd smelled so good.

But this was Nash's fear-memory, not mine, so I shouldn't have been surprised when what I remembered didn't happen next. Instead of kissing me and touching me and looking at me like the world suddenly existed only in my eyes, this fear-Nash climbed on top of me and . . .

The fear-me tried to stop him, but then he leaned down and whispered something in my ear, and my hand fell limp at my side. I stared at the ceiling over his shoulder as his mouth and hands wandered.

And that's when I understood. He wasn't scared of *me*. He was scared of *himself*. Nash was terrified that he'd Influenced me. *No!*

I pulled away from him and stared, my lips still warm from his. "No. Nash, that's not how it happened."

His brow furrowed. "What did you see?"

"Us. That night . . ." I swallowed, then met his gaze so he could see the truth in mine. "You're afraid that you *made* me."

He closed his eyes, and his head fell against the back of the chair. "Or that I *will* make you."

"But you didn't. You never have, and you never will."

He lifted his head, and now his gaze was searching. Worried. "How do you know? *I* don't even know I'm doing it half the time."

I frowned. "What are you talking about?"

"I'm pretty new at this, Sabine."

"Yeah, me too."

"No, not *that*." Nash shook his head and started over. "Well, that too, but that's not what I meant. Male *bean sidhes* are born

with a little bit of Influence, but we don't really come into our full potential until puberty." His face flushed, but his jaw line was firm—he was determined to spit out whatever he had to say. "Anyway, I'm not very good at controlling it yet. Tod says that's normal, and I'll gain a lot of control in the next couple of years, but right now I still . . . accidentally . . . Sometimes I make people do things without meaning to. And I don't want that to ever happen with you."

I kissed him again because I couldn't think of a better rebuttal. And when I pulled away, he looked a little calmer. "Nash, you don't Influence me. I don't think you *could*, even if you wanted to. I'm not exactly a pushover. Not neutered, remember?" I smiled and was relieved to see him grin in return.

Nash laughed out loud, and I kissed him one more time before climbing out of his lap. "Well, I guess you're not the problem," he said, as I settled onto the edge of the bed again.

"Huh? Oh. Yeah." I'd almost forgotten the point of our little experiment. "So, if it's not me, it's them, right? Or something that's happening to them."

"What could be happening to them?"

"I don't know, but the last time I felt that kind of mindless acceptance was when you Influenced the ticket guy into letting us watch *The Last House on the Left* at the movie theater. He felt like these girls felt. Like he was at peace with a decision he hadn't even made for himself."

"You're saying someone's Influencing the Holser girls?"

"No . . ." I frowned again. "There aren't any men on the staff—much less *bean sidhe* men—and anyway, I'm pretty sure I'd know if that were happening. Besides, Influence wears off almost as soon as you stop talking, so it couldn't be any of the dads visiting today, because none of them were outside with the girls I tasted. This is something else. It just *feels* similar to Influence."

"Sabine, whatever it is, it'll probably wear off. It wasn't like this the day you got here, right?"

"Right." BethAnne had felt anything but calm and accepting.

Nash nodded. "And you can't swear it was like this yesterday. Chances are everything will be fine tomorrow, and you'll gorge yourself on some poor girl's agoraphobia."

After BethAnne's nightmare, such a simple fear would be a relief. "And if you're wrong?"

Nash sighed. "I'm not going to talk you out of digging into this, am I?"

"Why would you try? A girl's gotta eat."

He leaned forward with his elbows on his knees. "Sabine, you're supposed to be lying low. It works the same way in here as it does out there." He gestured toward my window, to indicate the outside world. "Your best chance of survival is to go completely unnoticed by humans."

I raised my eyebrows at him. "More of your mom's advice?"

"She's eighty years old, Sabine." Though she looked less than thirty. "She knows what she's talking about."

"Not this time." I shook my head firmly and pushed his hands away when he tried to pull me closer. "My best chance of survival is not to starve to death."

"Why do I get the feeling you'd refuse to leave this alone even if you weren't hungry?"

I shrugged. "At least it'll pass the time."

"You have to learn to let things go, Sabine." He took a deep breath and met my gaze, then spat out what was really bothering him—the reason for the frustration I could taste in the air around him. "You should have told me about Tucker. I would have handled it."

"Nash, that was months ago. And I don't need you to handle things for me." Besides, knowing what I now knew about his tenuous control, I couldn't help thinking that if *he'd* handled it, Tucker would have gotten a sudden, irresistible urge to walk into rush-hour traffic. "I just need you to be here."

"I know." He sighed again and leaned forward and pulled

something out of his back pocket. "This is for when you need me and I can't be here." He handed me a small, slim flip phone. The pay-as-you-go, over-the-counter variety. "They'll take it away if they see it, so leave it on silent and be careful. But call me if you need to talk."

I didn't know what to say. So I kissed him, and when I finally pulled away, he stood. "Does this mean you have to go?"

"I need to be home before my mom gets back. Walk me out?"

I nodded reluctantly, and we moved down the hall and out the front door with a respectable space between us, like any normal brother and sister, even though I ached to be so close to him.

In the parking lot, I gave him a hug, holding him tighter and longer than I probably should have. "Come see me next weekend?"

His eyes looked weird again when he met my gaze, like the colors weren't quite steady. "Nothing could stop me, Sabine."

...

On my way back into the building, I was still thinking about Nash and wasn't watching where I was going. As I rounded the corner onto the front porch, I collided with Becky—one of the day-shift techs—coming up the steps from the other side. She stumbled and dropped a grease-stained paper bag on the step.

"Sorry," I mumbled, bending to pick it up. The bag smelled like French fries, and my stomach rumbled. But when I handed it to the tech, her hand brushed mine, and I froze beneath the onslaught of images.

Becky, on the floor of a dirty public restroom, vomiting thick streams of greasy, half-digested food. Over and over.

Becky, lying in a hospital bed, her flesh so bloated and distended that it hung over the sides. Her face swallowed by fat cheeks and voluminous chins. In the hall, the nurses laughed and joked about Becky the Blimp, just like the kids had in junior high.

On the steps of Holser House, Becky pulled the french-fry bag from my grip and frowned at me like I'd tried to steal her food—exactly what she was afraid of.

I stared after her as she stomped through the front door and took off toward the staff break room, but I'd already half forgotten her fear. All I could think about as I wandered into the building was that whatever was happening to the Holser girls *wasn't* happening to the staff.

Hmmm . . .

* * *

By that night, my dark hunger was gnawing at me from the inside again, much worse than it should have been by that point, demanding that I feed. And I tried. Fighting chills from the cold, hollow ache inside me, I Sleepwalked into sixteen of the nineteen other residents' rooms, starving for a taste of fear. I would even have taken a generic naked-in-the-classroom nightmare, but I found nothing. Not one of the natural sleepers—the last three were medicated—gave up even a trickle of discomfort.

Something was definitely wrong, and I wouldn't make it much longer without feeding. Not with my hunger accelerating for no reason I could figure out. That night, I could only lie in bed and shiver in spite of the warm Texas night, until it was light enough to get up.

Sunday morning, I devoured two helpings of everything at breakfast, hoping that the extra human food would help keep me running until I found a way to fulfill my other, darker appetite. Unfortunately, Greer noticed me shivering while I shoved food down my throat, and when I dumped my trash and set my dirty tray on the stack, she called me into the kitchen.

"Are you okay? You look pale." She tried to feel my forehead, but I jerked away as soon as her fingers touched my skin. They were scalding, and her touch brought with it only a glimpse of curiosity and a smudge of concern. "Sabine, you're freezing! You

need to go to the doctor."

I shook my head without meeting her gaze. "I'm fine."

"You're not," she insisted. "But you don't have a fever, and your appetite seems fine." She hesitated, glancing around the kitchen, then finally turned to pour a mug of coffee from the half-full pot behind her. "Normally, I wouldn't give coffee to a fifteen-year-old, but this might help warm you up. There's cream and sugar on the counter."

I poured both until the coffee looked like melted ice cream, but it still tasted bitter. However, by my second mug, the chills had stopped, at least for the moment.

"Is there anything you want to tell me?" Greer asked, when I finally pushed the empty mug away. "Are you on something?"

More like *off* something. But I only shook my head.

"Why don't you go lie down," she suggested. "And if you're not feeling better by tomorrow, you really need to tell Ms. Gomez, so she can get you in to see a doctor."

But if I wasn't feeling better by tomorrow, there would be nothing Gomez's doctor could do for me, short of putting me out of my misery.

•••

That night, the cold was so bad I could hardly think, the shakes so strong I felt like I was convulsing. How could the hunger have gotten so much worse, so fast?

It couldn't have. Not naturally. So I got out my cell phone and autodialed. He answered on the third ring.

"Hello? Sabine?" Nash said into my ear. His voice sounded warm and groggy from sleep, and I wanted to roll in it. Wrap it around me so I could share his heat and vitality.

"Yeah, it's me." My teeth chattered, even though I'd pulled the covers up over my shoulders, and I couldn't make them stop. "It doesn't make sense. *Everyone's* scared of something."

"Huh?" He cleared his throat. "Oh. Still no fear?"

"Uh uh. There should be plenty to eat here, but there's nothing and I'm cold and it hurts."

"But this is only the third night, right?" He sounded more alert, and springs creaked as he got out of bed. "You've gone longer than that before, haven't you?"

"I've gone a week, several times. But I can't now. Something's wrong with this place. There's no fear here. There's nothing much left of what I took from BethAnne. It's nearly gone, and I'm almost empty, like it was never there. I'm cold, Nash, and I'm scared." The irony of that last statement was even more terrifying.

"Okay, let me think," he said, and I recognized the soft click of his desk lamp.

But I couldn't think. I didn't have the energy, and I wouldn't until I'd fed. "I have to get out of here. Can you come get me?"

"If you leave, you'll get arrested again."

"If I stay, I'll die." I knew it, even if I couldn't explain it. I was getting colder by the minute, like a corpse cooling on the undertaker's table. Something was draining what little energy I had left from BethAnne's nightmare. Was this what she felt like when I fed from her? Was she cold and empty and lonely?

"Sabine, you're not going to die. Just give me a minute to think."

"I have to find something to eat. If you can't come get me, I'll go out by myself and meet you somewhere in the morning." And the truth was that I couldn't come back, if it was only going to happen again. If something was going to drain away the energy I'd stolen fair and square.

"You can't walk around in the middle of the night by yourself. Especially if you're sick."

"Nash, *I'm* the only thing out there to be scared of."

"Tell that to the bus that runs you over, or the drive-by bullet that doesn't bother to look deep into your scary eyes. I'm getting dressed right now. Promise you'll wait for me."

"I swear. Hurry." I flipped the phone closed and pushed the

covers back, mildly surprised that the chattering didn't get worse. Until I realized that the cold was coming from inside me—the covers made no difference, either way.

I'd slept in my clothes, hoping to preserve warmth, so all I had left to do was pull my hair into a ponytail and step into my shoes. And wait. It only took five minutes of shivering and staring at my bedroom door for me to decide I'd rather wait outside.

I snuck out of my room and closed the door softly, then started down the hall with my arms crossed tightly over my chest, grateful that my sneakers didn't squeak on the floor. The night-shift tech was asleep, sitting up in the common room, lit by the game show she'd been watching.

This is too easy, I thought. And I was right. I was halfway across the main room when a door creaked open behind me, and I froze.

"Sabine?"

I turned slowly, still shaking from the cold, to find Kate Greer, the cook, staring at me. One of her hands was still on the cafeteria door, which she'd just locked. At two in the morning.

"Are you okay? Still sick?" she asked, brows lowered in a frown that looked more irritated than concerned.

"I just couldn't sleep."

"You . . . couldn't sleep?" Her frown deepened, and she glanced at the tech still passed out on the couch. "Come in and let's see if I have anything that will help." She unlocked the cafeteria and shoved her keys into her purse, then held the door open for me.

Great. How was I supposed to meet Nash if I couldn't get rid of her? Fortunately, the drive would take him at least forty-five minutes, even with virtually no traffic. So I brushed past Greer into the empty cafeteria, dark, but for a single light shining in from the kitchen.

"You're shaking! Let's get you something warm . . ."

I followed her into the kitchen and sat at the prep table when

she waved one hand at the folding chair next to it. "Why are you here so late?" I asked, still shivering as she poured milk into a microwavable mug.

"Just finishing up some work." Greer set the mug in the microwave and pushed several buttons. "So . . . you can't sleep, you're pale, and you're obviously cold. Any other symptoms I should know about?"

I shook my head, and she watched me while the mug rotated. When the microwave buzzed, she took the milk out and stirred powered cocoa into it, dropped the spoon in the sink and handed me the mug. Her fingers touched mine, and the sudden flash of fear, pain, and anger nearly blew me out of my chair. But the realization that came with it was a million times worse.

None of what I'd felt was hers. It was *theirs*. All of it.

My eyes went wide, but hers only narrowed further. She nodded, like something mysterious finally made sense. But the only thing I understood was that *she* was the problem. Whatever was wrong with the girls at Holser was wrong because of Kate Greer.

How could I not have seen it? She wasn't working the night I'd fed from BethAnne, and she was the only one not scared of me the next day. What the hell was she doing to them?

She leaned against the counter, lightly gripping it with both hands. "Okay, you're obviously an empath of some sort, and based on the situation and your symptoms, I'm guessing . . . a *mara*?"

I blinked, as stunned by her casual utterance of my lifelong secret as by the fact that she knew what I was. And finally, I nodded, for lack of any better response. "So what the hell are *you*?" As hungry as I was in that moment, I could never have drained twenty girls at once, much less over several nights in a row. How had she?

Greer raised a brow at my language, then waved away the question, as if the answer didn't matter. "I'm a fellow empath, of course, though of a slightly different variety." She smiled and

opened the industrial-size fridge for a can of soda. "Wow. A walk-ing Nightmare. Do you have any idea how rare you are, especially these days? Few women have seven kids anymore, much less seven daughters in a row. I'm guessing your parents gave you away?"

"Like a naughty puppy," I said, numb, yet still shivering while I sipped my hot chocolate.

"I've only met one other *mara*, and she was old as dirt. Still scary as hell, though. You could have learned a thing or two from her."

"Wait . . ." I interrupted, as something she'd said finally sank in. "Seventh daughter?"

"Yeah. You know, 'And the seventh daughter of the seventh daughter shall be born a night-hag, and she shall feed from the fear of the innocent as they slumber . . .'" Greer stopped and raised both brows at me. "You haven't heard that, have you?"

"No." *And I'm* not *a hag.* I took another sip, then stared up at her, my mind spinning. "So . . . I have six sisters?"

"Oh, no, not anymore." She frowned, like that should have been obvious. "Not if they gave you up. *Maras* are always born to human families, and it's really hard for humans to believe they're not the top of the food chain. And that their precious baby girl is literally a thing of nightmares. So the seventh daughter is almost always abandoned."

Abandoned? I'd known it, of course, but hearing it outright . . . it kinda stung.

"A couple hundred years ago, there would have been others of your kind to take you in and teach you. But today . . . well, with the popularity of contraception and termination, there are fewer and fewer of you born. Especially in the U.S. So you have to fend for yourself."

She drank from her can and gestured with it. "You know, I knew there was something different about you. The others are like drops of rain in a puddle, but you're a river of fear and resent-

ment. Though based on the looks of you, I'd say that river has nearly run dry. Sorry 'bout that. Collateral damage."

"You're . . . stealing their fear?" And clearly stealing what little I'd collected from them, as well as what I produced on my own.

Greer's eyes flashed in irritation, and her gaze narrowed again. "I'm not *stealing* anything. I'm flushing out the negative energy and replacing it with acceptance and peace—exactly what girls like you need." She hesitated, then gave a little chuckle. "Well, not girls like *you*, obviously. But the others . . ."

What they need? Who was she to decide what they—what *we*—needed?

"But that 'negative energy' is half of who they are! They've been through a lot. They've *earned* a little anger and aggression." I know I had! "You're turning them into . . . zombies!"

Greer's frown deepened, and another chill ran up my spine. "I'm turning them into respectable young women who finally have a chance to make something of their lives. How many of them would even be *thinking* about college and careers if they were still on the self-destructive paths that put them here in the first place?" she demanded, and I felt my temperature drop at least another degree. Goose bumps popped up on my arms, and I swayed on my chair.

She was draining me where I sat!

"This is a mutually beneficial arrangement, and I've made Holser the top halfway house for girls in the state. They should all be grateful to be here!"

Wow. Was she serious? Regardless, she was clearly pissed, and the angrier she grew, the weaker I felt. At this rate, I wouldn't be able to stand up by the time Nash got there.

"What do you do with all the 'negative energy'?" I asked through chattering teeth, trying to calm her down and buy myself some time.

"Well, I need some of it, obviously. A girl's gotta eat, right?"

She grinned and patted her flat stomach, as if we'd just shared a great joke. Nausea churned in my guts at the realization that I'd said the same thing to Nash. "The rest of it I sell, or trade for the healthier energies I'm replacing it with. Fortunately, the dark stuff sells for much more than the shiny-happy feelings, so I still pull in a tidy profit, even after expenses."

"You can sell fear?" I asked around still-chattering teeth, trying to hide my growing revulsion.

"Of course." She shrugged. "And despair and pain and anger and everything at the opposite end of the spectrum, too. Everything is food for something, Sabine. You'd know that better than most."

"I guess." But with her words, a new world had just opened up in front of me, and its dark, gaping maw threatened to swallow me whole. I didn't know how to exist in a world where I wasn't the scariest thing around. I wasn't sure I wanted to. But the new fear that realization should have triggered in me was gone almost before I'd felt it, leaving me light-headed and hollow.

Greer was taking it—all of it—before it could even ripen. And along with my emotions, she was stealing my energy, my very life force, much faster than she took from the others. Whether she meant to or not, she was killing me.

Keep her talking, Sabine . . .

"So . . . you're like me?"

"I'm an empath, yes." She looked irritated at having to repeat herself. "But not like you. I am an *emovere*. By replacing what I take with much healthier emotions, I'm making the world a better place, one rehabilitated delinquent at a time.

"You, on the other hand . . ." She smiled at me in nauseating mock sympathy. "You can't help what you are, but the truth is that you provide no benefit to anyone but yourself. You're a dirty little parasite, sucking people dry in their sleep. Like a giant bedbug." Greer set her soda can down and leaned against the counter at her back. "You're lucky, you know, Sabine. Most people wouldn't

hesitate to squash a bedbug that had burrowed into their home. But I don't want to hurt you."

A statement unsupported by my steadily dropping temperature.

"But you can't stay here, obviously." She shrugged, like we were friends again. Greer gave new meaning to the word "unstable." "One more night, and I might have accidentally drained you dry."

"What?" Her alternative to killing me was to kick me out of my court-mandated halfway house?

"I think the best thing would be for you to leave tonight. Go find some sleeping drifter and have a good meal. The staff will report you missing in the morning, and when the police pick you up, Gomez will send you to Ron Jackson. Problem solved." She brushed her hands together, like she was brushing dirt off her palms.

Was I that dirt?

No. And she couldn't brush me off either.

"Hell no." I said, my hands curling into fists around the edge of my metal seat.

"What?" Greer looked genuinely confused by my refusal.

"I'm not going." I stood, struggling to keep my jaw from chattering, but my legs were steady, since she seemed to have stopped actively draining me. "I'm not going to prison just so you can keep selling stolen emotions on some weird-ass black market. This is where the judge sent me, and this is where I'm gonna stay, until the director decides to release me."

Greer's jaw clenched in fury, and the blue of her irises darkened rapidly. "I can make your stay here very unpleasant, *bedbug*. And very, very short." Her eyes narrowed to mere slits, and pain exploded in my center. If felt like the air was being sucked from my lungs. But Greer wasn't taking air. She was taking the very last of the energy generated from my emotions, and when that was gone, Ron Jackson would be the least of my worries.

"Leave her alone, or I'll make sure you're never seen in the human world again," a familiar, masculine voice said, and I turned to see Nash walking toward us from the cafeteria.

"Nash, no! She's an *emovere*."

"You should listen to your girlfriend, little *bean sidhe*," Greer growled, her eyes almost solid black now. But my pain ebbed when she focused on him. "Your honey-voice won't work on me."

But somehow, Nash was unfazed. "Leave her alone and back the hell off, or you'll spend the rest of your short life in the Netherworld."

Greer laughed out loud. "Take one more step, and you'll spend tomorrow night at your own funeral, little boy."

Nash glanced at me and winked, like he had a plan. Then he took one step forward.

"No!" I shouted. He'd forgotten to actually *tell* me the plan!

Greer focused a wicked black-eyed stare at him. Nash crumpled to the floor.

I dropped to my knees at his side, and the minute my hand touched his face, I realized he was still alive. She hadn't completely drained him. His fear called to me like a lighthouse on a foggy night, but I pushed past that to his periphery emotions. The ones I normally wouldn't touch. Even unconscious, Nash was still furious at her—and still in love with me.

"What is wrong with kids today? You never do as you're told," Greer lamented, as I leaned down and kissed Nash. And this time I fed from his other, stronger emotions though they tasted bitter compared to his sweet fears. And when I sat up, I was no longer shaking. My teeth no longer chattered.

"Take your boyfriend home before I drain you both," Greer said. "And consider this your one and only warning." She twisted to reach for her soda, as if we weren't enough of a threat to interrupt her caffeine fix. The moment her back was turned, I lurched to my feet. I grabbed a lunch tray from the stack on the counter and rushed her.

As she turned toward me, I swung the tray. The edge slammed into her cheek. Bone crunched. Her soda can went flying. Kate Greer fell backward and landed face up on the linoleum. Her head smacked the ground, and her eyes fluttered shut. She was out cold.

For a moment, I stood in shock. Not over what I'd done—it wasn't my first time wielding a lunch tray—but that it had worked. Then I dropped onto her chest, put my hands on either side of her face—the right side of which was now soft and lumpy—and drank long and hard from the well of fear she'd filled earlier that night.

She was glutted with it. Fat and lazy on the inside, and high on her own power. She was also delicious, and I was a poor kid in a candy store, stuffing myself because I knew I might never get a second chance. How often does one even meet an *emovere*?

The more I drank, the better I felt, physically. But the angrier I got. She'd hurt those girls, who couldn't defend themselves from a predator they didn't understand. She'd tried to send me to prison. She'd threatened to starve me if I didn't go. And she'd tried to kill Nash.

So I drank. And I drank. I fed until I had all the fear she'd amassed. I fed until her cheeks went cold beneath my fingers. I fed until her breathing grew ragged and labored.

"Sabine!" Nash pulled on my arm, but I barely heard him. "Sabine, stop! You're killing her." But that was the point. She'd tried to kill him, she *would* have killed me. *Poetic justice.*

"Sabine, I said stop!" That time Nash hauled me off of her, then pulled me away. He wrapped his arms around me and turned us so that his body blocked hers from my sight.

For several long moments, I could only breathe deeply and ride the high surging through me, like bolts of lightning striking me over and over. It was unlike anything I'd ever experienced, and it felt good. I felt hot and alive and powerful. *Scary*-powerful.

Did Greer feel like this every night? No wonder she wouldn't leave! Who could give up that kind of power and . . . feast? And if I

hadn't wound up at Holser, she never would have been caught. She could have gorged forever, convinced that she was shaping the next generation, while stuffing herself and her wallet on the emotions of neglected, abused delinquents.

And now, so could I . . .

No. That was my stomach talking. The sweet, succulent fear. But I didn't need anywhere near as much as she had taken, and neither did she.

Nash pulled something from his pocket, and distantly I heard him speak into his cell phone. "Tod? I need you to get Mom and bring her to Holser House." He paused, and his brother said something over the line. "Well, wake her up! It's an emergency. An *emovere* just tried to kill me and Sabine. Mom has to take her to the Netherworld before she wakes up, or we're all in trouble."

Tod cursed over the line, then said something that sounded like an agreement. Nash hung up and shoved his phone back into his pocket. His hands slid beneath the back of my shirt, and his skin was blessedly cool.

"You're burning up, Sabine. What happened?"

I took several deep breaths, and when I could speak—when I could think straight again—I pulled away to look at him. "I took too much. And it wasn't just fear. She was so full of anger! Everything she took from them, and I drank it." And that's when it hit me. "I would have killed her. Nash, I would have killed her if you weren't here." Then I would have gone after the girls. All of them. Not just what I needed to survive. Because it felt so *good*. They were going to shun me anyway, so why not give them a reason to?

Because you're not a monster. Not really. Not yet, anyway. But I could be . . .

I saw my own true fear in that moment. I was afraid of *myself*. Afraid of what I was capable of. Of what I still wanted to do, with the power still buzzing through me.

Was Greer right? Was I just a parasite, feeding on the weak in their sleep? Was I nothing but a monster?

No. Not as long as Nash saw something else in me. Even if I couldn't trust myself, I could trust him. To see the truth, and to hold me in check. But without him . . . ?

"Promise you won't leave me, Nash," I whispered. "Promise me."

"You know I won't." He whispered it in my ear, his cheek cool against my overheated face.

"Say it."

Nash stepped back and lifted my chin so that my gaze met his. "You're stuck with me forever, Sabine."

"Good," I whispered. But in my head, I heard what I didn't dare say, even to him.

Because I'm not sure what I'd become without you . . .

Vermillion

BY DANIEL MARKS

"This is Amie Shin." The Station Agent gestured in the direction of a petite Asian girl bunched up at one end of the settee like a snowdrift.

Unlike so many in Purgatory, where a quick rub of ash sufficed to dim the glare of their souls, this girl was immaculately painted, her face powdered white, her brows dark with kohl, a deep spot of crimson dotting her tiny pert lips. If it weren't for the bold glow of memory burnishing her eyes, she might have passed for living.

She untangled her legs from underneath her and crossed the slickly polished stone of Manny's office, her ornately embroidered robe fluttering around her and slippered-feet softly shuffling. Extending her hand and nodding sweetly, she said, "I've heard much about your thievery."

Velvet slipped her hand into Amie's and squeezed. "Pleased to meet you . . . I guess. I won't lie, I've never heard of you."

She noticed a sinister assessment in the girl's eyes that traveled all the way down to a grip that lingered longer than any handshake known to man. Velvet jerked away and rubbed at her hand uncomfortably.

She spun toward Nick, widening her eyes to indicate that they might be dangerously close to a crazy person. "Um . . . this is my boyfriend," she said.

Ever the people pleaser, Nick stabbed his arm between them, a big Prom-King smile plastered on his lips, but not for long.

"I'm Nick," he said.

His hand hung in midair. Amie recoiled from it for a moment like he'd slapped some roadkill onto the floor between them. A smile flittered on her lip, brief as a facial tic, and then it was gone. Nick withdrew and gave Velvet a quick glance that verified her assessment that the girl was likely criminally insane.

Amie backed away and curled up again on the couch, glaring at them both. Velvet shivered. Nick gulped audibly.

Manny raised an eyebrow and crossed to the other side of the mammoth room. A study in gray Hollywood glamor, the gun-metal-colored silk gown draped on her slim figure like a cascade of water, and the short train was shirred elegantly. Her hair coiled about her lovely face in perfectly coiffed waves. She flipped open a carved wooden box, set atop a mirrored bureau, and pulled out a pale pink envelope and a slip of folded paper and retired to her writing desk where she jotted notes as they talked.

"We've uncovered an issue," she said, voice echoing across the expanse. She tapped the edge of the envelope into the palm of her hand. "A haunting, of course. But this one is marked by both its chronicity and audacity. Amie was sent to fill us in on the details, so I expect she'll do that."

Manny wove her hands together and gazed across the temple of her index fingers.

Velvet and Nick watched Amie as she rose and paced back and forth between the settee and the Station Agent's kidney-shaped desk, weaving in between the columns of light cast by the gas lanterns, like a vampire would daylight.

"The tremors started only a couple of weeks ago. A light rumbling soon gave way to more moderate shaking and the appearance of the inky shadows rushing into Vermillion like a dense fog," Amie said.

"You got yourself some shadowquakes." Nick flopped into the armchair and pulled Velvet into his lap, hand resting gently on her stomach.

Velvet snuggled in and yawned. "Obviously."

Amie stopped for a moment and glowered before Manny encouraged her to continue. "You must understand, we run a very tight ship in our district and hauntings have declined rapidly in the past quarter. So it comes as a surprise, but not nearly as much of a surprise as who we believe is causing the disturbance."

The girl paused dramatically, scanning their faces. Probably checking to make sure they were enthralled.

Holy crap, Velvet thought. *She's totally full of herself.*

Normally, hauntings are a pretty simple fix. You can count on a shadowquake when there's some sort of psychic meddling going on in the world of the living, but that's not always the case. Velvet knew from experience that ghosts traveling through the cracks could create just as many, if not more, problems than any medium, fortune-teller, witch, or telephone psychic ever could. But, you merely had to scare humans badly enough to put a stop to their shenanigans—a well-placed undertaker and a corpse will suffice, on that count—or just snare the ghost and bring it back to the City of the Dead for a proper comeuppance. *Who in the business didn't know that?* Velvet wasn't sure how they did things in Vermillion, but the Latin Quarter had a massive cellar full of ghosts who were absolutely, positively sorry for what they'd done.

"So who is it?" Velvet asked, taking the bait.

"Our undertaker, Abner Conroy."

It was as though the news stripped the room of oxygen, of sound. Velvet glanced at Nick. His mouth hung open, horrified at the possibility that his counterpart in Vermillion would perpetrate such an offense. Though they were both adept at possessing bodies, Nick's expertise was in raising the dead, not burying them as his job title implied. They didn't make the rules, any more than they picked their occupations. If they had, Velvet would have christened Nick 'The Zombie Guy,' which is way more appropriate. But that's neither here nor there.

"How do you know?" Nick snapped.

"We've long suspected Abner." Amie tossed a hand flip-

pantly. "Well, for the past two weeks, anyway. He was never quiet about his desire to join the revolution, so we were surprised he didn't vacate Purgatory during that exodus with the rest of the criminals. Now he's gone missing. It's been two weeks and the shadowquakes have increased. So what do you think? Who else could it be?"

Velvet pushed herself off Nick's lap, bristled the crinoline of her skirt and straightened the stocking seam rising from her combat boots. "You're sure he hasn't moved on to another of Purgatory's boroughs? You've gone in? You've searched?"

"Of course, we've searched," the girl spat. "We're no amateurs . . ." She struggled for a word. ". . . Miss."

Manny's eyes narrowed in Velvet's direction. She took it as a cue to ease the tensions building since their introduction to the strange and possibly schizophrenic girl. The last thing Velvet wanted to do was get on the Station Agent's bad side. Manny had nearly as bad a temper as Velvet's.

"Of course not, Amie. I only meant to cover the bases," Velvet smiled.

Amie straightened and gave a little nod of acquiescence. "Okay."

"So what is it your team needs from us?" Velvet asked.

"Well, I'm not convinced we need you," Amie said huffily. "But our Station Agent is of a different mind about all this, and we are rather busy, just now."

"What does your Station Agent want, then?" Nick sat forward on the chair, elbows resting on his knees and head cocked to the side. He had that easy comfort about him that Velvet never quite got a handle on, as though he'd never be out of place anywhere . . . even in death. Plus he was smokin' hot. She never turned down a chance to ogle him, profusely.

"He wants you to go in and search, though there's really no need. I've personally exhausted every trail." Amie's voice was condescending and haughty, two words Velvet imagined were

carved into the girl's headstone.

Actually, she was kind of sure of it.

Velvet sneered at her.

Amie glowered back.

"Velvet and her team are the best we have," Manny said, breaking the tension. She folded the stationery and slipped the paper into the envelope. "See that this gets to Howard Barker at the Temple of the Nomadic Star."

Velvet gripped the corner of the envelope and tugged but Manny didn't let go. She glanced up. The Station Agent had a serious look gracing her normally placid face.

"And don't open it please."

"What? Of course, I wouldn't." Velvet chuckled uncomfortably and glanced at Nick, who shrugged in silent judgment. "Really? You have to ask?" She turned the envelope over between her fingers, examining Manny's luxuriant cursive. Letters are so romantic, she thought and shot a suspicious glance in the Station Agent's direction.

The woman cocked her brow, daring Velvet to ask.

"Now, Amie will accompany you on the journey to Vermillion. She's to be your guide. I'm sure that won't be a problem."

"Oh no, not at all," Velvet said. But what she meant was:

Huge problem. Ginormous problem.

• • •

The next morning came terribly early.

Velvet set her bags on the dark platform and sneered at the commotion coming up the ramp. Amie had somehow coerced Nick into carrying her luggage—the biggest trunk in the world. Probably via a little *helpless woman* routine that made Velvet want to throw up nerve endings in a nice wet sparking pile . . . preferably all over Amie.

Nick was, of course, polite about it, but underneath, Velvet searched for a clue that he was seething with irritation, as she was.

He'd better be, she thought.

"Thank you sooo much," Amie said, her face tortured into what was supposed to be a pretty smile but looked like constipation, as far as Velvet was concerned. "I don't know what I'd have done, if I didn't have a strong man to help. I suppose it should teach me to pack lighter, huh?"

Those things at the ends of Velvet's arms were called fists, and she was pumping them furiously and debating whether to hammer them into the girl's face. It seemed like the only logical response. *Stereotype much?*

Nick put the epic leather trunk down next to his girlfriend's carpetbag. Velvet reached down and made sure there was a gap between the two, even just an inch—you never could tell where the dreaded *asshole* virus would strike next, so precautions are often necessary.

"Good morning, Amie." Velvet choked the words from her vocal chords. What she'd wanted to say was: *Are you wearing skin-colored headphones? Because those ears are massive! Damn.*

And at least that would have been the truth. With ears as large as Amie's, you don't wear your hair back. It's just not okay. Ever.

"Ah." The girl's face brightened dramatically when she saw Velvet. "You look so pretty today, with your hair up like that."

Yes, Velvet thought, *I have normal, human-sized ears. I can wear it like this.*

Amie reached up and stroked a length of dreadlock hanging from the pile atop Velvet's head. Velvet resisted the urge to jerk away and simply eked out a curt smile.

Nick ran up next to them, his blond hair flopping about on his forehead and a grin plastered across his face that she hoped wasn't genuine, though she suspected actually was. It was her curse to be in love with someone so nice. And the fact that he was legitimately hot—and not just average, as all her *living* boyfriends had been— filled her with two things: pride and proprietary jealousy.

Her eyes ricocheted off Nick's brilliant smile and back toward the girl who was eying not Nick, as she'd suspected, but . . . her. Amie was watching her in an odd, assessing way.

"How long did you say this trip would take?" Velvet asked.

"No more than a day. So, plenty of time for us to get to know each other. Won't that be great?"

"Awesome," Velvet said sarcastically.

Nick on the other hand was excited. "Can't wait. It gets so boring hanging out in the Latin Quarter. Same old ashen souls wandering the streets every day. 'Hello, how are you?' 'Fine and you?' Ugh. Vermillion, though. Now that sounds exotic to me. Like Chinatown or something, but with less hobos."

"Mmm. Sweet and sour," Velvet said. "Remember that?"

Of course he did. Everyone in the entire City of the Dead could get in on that conversation as though someone had wheeled up a watercooler or screamed "gossip!" in a crowded cafeteria.

"The barbecue pork with hot mustard was my favorite." Nick's eyes rolled into the back of his head as he searched for the pleasurable memory.

"Fried chicken feet at Uncle's Dim Sum." Amie added, trying to join in.

Velvet startled, her mouth agape. "Chicken's feet?"

"Oh yeah, they are delicious . . . and so crunchy. You could just suck the skin right off the bone . . ."

The girl continued to wax nostalgic about her disturbing meal, while Velvet glanced at Nick, happy to see that his face was a sour as hers. Uncle's Dim Sum must have been a mental institution. Maybe Amie just *thought* it was a Chinese restaurant. She seemed easily confused.

Nick leaned over to Velvet and whispered, "Um . . . no. That's so not delicious."

Thank you, Velvet thought. *Chicken's feet are for one thing, so that chickens can walk around a barnyard. What's next, a big plate of fried beaks? Gross.*

She glanced back at Amie and noticed that, at some point during the exchange, she'd stopped talking about gross things that weren't actually food and was staring directly at the two of them. Velvet shuffled her feet uncomfortably.

"That's probably something you have to be brought up eating. It just kind of sounds . . . " Nick searched for the word. "Different. To us. You know?"

Amie's face softened, and she nodded, agreeing. "Sure."

Thankfully, the funicular creaked into the station at that moment. A rickety wooden car with several doors down each side, each fitted with fringed café curtains and brass handles, jerked and heaved as it came to a stop before them. The doors opened and a fresh crop of souls, not an hour between their death and arrival in Purgatory, flooded out onto the platform. They were truly strangers. As strange as they come, ash spread on their skin in a sloppy amateurish way and the glow of lingering nerves beaming from patches of cosmetically neglected flesh. Souls who've been around know to ash generously. The glow can be a real eyesore.

Suffice it to say, they looked a mess.

And for once, Velvet was glad she wasn't responsible for their education.

She glanced at Nick, and thought of their first meeting, months ago, in that gothed-out storefront, amidst tons of black candles, stuffed ravens, and one unscrupulous fortune-teller named Madame Despot who was in possession of an imprisoned soul—a sixteen-year-old sporto guy, the kind Velvet wouldn't ever have even talked to had she been alive. Nick. Velvet and her team had been sent to free him and arrest the Madame.

At the time, Velvet was in the body of a particularly crotchety-looking nurse in her mid-fifties, so it was probably a tad inappropriate to be crushing on the unnervingly hot spirit that spilled out of Despot's shattered crystal ball. It's not that she was being pervy, exactly, it's that she wasn't in her seventeen-year-old ghost

form. But that didn't stop Velvet from eyeing Nick greedily. Even balled up in a fetal position, sandy hair tussled and blue eyes drilling into her brain like lasers, Nick was mesmerizing. And he'd taken to the afterlife so quickly, with aplomb even.

New souls sort of shuffled and moped. Nick stood proud, broad shoulders erect, like he were still alive, and in many ways, of course, he was. More alive than anyone she'd ever known. She'd saved him that day, and later he'd returned the favor. She guessed they'd saved each other.

He tossed their bags on the rack atop the funicular and opened the door for the two young women.

"Such a gentleman," Amie said.

There was something in both the words and the tone that irritated Velvet. Though at that moment, nothing the girl said would have filled her with a warm happy feeling.

Velvet slipped into the funicular and sat back on the long bench, making sure she was between Nick and Amie—there'd be no casual brushing of hands or flirting on her watch.

Not. A. Chance.

The funicular, really no more than a low-tech train pulled along on a single rail, ambled a path through the boroughs, districts, and shantytowns of Purgatory. The Latin Quarter, where they lived, gave way to Little Cairo with its flapping awnings and wide-open markets. In the real Cairo, there'd have been the rich scent of spices piled high in metal bowls, instead of the fragrance-free pigments sold in the City of the Dead. Fantastically colored wool carpets were replaced by stacks of newsprint as tall as the biggest men, some teetering, threatening to fall on the women underneath, rolling them into tubes for the dusty souls to carry home.

Little Cairo spilled into Hipstertown, which despite its name was more longhaired-hippie-types and less expensive-cocktail-bars-with-sidewalk-verandas-and-tons-of-chain-smokers. Though, Velvet had heard that the Salons there were quite

risqué. Only the most irreverent souls ended up settling in Hipstertown. She watched its denizens with speculative intent as the gears and pulleys cranked underneath the car. It shuddered forward past the smirking souls in tight pants and Hello Kitty backpacks, stolen and brought across the gap by their resident Collector, Booda Khan.

"Are you watching for Booda?" Nick asked, leaning toward Velvet. His foot was propped on the bench ahead of them casually, his ankle glowing from the break between his cuff and the wingtip shoes he wore, sockless.

She shrugged, "Of course. He's a legend." Velvet glanced at Amie who was, likewise, eying the bit of flesh Nick was selling.

"Like the religious guy?" the girl asked. Making deliberate eye contact with Velvet, or so she presumed, so as not to eyeball Velvet's boyfriend any longer than would seem unusual or slutty.

"He's only the coolest operator in Collections today," Velvet said. "How can you *not* have heard of him?"

The girl shrugged. Her eyes traveled down the length of Velvet's body, lighting on the silver buckle of her pants. "That's pretty."

Velvet looked down at the intersecting loops that formed the symbol for infinity and smiled. "It is, isn't it? A friend brought it back from the world of the living."

Amie sat up straight. "A boy?" she asked suggestively, eyes drifting toward Nick.

And before Velvet could stop herself, she let it escape. "Yes. His name was Porter."

"Ahem," Nick's eyes were all squinty with suspicion.

"It was a long time ago," she said. "He's not even around anymore. Dimmed and moved on, back before you showed up."

"Hmm," he grunted and crossed his arms across his chest, clearly done with the conversation and none too happy to be in competition with a dead boy, or even a dimmed one as the case may be.

She neglected to go into details. Velvet had been quite fond of Porter, not in love with him mind you, but in a deep . . . *like*, let's say. She'd been holding his hand as he dimmed, the light going out within his soul, eyes darkening, his pale translucent flesh crumbling away like a burnt husk, collapsing. If she'd been nostalgic, as so many are, she'd have honored his passing by spreading his ash on her skin. But she had the silver belt buckle instead and that was plenty to remind her of their brief time together. Of their sweet kisses.

Velvet glanced in Amie's direction and found her grinning evilly. Nick had amped up his irritation to a full glower. In fact, he wouldn't even meet Velvet's gaze, no matter how hard she tried.

"Oh Nyx," Velvet cooed, using his secret pet name. She attempted to slip her hand into his, but he pulled away, glaring out the window at the passing scenery.

Velvet fumed.

This girl wasn't going to drive a wedge between her and Nick, Velvet would see to that. But that seemed to be exactly Amie's plan. Though for what reason, she couldn't imagine. They'd just met, after all.

It usually takes at least three days for people to hate me, Velvet reminisced. Of course, her own judgments ran much quicker than that, and she had Amie directly in her rifle sights.

"You're dead meat," she mouthed at the girl, who merely cocked an eyebrow and continued to smirk.

Velvet rolled her eyes and huffed. Staring down the center of the car, she prayed for a violent derailment.

When Velvet finally ventured a look out the windows again, the first thing to catch her eye was the fading red-lacquered glory of the Pagoda of Vermillion rising high into the sky like a monument. It was in full view, despite the fact that they were technically still traveling through the shacks of Boondock Holler, apparently the place hillbillies went to die. Seriously. Velvet saw no less than three toothless souls with banjos. It was quite fasci-

nating in a National Geographic, don't-break-down-here-if-it's-the-last thing-you-do sort of way.

"Your neighbors are colorful, at least," Velvet snarked.

"They are a wonderful, welcoming group. I do adore them." Amie said sweetly.

Velvet glanced at Nick to find him pleasantly agreeing with the girl. So she sank back into the bench cushion. *Of course*, she thought. I'm *the jerk. That's me. Of course!*

"So, Amie. Why don't you tell us about this errant undertaker we're supposed to capture. Do you know him well?"

She nodded.

"You didn't chase him off, did ya?" Velvet winked at her opponent. "I mean with your sparkling personality."

Amie grinned mischievously. "He's handicapped."

Velvet's breath caught in her throat.

The girl went on, "He can't run at all. He wheels himself around in an antique wooden desk chair. It's quite empowering really. Gets him where he needs to go."

She glanced at Nick, whose only response was, "Nice going."

Vermillion's funicular platform was completely deserted except for a pair of bored adolescents, hands jammed in the pockets of their jeans. When the train car stopped, they rushed to pull the luggage from the roof rack and trailed behind Velvet and Nick, as Amie stomped off ahead.

Amie led them under the high lacquered arch in the stone wall. The ends of the crosspost depicted dragons breathing fire, though the intensity of the flames was diminished by a thick coat of ash settled in their grooves, like some knick-knack you'd find in your grandma's dusty house. Beyond this, the courtyard of the temple complex spread out like a tent city. A hodgepodge of low structures with corrugated metal roofs—unlike the blue tile Velvet remembered from Chinese action movies—lined up in tight rows. Candles flickered inside cheap dollar-store paper lanterns, a few of them burnt down to expose the wire coil forms that made

them look like globes.

Salvaged and often shoddy fixtures and building materials were a sad reality in Purgatory. Most everything needed to be stolen from the land of the living and brought through the cracks between the worlds without being noticed. Oddly enough, the need for subterfuge was the reason the dead were so well-dressed. What else could be misplaced so easily but couture clothing that never sold because of its outlandishness? Velvet hated such extravagant rags, preferring simple factory seconds and combat boots.

A timeless classic.

At the far end of the passage, an open pavilion revealed itself. Inside, sitting cross-legged by a low table, flipping through no less than three books at once in a flurry of page turning, was a middle-aged man in an argyle sweater and wool trousers. Unlike so many they'd passed in Vermillion, this soul left his skin unburnished of either powders or ash. He glowed a vivid amber and, noticing them, brightened both in flesh and smile.

"Amie," he called, rising from the floor elegantly. "Bring our guests up here this minute. I've been so excited to meet Jayne's charges."

Velvet noticed two more things about the man. He spoke in a refined British accent and he'd referred to Manny by what she assumed was her first name. Jayne. It was weird to hear it. She'd heard people call her "Mansfield," and many of the older souls talked about her pin-ups and movies when she'd been a living person, but never to her face. You just didn't do that kind of thing with a Station Agent. Whether she was a sex symbol or not earth-side, dead she was a government official. One with certain charms, certainly. And by charms Velvet meant the dagger-like vessels that hung from the hundreds of keys in the Agent's office. It just wasn't sexy to watch her gouge a man's thoughts from the center of his forehead like she was picking pineapple out of some sweet and sour pork.

Sweet and sour. Mmm.

"I'm Howard Barker, the Salvage Father of these little heathens." He gestured playfully in Amie's direction.

The girl grimaced and planted her hand on her hip. "What did I tell you about those racist comments?"

"Hush girl, we're all souls now. Dead is dead and that's all that matters."

"Pleased to meet you, sir," Velvet said and then remembered the envelope. "Oh wait. Manny gave me something for you."

Nick rushed forward to shake the man's hand politely as Velvet dug in her pockets for the correspondence.

"Nick Jessup," he said.

"I've heard tales about your exploits. The both of you. You're quite famous now."

Velvet pressed the envelope into his palm. "Well, I don't know about that."

Barker retraced his steps to the short table, picked up an opener and slit the pink envelope open like he'd skewered an opponent. He read the letter silently, closing his eyes once he'd finished and holding the note to his heart.

Just as Velvet suspected. A love letter.

It was difficult to imagine Manny cultivating any sort of relationship, with all of her responsibilities as an agent, but clearly there was something going on between these two. If she'd had any doubt, the expression of complete serenity on Howard's face confirmed the truth.

Velvet wasn't sure what to say—she couldn't just ask if they were getting it on—so she opted for the next best thing: changing the subject entirely. Scanning the room, her eyes lit on a desk and behind it a wooden chair on rollers. She cocked her head, layered on the most sympathetic expression she could conjure and said, "Oh, that must be Abner's chair."

Amie began to giggle immediately.

"Whatever do you mean? Abner's chair?"

Velvet should have caught on, but by the time Amie's giggle had turned into full-blown and very mean-spirited laughter, she'd already started to speak. "You know, the one he'd roll around in, what with his . . . handicap?"

"I assure you, there's no such thing as a disabled spirit," Barker gruffed. "If you're looking for some reason to pity the boy, then I'm not sure you're the right one for the job."

"I . . . uh . . . I," she stuttered, glancing again at Amie's hideous grin.

"Well." He slipped the folded piece of paper back in the envelope and trapped it in his pocket. "You'll be needing to get some rest, I suspect. As you're clearly suffering from exhaustion."

Nick, thank God, intervened. "It must have been the fumes from the Boondock Holler bogs or something. Velvet will be fine in a second, sir. I swear."

Barker softened, brows lilting in a clearly paternal way. "Of course."

Velvet glared at Amie, raising her fist threateningly as Barker turned away and sank onto his knees in front of the table again.

"I take it Amie has filled you in sufficiently?" he asked, fluffing the silk cushion before settling in.

"I have." Amie's stare dared her to disagree.

Velvet smirked—vengeance would be hers like a new pair of combat boots. No one pulled a prank like Amie's without retribution. "She's told us the bare minimum, I'm afraid, and about some things there's likely been a misunderstanding. What we do know is you have an undertaker on the haunt and a need to reel him in."

"True, true," Barker said. "Mr. Conroy has been in the daylight for several weeks now. His team started noticing his absences and, when confronted, he'd lie that he'd been taking a walk or welcoming the recently dead. Later, we found that he'd been missing for hours on end. Those hours turned into days. Those days into a week. Not to mention the shadowquakes, but I

don't have to tell you about those."

Velvet shuddered. They were still rebuilding after the last big shadowquake in the Latin Quarter. They were just lucky to still have a dorm to house the team—half of their block had crumbled like Gorgonzola on a salad.

"How long has he been earthside this time?" she asked.

Barker turned to Amie for the answer.

"Nine days or so," she sighed, a look of concern on her otherwise miserable face.

"That's a long time," Nick said.

"Yeah, it is. We really need him back, too. Abner's absence has had a disheartening effect on both Amie and our poltergeists."

Velvet's team had a pair of poltergeists, too. Logan and Luisa were a brother-and-sister act known for their impressively vicious fighting skill and dogged loyalty. In that moment, Velvet missed the two terribly. Not least of all to have some other friendly faces to offset Amie's near constant venom.

"Can we speak to them? Your poltergeists?" Velvet asked, ignoring Amie. From the corner of her eye, she saw the girl shift, her hand propped on her hip like a warning.

That made Velvet smile.

"Tomorrow," Amie intervened. "They're probably sleeping just now. Don't you think, Howard?"

Barker shrugged. "How would I know?"

The girl rolled her eyes and then stared back into Velvet's scrutinizing gaze.

"Could we check?" Velvet pressed.

Amie huffed and turned to the two boys who had lugged her trunk from the platform. "Put that in my room while I take these strangers to meet Ho and Charlie."

Velvet thought she heard the boys mumble the word "witch," though it was undoubtedly and deservedly something a little harsher. Either way, they were right and Amie deserved it. They stumbled off in the direction of one of the little residences,

and Amie stomped off in the other, neglecting to say good-bye to Howard or even direct Nick and Velvet to follow her.

Amie was right though, Ho Min was asleep, but the other team poltergeist, Charlie, was up playing cards with a table of grouchy-looking men. He was a kid of no more than ten when he died, if he was a day; most poltergeists were small and nimble—perfectly suited to their profession as troublemakers. Charlie brightened when he saw Amie approach and, grinning devilishly at the gathered men, tossed his cards on the table.

"Ace-high flush, gentlemen."

The men groaned, slapped the table, and cursed.

"That's called getting your ass handed to you." Charlie gathered the stacks of pressed-paper coins in the center of the table and shoveled them into a cloth sack he produced from the pocket of his robe. "And with that, gentlemen, I'm off to see what my friends want."

More groans.

Velvet liked the kid instantly. She liked any kid that was a little rough around the edges and didn't mind showing it. Filled her with a sense of warmth.

"You cleaned them out," she said. "Respect."

Charlie nodded proudly and looked her up and down. "Thank you, and respect right back. That body is slammin'."

Velvet gulped. Despite being dead for three years, it always slipped her mind that the "kids" in the City of the Dead might not actually be so child-like. Take this little card shark, for instance.

"So you've been around, I take it?" Velvet smirked.

"Long enough." Charlie slipped past, patted her on the butt, and kept walking.

Velvet leaned in to Nick's ear. "I'm liking that kid less and less."

"I think he's pretty funny."

"Whatever."

Amie stood where she was, not even attempting to stop the boy's retreat. Velvet had to dodge around her to follow Charlie, sprinting down the stone path between the outer wall of the compound and a row of well-appointed houses with gaslight instead of candles, casting warm glows against the painted stone walls.

"Hey," she called, Nick beating the ground with his feet as he caught up. "Wait a minute."

The boy ducked into the last house on the left, letting the canvas fabric in the doorway flap close behind him. Velvet poked her head in without knocking.

"Dude, that was too rude." She pointed at herself and Nick. "Guests here. You understand that concept?"

"Yeah. Yeah. What you want?" He emptied out the sack and started to count the coins on his unmade bed, the covers coiled up on the floor like a dog's chew toy.

"What can you tell us about Abner Conroy?"

"He's an okay guy."

"Okay?" Nick asked. "But he's a dirty haunter."

Velvet glanced at Nick, brows raised. He shrugged. His heart wasn't in those words and never would be. In fact, the two of them would have never found each other, would have never fallen in love, if it weren't for the fact that Velvet was a "dirty haunter" herself. Though, she couldn't be blamed, could she? It's not as though her killer could just be allowed to go on torturing and murdering young girls. Velvet wouldn't allow it. But that issue had been cleared up long ago, or at least a few months prior, when Manny had found out Velvet's secret.

"Whatever. Like I give a crap whether he haunts. I've got a job to do, and I do it well. We're all just killing time until we dim out and move on. What's the harm in slipping through to the other side? It don't hurt nobody."

"Except sometimes it does."

Velvet thought about the shadowquakes that happen when souls set their minds to a little mischief in the land of the living. It

was bad enough with all the psychics and the mediums trying to interfere in Purgatory, but add some dead apples to the mix, and it was a recipe for trouble.

Charlie shrugged and finished his counting. "One hundred and eighteen pieces."

"Sweet." Nick whistled.

Charlie nodded in his direction.

Nick stepped forward. "You don't sound like you blame Old Abner for taking off."

"Well no. Not with . . ." He stopped mid sentence.

Velvet thought she saw his eyes dart toward the doorway. But when she slapped the curtain open, no one was there, listening or otherwise.

"You were saying?" she asked.

"I wasn't saying nothin'. Abner's just gone. Isn't it up to you guys to find him anyway? We've got missions and stuff to deal with. Being down a team member doesn't exactly lighten the work load."

He stood up and stripped off his robe immodestly.

Velvet pivoted away and dove head first through the curtain.

She heard Nick saying his good-byes and then he ducked out too.

"That was weird."

"Uh . . . yeah," she said. "I could have gone a lifetime without seeing . . ."

"I meant what he was saying about Conroy."

Back in the open area of the courtyard, they found Amie, changed into a satin tuxedo and top hat, her hair coiled about her face like a caress. She sat atop the table with her legs crossed and skirt slit open to reveal surprisingly long legs for such a short girl. All around her sat the card players, the gloom of their loss replaced by wicked laughter. Glancing across the room and eyes lighting on Velvet, Amie launched into a fit of evil giggles.

Velvet was pretty sure *she* was the butt of the joke.

Amie led them to a tiny gate that opened up into a field. There were so few areas of Purgatory that weren't occupied by some sort of construction so Velvet was surprised to see a paper garden. Origami trees made of twisted metal and newsprint leaves surrounded them like an orchard and beyond that a crude stone wall beset with crepe vines and a small bronze door, no taller than if it had been made for dogs or dolls.

"What's that?" Nick squatted and peered into the shadows.

Amie knelt down next to the door, steadying herself on the iron ashpot standing nearby—a returning soul always returns fresh and clean and bright . . . blindingly bright—and produced a shiny bronze key from her pocket. She cranked the lock and opened the door, revealing a thin crack in the limestone behind it. No ordinary crack, obviously. Not like the ones you jump over to avoid breaking your mother's back, or the kind to which you "just say no" when propositioned by a slimy guy in the 7-Eleven parking lot.

In Purgatory, cracks were doorways. Usually.

The majority of cracks in the Latin Quarter were safely protected in caves, behind big wrought-iron gates. The ones that developed later from manipulations and shadowquakes had since been sealed—or rather, most of them had.

Velvet glanced at the little door, hinges glinting in the low light of the garden.

"So this is the way, then?" Velvet asked, not really expecting a response, and not really getting one.

Amie simply gestured to the spidery crack in the limestone and stepped aside, rolling the key between her fingers.

"You wouldn't lock us in there, now would you?" Nick joked, unbuttoning his vest, and drawing the attentions of both girls.

Velvet lingered on the shimmering glow of her boyfriend's chest, until she felt another set of eyes perusing the merchandise, however.

She snapped in Amie's direction. "We've got it from here,

thanks. Unless you'll be accompanying us?"

"Why would I?" Amie retorted. "You're so *good* at your job."

"Then maybe you should run along and give us a little privacy?"

Amie arched her neck and peered around Velvet at Nick, who continued to undress. Velvet stuck her head directly in her way. "Seriously. It's called loitering, look it up."

"All right," Amie threw her hands into the air. "I was just trying to be helpful. But you're the big Body Thief, aren't you?"

Velvet rolled her eyes and wished for the girl to simply disappear. Then she pivoted and shielded Nick's body as it thinned and stretched, becoming less corporeal by the second until, finally, he slid his whole self into the crack, like a letter into a mail slot.

"Stay away from him." Velvet warned.

"Oh," Amie cooed. She held up her delicate white fingers and brushed them against Velvet's cheek. "And what if it's not Nick I'm after?"

Velvet shrank back, and the girl cackled viciously, turning and striding back through the garden happily. She may have even been humming.

Doesn't she know I'll hurt her? Velvet fumed.

• • •

Slipping through cracks doesn't really feel like travel. It doesn't feel like anything. One minute you're stretching out, naked as the day you were born, only slightly less . . . *there* than you were before, and the next you're popping out on the other side, looking exactly like you did the moment before you died.

Like a memory.

It might seem silly to strip down to your birthday suit for the process, but as Velvet knew from experience, when a soul pops back into the City of the Dead, it's kind of nice to have clothes that haven't been shredded to ribbons. It's hard enough for Collectors like Booda Khan to bring clothing through into Purgatory,

but getting them back out is another thing, entirely.

The crack let out into a bright bustling kitchen, white floors scuffed with black rubber, and men and women in tomato sauce-spattered chef whites. It took a bit of hunting to pick Nick out of the clamor, especially when Velvet could only see the back of his body, transparent and protruding from the far wall like a piece of modern art, meant only for her eyes. Or any other ghost's, she supposed. But, to get to him, they'd have to go through her first.

"Nick!" she shouted over the din of the kitchen.

He thunked out of the wall and waved excitedly. "Over here."

"Could you believe that bitch?" Velvet asked as she slipped her arm around his waist, or through it, as was the case. Souls in Purgatory were at least solid. In the "daylight"—as they some-times called "being on earth"—souls were opaque and flimsy as smoke. She had to make a conscious effort to give her hands enough form to touch her boyfriend.

Nick shrugged. "What I can't believe is how good the food looks. Reminds me of Sal-Antonio's on First. They had the best braciole in tomata gravy." His voice took on that affected Italian New York accent that you hear so often on TV.

Velvet glanced at the trays that passed and marveled at the shiny silver domes covering them. "Fancy," she noted and stuck her head through the wall.

On the other side, the dining room was packed with hun-dreds of hungry diners, cramming forkful after forkful of deli-cious-looking food down their salivating maws. She watched a plate of linguine with clam sauce being delicately served to a nearby patron, a staunch and starched gentleman in a pin-striped suit with a cloth napkin shoved into the neck of his dress shirt. He already had his fork in his hand by the time the plate connected with the tablecloth.

"Enjoy-a!" the waiter pronounced and trotted off with a little skip.

It was too much to take. They'd been talking about sweet and sour pork and stuff and now all this yummy food? Velvet couldn't resist.

She glanced at Nick's head sticking out of the wall next to her like a hunting trophy. "You thinkin' what I'm thinkin'?"

"Probably."

"Well I'm thinkin' we do a quick little possession and fill our mouths with some yum."

He nodded. "Then yeah. We're thinkin' the same thing. Yeah."

They didn't need a count of three, just rushed forward. Velvet dove headfirst into Mr. Pin-Stripe Suit, his cheeks already puffed out with creamy, garlicky clams. He was in a state of such taste-bud ecstasy that he barely noticed Velvet locking his mind away and taking possession. She always imagined encasing minds in an imaginary box near the subject's left ear. Whether there was a box or not, she could care less. The visualization was the important thing, you understand.

Nick struck out for the man's date, a woman in a poofy gown. She could have been his daughter, but she wasn't—Velvet felt the girl's hand on the man's thick knee the minute she slid him on like a new outfit. She watched as Nick took hold of the girl's brain and jerked her hand away prudishly.

"It's just me, knucklehead." Velvet chided.

"Yeah," he said. "But right now, you're kind of a guy."

Velvet ignored him and glanced down at the plate. *Swoon*. It was hard to figure out what to do first. The extent of a Purgatory-bonded soul's nourishment was the entertainments they took in at the weekly Salons. But this. *This* was real food. And she planned to cherish the experience.

She scraped a clam out of its shell and spun it in the creamy sauce, plunging the tines of the fork deep in the noodles and spinning. She didn't much care if she was making the guy look like a pig or not. She shoved the giant ball of slippery noodles and

seafood into his mouth and chomped like a pig at the trough. The garlicky goodness exploded throughout her senses, and she closed her eyes, munching quietly as the clamor of the room was washed away in her rapture.

"Oh, oh. I think that's our guy!" A woman's voice stuttered.

It took Velvet a second to realize the voice came from Nick. She opened her eyes to see Mr. Pin-Stripe Suit's date, face smudged with chunks of marinara and noodle debris, pointing across the room. Velvet followed her gaze and noticed a man, wearing sunglasses and a waiter's uniform, shoving his arms into a raincoat.

She shoved one more forkful of pasta into the man's mouth and gave it a final loving chew before dispossessing the body and darting through the room after their prey. Turning around mid-run to scream for Nick, she noticed she was waist high in the center of one of the round tables, a fluttering hurricane lamp glowing inside her abdomen.

She chuckled a bit at the sight.

Once Nick had given up on his food—the man's date spasmed a bit as he disentangled from her—he joined her, running flat across the restaurant. Nick wasn't nearly as proficient with the living as he was the dead. *You should see him maneuver a corpse, though*, Velvet thought. Fast zombies *do* exist. At least when Nick was working on them. But she didn't have the stomach for the job and, thankfully, she'd only had to steer a dead body once.

Velvet darted for the door, Nick hot on her heels.

They sped out the front door and into a dark rainy street. Huge drops pelted off car roofs in sharp *tink*s, a salty wind blew, and the shadows of young lovers holding each other under umbrellas stretched toward them like freaky mushrooms grown up out of the sidewalk.

There was no sign of Abner Conroy.

"Do you think he saw us?" Velvet asked. "Or *you* rather, since

you were pointing at him like you'd seen an alien or something."

"Um . . . I was distracted."

She nodded. "Mmm hmm. Well, he's definitely working in the restaurant. So close to the crack, he's literally *on top* of it. It doesn't make sense that the Vermillion team couldn't find him."

"Maybe they weren't looking," Nick suggested.

Velvet thought about that for a moment. They *had* said they were terribly busy. But what had she and Nick really seen? The kid spent his evening conning old souls out of their paper coins, Amie was busy all right—being a bitch and a tease, to put it mildly— and the other poltergeist enjoyed her snooze time. Not quite as active as Amie had led them to believe, it's true.

"I think you're right, but we'll have to get to the bottom of it tomorrow. Tonight we'll have to go back and endure some more of Vermillion's warm and cheery hospitality." She turned, and they padded back into the restaurant.

...

Velvet slipped her feet between the horribly scratchy sheets draped over her thin canvas cot, a far cry from the comfy pillow-topped mattress that she'd earned in the Latin Quarter Salvage dorm as the leader of the team. It was like she was in the military or something. Clearly Vermillion had something to learn about comfort.

She'd hardly made a dent in the paper-thin pillow supplied before she heard a soft rap of knuckles against wood.

"Are you busy?" Nick was no more than a shadow in the doorway, barely visible if it weren't for the glowing orbs of his eyes.

"Nope just thinking." Velvet slid her legs out from under the flimsy afterthought of a blanket and reached out for him.

A moment later they were in each other's arms, Nick's lips pressed against her throat, into the clefts of her shoulders. "Whatcha thinkin'?" he murmured.

Velvet pondered the question. *What had she been thinking?*

Nick didn't wait for an answer. He pressed soft kisses onto her eyelids, down each cheek. He covered her mouth with his, nibbling at the flesh there, beseeching her with tiny invasions from his tongue, cradling her head to pull her more deeply into his affections.

Oh my God, she thought.

The boy could kiss. But he could also make her forget.

From the first days of their acquaintance, Nick was her biggest distraction. A welcome one, at the time, but dangerous. Loving him put everything she held dear at risk: her job, her friends, her reputation. It was against the rules to fraternize with your team members. So they hid. Making out in the shadows. Sharing kisses in those brief moments of privacy.

Lucky for them—and it *was* that: pure luck—a wicked turn of events and a show of heroism allotted some leniency. Manny had pulled the necessary strings and now they could be together openly.

Lucky.

But even then, wound up in shrouds of blankets like a pair of mummies, Velvet and Nick couldn't be entirely open about their love. The dorm was quiet. Their voices had to be hushed.

"Nyx," she whispered his secret epithet, the word stretching out into a whimper.

A smile played across the boy's lips, the flesh around them rubbed clean of ash and glowing like the blush from a slap. "Velvet," he moaned and trailed the tips of his fingers down to her waist.

Then the bed began to shake, but it had nothing to do with them.

"Nick," she said.

He hummed some unintelligible response into the flesh of her neck.

What started as a low rumble from deep beneath them, soon

shook the walls of the cinderblock cell. Grits showered from gaps in the rattling metal roof. Screams filled the air.

"Dammit!" Nick yelled and in an attempt to scramble from the bed, crashed to the floor, dragging Velvet off, too, their feet twisted in the bed sheets.

She was about to shout, "Shadowquake!" But the darkness was already coiling around the gas lamp outside the door, squeezing the last of the light and casting Velvet and Nick into the darkest of shadows.

They bumped into each other, stumbling. Velvet replaced her pajamas with a pair of tights and her plaid skirt. She crammed her feet into her unlaced boots, while Nick buttoned his shirt and hurridly tucked it into the waistband of his pants. She wiped the ash from her hands and forearms onto the scratchy sheet. Then she held her hands before her like a pair of lanterns. Nick looked up from tying the laces on his wingtips and squinted.

"We gotta hurry," Velvet said, pushing past him. "We might be able to catch Conroy in the act, bust this case wide open, and get out of this hellhole!"

But shortly after taking their first wobbly steps into the slender alley between the cottage rows, the shaking and darkness subsided. The inky tentacles that always accompanied shadowquakes receded into the dark corners of walls, into the eaves.

Velvet's heart sank. Time was running out, they needed to cross over quickly.

The courtyard was a flurry of activity as they raced through it. Barker gathered the bulk of the temple's residents under the pavilion. Charlie and a girl, Ho Min, flanked him.

"Is there anyone missing?" Velvet yelled in the man's direction.

"I haven't seen Am—" he started.

"I'm here!" Amie yelled from the back of the crowd glowing bright and totally free of ash.

Velvet pulled Nick close. "You see that? Either she's got a

great skin care regimen, or she's fresh from a trip through the crack."

Nick nodded.

Velvet glared at the girl. Amie stared right back, a crooked smile curled onto her lip like it was caught on a fishhook.

"I'm going back. Stay here and watch her. I don't trust her for a second, and something's wrong." Velvet raced off.

...

Velvet didn't have to search for the source of the shadowquake after all.

She stumbled out of the crack and into a destroyed version of the busy kitchen they'd passed through earlier. Gas stove-top burners raged with flame, but their pots were overturned on the linoleum floor, crimson sauce splattered up the walls like blood spray on a forensics TV show. Knives and carving forks protruded from the ceiling and, as Velvet looked closer, she saw a carrot sticking out of the wall.

Pretty stereotypical haunting-type stuff, she thought. But it seemed a little over-the-top. Most hauntings didn't show any outward signs, but rather were simple unwarranted possessions. This one seemed—she took another look around—amateurish.

On the far end of the kitchen, near the swinging doors, sat the waiter she'd assumed was being possessed by Conroy.

Approaching him, Velvet realized if this were the same guy, the undertaker had since disposed of his body. It was empty. The eyes were flat, dim—no ghost, no matter how skilled, was able to mask their glow through a body's eyes. She glanced around the room for signs of another spirit lingering in the shadows, to no avail.

Just then, the swinging doors crashed open and a petite, young waitress with short-cropped brown hair like a pixie and a nose as narrow and blunt as a pencil eraser ran into the room.

"Emile, the police are here. They want to talk to you."

The waiter's face fell into his palms, and he shook his head, groaning.

Pixie Girl squatted beside him, concern spread across her features. She pulled a napkin from her apron pocket and dabbed at a trickle of blood trailing from the battered guy's ear down his neck.

"Just tell them what we all know," she whispered.

Velvet leaned in closer, intrigued.

Emile, as the waiter's name apparently was, slapped his hands against his thighs and glared at the young woman, furiously. "They're not going to believe that all this . . ." He flailed his arms about.

Pixie Girl's eyes followed his. She chewed at her lip, discouraged.

". . .That all this was done by some invisible entity. They just won't."

So they know, Velvet thought.

The amount of energy it took to do the kind of damage on display at Il Fortuna was definitely enough bad juju to cause a shadowquake but, clearly, from the looks of Emile, the kitchen hadn't been the target. The haunting wasn't about the restaurant at all. As though they'd heard Velvet's epiphany, the two waiters continued:

"But it's not been just this once," Pixie Girl said. "And it's always you that gets hurt. Look at you this time! Your black eyes were just beginning to fade, too."

Emile nodded, clutching at his hair. "I know. I know. But it doesn't matter. They'll just think I'm crazy. Better just to lie and say it was a vagrant or something."

"Maybe you should ask for some time off. Get out of here."

"I need the cash. The tips. It's not like there are jobs out there, you know."

From the dining room, Velvet heard the sound of heavy boots stomping, getting louder as they approached; the cops coming with their questions.

Questions. She had some of her own. *What did Abner have against this particular guy? Who was this waiter anyway—this Emile?*

She listened through the police officer's bland and patently uninteresting line of interrogation. When none of her questions were even remotely touched upon, and the restaurant had emptied out and darkened for the night, Velvet slipped back into the perplexing world of Vermillion. She was going to figure that place out, if it was the last thing she did.

· · ·

The courtyard was quiet.

She didn't notice a single ashen soul upon her return until Barker coughed from the shadows. A second later she saw a match flare and the wick of incense begin to glug its pungent smoke into the air.

"Come." Barker beckoned, patting the cushion next to him. "What have you learned?"

She padded over and sank down. "A whole lot and not enough, I'm afraid. Abner apparently has a grudge against some guy named Emile, a waiter at a restaurant called Il Fortuna. He was beaten bloody tonight by an 'invisible entity.' His words, not mine. The place was a wreck, too. Abner is a pretty angry guy."

The words felt false in her mouth. What had the little card shark said? Abner was an okay guy. It was like they didn't even know him. Velvet and Nick were close friends with their poltergeists. They *knew* each other. These people seemed to be skirting around the issue. Hiding something.

"That's unfortunate . . . ironically." Barker spun the stick of incense between his fingers until the smoke spiraled like a ribbon on a present.

"Do you know if Abner had any connections to that place?" Velvet asked.

"Not at all. But I'm certain you'll find out."

"I wish I was so certain." She glanced around. The place was

deserted. She didn't notice even the creepiest resident of the temple complex lurking. "Where is everyone, anyway?"

"I sent them to bed." A glint from the nearby gaslight caught in Barker's eye, as he stared at her, contemplating his next statement. "You know, Abner was very close to Amie."

The tiny hairs on Velvet's neck stood up at the mention of the girl's name. "In what sense?"

"I think he had a crush on her. She, being Amie, had very little interest in him. In fact, as I'm sure you've noticed, our Body Thief can be a bit abrasive. I suspect," he paused. "I suspect she has some unresolved issues from her death. She 'struggles,' if you know what I mean."

"We all do. It's no reason to be a . . ." Velvet was going to say 'bitch,' but thought better of it. ". . . mean person."

Barker shrugged.

"So I guess I should talk to Amie." Velvet sighed.

The man shrugged again and stubbed out the incense. "In the morning. It's quiet now, and I don't expect it'd stay that way if you confronted her this evening, considering the animosity I sense brewing."

Velvet took that as a cue to head back to her bed. She thought about Barker's final words. About the "animosity." Why was Amie so hateful toward her?

The girl had made it perfectly clear that she was engaging their services under duress, but what was it specifically that bothered her about Velvet and Nick?

• • •

"Velvet?" Amie's horrid voice crept in, destroying the quiet solitude of Velvet's cell and waking her . . . rudely.

She pushed herself up on her elbows and sighed. "What do you want, Amie?"

The girl slunk across the shadowy room and sank onto the foot of the mattress.

"It's just that I feel like we have quite a connection, you and I." When Velvet didn't respond, she continued. "Since we share the same job and all."

Velvet stared. She had no clue what the girl was talking about. *Didn't Amie hate her? Hadn't that been established?* They *were* both Body Thieves, that was true, but beyond that, as far as she could tell, they had absolutely nothing connecting them. Since Velvet wasn't a complete skeez.

"You look pretty in the soft glow of the candle light." Amie slipped her hand under the sheet and inched it toward Velvet's calf.

She threw the sheet off and glared at Amie's hand, then up to her surprised face and back to the hand. Velvet was glowing all right, but this time it was the furious glow of the remnants of her nerves being pushed to the far side of *enough*.

"What do you think you're doing?" Velvet demanded as the girl snatched her hand back into her own lap and hung her head in shame. Then Amie broke into sobs and darted out of the room.

What the heck was that about? Velvet wondered. *Apparently it's crazy time.*

Was she putting out some sort of lesbian vibe? She knew she could be a little butch, but she liked to think of that as assertive. And she certainly thought other girls were pretty, because they were—some boys too. But she'd never made any passes at Amie, unless the girl viewed contempt as a come-on.

Velvet decided she wouldn't be able to sleep unless she got to the bottom of this. She hopped out of the sorry excuse for a bed, out the door, and into the open-air hall. Behind the thin doors and drapes that rustled in the doorways, she heard the soft snores of sleeping souls; saw the flicker of candles and the acrid scent of incense wafting through Vermillion's air from the balconies of the massive pagoda.

She crept toward the far end of the row, half expecting Amie to jump out from the shadows and pin her to the wall with a kiss

as unwanted as a tissue full of ether. Or scurry past with someone's bunny, ready to boil it alive.

Outside the canvas flap draped across Nick's doorway, Velvet
heard whispers, soft cooing.

She shook her head, the ire rising inside her like bile, thick as
curdled milk.

You didn't run far, did you Amie?

Bitch.

Craning to listen, Velvet curled her fingers around the tattered edge of the curtain and gripped it with such intensity her
knuckles glowed a metallic color in the cracks of her skin. "You're
so beautiful Nick," the girl whispered. "So strong. What do you
see in that girl? That horrible ugly girl?"

What the hell? Um . . . no. This was not happening.

Velvet tore at the curtain with such force the rod holding it
dislodged from the wall and clattered against the cobbled hall.
Inside, Amie gasped and fumbled to cover her nude torso with
the edge of Nick's blanket. The boy looked genuinely stunned,
the light from the globes of gaslight on the far wall lit up a face so
groggy that Velvet could almost mistake it for deep sleep—if she
didn't know better.

If she didn't know what Amie was capable of.

Dirty whore.

She wouldn't have been surprised in the slightest to find the
girl smothering Nick with kisses.

"What's going on?" Nick growled, inching up onto his elbows
and grinding sleep crumbs from his eyes like a four-year-old.

"Why don't you ask your *friend*?" Velvet didn't like the sound
of insanity creeping into her voice, the high-pitched lilt of the
super jealous didn't suit her and she knew it.

"What?" Nick startled and jerked his feet up and away from
Amie. "What? What?"

"Oh for chrissakes!" Velvet shouted. "Cut the crap, Nick. I
heard her. I *saw* her!"

"It's true, Nick," Amie sighed. "She was right outside. She knows everything. It's useless to deny it. Tell her." She urged him with a sympathetic nod.

Velvet simmered. Eyes darting from the girl to Nick, back again.

"Tell her what?" he howled, slapping the mattress angrily.

The girl simply shrugged, letting the sheet fall loose from her nakedness.

Velvet cringed, turning to search Nick's face, watching him go from tense teeth-grinding anger to a shocked realization that he was caught, no doubt.

His mouth dropped open.

"You don't deny it then?" Velvet challenged. "You've done things with . . . this . . ." She flipped a hand in Amie's direction. "Walking STD?"

"Hell, yes, I deny it." Nick snatched the sheet away from Amie and bound it around his waist, hiding the lucky clover boxers Velvet had given him for his birthday, but not his magnificent torso. It would have been easier to be disgusted with him, if he didn't look so hot, but Velvet was pretty sure she could still manage it.

He rushed across the floor toward Velvet. "I don't know what kind of game she's playing." His head whipped in Amie's direction, and he yelled at her. "Put your top on! Jeez."

Velvet turned and stomped outside, her feet tangling up in the drape and nearly tripping her. She would have fallen flat on her face if Nick hadn't caught her mid-dive and twirled her into his arms.

"You're crazier than her if you think something happened in there!" he shouted, eyes wild with terror.

She jerked her head away, staring off down the passageway.

The dead are nosier than you'd imagine. Soon after the yelling started gray heads were poking out of doorways and around corners, whispering intently, hot for some new gossip.

Vultures, she thought.

She pushed Nick away. "Just stay away from me, unless you want to be picking nerve endings out of your smashed skull."

Letting go of her, Nick crossed his arms and glared. "Fine!"

"Fine is right," she mumbled over her shoulder as she marched back toward her room, glowering at each and every startled soul on the way and slamming the flimsy door behind her.

A crack splintered up its shoddy center.

Velvet glowered back at it and flinched.

She wished they'd never come to Vermillion. And more than that, she wished they'd never met Amie Shin. And more than *that* she wished Nick had never laid eyes on the skinny bitch.

Amie.

This was all her fault, after all. *Of course, how hard is it to push a tiny Asian girl off your junk? Damn boys and their weak fortitude. It was all only a matter of time*, she supposed. It's not like she'd ever had a relationship work out.

Even when she was alive, boys had been a fleeting quantity. All façade. And all the same inside. Pervs.

But she'd thought Nick was different. She was sure of it.

She glanced up at the door and whispered, "If you're different Nick Jessup, you'll knock on that door in the next five minutes."

Velvet lay on her side and stared at the crack and waited.

And waited.

Until finally she drifted off to sleep.

•••

In the morning—or what passed as morning in Purgatory: just a different shade of night, as far as anyone could tell—Velvet piled her dreads atop her head and bound them in strips of leather from her suitcase. She smeared her face and arms with ash where it rubbed off on the flimsy pillow overnight, covering the soft glow of her flesh. Outside of her quarters, there was movement, a

scuffing against the cobblestone path.

The dorm coming to life, she imagined.

Freshly gray souls gathered themselves up for the day, readying to bind paper, go on collection runs through sanctioned cracks into the world of the living, or join up with their salvage teams, lining up to get instructions for the day from their Station Agent.

She found she missed Manny and her friends in the Latin Quarter dorms, but most of all Luisa, one of the twin poltergeists on their team. She'd have helped her to think this whole Nick/Amie thing out.

Velvet peered up at the towering pagoda; its faded red paint chipping away like dry skin. She noticed a faint hue on the cobble at her feet and wondered if the whole of Vermillion were sprinkled in the color, if it all came from the pagoda or if there was something else at play here.

She wondered lots of things.

Whether Manny and Howard met in Purgatory or whether they knew each other when they were living. She imagined that the card players in the courtyard were previous participants in the World Poker Tour that seemed to be on TV every day when she'd come home from school when she was alive.

But mostly she wondered about anything, just to stop thinking about Nick.

It was a pleasant morning otherwise, and she found herself wandering uninterrupted into the secret paper orchard behind the temple compound. Gravel grated under the soles of her combat boots, and the paper leaves and wire branches crinkled in the dark breeze. Overhead, the sky glowed with passing souls, like shooting stars. There seemed to be thousands that day, speeding past. Constant reminders that the rest of them were all stuck in the City of the Dead until their time came to dim and fade away.

The souls mocked her—all blinky and happy. She imagined them flipping her off as they passed on to heaven, or wherever.

Jerks.

"They're beautiful," Nick said as he stepped into the garden. Velvet said nothing.

He didn't try anything as stupid as touching her. He had enough sense to know she was still angry. But he did keep talking. "I don't know what you heard last night Velvet, but you have to believe me, I was asleep."

She shrugged as though she didn't care. As if the whole thing were behind them and they'd moved on to a strictly business relationship, for that was all it should have ever been.

For chrissakes, they *worked* together.

"We have a job to do," she said and strode off in the direction of the little bronze door.

But when she got there, she realized she'd have to disrobe in front of him. In front of the one who'd wronged her. She suddenly felt vulnerable and clenched her arms around herself.

"You've got to give me the benefit of the doubt here!" Nick lunged in front of her, forcing eye contact.

Or attempting to.

She looked away. *Did she have any doubts? Was there reason to believe he hadn't been involved?*

Only one.

Amie had gone straight to him, after Velvet had shot her down. That part didn't make sense. But the stuff she was saying was so ugly. And, well, she had been as topless as a diseased stripper, too.

She shook her head and opened the wooden hamper next to the metal door in the wall. Starting to pull her boots off, she nearly fell over, but Nick was there to steady her. His strong hands on her shoulders, his breath on the back of her neck, lips so close to that sensitive flesh.

"I love you, Velvet," he whispered. "And this thing with Amie isn't going to change that. And your doubts aren't going to change that. And Amie sure as hell isn't going to change that."

Something in her softened and she craned her neck a bit and nodded that she'd heard him.

Softened but not accepted.

Velvet stuffed her clothing into the box and used the key to open the little door, revealing the portal crack behind it.

...

A moment later they were speeding through the freshly cleaned kitchen. Hair-netted sous-chefs chopped onions into piles like anthills, and pots of sauces were lined up on the stoves bubbling with salty tomatoey lava and rich cream. It must have been lunch. Fewer customers ringed the white tablecloths, and only a handful of waiters bustled around, none of whom was Emile, hiding his bruises behind sunglasses.

"Where are we headed?" Nick spoke in as delicate a manner as someone as deep in crap as he was should.

He was getting good at this part, Velvet noted. Meaning: dancing around the issue at hand. Of course, he'd said everything he needed to, regardless of its implausibility. And to be honest, Velvet's doubts were gaining on the circumstantial evidence. No matter how she played it out, the timing seemed off.

What was the girl up to? Trying to seduce both of them?

That was just plain weird, if not the most slutty thing *ever*.

She didn't answer and, instead, swept through a door marked OFFICE and straight to the single file cabinet in the dark room.

"Whatcha doin'?" Nick asked.

Velvet traced the word EMPLOYEES on one of the drawers and forced her head through the metal, cramming her hands in the sides of the cabinet. Ghosts don't glow enough to draw attention to themselves in the daylight, but in a pitch black space, it was enough. She thumbed through the files until she found Emile's address and withdrew.

"2622 Colonial. Let's find the waiter."

She ran from the room, an idea starting to form in her head. *Why had they been called to find Abner Conroy, when clearly Amie was not a busy salvage team? Why couldn't Amie's team find him them-*

selves? Why couldn't Amie's team provide some, even a little, protection to Emile?

"If Amie and Vermillion really needed our help, why has she been so mean?" Velvet asked as they ran down the street. "And then alternately so aggressively sexual . . . and not just with you?"

Nick's brow arched.

"What do you mean?"

Velvet stopped, shrugging limply. "Before I caught her in your room, she'd come to mine."

He shook his head, the idea not quite catching. "Amie came on to you? What?"

Velvet ignored the panicked tone in Nick's voice and, in one smooth sidestep, plunged into a stranger waiting at the bus stop, asked a passerby for directions to 2622 Colonial, and stepped back out, leaving the person only slightly confused.

Velvet stared at the woman she'd just recently possessed. Her face was scrunched up like she thought something was wrong but she couldn't quite put her finger on what it was.

And that was it. That was the thought bouncing around in Velvet's head, just underneath all the Amie-anger.

"She's trying to confuse us," she said.

"Sexual subterfuge!" Nick shouted.

Velvet shook her head. "What?"

"It's like this," he said, suddenly animated and waving his hands around wildly. "You watch enough spy movies, and you start to catch on. Amie is like Mata Hari."

"Who's that?"

"She was a double agent in World War I. Seduced guys on both sides of the war and funneled information back to Germany. Eventually they beheaded her."

"I know someone in need of a good beheading." Velvet started in the direction of Emile's apartment.

"So yeah. She's using both of us, but *for the same purpose.*" He said the last words emphatically, as though he'd figured every-

thing out and was exonerated entirely.

Velvet didn't have the venom in her to correct Nick—it wasn't like Amie was getting valuable information from them, nor were they on opposite sides of a war. She waived it off. "And what about Abner Conroy? Or Emile? How do they fit into all this?"

Nick shrugged, sheepishly, scurrying along beside her. "Don't know."

"Well then, we better find out because I've no intention of spending another hell night in Vermillion." Velvet stomped back toward the restaurant. "This ends today!"

Emile was just leaving his apartment as Velvet and Nick slipped through the wall. Nick stared at the sheer amount of bruises on the guy, and they both noted he was walking with a limp as he stepped outside and locked the door behind him.

Emile's studio was simply decorated, a futon on a wooden frame seemed to function as the only seating in the place. Besides a TV and a small dresser with a few framed photos, the place was bare.

Nick wandered over to the photos and stood there, mouth hanging open.

"What?" Velvet asked.

He simply pointed at one of the photographs.

In it, Emile was all smiles and bruise-free, his arm around a petite Asian girl, her black hair pulled back in a tight chignon.

Amie.

* * *

At about five o'clock, Emile and his sunglasses limped into Il Fortuna and gave his jacket to the coat check girl with a wicked wink. Her response was a likewise lascivious *meow*, which grossed Velvet out but coaxed a saucy "ooh," from Nick.

Velvet spun around and elbowed Nick in the ribs, or through them, actually. "Follow him!"

They popped out from their hiding place inside the coat-

checked coats, and Nick ran straight through the girl's desk after Emile, while Velvet took a moment to come up with a plan.

She knew she was going to have to possess the girl—Willa was the name on her name tag—but for what purpose? Velvet thought a moment, and then a broad grin spread across her face. Obviously Emile and Willa had some sort of relationship. She'd use that to get the goods on Amie, once and for all!

She hunched down beside Willa's back and thrust herself up, through her and inside her as if Willa was a tight-fitting dress that Velvet had to shimmy into. The girl twitched a bit, but that was to be expected—Velvet was a big girl.

Good thing ghosts don't cause stretch marks, she thought.

With no more than a "What the . . . ?" from Willa, Velvet constricted Willa's thoughts into that imaginary box and took her over.

"So easy," Velvet said. The voice came out child-like and irritating to her ear. "Oh God. Nice baby voice."

She glanced down behind the desk and found a sign that read, BE RIGHT BACK, AMICIS. Velvet left her post and skipped toward the dining room.

There she saw Emile running; being chased was a more accurate description. A man in a mustard-colored blazer and a bushy goatee rushed toward the waiter with a fork, eyes blazing like someone had set fire to his brain.

Must be Abner.

"Abner!" Velvet screamed, but neither the man nor the ghost inside him seemed to hear anything.

They bolted, one after the other, through the swinging door into the kitchen, followed by an opaque presence she hoped was Nick. Velvet scrambled after them and bolted into the busy kitchen in time to see them all pass through the metal exit door.

There was a brawl going on in the dank shadows of the dusky alley. Colonel Mustard, both possessed and incredibly pissed off, pummeled Emile with fists the size of Easter hams. Emile,

defending himself valiantly, seemed to have picked up a ghostly passenger of his own. His eyes radiated in the shadows, freckling his bruised cheeks with rays of light.

Nick?

"Stop it, Abner!" Velvet shouted at the goateed Colonel Mustard. "We've got you now."

Emile ducked another punch, bobbing toward her and getting enough of a gap between him and the other guy to shout, "That's not, Abner," in a thick British accent.

"Why are you talking like that, Nick?"

"I'm not Nick, I'm Abner!" The ghost inside Emile shouted.

Velvet flinched. "Then where's Nick?"

At that precise moment, the door banged open and a little girl rushed out, fists balled and ready for a fight, the blunt end of pizza crust bouncing from the corner of her lips like a cigar.

So if Abner is in Emile, who's in the Colonel . . . and the kid?

Colonel Mustard stopped dead and exploded into laughter. "You're all ridiculous. You should hear yourselves."

Abner/Emile rushed forward and pushed the Colonel through the open doorway and back into the kitchen, pulling the door shut and bracing it closed with a broken piece of board from a stack of pallets so the Colonel was trapped in the kitchen and couldn't get back into the alley.

"So what's going on here?" Abner asked. "Who are you? And who's this?" He pointed at the little girl.

"My undertaker, Nick, is my guess," Velvet replied, staring at the girl and shaking her head, judgmentally.

The little girl pushed up her sleeves, as though she was about to start throwing punches. "We know everything, Abner."

"And what's that? What do you think you know?"

Velvet interjected. "We know that Amie had some kind of relationship with the body you're possessing. If it's some kind of sick domestic violence thing then, seriously, you two couldn't have played that out without getting an innocent living person

involved? That's really low."

"No doubt," Nick said, shaking his head. "Do we haul you back to Vermillion, or get you a guest spot on *Oprah*?"

Abner scowled and reached for his belt as though he'd go after the little girl/Nick, but the door behind them boomed and clattered. The board shook and shifted, threatening to fall loose and unleash the big brute from the kitchen.

"She'll break through soon."

"She?" Velvet echoed.

"Amie." Emile/Abner sighed and shook his head.

Abner shook his head. "I'm protecting this body."

"Just not very well?" she asked.

"Listen, Amie and Emile were together . . . before she died. After she was gone, she couldn't let him go. She found a way back earthside, through that crack you two traveled through, and when he wouldn't accept her advances—she'd possess a variety of different girls to try to tempt him—she started to act out. Violently. So I intervened, of course." He shrugged. "Well, as often as I could."

"But why are you even here, Abner?" Velvet asked. "You could guard the crack from the other side, you know? Or even tell someone and get the crack filled in. Alerting Barker about all this might have been helpful."

"I—" Abner started.

"The whole thing is pathetic," Nick said, balling the little girl's fists up and scowling furiously.

The little girl looked like she was going to throw a tantrum, and Velvet almost giggled at the thought. She wished Nick could see himself and the spectacle he was creating, but in that moment, a crackling sound issued from the kitchen, and while the door didn't move a bit, Velvet knew someone was about to pass through it. Someone terrible.

Someone slutty.

Abner was already moving away, stumbling toward the green

Dumpster. Afraid. Velvet and Nick stood their ground.

Tentacles of white smoke spilled from the cracks around the door, spreading over the brick like a vine, curling and undulating and, worst of all, thickening to the size of tree trunks. They weren't dealing with Colonel Mustard anymore.

It wasn't the first time they'd encountered a banshee—the more a ghost haunted, the more evil it exuded, the more it was deformed and ravaged by its own intent. But Amie didn't look right. She had too many arms and legs, and they were really stinking big. When she pulled her head and torso through the door, though, Velvet could see that it was definitely Amie. But she was different. More voluminous.

"Gee Amie, you look so much . . . fatter earthside," Velvet said without really thinking.

The girl banshee hissed and flicked a tentacle out with a whip crack that cut a blood red line up Willa's arm. Velvet was stunned. Her mother had always told her that her mouth would get her in trouble one day.

Or on many days, concurrently, as she'd discovered.

"Watch your mouth," Amie shrieked, the sound echoing off the walls like the squelch of a poorly tuned guitar.

"Hey," Velvet hissed. "You're the one in the wrong here. Beating up your ex-boyfriend."

"What else could I do? He was going to leave me!"

"You're dead!" Velvet shouted. "*You're* the one that left."

Amie twisted and writhed, even as a banshee she was dramatic and irritating. "Yeah, but only temporarily," she whined. "I was there for him. I came back."

"And I'm sure he appreciated that," Velvet said sarcastically.

Velvet clutched her bloody limb and backed away. She couldn't let Amie hurt Willa's body. Not again.

She spun and dashed for the street end of the alley. Behind her, bricks clacked against concrete and Abner started shouting, "They're onto you Amie!"

Velvet dispossessed Willa mid-stride, and the girl continued to jog a few steps out onto the sidewalk, shaking her head a couple times before noticing her dripping arm and dashing toward the front of the restaurant.

When Velvet twisted to peer back down the alley, she froze. Amie was orbiting Abner like a solar flare, her gaseous tendrils wafting in the breeze like toilet paper off a tree that had been pranked. Conroy wasn't giving up any ground. Nick's little girl was nowhere to be seen and though Velvet felt woefully unprepared considering the turn of events, she knew they couldn't let anything happen to the child Nick had possessed.

"Nick!" she screamed, expecting to see a tiny hand gesture from one of the piles of rubble littering the alley. But there was none. The door to the kitchen was slightly ajar. She hoped he'd gotten the girl out of there and to her safety, but as she approached, readying herself to launch at the banshee, the door slammed open. The little girl rushed out, pigtails slapping the sides of her head, a big empty saucepot in one hand and its lid in the other.

Nick was thinking ahead. They'd need a metal container to hold her. But his timing, as usual, was a bit off. One smoky banshee tentacle shot out and flattened the little girl to the wall. The pot went clattering off the pavement, rocking back and forth to a standstill.

Velvet rushed forward, all her thoughts focused on her hands, on making them a solid enough entity to connect with the banshee. Beside her, she saw Abner disconnect from Emile and crouch; the freed waiter ran in the direction of the door.

Abner was older than she'd expected, in his ghostly wavering form. He looked like a college student really, in an argyle sweater, jeans, and penny loafers. His hair was short enough to have been shaved, and he wore glasses over eyes that were probably too large for his head, unless you were into Japanese anime.

She and Abner both lunged, tackling Amie's contorting form

at chest height. Velvet wrapped herself around Amie, holding the banshee with her legs as though riding a horse, squeezing against her. Velvet stole a glance upward. Abner climbed higher up the banshee's undulating frame and promptly head-butted her.

Amie wailed dramatically, her tentacles beating them across their backs. "Let go! I'll kill you!"

Velvet thought she heard a *thud*, and when she peered down from the struggle, saw Nick's little girl stealthily forcing one of Amie's tentacles inside the metal pot.

"Abner!" Velvet cried. "Pull!"

The action was akin to wringing out a wet towel. The more they twisted and tightened on the banshee's struggling form, the thinner she became until, high above, Abner was whipping about the evil witch as though he was a flag on a pole.

"No!" Amie screamed. "Noooo!"

They were making headway.

They had to.

Nick yanked at the smoky trunk of the banshee, scrolling her into the pot like a hose on a feeder. Amie shrieked with anger and tried to pull herself away. Unable to dislodge herself, she fell finally, the entirety of her smoky mass dropping straight into the pot. Nick slapped on the lid with a wet tomato saucey squish.

"Nice choice going with a dirty pot," Velvet admired.

The little girl nodded and wiped her marinara covered hands on the yoke of her dress. "Now for you, Abner. Are you going to go quietly?"

"Hey, guys," Abner said. "You got me all wrong. Every time I tried to sneak back out to tell people about what she was doing, I'd bounce right back. It's like I'm trapped here or something."

"You're locked in," Velvet said. The vision of Amie with the shiny bronze key scrolled through her head.

"What?" Abner cocked an eyebrow.

"She's right, the crack is covered up by this metal door. Amie had the key. She was reluctant to even have us slip through."

Velvet nodded. "Definitely reluctant. But it's open now or she wouldn't have been able to get through herself. You can go on back and explain what's been happening." She jabbed a thumb in the direction of the pot. "We've got some work to do to get this one off to the Station cellar where she belongs."

Abner smiled and reached out his ethereal hand. Velvet made the effort to touch it, despite being exhausted. The show of effort was the thing. People shake hands all the time—it's easy and familiar—but when a ghost does it you know it really means something because they have to focus all their intentions on the action.

Nick stepped out of the girl and offered his own hand. The little girl wandered around for a moment, not sure what was happening. After he shook Abner's hand, Nick glanced at Velvet—more of a gaze, really—a sad smile curled on his lips. He lingered a moment, and then repossessed the girl, to walk her back to her parents, presumably.

"I really thought he'd cheated on me with Amie," Velvet said, but Conroy just shook his head.

"Why would he when he's got you?"

Velvet cringed, who was this guy, a relationship counselor? "How do you know?"

"Jesus, did you see the way he looked at you? He's so into you, it's scary."

"You think? Like serial killer scary?" she asked. The conversation was getting a little too serious with this stranger.

But then he said, "Yep," and started to walk toward the door.

"Hey," Velvet called after him, chuckling. "Where's the closest morgue, or cemetery?"

Abner grimaced, holding his stomach, sympathetically. "County Coroner is on Fourth. Two blocks that way." He pointed.

"I know what you mean, disposing of these things . . ." she gestured toward the pot. "It isn't my favorite thing either, but this one I don't think I'll mind too much."

He nodded and waved as he disappeared through the door.

It's true what they say. Anyone can thieve a body, but it takes a real specialist to be an undertaker. There are the worms and flies to deal with, obviously, and the smells. She didn't begrudge Nick a single thing.

...

Later, after the flies Nick had accelerated from the Jane Doe at the morgue had carried Amie to her prison under the pagoda—in tiny, incredibly gross, bite-sized portions, no less—Nick and Velvet held hands and took a long walk on the nearby beach.

"You know I'd never do that to you, right?" Nick said, pulling her close and pressing his lips against hers.

"Chase me into the world of the living with your tentacles?" she kidded.

"I got your tentacles, right here." He smiled and held out his arms, then chased her up to the boardwalk and back toward the restaurant.

Back in Vermillion, the compound was in an uproar, people chattered back and forth about the events of the day, about Amie's deception and treachery and the stranglehold she'd had the community under with the shadowquakes.

Howard waved them into his quarters and held his hands out. "Please accept my most genuine apologies," he said. "Manny and I debated letting you in on the plan, but couldn't risk Amie catching wind of it, lest she elope and evade capture. Which, by the way, was brilliant salvage work. Simply brilliant."

He handed Velvet the pink envelope from the robe of his pocket. Inside folded twice was the letter from Manny.

Dear Howard,
You're quite right. This girl is a master of manipulation. In our short time together she has attempted, on no less than two occasions to determine the whereabouts of our keys. No doubt to unleash her fellow ban-

shees in our cellar. A most heinous criminal, who I have no doubt in my
mind, Velvet and Nyx—as Nick is sometimes called—will be able to
find out and dispatch. I pray for the safekeeping of your salvage team
and your missing undertaker. Let's hope that all shall come to their just
rewards in a timely fashion.
Sincerely,
Jayne

Velvet slipped the note back into its envelope. "You know, I thought this was a love letter."

Howard chuckled briefly and then waved a quick good-bye.

"You know what?" Nick whispered in her ear. "He didn't deny it."

And he hadn't.

The Hounds of Ulster

BY MAGGIE STIEFVATER

This is not my story.

My name is Bryant Black. I'm nineteen years old, I worship Paddy Keenan (you don't know who he is, and I'm okay with that) and I don't embarrass myself on the guitar. I lift weights, I like to think I am moderately talented with my tongue (if you take my meaning), and around my left bicep I have a tattoo of the Ouroborous—a snake eating its own tail. I consider myself pretty interesting, although I'm a bit on the biased side of the department.

But this story still isn't about me. Nobody's interested in the ones that got away.

This story is about my best friend, Patrick Sullivan.

(I miss him, still.)

...

This is the scene: we are seventeen and we are going to change the world. Sullivan—no one who knows him worth a damn calls him Patrick, which is his father's name and his grandfather's name and, if he is nothing else, he is not his father nor his grandfather— has his fiddle and I have my guitar named Cú Chulainn and we are punk Irish gods in our D.C. suburb.

I should tell you about Cú Chulainn because, like most things that are cool, you probably haven't heard of him. Cú Chulainn means "the hound of Culain" but most people called him "The Hound of Ulster"—not that you care, but that's okay. In Irish legend, he was a mighty warrior who was famous for, among

other things, his warp spasms (these are fits of rage). During a warp spasm, Cú Chulainn'd grow so agitated that his body parts would move all around by themselves. He'd get an arm coming out his chest or his eyes wandering down to his neck, his legs all changing sizes and shapes, his skin boiling, and then he would go out and kill his enemies.

Must've been some pretty freaky shit to behold. Can you imagine pissing off some massive Irishman, and right before he kills you, you can literally see his balls in his eyes?

Some days, being an Irish punk god in D.C. is not the easiest thing in the world, and on those days, I wish that a warp spasm was in my future.

Okay, see, that. This is the sort of thing I used to say casually. That I'd like a warp spasm or a lucky charm or a bolt of lightning to strike mine enemy to the ground. The usual turns of the phrase. But now, I'm more careful. You never know when you might get what you wish for. But back then, when it was me and Sullivan against the world, I hadn't learned that yet. Seventeen is criminally younger than nineteen, and I knew everything I needed and nothing about using what I knew.

But like I said, we are seventeen, we are gods, and we are slowly taking over the hearts and minds of D.C. with wickedly fast reels and power chords. Oh, I know you are doubtful, but that is because you haven't heard Sullivan on his fiddle. When Sullivan plays a sweet set of jigs, girls' clothing *literally* melts off. It's pretty fantastic. There is no one that can bend a tune like him in fifty miles. A hundred. Nobody this side of Baltimore, anyway, and definitely no one down all the way to Richmond. I think it's a fact that his has the fiddling crown pretty much sewn up for the tri-state area, and it's not just me that thinks so. To hear Sullivan play is to have a story to take home and tell your friends.

I know no one sees me when we are playing together, even if I did use a Sharpie to draw a gnome blowing fire on my guitar, but I'm okay with this. I am utterly confident in my Irish punk gui-

tarist status, and a good guitarist knows when to hot dog and when to just stand back and support the wickedness that is your best friend's musical wizardry. And let me tell you, there is nothing sweeter in this world than the moment when it is the two of us on some greasy stage of some open mic night, him leaning toward me and me leaning toward him, and we are riffing off each other, Cú Chulainn howling with electric fury and Sullivan's unnamed fiddle singing high above it. Together we are so much more than either one of us is alone.

I never thought the music was dangerous.

• • •

Should I back up and tell you about us, or should I tell you about *Them*? I don't know how long they were listening to us. Months before we earned our place at Mullen's, I think. Way before Sullivan applied to Julliard, that's for sure.

Ha, look at me, even now. I still can't bring myself to say what They are—just this word, so coy: *Them*. I can't name *Them*. Not out loud. I know that They hate the word we use, that hearing it spoken infuriates them. And fury is a terrible thing when They have it. But I should be able to say it, now, with impunity. They have no interest in me. Not any more.

So here it is. This was all because of the—

I still can't bring myself to say it.

• • •

Let me tell you about Sullivan's dad, the one Sullivan was so sure he wouldn't be. Patrick John Sullivan II, or P.J. as he was known. Sullivan's mom told me once—oh, she was a good one for talking, 'specially with one or two drinks in her, she was hilarious, if platinum blond, fifty-year-old women saying stuff they shouldn't is your idea of a good time—that Sullivan's dad grew up so poor that his house back in Ireland didn't even have a real floor, just a dirt one. I Googled that shit, because I didn't think that people still

had dirt floors in this century. Because even though Sullivan's father looks old as a block of rock (they'd had Sullivan really late), he was definitely born sometime in the twentieth century. Dirt floors seem pretty feudal (now there is an adjective you don't get to use very much). And Ireland is not exactly the African bush. But Google supported Sullivan's mom's story, so dirt it was. Sullivan's dad, had officially been dirt-poor.

Sullivan's mother told me that back then, they were superstitious. They put out bowls of milk for luck and tucked iron nails in their pockets when they had to walk out on Midsummer's night. And there was all this stuff about things you threw over the threshold on the New Year's Eve and places you just didn't go because it was not done. I always thought all the superstitions were sort of cool. I mean, what did they think was going to happen?

"Bad luck," Sullivan's mom—her real name was Dolores—said. "Or worse. Probably worse."

Definitely more intriguing than terrifying. There is a fairly recent slip jig I know—it's a pretty tight slip jig, from the fifties—that was supposedly given to the musician by the . . . I can't say it. I *still* can't say it. Anyway, he said he didn't write it. He said it was *given* to him. And I have to admit, I was attracted to that idea. I mean, sublime music handed over by supernatural creatures? You don't have to be a punk Irish god to appreciate the coolness of that.

But Dolores Sullivan, platinum blond businesswoman of the future, doesn't believe in any of that stuff, now. There are no bowls of milk or upside-down horseshoes over her doors or open scissors hanging from strings. There is just Patrick Sullivan II, who is not the nicest of people. He doesn't curse or throw things or hit, but he does drink, a lot. And he also . . . broods, I guess. Dolores calls them his "dark moods." Sullivan calls them "being a lazy asshole." I can see how both interpretations are correct.

When he's brooding, P.J. has two tendencies: he remains for hours in the frayed ivory wingback chair in the living room, and he

says nasty, true things. Once I came over to get Sullivan so we could go cruise the streets by the college to eyeball hot undergrads, and as we left, his father told Sullivan that he'd been an accident. That he and his mother never meant to have a baby so many years after his older brothers, and that if P.J. had known back then that he'd be supporting a kid when he was sixty he would've wrapped the cord around Sullivan's neck when Sullivan came out.

It's a pretty terrible thing to say, looking back on it.

But his father said it in that joking way that guys do, so that you can't be sure if they're just trying to be funny. We both knew that he wasn't trying to be funny. But because he said it that way, I couldn't get properly defensive on Sullivan's behalf.

Sullivan never got angry, either, no matter what P.J. said, whether he said that Sullivan had a monkey's face or that he was destined for prison. Sullivan would just get glib and high-strung. I kind of liked him, actually, when he was keyed up like that, because when he was, he got really funny and very, very good when we played music, but it wasn't a good idea to let him drive. Because when he was like that he drove too fast and too far, and once, we ended up near Philly with a tenner in my pocket and a quarter tank of gas, and we both had to dig under the seats for change to have enough gas to get back. And we laughed like crazy people and busted illegally through one toll booth because we didn't have the change, and Sullivan was wild and high as a kite and never said a thing about his father. And I didn't say anything, either, because I didn't want to ruin his mood with that crap.

So we were the wild, brilliant punk gods of Alexandria, and we never said anything about Sullivan's family. I didn't want anything to change.

(I know, okay? I know.)

...

Sullivan kept getting better. He was a genius on that fiddle, man. At school, he played it as a violin, and he did the shock-and-awe

thing with dead Europeans like Vivaldi when he was supposed to, but if you wanted to lose yourself, you asked him for a reel.

God, he was good.

I used to be jealous of his fiddle. When we were nine, I broke Sullivan's arm with a baseball bat from his brother's room. He'd been practicing his fiddle all summer, and I had come over to confront him about it, and we'd fought. I hadn't meant to break his arm.

I'd meant to break his hand.

Sullivan told his parents that we'd been wrestling and that he'd fallen on the headboard of his bed. His father called him a clumsy little bastard. I didn't argue. Later, I drew a picture of Cú Chulainn on Sullivan's cast, and he told me that I owed him a broken bone, someday. I knew it was true.

This is the way that Cú Chulainn got his name: when he was young, he killed the guard dog of Culain out of self defense, and Culain got all snively and sad over the brute's death, so Cú Chulainn promised to guard his castle in the place of the dog. So he changed his name and became the hound of Culain.

After I broke his arm, I told Sullivan that we ought to change our names, like Cú Chulainn changed his name after killing the hound. Sullivan said he was going to be just Sullivan, no Patrick. I said I was going to be Bryant, after my favorite guitarist's last name. We spat and swore on it.

• • •

Usually it is me that goes looking for Sullivan. I'm not saying he never comes over to my house before we head out to make trouble, but I know I'm the needy one. Plus Dolores makes killer peanut butter cookies (my mom's allergic to peanuts, which should be a felony) and there's always the chance that I can pinch some when I drive over. But one sticky summer evening, as I am cleaning the garage (even punk gods have chores) and my kid brothers are kicking ball and riding their bikes in the street

because Mom told them not to, I hear their joyous cry:

"Sulllllivan!"

And there he is, striding down the sidewalk with his hands in his pockets, shoulders hunched, striding fast in that way that tells me that tonight he will be playing like the devil. His fiddle case is strapped over his shoulder. I leave the lawn mower orphaned in the middle of the garage and come out to meet him. My kid brothers are riding their bikes around him in circles.

"Hi," I say, wiping my greasy hands on my pants. I smell like rocket fuel.

Sullivan's eyes have a hooded look. He stands there, hands still stuffed in his pockets, and he says, in a dangerous way, "Let's go to Mullen's."

Let me tell you something about Mullen's. It's a pub, the sort of pub that is legendary, that hosts sessions every Thursday night. A session, or a *seisún*, if you want to be all Irish and snobby about it, is basically a pissing contest for Irish musicians. Okay, it's not really. A real session is supposed to be about a bunch of Irish traditional musicians jamming together, playing common tunes and having a great time. But the session at Mullen's, which is the best in D.C., isn't like that. It's about who can play the fastest and who can sing the highest and who can say *you play like cow shit* in Irish. It's an elitist club for Irish music geeks, and both of us want desperately to be in it, just to say we are.

"Ha," I say, even though it is clear from the way Sullivan is just standing there, oblivious to the bikes circling him, that he isn't joking.

A year and a half ago, before I had my full license, my dad had driven us to Mullen's when we heard they had a rocking session. We'd been to a couple of lousy ones at other pubs, all old drunk men squeezing accordions and singing "Danny Boy," so we were psyched to find a good one. Once we got there, though, and found the session in the back of the pub, we hadn't even gotten to take out our instruments. Lesley Nolan, the bastard fiddle player

who leads the session, paused between tunes to chew out a con-certina player who missed the B part on "The Apples in Winter," telling him to get out of the pub before he embarrassed himself. Then he noticed us standing there, hopeful with our instrument cases, and he snarled at us, "the session's closed to new players."

We'd popped back in a few times since then, lingering at the door to listen, but it was the same old regulars, whipping along with such proficiency between sets that they had all played so often that the seams between tunes were invisible. The only time we saw anyone new was when they let in that new bodhrán player, but I heard he played for a pro band back in Chicago, so he didn't have to prove anything.

But for us, Mullen's stayed out of reach. We were relegated to open mic nights and college bars. Bookstores, cafés, sidewalks, train stations. We were good, good, good, but we never even got the chance to show what we had at Mullen's. Even watching the musicians of the Mullen's session talk and laugh together, con-versation for no one else in the pub, rubbed my hairs the wrong way. They could all screw their traditional selves, that's what I thought. Pompous Mullen's and their club. The lot of them and a bus token would get you a ride.

Now, standing in my driveway, Sullivan says, "It's time." He jerks his chin up and I see that his eyes are wild and intense. To not play with him tonight, somewhere, would be a crime. I can talk him out of Mullen's on the way.

"I'll get Cú Chulainn," I reply.

...

At first, it is not *Them*. It is *She*.

She is beautiful. When I first saw her, I thought she was too old for Sullivan, though when I looked again, I couldn't say why I thought that. She makes my chest feel strange—when I first met her, I thought, so this is what heartsick means. She made me feel . . . wanting. Not like wanting a specific person or thing. It was

that I wanted everything, anything that I couldn't have, everything out of reach.

With the benefit of crystal-clear hindsight, I think I knew, right off, that she was no ordinary girl.

What I definitely knew was this: when I saw the way she looked at Sullivan, that first night, the ground beneath our friendship felt suddenly fragile. It was the first time I considered the idea that our ascendancy to punk god status might not be as inevitable as I had thought.

And I saw him look back, his eyebrow quirked, thinking.

She scared me for so many reasons.

...

So here we are at Mullen's, because I couldn't talk Sullivan out of it, and we're heading back through the building towards the session, because Sullivan is high on his mood and can't be talked out of it. The pub is full of cigarette smoke and the scent of a decade's worth of spilled beer. It is hot as the Dominican Republic outside the pub and several degrees warmer than that inside. I'm already sweating. We do the perp walk past the bar, and the heads turn to watch us, expressions curious at best or sardonic at worst. We're young and unfamiliar, and we're carrying instrument cases. Last year, I ducked my head and stared at the floor as I walked past the bar stools, but this year is different. *We* are different now, Sullivan and I. I stare back at the onlookers and Sullivan gives one of them the finger.

As we approach the back room, I can pick out the tune of the reel they're playing—"The Hare in the Heather"—and it's clipping along nicely. Maybe a little too fast to be really sexy, but hey, that's how some people roll. Last year, this was the bit where we'd come in and hung at the side of the room, waiting for a pause between tunes to ask Lesley if we could sit down.

This time, Sullivan has already pulled his case in front of him and partially unzipped it by the time he strides into the back

room, like it's a weapon case and he's a Mafia hitman about to pull out his Tommy gun and waste everyone. In a way that's true. His fiddle is a weapon. He draws it out in the space of a breath. Half of the session players have their backs to him, unaware of our presence, and the other half hesitate slightly when they see him. But they don't stop. It would take more than us to stop a set in midplay.

Sullivan draws his bow across his strings and it wails a long, slow note from a high, high E down to the E that begins the measure they are playing. It's a battle cry, that note. He rips into "The Hare in the Heather" with them. He doesn't wait for permission. He doesn't move from his place just inside the door. He just hauls ass on his fiddle, it singing loud and sweet and fast, rolls falling from his finger like a bird calling to the heavens.

I sure as hell am not leaving him there on his own, so out comes Cú Chulainn—no time to really tune, though the B string could afford to come up a bit—and then I am half-strumming, half-fingerpicking my way along with him. The strings sound watery and clear under my pick. All of us playing together sounds like something you'd buy off a rack. It sounds like nostalgia made flesh.

At the end of the reel, everyone else stops playing and Lesley drops his fiddle from his shoulder. He gives Sullivan a look which clearly means *okay, now stop, you pissing usurper, I'm going to kill you*, but Sullivan doesn't stop playing. He charges into another reel, and I follow him, counterpoint my swagger to his sweetness, and then let his fiddle chastise my guitar into submission. We two are louder than all the other session players combined. We fill the room. We fill the pub. Sullivan is sawing away so hard that there are loose hairs floating from his bow. I am sneaking a bit of sly tuning in between riffs, my hand snaking up to twist a peg to brighten my B string. Sullivan buys me time with some dirty bowing—the bow goes *scuff, scuff, scuff* on his fiddle like someone laughing in time with the music. People have come in to stand

behind him in the doorway to listen. It is wild and brilliant, everything that the fever in his eyes had promised before.

We come to the end of the set—Sullivan doesn't have to tell me we're done, I know it, because we've jammed together so often that his fiddle and my guitar are nearly one instrument—and we stop.

Lesley Nolan looks at Sullivan and I. He's a square, grayhaired man, sharp corners and deep set eyes. Beside him the bodhrán player is surrounded by a cloud of smoke from a cigarette that dangled from his lips even while he was playing the drum. There's a long pause, during which the accordion player takes a mouthful of beer. We can all hear him swallow.

"Sit down," Lesley says.

Sullivan says, "what?" although he knows perfectly well what Lesley said.

"Sit down," Lesley says again. And to the others, "make some room for them."

The others shift and push around on the chairs and the corner booth. The table in front of them is a mess of full and half-full beer glasses; the glasses are jostled together, impossible to tell whose is whose. There are hands shaken, names exchanged (I remember none of them), we are brought sodas by a waitress who doesn't ask to see our licenses.

"Patrick Sullivan," Lesley says, as if trying it out.

Sullivan says, "Just Sullivan. And this is Bryant. Black."

"And you want to play some tunes," Lesley says.

"That's all we want," Sullivan says.

Something draws my attention to the doorway, then, and that's when I see her for the first time. She's standing at the threshold, and like I said, the first idea I get of her is that she is a lot older than she really looks. I only watch her for a moment—her hair is light, light gold and her eyes are the color of my father's blue work shirts, and she is beautiful in a way that hurts. She's so out of place that it is unsettling. Or dis—discomfiting? Is that a

word? Sullivan uses forty-point words like that and I try to remember to use them to make them my own. Anyway, I feel discomfited, if it is a word, with her standing there and Sullivan looking at her. Then someone says, "Bryant?" and the next time I think to look, she's long gone.

•••

Sullivan calls me that night, at four-oh-seven in the morning. The phone doesn't wake my parents since it only rings in my room. I have held my good grades ransom and one of the concessions my parents had to agree to was a personal phone line. (My father said, *I thought I only had to worry about multiple phone lines if I had girly girl daughters*").

Sullivan's voice is hushed and it's clear he's come down from his musical high of earlier. "You sleeping?"

"Never," I reply. "You?"

Sullivan thinks this over. "That was something, wasn't it, at Mullen's."

"Something? That was nothing," I say. "They had it coming a long time. You could play circles round Lesley Nolan."

"Ha," Sullivan says, but I can tell he's pleased. He is silent again, but I don't hang up. Hours we've spent like this, on the phone in the short hours of the night, a dozen words exchanged over the course of a few hours. Sometimes it's just enough to know you're not alone with your thoughts.

Still, I have no deep thoughts to keep me awake and so sleep pulls at me. I am halfway dreaming, halfway to Mullen's pub again in my head, when Sullivan says, "I asked a girl for her number."

I open my eyes and watch the lights from a passing car stripe across my bedroom ceiling; it's still hot and the windows are open and I can hear the engine become louder and then softer. "Come again?" I say, because I am not sure if he's really spoken or if it was a Sullivan in my dream.

"When we were standing on the sidewalk, after, I asked a girl

for her number."

I say, "I didn't see you talking to anyone."

"You were talking to Gerald."

I don't remember anyone's names. I talked to a lot of people. I hadn't really considered the idea that Sullivan was having equal but separate conversations at the same time. I have a brief thought that he means the girl I saw standing in the doorway, and the concept fills me with horror. "Did she give it to you?"

"No," Sullivan says.

"Good," I say.

"Good?"

"No," I reply. "Not good. Why did you ask her?"

Sullivan doesn't answer. I wait for him to clarify, but there is nothing but heavy, heavy silence. I realize that this is the reason that he called. It was not Mullen's that was weighing on him, but this girl. I am preoccupied by this, actually, Sullivan giving some girl more importance than our long-awaited Mullen's siege. Sullivan has had strings of meaningless girlfriends.

There are bugs humming outside, and normally I would sleep through them, but they keep me awake now.

Sullivan says, suddenly, plaintively, "Bryant? Are you still there?"

I have never heard him ask me that before.

"I'm here."

His breaths are audible. I can feel the quiet stretching out long and thin again, so I interrupt it. "What is it, Sullivan?"

I think that he might not answer, but in the end, he says, "You wouldn't have let us go to Mullen's if it wasn't a good idea, right? I mean, even if I'd said I wanted to, you would've stopped me if it was a really ridiculous concept."

"Of course." I think this is true. "Of course, Sullivan, I got your back."

"Good."

I am aware that the hairs on my arms are standing up. I have

a sudden, creeping sensation that I should shut my bedroom window, because although I have not heard anyone approach, the insects outside have gone quiet, and I feel watched.

I say, "We're going to Mullen's next week, right?"

"Yes," Sullivan replies. He pauses. "Don't hang up."

I don't, and the morning is a long time coming.

• • •

Cú Chulainn has a lot of stories told about him—when you're a guy who changes shape and flies into rages that make you kill both friend and foe, people tend to remember you. One of the stories is that there was a prophecy about him (really, in the old stories, you're nobody unless you have a prophecy attached to you) that said he'd be a great warrior but that his life would be short. There's always a trade-off in the old stories. You're wicked hot, but you have to turn into a swan overnight. You can have all the land in the country, but you have seven toes on your left foot. Or you are an awesome warrior, but you're going to die young.

Everyone remembers Cú Chulainn for the guy he was when he was whacking off people's heads or pulling dragon's hearts out through their nostrils or strangling random terrible hounds.

No one remembers the Cú Chulainn between the warp spasms. He could've been the nicest guy in the world.

• • •

If you are into that mother–son bond thing, the one between Sullivan and Dolores would make your black heart bleed happy. I mean, I'm not saying that I don't get along with my mother— I love her, I do—but Sullivan and his mom are the sort of thing that Hallmark commercials love. He tells her that her new sweater looks really good on her and she dabs tears away from her eyes as she tells him that she's really proud of him. It's all very sappy and supportive and I'll admit it, it's a fine thing to behold.

Anyway, because Sullivan loves his mother so much, I love

her too, and because I spend so much time over at her house, I like to think it's mutual. So when I come over one afternoon and Sullivan's not there, Dolores makes me a cup of tea and sits me at the kitchen table. I have to push aside piles of bills and magazines and Dolores' laptop to find a space for the saucer. Because it is after four p.m., Dolores makes herself a gin and tonic and sits across from me. It is several weeks after our conquest of Mullen's and though we've returned every week, we've discovered that it is more fun to conquer a kingdom than to hold it. I'm ready for the next battle.

"Bryant," she says, "Have you ever thought about, you know, doing something with your hair?"

In the Middle Ages, when foot soldiers needed to defend themselves against mounted soldiers, they would draw down into a ball and point their spears outward. It was called the hedgehog. My hair looks like that. I consider it my finest feature.

"Not really."

Dolores expertly tips back her gin and tonic. It's rewarding to watch a someone who's really good at it drinking. She says, "Sullivan got into Julliard."

I don't say anything. I mean, I knew he would, because he's Sullivan. But I hadn't really prepared for the actual event. The thing is, I know I am invisible when I play with Sullivan, because I am a minor star to his brilliant sun. But the thing I am not sure about is whether or not I will stay invisible without him. I don't think I can handle that.

"I guess I'm hoping my New York college aps go well," I say.

Dolores gets herself another drink. "Do you know about this girl Sullivan is seeing?"

It is like this: I have no lungs.

"That's what I thought," she says. "She's different from the others, then."

He has always told me about his girlfriends. This feels like betrayal. I wonder if he is out with her right now. I wonder how

many times when I've called over the last four weeks he has been with her. Mostly, I wonder if it is that girl from Mullen's.

Dolores opens her laptop, which powers up instantly, and turns it around to face me. It's an eBay page, and she's buying a horseshoe. There's another window open to a search engine, and she clicks over so I can see what she's been looking at.

Protection against faeries says the text in the search engine. She can type it, even if she can't say it. I'd like to say I'm incredibly shocked, but I have an Ouroborous around my arm and a guitar named Cú Chulainn. I could be convinced of a lot of things. And to see that girl at Mullen's was to be a believer.

She asks, "Do you think Sullivan is too good?"

I don't reply. We both know the answer to that.

...

That night, I dream I see them together. They are in a midnight garden covered with long, delicate purple flowers that look like candy. She sings a song into his ear and he listens, half a smile on his face. I hear strains of the song and it is wild and beautiful and *other*, and even from far away, on the other side of the dream, it makes me crazy with wanting. I can only imagine what it is doing to him. He says to her, "I want to know more." She says, "*More* is not a safe place for you." He replies, "Safe has never been important."

I know this is true, but the fact that he's saying it to her instead of to me hurts. Not hurts like in a dream, but hurts like it's real life and I'm awake. I dream that he kisses her and it's the *way* he kisses her that makes me wake up.

Lying in dark, I reach for the phone and I call him, but he doesn't pick up. I know it's because the dream was real. He's not in his room but in some dangerous garden far away from a world that includes my guitar, Mullen's, and gin and tonics at his mother's kitchen table.

I get out of bed and go into the bathroom and in the ordinary silence of night. I shave my head. I feel invisible.

It is eight thirty p.m. and the street in front of Mullen's is greasy with rain. It is our sixth week coming to Mullen's, and Sullivan told me he would meet me here instead of riding with me. He had *things to do*.

I feel like I am nine again and I want to smash his hand with a baseball bat, but this time, it's not his fiddle that he's leaving me for.

I consider getting back into the car and driving home. But then I would just be sitting at home waiting for him, and that has been the story of the last two weeks. And let me tell you, it's a boring story.

The pub door shuts behind me and I hear someone thumb a lighter to a cigarette. "Bryant? Is that you?"

I turn and it's the bodhrán player from the session, the one who had his big-ass band back in Chicago. He sucks in on the cigarette and eyes me. "I almost didn't recognize you without your hair. Well, if anyone can pull off the shaved head, you can."

"Thanks," I say. I am thinking about Sullivan kissing the girl.

"It's good job you're here," the bodhrán player says. "Session's half-dead tonight, and we could use a pulse."

"Sullivan might not be coming," I say.

"Psh," the bodhrán player says. "We need another fiddler like we need a hole in the head. You're the one who rocks this place." He stubs out his cigarette on the dirty wall beside the door.

I'm not one for fishing for compliments, but I say, "Come again?"

The bodhrán player flicks the cigarette off into the night. "You make him look good. Crying shame we didn't have you in Chicago." He holds the door open for me. I feel like my brain is exploding. I feel like I need to readjust the lens through which I look back on my entire life.

I follow the bodhrán player—I still don't know anybody's

names, least of all his—and they make a place for me at the table in the back. *Thank God* someone says. *We thought you weren't coming.*

We play so fast the notes trip over each other. We play so well the paint on the walls blisters. We are so amazing that the whole city falls quiet and listens to us, from Baltimore to Richmond. We play so wondrously that other musicians write *other* tunes about how great our tunes were that night.

I hope that wherever Sullivan is, he can somehow hear us, and he knows that music can sound like this without *her*. Without *Them*. He only needs me.

• • •

At Cú Chulainn's worst, when he was in his warp spasms, his blood would start to boil. They used to put him into barrels of cold water to cool him down after he'd gone all battle-rage, and he would explode the barrels with heat until finally he achieved room temperature.

By the time I get to Sullivan's house after the session, my blood is just about hot enough to cook a chicken. Fifteen years I'd known him and never stood him up.

I sit myself on his front step and I wait. I am still humming with the music from before. When he finally appears, emerging from the night, hands in his pockets, he doesn't seem surprised to see me.

I stand up to face him, not letting him past me on the stairs. "You want to tell me where you were?"

I can smell it on him, though—clover and spring and flowers, all of them out of season for a D.C. fall. He's been with her.

"I'm sorry," he says, but not in that way that means he actually is sorry. The way that means he's sorry he has to say sorry.

"You told me to tell you when you were doing something stupid," I say. "You're doing something stupid."

He stares at my hair. "I want something more," he says.

"Then we'll go find it."

"Something more than that," he says. "Something more than *here*."

"And I'm telling you that what's she's offering is a cheat," I say. "Short cut. Is that what you want? Or do you want to earn it yourself?"

Sullivan eyes are still fixed on my hair, or rather, the lack of it. "I'll never get to that place without her. Without *Them*. I'm sorry." And this time, I can tell that he really is sorry, because he's made up his mind.

I feel my blood reach boiling point. Everything inside me has shifted to something else and I'm no longer the same person I was five minutes before.

I smash my fist into his face.

I *hear* the bones in my hand hit his cheek, like knuckles being popped. Sullivan stumbles back, holding his face. I am ready to hit him again, fueled by the memory of him kissing her. What I can see of his expression around his hand is shocked as he realizes I'm about to hit him again.

"Anne," he says. "Anne, please."

I haven't heard my real name in almost a decade.

My fist slowly drops to my side. I'm aware that it's throbbing and painful. I think I've broken my hand on his face.

"Anne," he says again. "I'm sorry." And this is a third kind of sorry.

My mind is still churning with the sound of my real name in his mouth. With the memory of one night eight years ago, a girl holding a baseball bat and a boy cradling his broken arm.

"I've broken my hand," I tell him. "On your face."

He lowers his fingers from his cheek; it's turning purple already. "Then we're even."

"We're not," I say. "Don't go with her, Sullivan."

"Anne—"

"Don't call me that," I say. "I haven't been Anne in a long time. Should I start calling you Patrick again?"

He looks away. He's already changing, I see now. He needs a new name entirely. Maybe she's already given him one.

We were punk gods of Irish music, and we were going to change the world. It was supposed to be the two of us against the world.

(I miss him, still.)

Many Happy Returns
A Generation Dead Story

BY DANIEL WATERS

I think I love him, Daddy, is what she'd said. This was what Cal was thinking about when he heard that the van had gone off the road.

There were five young people in the van, but that number had not been easy for the initial officers at the site to determine. Not at first. Some of the bodies had been thrown from the vehicle, probably when it caromed off the red oak, but possibly after, when it slid careening down the culvert and tipped over onto the passenger side. But even before there was an accurate count, many members of the Sanders volunteer fire department were crying. Cal Wilson was the Sanders town constable, and he was trying his best to keep from coming unglued, but it was difficult. He knew at least two of the teens who had been traveling in the van. He knew they'd been in there because he'd waved good-bye to them as the van had pulled out of his driveway.

It would be Christmas in two weeks.

They had to cut the van open. They peeled the roof back like the lid of a can of pudding. There were two teens still in the vehicle. Two more by the tree, one in the culvert. Everyone on scene was thinking alcohol was involved, but no one wanted to say it. The emergency personnel were gentle, as though they were lifting babies from cribs rather than bodies from a wreck.

The living wouldn't look at each other, and as soon as vitals were checked, and found to be defunct, they would not look at the dead, either.

"Donny," Mike Smolenski, the newest volunteer, was not much older than the kids who died in the wreck. "I think I saw this one move."

Donny glanced over at "this one," a girl he knew. Not well, but enough to feel and predict all the resonance her death would have. He knew many of these kids, by sight if not by name, and he knew that no matter what happened in the next couple days, this would be the accident that they would be talking about fifty years from now, the crash that would be etched into the town consciousness permanently, as though with a rusty nail. This would be like the day, twenty-seven years back, when the O'Briens' horse barn caught fire and five horses burned to death. The only thing people talked about when they talked about that fire was the sound of the horses screaming.

There wasn't any screaming now, on this night. Not yet.

"She's moving, Donny. I really saw her move." Mike sounded terrified.

"Too early," Donny said. He had heard of some coming back that fast, but more typically, it would be anywhere from six hours to a day. There was the one time that a kid, a drowning victim, had sat up in the back of the ambulance, unable to talk because water had filled his lungs. But all the others, that Donny knew of personally, took their time about it.

He'd just never heard of one coming back that fast. They weren't sure how long the bodies had been there, but the trucker who called it in said that the snow hadn't filled in the tire tracks yet, the treads like a long black snake uncoiling off the road. Donny'd arrived seven minutes later, and Cal rolled up three minutes after that.

"She's moving. Her eyelids are moving."

Donny went to her. He felt for a pulse, and it wasn't there it

wasn't there and then it was. Faint. An echo of life.

Donny swore. "We've got one still alive!" he said. "Alive!"

He yelled orders, people moved. Cal Wilson was running. Mike moved. Other than she-of-the-fluttering-eyelids, none of the other bodies on the ground had moved.

Cal Wilson ran over too. The girl on the ground was bruised and bleeding, but she wasn't his. Hope, like love, can be a dagger in the heart.

Not his. Not Mandy.

She was still in the front seat of the van.

...

They made Sanders High School the center for grief counseling. There were those in the area who thought that was an idiotic idea, seeing the school as a large brick-and-chalk-dust reminder of those very kids they'd just lost, but there were others who understood. Sanders High School, for many, was the last remaining edifice that held some sense of the community that Sanders once was. It was where Mayor Marshland had town meetings. It was where the rotary club met. It was where the spaghetti suppers and the fundraisers and the socials were held. It was where Alma Gustavson held adult ed classes in macramé and needlepoint.

It was where the dead kids had gone to school.

No one could fault Mr. Stockton, the school's guidance counselor, for his breakdown early in the day. He was qualified to help the graduating seniors, all twenty-nine of them, to locate and apply to college, or to help them find placement with one of the few local businesses within city limits or in Wells, the larger town that the van had been returning from. He'd known these kids well, and one of them especially well, having guided her through a troubling situation at home. Four kids D.O.S. in one accident, with a fifth comatose and most likely crippled for life in a bed at Wells hospital. Who could provide guidance or counseling for that?

A "grief specialist" from Boston was brought in. Again, there was talk, and grumbling, but at the end of the discussion most agreed that it was necessary. This way the town could pour all of their grief—and their resentment, and their hatred—into this person and then send her back to Beantown with her check and never have to see her again.

Cal Wilson took a seat toward the back of the room at a respectful distance from the other grieving parents. A few seats ahead of him, Bill Trafton lifted his hand in a curt wave of acknowledgment. Bill owned Sanders Hardware downtown. He was also a volunteer fireman who was fortunate enough to have missed the call the previous night. Cal was glad it was he, and not Bill, that had found his son Curtis lying in the snow.

Chuck Barnes looked back at him but didn't acknowledge him at all. Chuck's wife didn't even turn around.

They started the meeting with introductions—of the parents, the counselor, and various town functionaries who wished to bear witness to their grief. After a brief shuffling of feet and staring at the floor, the woman from Boston started the session.

"Good evening," she said. "Let's talk about why we are all here."

She pronounced the "r". She was wearing a sharp suit that set her apart from the grief stricken, who were mostly in sweatshirts and jeans. Mayor Marshland was worried that she wasn't a Bostonian at all, but a New Yorker in disguise.

"We don't know for certain why they come back sometimes, or even if they will come back." She stopped, and smiled. She was a small woman, young, with glasses and long chestnut hair.

"But we know that the possibility exists, and we should talk about what will happen if they do return."

The parents of the children were silent. It was difficult to tell what they were thinking—whether or not they felt as though they were being counseled or if they were only a moment away from dragging the lady from Boston out into the street. But the woman

thought she knew.

"I know what you are thinking. I'd be thinking the same thing if I were in your position. All the things going through your head. Is my child coming back? Is he not coming back? Do I want her or him to come back? Will he or she be different? The same? What will I do?"

She paused and looked at each of the parents in turn.

"You are wondering: what will happen if my child comes back from the dead?"

Cal nodded along with the others, but that isn't what he'd been wondering at all.

He wished he'd stayed with Laura Davis at the hospital. Laura's son Stevie had been in the far back seat, the only boy without a date. Cal had offered Laura a ride—he supposed they were friends, at least their kids had been friends for a few years—but Laura said that she wanted to be there when Stevie "woke up." That's how she'd put it. *Woke up.* As though her son's death was just a bad dream they were sharing, one that would vanish the moment he opened his eyes.

The doctor said that it was too early for any of them to start coming back, that she should go talk to the trauma specialist, but Laura wasn't having any of it.

"Doctors don't know jackrabbit about it," is what she'd said. *Jackrabbit.* She'd be sitting in the hospital with a mystery novel and the largest cup of coffee she could get from Dunkin' Donuts, while Cal and the other parents were listening to the woman in the expensive red suit tell them how they felt.

"I'll call you," Laura had told Cal, her eyes clear as she looked up at him from her blue vinyl seat. He wanted to hold her hand, to hug her, but in the end he stood there like a statue. Laura lost her husband in a fishing accident a few years ago, and Cal had spent the last few months wondering if enough time had passed for him to ask her out.

"Call me?" he said.

"You'll be the first to know," she replied. Ice clicked in her giant plastic cup. She drank her coffee iced, even in January. "If anyone wakes up."

"Oh," Cal said. "I'll . . . I'll take notes for us."

It was the sort of stupid platitude that he regretted immediately upon speaking, but Laura's eyes softened for the briefest of moments, making him glad that he'd at least said something.

Wake up, he thought. *Please, Mandy, please wake up.*

Cal realized that the trauma counselor was still speaking, was ticking off all the different things that you could expect if your child returned from the dead.

"They will be slower. They won't be able to move the same way that they could move in life. Some of them will not be able to speak, and most will not sound anything like they used to."

Something unraveled in Cal's chest. He loved many things about his daughter, but the sound of her voice was very high on his list. Her always-reliable "Hi, Daddy!" when he got home from work was quite often the highlight of a hard day. Those two simple words washed away his wounds.

But "I think I love him, Daddy," had a different effect on him at the time, he recalled. His initial reaction was one of shock, as though Mandy had dropped an obscenity. His second reaction was one of concerned amusement. He liked Jake but doubted sincerely that the boy could sustain his daughter's interest over the long haul.

Love? he thought. *You don't know jackrabbit about love.*

• • •

Cal saw Jake's father Chuck Barnes scowling beneath his trucker's cap. His wife sat cowering beside him like a plump beige mouse taking shelter under a cabinet. Mandy and Jake started dating last March, nearly a year ago, but it wasn't until last week that Mandy had informed Cal that she was in love with him.

Jake had been driving the van when it left the road. Mandy

had been sitting next to him in a new sweater she'd bought just for the party. He was her first real boyfriend.

The woman from Boston cleared her throat, as though she'd noticed that Cal's attention had been drifting.

"Their lack of mobility and their inability to communicate immediately can be very difficult to deal with," she said. "In most cases you can expect them to make incremental improvements in both of these areas. Some differently biotic people have shown marked improvements over time, to the point where many of them can move and talk nearly as well as they did in life."

Sandy Trafton raised her hand, Bill's arm tightening across her shoulders. The grief counselor gave her an encouraging nod.

"Why do some differently biotic people make improvements?" she said, her voice raw from crying. "How can we help them?"

That, Cal noted, earned a pale smile from Mayor Marshland.

"I'm afraid that we don't understand the *why* of almost anything that concerns the differently biotic," the counselor said. "Some studies indicate that db people respond favorably to encouragement and support." Here she paused, her eyes flitting across the room as though to gauge who would and would not be providing encouragement and support. She stopped upon Chuck Barnes, who had crossed his thick arms, resting them upon his belly.

"Love," she continued. "They seem to respond to love, just like any teenaged child."

Cal saw Chuck make a comment that only his mouse-brown wife could hear. Chuck did not seem to notice his wife recoil from the comment as though from a blow, nor did he seem to notice the tears that were coursing down her pale cheeks.

"So we know a little about the how, but not the why. Since teens began returning from the dead—and new research indicates that the phenomenon may have begun as many as five years ago, much before the Dallas Jones incident—we have tried our best to

study the phenomenon, but various . . ." She trailed off, again settling her eyes on Chuck. " . . . social forces have made a serious
scientific inquiry difficult."

Cal didn't really care about a serious scientific inquiry. He
just wanted his daughter back.

He wondered how he would have felt had something happened to her prior to the whole db phenomenon, back in the days
when there was absolutely no hope of her returning. Would he
have just let the massive tide of grief roll over him in one annihi-
lating wave?

Mandy was dead. No matter what happened, Mandy was
dead. But it hadn't hit him yet, not in the way it should have,
because he could still allow himself to believe that she was coming back. He could still deny what had happened to her because
he could still hold hope that she would open her eyes and return
to him.

But not everyone came back.

The grief counselor was still talking about other changes that
could occur when she said something that snapped him out of his
thoughts. "But perhaps the most traumatic aspect of a return that
a parent can deal with is the lack of expression."

Cal watched Bill's hand moving in slow circles on his wife's
back and tried to swallow back the lump forming in his throat.

"Your child, if he or she returns, will not express emotions in
the same way that they used to. Their facial muscles simply won't
work properly, and so much of the communication that used to
pass between the two of you will be gone. You mustn't confuse
their inability to express these emotions with their not having
them. I assure you, your child will be just as sensitive as they were
in life, they just will not be able to show it. Do not get discouraged when your child doesn't seem to be responding to your
efforts to reacclimate them to 'life.'"

She paused, her smile and voice softening.

"Don't stop showing them affection and love. Your child most

likely will not be able to smile, or frown, and will not be able to communicate the thousand little things that we can communicate with our eyes and mouths. It may not sound like much now, in light of what just happened, but dealing with the lack of emotional responsiveness and expression will be one of the most difficult things you will face as the parent of a differently biotic child. If you have ever tried to talk to your child when they were playing a video game or engaged in the Internet, you can imagine what I'm talking about. You will be able to see your child's face, you will be able to see them move, but when you speak to them or hug them you will get the sense that they aren't really there."

"That's because they *aren't* really there," Barnes said, his gravel voice rumbling around the room like the cough of an old pickup truck.

"I'm sorry?" the counselor from Boston said, her face going blank much like the db children she'd just been describing. Cal had been expecting this from Chuck. He was more interested in the reactions of the other parents than in Chuck's predictable meltdown.

Chuck stood up, a sight Cal had gotten used to in town meetings when Barnes felt a school budget needed to be voted down. "They aren't really there. They're dead. And they aren't 'coming back' or 'returning' or any of the above. What 'comes back' isn't our children, and the sooner everyone in this room is aware of that, the better."

"Mr. Barnes . . ."

Barnes leveled a squat, calloused finger at her. "Don't interrupt me, missy. You've said your piece, and now I'm going to say mine. I think it is a disgrace the way that you are playing upon these poor people's grief and loss to get them to subscribe to your warped worldview. My wife is sick—just sick—over this and you aren't helping. Our children are dead. Dead. There's no such thing as a return from death. What inhabits their bodies after they pass on is not of this world."

"You are upsetting my wife," Trafton said, quietly, but loudly enough for Cal to hear the tremor in his voice. "If you don't want to discuss this, why don't you just leave."

Chuck laughed, leaning forward against the table that was too small for him. "But I *do* want to discuss this. I want to discuss what we should do if demons infest our children," he said. "We should burn them. We should burn the corpses right now before they even start to come back."

Sandy burst into a loud wailing that filled the room with her pain. Trafton came up out of his chair, and Cal could see his arms shaking with rage and frustration. Chuck Barnes, hardened from years of physical labor, and outweighing Trafton by a good forty pounds, simply looked at him and shook his head. He got to his feet after a moment's deliberation, and Cal saw that he was smiling. Certain men took an enjoyment out of casual violence.

Cal wasn't one of them, but sitting there, he decided that he would beat Chuck Barnes within an inch of the life their children had just lost if he did anything more than smile at Bill Trafton.

"Mr. Barnes," the grief counselor was saying, as though she could talk the men back into their seats. "It is now illegal in the state of Maine to harm the differently biotic. It is also illegal to . . ."

"Laws! Laws!" Barnes said, his eyes, full of contempt, still fixed on Bill Trafton. "You think passing a human law makes something all right?"

". . . interfere with the body of a deceased young adult before the requisite seven days have passed."

Chuck, as though satisfied that all Trafton could do was stand there and shake, cast a quick glance at Cal.

"You people can wait around for your dead children to come back to you, but it is never going to happen. And if I was a younger man who didn't have four mouths—*living* mouths—left to feed, I'd be taking it upon myself to make sure that the dead remained uncorrupted by whatever creatures of hell are planning to take them over."

He grabbed his wife's hand and pulled her toward the door. The mayor and the grief counselor called for them to stay, but Barnes' progress was swift and inexorable.

Cal watched them leave but the scene had ceased to register upon him. Instead, he focused on the memory of his daughter's voice.

I think I'm in love with him.

...

When Cal returned home, the first thing he looked at was the answering machine in the kitchen because just about the only person that ever called him was Mandy.

The red light was winking at him.

Without taking the time to take off his coat and hat, or even to let go of his keys, he punched the button with a shaking finger.

"Hello? Hello, Cal?" A female voice, but not Mandy's. It was Laura. She sounded like she was crying, but there was warmth in her voice, a ray of sunlight piercing clouds.

"Cal, he came back. My boy came back."

A dull pressure formed against the backs of his eyes . . .

He was happy for Laura—jealous of course, but happy as well. She'd been the smart one, the one to ignore the "counseling" and the stupid group-hug (or *hate*, in the case of Barnes) session, to do the only thing that really mattered—stay and wait for her child. He dropped his keys on the kitchen counter where they landed with a jangling clunk.

Maybe Laura's presence helped her son find his way back, Cal thought. Maybe, from whatever pocket of space that Stevie existed in, he'd been able to hear his mother's coffee-fueled heart beating, and he followed the sound back into his bruised and lifeless body.

Laura didn't say anything else, but there was a long pause at the end of the message before she hung up.

Cal picked up his keys and drove back to the hospital.

...

He woke up, blinking and disoriented. Someone had covered him with a blanket during the night, and he realized that he had clutched it to his chin with curling fingers. His mouth tasted of the gum of a thousand envelopes.

"Hey, Cal," a voice said. Cal patted his breast pocket for his glasses, but even sightless he knew who the voice belonged to. It was Bill Trafton. "I've got a coffee for you here if you want it."

"Bill," Cal said, sitting up and pulling on his glasses, which were spotted and dusty. "Thank you."

"I hate the waiting," Bill said, holding out a large coffee. "I'm sorry if it's too cold; I thought you'd have woken up awhile ago."

"I'm awake," Cal said. He accepted the cup and took a long sip. Silence stretched out between the two fathers.

"I guess we'll know in the next seven days, right?"

Cal took another sip. "I guess so."

"Stevie Davis came back," Bill said. Cal thought he was trying, and failing, to sound cheery and optimistic. "There's an article in the paper about it and Laura called Sandy last night."

"I heard. That's great."

"Yeah, isn't it? I went upstairs and talked to the Franks," Trafton said. "Amber still hasn't . . . she's still comatose. Both her legs . . ."

He stopped when he saw a nurse running toward them, the slap of her sneakers against the burnished floor of the corridor rising in volume. She was young, and not one of the medical staff Cal had spoken to when he'd first arrived. He and Trafton rose from their seats.

"One woke up," the nurse said, breathless. "You should come. One of the boys woke up."

One of the boys, Cal thought. But he followed Trafton down the hall anyway. They were running by the time they reached the boy—a large, stumbling figure in a pale blue hospital gown. He was with a nurse who was encouraging him to walk, but the look

on her face said that she didn't really want to touch him. The boy weaved like a drunk. When he turned his face to them, they saw that it was Jake Barnes.

Trafton slumped against the wall, shuddering with the failed effort of holding his emotions in check.

...

I wanted to see her, but they wouldn't let me see her. There were still two bodies beneath sheets in the cold room but they were vague, almost shapeless. They could have been anybody at all but I wanted to know. I knew that I was dead and I wanted to see who else was and I hoped it wasn't Mandy. I tried to approach the bodies but the nurse's hand was firm on my shoulder as she steered me towards the door. I couldn't tell that the bodies under the sheets were Curtis's and Mandy's but when I saw their parents outside the door of the cold room I knew. I knew and I tried to go back.

When I saw Mandy's father I tried to return to the cold room and find her and help her come back. I don't know how I could help her come back but I thought if I held her or if I kissed her she would awaken like Snow White like Sleeping Beauty like any of the fairy tale princesses who'd fallen into a magic slumber.

But what I'd returned from didn't feel like slumber. There was pain, there was raw ache when I moved, each muscle felt twisted and dry, like overcooked bacon.

But they wouldn't let me return. "It isn't permitted," the nurse said. As though saying so made it real, as though all manner of permissions hadn't been revoked or granted. I could have forced her but then what? That's what I thought. I wasn't thinking about being dead—that would come later—I was just thinking about seeing Mandy again. That's all.

I tried to speak but I couldn't make any sound at all. My tongue was like a mouthful of cold meat; I could feel it lying there, pressing against my teeth, but I couldn't move it at all.

When I fell, it was Mandy's father that lifted me up. There was

something in his eyes, some message, but it wasn't one of fear like with the nurse.

"Come on," her father said. "I'll take you home."

I followed. But I knew there was no home to return to.

...

Cal sat in the truck with the engine running as Jake got out of the cab. Cal had started to get out himself, but Jake's hand—surprisingly gentle—fell upon his arm, and the boy shook his head. Jake didn't say anything, but Cal didn't think there was really anything *to* say at that moment.

I think I love him, Daddy.

Cal watched him make slow, shuffling progress through the snow toward his front door. He was about halfway across the front lawn when the door opened, and his father strode out onto the steps. Chuck was wearing a tattered sweatshirt and paint-splattered jeans tucked into the tops of work boots he'd not had time to lace up. He was holding a shotgun.

"Get out of here!" he yelled. Like he was shooing an animal. He waved the shotgun in a tight arc. Behind him, Cal could see his wife holding back one of Jake's younger brothers—Andy, he thought—and trying to cover his eyes with her hands, as though she was afraid that he'd turn to salt.

"Go on! You aren't welcome here!" Cal could see the heat rising from Chuck's head and shoulders even across the yard, as though there were a tiny furnace being stoked within him. Jake stood rooted in his tracks, motionless. Chuck brought the shotgun up.

"Don't do it, Barnes!" Cal called out, opening his car door.

"Do not move, Cal Wilson," Barnes said. "I have a right to defend my property. I have every right."

Cal watched the man's eyes and the barrel of the gun. They were both steady and insane, the eyes of a fanatic who'd found his purpose. Cal had left his own gun at home.

"He's your son, Chuck."

"My son is dead," Barnes replied. "Whatever this thing is, it isn't my son." He cocked the hammer on the shotgun and spoke to the boy. "This will be the last time I tell you. You aren't welcome here."

Jake took a step backward, as though he wanted to be certain that his father knew he was going. Then he turned away.

Cal remained by the truck, wondering if he should call to Jake. But before he could, the boy shuffled away—away from his family, from the road, from Cal and his waiting truck—and into the woods across the street.

When he was no longer visible through the trees, Cal turned back to see Barnes squinting off into the distance. Cal watched him spit into the snow and return to his house, his voice audible through the closed door as he shouted at his wife and remaining children.

Cal returned to the warm cab of his truck and drove back to the hospital.

...

"The Franks would like it if you visited them sometime today, Cal," Sandy Trafton was telling him. "Amber regained consciousness a few hours ago. It's almost like a miracle."

He could hear the anxiety in her voice, and he watched her involuntary glance toward the room where their dead children were waiting.

"Maybe I'll do that," Cal said, rising to his feet. The joints of his knees popped like a sheet of bubble wrap. "Can I get you something from the cafeteria on my way back? Coffee, or a sandwich?"

"No, thank you, Cal." She gave him directions to Amber's room, and he walked away.

You should have stopped the boy, he thought, passing doctors and people he knew from town, all of whom gave him a wide

berth, as though it were he that had returned from the dead. *You should have stopped him and you didn't. What would Mandy think of you?*

He knew what she'd think. And she'd be right to think it.

He'd been angry when he'd waved them good-bye. Angry and jealous. Because from the moment that his daughter—in her soft, cautious way—said that what she felt for Jake might actually be *Love,* capital L, Jake had ceased to be the boyfriend and had instead had become the boy that would take his little girl away from him. He knew it was wrong, but as he stood there, grinning through gritted teeth and waving like an idiot as they pulled away, that was what he'd been thinking.

And, in the end, he'd been right. Jake Barnes *had* taken his little girl away from him. Forever.

No. No, she'll come back. She has *to come back.*

He'd arrived at Amber Frank's room on autopilot. Her father—Cal couldn't recall his name—saw him and rushed over to shake his hand, at once thanking him for coming and offering condolences for his loss. Cal imagined that he was so numb that he couldn't feel either the kindness of his words or the pressure of the other man's hand.

"Amber wanted to talk to you, Officer Wilson," Mr. Frank was saying. "I realize this is a very, very difficult time, but once she started to get a sense of where she was and what happened to her, it became very important that we contact you."

Cal nodded without really comprehending what the man was trying to say. He allowed Mr. Frank to guide him into his room where Mrs. Frank was sitting by her daughter's bedside. Cal looked down at the girl in the bed. Her face was mottled and bruised, her cheeks puffed and swollen. Cal closed his eyes, remembering how her legs had been twisted when they'd found her in the snow.

"I can come back later," Cal whispered to Mrs. Frank, who shook her head as Amber tried to speak. Her eyes were so swollen

Cal hadn't been able to tell that she was awake.

"You might have to lean close," Mrs. Frank—Helen, he remembered—said to him. He lowered his head toward Amber.

"Jake," she whispered. "Jake."

Cal closed his eyes and opened them again when the vision inside his head was of Jake and his daughter, driving away.

"Jake . . . wasn't . . . drinking," she said. "Mandy . . . neither."

Cal looked at her, and then at Helen, who was smiling at her daughter and patting her hand. He straightened up and cleared his throat.

"Thank you, Amber," he said. "Thank you for telling me. You get better, okay?"

Mr. Frank stopped him in the hallway.

"Thank you," he said. "It was really important for Amber to tell you that. From what I gather, she and the other boys had had a few beers, but Jake refused because he was driving."

"And Mandy doesn't drink," Cal said. His own throat was dry.

Mr. Frank nodded. "That's right. That's what Amber said. 'Mandy doesn't drink.'"

Cal turned to go, but before he could escape, Mr. Frank's hand was on his arm.

"I hope . . . I hope she comes back," Mr. Frank said, faltering as Cal's eyes met his own. "If that's what you want."

Cal didn't know if he should thank him or punch his lights out, so instead he just nodded and moved away.

It is *what I want*, he thought.

But three days later, she still hadn't come back.

...

Chuck Barnes found out about the milk and the peanut butter on toast on the third day.

The first few times, Andy had gotten away with it because Chuck was up earlier than everyone and out the door by the time

they all came down for breakfast, so he never saw Andy leaving it out on the deck. Nor did he see his wife Molly, once the children had all been packed off onto the morning bus, go out onto the deck in her housecoat and slippers to retrieve the milk and toss the peanut butter toast out into the backyard for the birds and the squirrels to eat. And he was never there in time to hear Andy's first words upon arriving home from school, which were: "Did Jake come and get his breakfast?" And he wasn't there to see him run to the sliding door and look out onto the deck for any sign or trace that his brother had been there. Nor did he hear Molly's assurances that Jake had, in fact, come home to have his breakfast. Andy was nine, but he still believed in both Santa Claus and the Easter Bunny; it wasn't such a stretch for his imagination to picture the arrival of his deceased brother coming to collect his breakfast, whom he had actually seen with his own eyes.

Andy was up early again on Saturday to fix Jake his breakfast. He was excited about it because he thought that if he sat really quietly just inside the door and behind the curtain, he might actually get to *see* Jake. If Jake didn't get scared, then maybe he could even *talk* to him. He really missed his older brother. If he saw Jake, he'd talk to him about school and TV and stuff, but Andy didn't think he'd mention that last night he'd cried a little at bedtime thinking about him. Jake had enough to worry about without knowing his brother was a crybaby.

Andy was proud of himself when he went downstairs into the kitchen and poured Jake a big glass of milk. So proud and so elated at the thought of helping Jake that he didn't hear his father flush the toilet down the hall and walk into the kitchen. Andy'd unlocked the sliding door and was just about to set the glass of milk down in a nice little pile of snow when his father's voice startled him so badly he spilled half the milk onto the deck.

"What the hell do you think you are doing?"

Andy didn't want to turn around. He wanted to keep facing toward the backyard, where at any moment Jake could be walk-

ing out of the woods, ready to take Andy away with him. Andy rose to his feet and blinked against the chill air, wishing it to happen.

"Turn around!" his father yelled. "Answer me!"

Andy turned, aware that the remaining milk was in danger of spilling because his hands were shaking. His father was glowering at him, the gray black tufts of his hair still wild from sleep. "I . . . I . . ."

"Out with it!"

"I . . . I was getting Jake his breakfast," Andy said.

His father struck him hard enough to send him to the floor. The glass broke beneath his hand, and he felt a hot bright pain as his palm was sliced open.

"He's dead, do you understand me? Dead!"

Andy tasted blood from a cut inside his cheek. Red drops rolled off his wrist and swirled into the pool of spilled milk spreading around the broken glass. It was in this way that Andy realized that some things, once broken, could never be repaired again.

...

There was a place in the woods where we used to go in the summertime, Mandy and me. A place that was near the lake but that you couldn't see from the lake and we used to like going there on the days where it was too hot for anything else. We must have gone there five times—no, I know, we went there exactly five times and each time we went it was better than the time before and when we walked back Mandy would hold her sandals in her left hand and my hand in her right and most times we didn't say anything at all the entire walk back to my father's van. But on the fifth and last time, the best time of all, she said "Summer's almost over." She said it like she was sad but then I looked at her and I said that it didn't matter, because summer is just a season, and that the only thing that was over was a season. That made her laugh a little and thinking back on it that might have been one of the smartest things I've ever said.

I tried to find that place in the woods and I walked and walked and walked and you'd think I'd be able to find it okay because I'd spent the best times of my life there. Literally, the best times of my life, now that my life was over. But I couldn't find it. I couldn't have imagined how differently everything looked with just a change of seasons.

I don't know what I was expecting to find there, even if I could have found it. Mandy wouldn't have been there. If Mandy had come back she would have been with her father. The only way that Mandy would have been there was if she didn't come back. Ever. This is what I was thinking but my thinking was so confused it was no wonder I couldn't find our place in the woods.

Eventually I stopped looking. I stopped looking and decided to go to the place where I thought that Mandy would be, not where she had been.

• • •

Bill Trafton's boy Curtis rose on the sixth day. His parents embraced him, and Cal could hear Sandy Trafton telling Curtis that "everything was going to be all right, everything will be all right." He watched their embrace from the couch outside the morgue. Curtis's eyes, unfocused and milky, found Cal's. Cal had to look away.

• • •

Mandy—beautiful Mandy—lifted herself up off of her hospital gurney. She walked down the hallway, one bare foot dragging on the burnished hospital floors. She left the hospital and then fell to her hands and knees at the bottom of the hospital steps, crawling along the snow covered streets until her left arm gave out and she had to push herself forward on her belly like a snake, with intermittent help from her legs. Hours and hours she crept along in this manner until she reached her home. But then it wasn't her home at all. It was the home of Jake Barnes, and when she lifted her still pretty face from the cement front steps, it wasn't to a gentle kiss and a warm embrace but to the cocking of a loaded shotgun.

•••

Cal cried out as he fell from his chair upon waking, hitting his head and bruising his hip as he landed. He was aware of other people in the hallway, some rushing toward him. But he was too tired and heartsick to feel any embarrassment. He remained where he'd fallen, his cheek cool against the hospital floor.

"Cal," he heard a woman's voice saying. Her hand was on his forehead, warm where all the rest of him was so cold. "Cal, are you all right?"

He opened one eye and saw Dr. Newcomb peering down at him with concern.

"I'm fine," he said, his voice unfamiliar to his own ears. "Fine."

She made as though to help him back to his chair, but he shook her off and seated himself again under his own volition.

She waited until he was settled and looking back at her. He could feel his throat constricting even before she spoke.

"Cal," she said. And then she spoke the words he had been dreading to hear.

"It's been seven days."

•••

He buried his daughter on the sunniest day of the month, just a few days before Christmas. He buried her next to her mother and wished that he could tell them to just open up his plot as well so he could crawl in.

There was a large turnout at the service, and just as many, if not more, at the gravesite. His friends, her friends, the dutiful, and the curious. He shook many hands and thanked many people but registered so few.

"We, uh, left Curtis at home," Bill said to him as he and Sandy stood shivering at the edge of the cemetery road. "We weren't sure it was, um, appropriate for him to come."

"Appropriate," Cal said. They were lowering his daughter

into the ground, and Bill was worried about what was appropriate. Cal couldn't remember ever feeling this tired.

"Curtis doesn't know what happened," Bill said. "He remembers that the radio was on and he remembers that he'd had a good time at the party, but he doesn't really remember what he did. Thank God he doesn't remember anything about the crash. He doesn't remember any of it."

"Thank God," Cal said.

"If you need anything . . . ," Sandy Trafton was saying. Cal thanked her before she could finish. He walked back toward his daughter's grave.

Laura was there with Stevie. She didn't say anything as she put her arms around Cal and pulled him into a tight embrace. She was crying when she let him go.

Her dead son extended his hand, and Cal took it, unable to feel its temperature through his leather gloves.

"Mister . . . Wilson," Stevie said. "I'm so . . . sorry. Mandy . . . was a . . . good . . . friend of . . . mine."

"Thank you," Cal said. The boy's eyes were blank and glassy and his expression was flat, just as the well-dressed woman from Boston had mentioned they would be. He was pale, bloodless-looking even in the light of the sun. Cal wished he could talk to the boy, ask him if he'd seen Mandy in those moments when he was on the other side.

"Cal, maybe you shouldn't be alone tonight. You could stay with me and Stevie, or . . ."

"Thanks, Laura," he said, her touch on his arm making him aware that he'd been staring at her son, searching for something in his eyes. "I'll be fine," he told her as he forced himself to look away.

"I'm going to call you, Cal," Laura said. Her thoughts were completely open to him. He could read them as easily as he could the words and names carved into the headstones surrounding them.

Lost his wife, lost his daughter, no real friends to speak of, carries a gun . . .

He didn't want her to worry, but he didn't know how he could convince her not to.

"I'm going to be watching out for you," she continued.

"I'd like that," he said, meaning it.

"Why don't you come to the car now?"

"In a minute."

He looked out over the cemetery, expecting to see someone who wasn't there.

•••

She was gone. Watching the cars file out of the cemetery in a long, laborious procession, he knew that she was gone. They'd said many things to each other and he'd meant it all, but in the end he didn't say the words that mattered most.

And now he couldn't say anything at all because that part of him wasn't working anymore. He sat down in the snow, leaned against a wide, flat headstone and concentrated on saying her name. And once he could say her name, he thought, he would say it over and over again.

•••

That night Cal stopped at the threshold of his daughter's room with the bag of presents that she would have been unwrapping in just a few days' time. He lightly tossed the bag in the center of the room, switched off the light, and closed the door.

•••

The phone rang that night, and he answered it, thinking that it was Laura. He didn't want to talk to anyone, not even her, but he didn't want her up all night worrying about him, either.

But it wasn't Laura.

"You should be glad, Wilson. You're the lucky one."

"What?" The words didn't register at first, only their tone.

He didn't recognize the voice at first, either. He'd never heard it over the phone before.

"You're the lucky one. Your girl had a nice, clean death. End of story. She didn't come back as one of those filthy monsters. Those abominations. Better she die than come back as one of them, or end up a paraplegic like the other one."

Cal knew that he should hang up on him but, in a way, the fury that he was feeling now was better than what he had been feeling, which was nothing at all. All he'd had was an emptiness, a void where feeling should have been.

"So count your blessings, Wilson. She's better off dead."

"Barnes," he said. "If you were here right now, I would kill you. Without any hesitation."

The man on the other end of the line gave a low, throaty chuckle. "I feel the same way about the thing living in my boy's corpse," he said, and then he hung up.

Cal listened to the dial tone for a while. He listened long enough to imagine that he could hear voices, crying for help, buried far beneath the drone. Barnes only lived ten minutes away.

...

Cal got into his car, but he didn't drive to Barnes's house. The moon was full, and the streets were empty. He took his time and was careful. Snow was falling.

Mandy had said she'd loved Jake, and Cal had just watched him walk away, off into the forest, lost and alone. His shame made him burn even more than the words from Barnes.

The cemetery was locked, but the stone wall near the gate was only waist high. Cal climbed it easily. The stones of the cemetery seemed to catch and store the moonlight among the spectral blue white snow. The only sound was Cal's crunching footfalls as he made deliberate progress toward his daughter's grave. Once there, he saw that it was covered by a blanket of new fallen snow. It made it look as though she'd been buried for years

and not for only a few hours.

He also saw the footprints.

A dark figure moved nearer, weaving among the stones. Cal watched as the figure seemed to coalesce out of the moonlight, its hospital gown glowing as it slouched against a mourning angel.

Cal had to swallow twice before he could get the words out.

"I've come for you," he said. "I've come to take you home."

Cal couldn't see what effect his words had, if any; the other's face was hidden in the shadow of the angel's wing. But then they were both walking forward, toward each other. Neither could say who took the first step.

Acknowledgements

"The Assassin's Apprentice" © by Michelle Zink. First publication, original to this anthology. Printed by permission of the author.

"Errant" © by Diana Peterfreund. First publication, original to this anthology. Printed by permission of the author.

"The Spirit Jar" © by Karen Mahoney. First publication, original to this anthology. Printed by permission of the author.

"Lost" © by Justine Musk. First publication, original to this anthology. Printed by permission of the author.

"The Spy Who Never Grew Up" © by Sarah Rees Brennan. First publication, original to this anthology. Printed by permission of the author.

"Dungeons of Langeais" © by Becca Fitzpatrick. First publication, original to this anthology. Printed by permission of the author.

"Behind the Red Door" © by Caitlin Kittredge. First publication, original to this anthology. Printed by permission of the author.

"Hare Moon" © by Carrie Ryan. First publication, original to this anthology. Printed by permission of the author.

"Familiar" © by Michelle Rowen. First publication, original to this anthology. Printed by permission of the author.

"Fearless" © by Rachel Vincent. First publication, original to this anthology. Printed by permission of the author.

"Vermillion" © by Daniel Marks. First publication, original to this anthology. Printed by permission of the author.

"The Hounds of Ulster" © by Maggie Stiefvater. First publication, original to this anthology. Printed by permission of the author.

"Many Happy Returns" © by Daniel Waters. First publication, original to this anthology. Printed by permission of the author.

Author Biographies

SARAH REES BRENNAN's first novel *The Demon's Lexicon*, a dark YA urban fantasy featuring magic, swords, and a cranky boy mechanic, was published in June 2009. It was nominated for the ALA/*YALSA* Best Books for Young Adults list, received three starred reviews, and a Carnegie Medal nomination. The sequel, *The Demon's Covenant*, came out in May 2010, and she is currently working on the third volume in the trilogy while being inspired by her muse—country music. She lives in Dublin, Ireland between a canal full of swans and a bakery full of muffins. www.sarahreesbrennan.com

BECCA FITZPATRICK is the *New York Times*–bestselling author of the paranormal thriller *Hush, Hush*. She graduated college with a degree in health, which she promptly abandoned for storytelling. When not writing, she's most likely running, prowling sale racks for reject shoes, or watching crime dramas on TV. *Crescendo*, the sequel to *Hush, Hush*, will be published in November 2010. www.beccafitzpatrick.com

CAITLIN KITTREDGE is the author of *The Iron Codex* trilogy for young adults, as well as the bestselling *Nocturne City* series, and the Black London series from St. Martin's Press. She collects comics, loves bad movies and good books, and is owned by two pushy cats. www.caitlinkittredge.com

KAREN MAHONEY gave up on her dreams of being Wonder Woman a long time ago, but has instead settled for being a writer of contemporary fantasy. This is her second published story about Moth, the teen vampire who made her first appearance in *The Eternal Kiss*. Her debut YA novel *The Iron Witch*, about a girl with iron tattoos and super strength (alchemy! dark elves! a hot half-fey guy called Xan!), will be published in 2011. She is

British and currently lives in London.
www.kazmahoney.com

DANIEL MARKS is the super secret pseudonym of a popular adult urban fantasy author. He lives in a highly classified and secluded location (a "house" in a "neighborhood") with his trusty body-guard ("wife"), and a cabal of evil minions (some "dogs"). He's currently hiring for a loyal henchman ("gardener"). Apply at:
www.velvetandnyx.com

JUSTINE MUSK is the author of the YA supernatural thriller *Uninvited*. She has also written the dark-fantasy novels *Bloodangel* and *Lord of Bones*, about a race of men and women descended from fallen angels who go to war against demons—and sometimes each other.
www.justinemusk.com

DIANA PETERFREUND is the author of the four books in the Secret Society Girl series, the first of which was named to the 2007 New York Public Library's Books for the Teen Age List and deemed "impossible to put down" by *Publishers Weekly*. Her young adult debut, *Rampant*, is a contemporary fantasy novel about killer unicorns and the virgin descendants of Alexander the Great who hunt them, and has been named one of the top ten children's books on IndieBound's Kids' Next List for Winter 2009.
www.dianapeterfreund.com

MICHELLE ROWEN is the national bestselling and award-winning writer of YA fantasy, paranormal romance, and urban fantasy. Her days (and some nights) are filled with writing about demons, vampires, shifters, faeries, and other worldly creatures who seem to want to tell her their tales. She's the author of the *Demon Princess* books for young adults, as well as the *Immortality Bites* and *Living in Eden* paranormal romance series. She lives in southern Ontario

with two needy cats and a poster of Robert Pattinson.
www.michellerowen.com

CARRIE RYAN was born in Greenville, South Carolina and attended Williams College and Duke University School of Law. Her debut novel, the *New York Times*–bestselling *The Forest of Hands and Teeth* (Delacorte Press for Young Readers, 2009), earned starred reviews from *Publishers Weekly* and *School Library Journal* and was listed as number four on IndieBound's Kids' Next List for Spring 2009. It was also a Junior Library Guild selection, a Borders Original Voices selection, and was nominated for the American Library Association's Best Books for Young Adults List. Her second novel, *The Dead-Tossed Waves*, is a companion to the first and was published in March 2010 with a third in the series scheduled for spring 2011. A reformed litigator, Carrie now lives and writes in Charlotte, North Carolina with her husband, two cats, and a dog.
www.carrieryan.com

MAGGIE STIEFVATER is the *New York Times*–bestselling author of novels for young adults, including The Wolves of Mercy Falls trilogy (*Shiver*, *Linger*, and *Forever* [July 2011]) and The Book of Faerie series (*Lament* and *Ballad*). When she is not writing about homicidal paranormal creatures and teens, she is also an artist and a musician, claiming both harp and bagpipes in her list of talents. She lives in Virginia with her husband, two young children, two dogs who fart recreationally, and a 1973 Camaro named Loki. She's an unapologetic Scorpio.
www.maggiestiefvater.com

RACHEL VINCENT is the *New York Times*–bestselling author of the Shifters series for adults and author of the Soul Screamers young adult series, about a teenage banshee trying to balance a normal high school experience with her new, secret supernatural world. A

recent transplant into south Texas, Rachel has a BA in English and an overactive imagination, and she consistently finds the latter to be more practical. Rachel is motivated by deadlines and chocolate, lives for a good pair of jeans, and is known to hand out mini-excerpts at random on her blog.

www.rachelvincent.com

DANIEL WATERS lives in Connecticut with his family. He is the author of the Generation Dead series, which includes *Generation Dead*, *Kiss of Life*, and *Passing Strange*. *Generation Dead* was shortlisted for the Sheffield Children's Book Award and was a 2008 *Kirkus* Best Book of the Year.

www.danielwaters.com

Michelle Zink lives in New York and has always been fascinated with ancient myths and legends. Never satisfied with simply reading them, she usually ends up asking, "What if?" Sometimes asking only leads to more questions, but every now and then, when everything falls into place just right, a story is born. Her first book is one of those stories. *Publishers Weekly* called *Prophecy of the Sisters* "a captivating tragedy," and it was also named to *Booklist*'s 2009 Top Ten First Novels for Youth. The second book in the *Prophecy* series, *Guardian of the Gate*, will be published in August 2010.

www.michellezink.com